Iris Gower is the author of the highly successful *Sweyn's Eye* series of novels. She has four children and comes from Swansea, where her family have always lived, and which she uses as the background for her wonderfully evocative novels of Wales and the Welsh people.

Also by Iris Gower

COPPER KINGDOM
PROUD MARY
SPINNERS' WHARF
MORGAN'S WOMAN
FIDDLER'S FERRY
BLACK GOLD
THE LOVES OF CATRIN
THE SHOEMAKER'S DAUGHTER

and published by Corgi Books

THE OYSTER CATCHERS

Iris Gower

CORGI BOOKS

THE OYSTER CATCHERS
A CORGI BOOK : 0 552 13688 3

Originally published in Great Britain by Bantam Press,
a division of Transworld Publishers Ltd

PRINTING HISTORY
Bantam Press edition published 1992
Corgi edition published 1993

Set in 10/11pt Monotype Plantin by
Kestrel Data, Exeter

Corgi Books are published by Transworld Publishers Ltd,
61–63 Uxbridge Road, Ealing, London W5 5SA,
in Australia by Transworld Publishers (Australia) Pty Ltd,
15–25 Helles Avenue, Moorebank, NSW 2170,
and New Zealand by Transworld Publishers (N.Z.) Ltd,
3 William Pickering Drive, Albany, Auckland.

Reproduced, printed and bound in Great Britain by
Cox & Wyman Ltd, Reading, Berks.

In memory of my dear friend and
fellow writer Julia Fitzgerald who
pointed me in the right direction

CHAPTER ONE

The seas were rough that morning, washing against the shore in short, angry gusts. The shells rattled furiously, dragged along the beach by the strength of the tide. The wind whipped white foam against the stark rocks.

Eline Harries hauled on the ropes of the open boat, straining to draw it towards the sea, her hands chaffing in the coldness, her back almost breaking.

She glanced over her shoulder at the women who were pulling the boats along the resisting sand so easily and frowned; they were gossiping good-naturedly together as though there was no hardship in putting to sea the small crafts in readiness for the menfolk.

Eline's arms ached and she paused for a moment to gather her strength, determined not to be defeated by the unresisting wood that seemed to sink into the sand as though in defiance of her efforts.

She envied the strength of the village women. These were wives of the men who were ready to face the elements, to bring in the oysters to the safety of the perches near the shore. And now she must try to be one of them, for she, too, was married to an oyster fisherman.

She sighed, that was possibly the only similarity between them for while the women of the village of Oystermouth were sturdy and stoic, used to the harshness of the sea-faring life, Eline was a country girl, born Emmeline Powell in the small, whitewashed cottage on Honey's Farm near Swansea. She was different and she was made to feel it.

'Come on, *merchi*, put your back in to it!' Carys Morgan was a short but stout woman with shoulders and

7

arms, bared now as she toiled, like those of a man, strong and well-muscled.

'Leave the girl alone,' Annie George shouted, 'she's not another Nina Parks and neither is she built like a Welsh dresser like you, Carys!' There was laughter and though Eline pretended to join in, she felt a sinking despair at the barrenness that her life had become over the past weeks.

At the age of seventeen, Eline had married Joseph Harries, a man older than her by twenty years. Joe was kind, a long-time friend of the family and a vigorous man in the marriage bed. But Eline didn't love him.

Why, she asked herself, had she married him? Was it because when Dad had fallen sick from working so hard on the hill farm, Joe had been there at her side, supporting and helping her?

When Dad had given in to the lung disease, Eline felt so alone and lost and, as she'd stood at his graveside in *Dan y Graig* cemetery, she felt there was no one left in the world to care about her. No one but Joe.

Joe had taken command then, he had been a tower of strength, taking charge of Eline's affairs, selling the small farmhouse, Honey's Farm, that had been in the family for generations because he deemed Eline too young and too frail to manage it alone.

And so she had come with him to the village of Oystermouth, to the gossip and suspicion of the other villagers who considered her an outsider and probably always would. It had been the widow Parks who had always been the one to take Joe's rowing boat to the water's edge.

There was no doubt that she resented Eline for taking the task from her and Eline knew that she had made an enemy. But Eline was Joe's wife, not Nina Parks.

Eline had felt more than a pang of loss when the money from the farm had gone to buy a fine, new skiff, but she realized she must trust her husband to know best; he was far older and wiser than she was.

The *Oyster Sunrise* was fine, clean and new, and Joe had been convinced that now he had two boats, he would make his fortune. Eline was warmed by his enthusiasm believing that one day, when he had made his fortune, he might take her back to the farmlands to live, back to her roots.

Joe's first boat was weathered and seasoned, well used and faithful. He had named it for Eline, shortly after her birth, the *Emmeline* he had called it and it was ironic to think that the boat was almost as old as she was.

The *Emmeline* was now bobbing cork-like out on the moorings, the sails were patched and faded, but it seemed they stood up well to the fresh winds that came in off the Bristol Channel.

'Day-dreaming again, *merchi*?' Carys leaned over her shoulder. 'Thinkin' of that fine man of yours, are you then? And who could blame you? Joe Harries always was a handsome buck, all the village girls fell for him, many would have married him given half a chance, but he was waiting for you to grow up, he always said so.'

Eline laughed. 'What if I'd been as ugly as sin, wouldn't he have changed his mind then?'

'Looks isn't everything, my girl,' Carys said sagely. 'If a man's got a notion in his head about something there's not much we women can do to change it.'

The boats were ranged now on the edge of the sea and the men were coming on to the shore drawn by an instinctive sense of time that had more to do with the sky and sea than with any clock. They were shouting to each other in loud jovial tones, bluff hearty men who loved the sea and all its moods.

The fishermen scarcely looked at their wives, engrossed as they were in the province of a wholly masculine domain where a man battled the elements to make a living. The sea was a man's mistress, his love, his life and she had all the attention on this blustery morning.

'The weather will be better soon, man.' Skipper George was a tall, rugged man, his face a startling red against the blue of his cap, his eyes far-seeing and wise. 'No doubt about it, the wind will die within the hour and we will have a fine haul, our dredges will be overflowing.'

'*Duw*, you're like a preacher there, man.' Joe Harries spoke warmly for George was held in great respect. He was the oldest fisherman in the village who`had seen more storms than most of them had lived years and had gathered the oysters from the lanes with an unerring skill, almost as though he could see the trails of oysters along the ocean beds.

Eline sat in the boat with Joe while he rowed towards the *Emmeline*; he was preoccupied, looking beyond her, examining the sky intently. In this light he appeared to be a stranger, far removed from the man who had laboured above her in the marriage bed only a few hours ago.

Eline was aware of the laughter of the other women as she took the oars from Joe, attempting to steady the boat while he climbed aboard the *Emmeline*.

Doggedly, she wielded the oars and awkwardly turned the boat which seemed heavy and unresponsive now, and made her way back to the shore.

The other women, their first task of the day over, retreated back along the shore towards the narrow road that wound through the village. Carys hung back, waiting, and then fell into step beside Eline. Carys was perhaps, being young, more sympathetic than the other women.

'There's goin' to be a new boot and shoe shop in the village,' she said importantly. 'You know them Grenfells from Swansea? Well, they've had workmen putting shelving and such in empty premises just outside the village.' She dug a meaty elbow into Eline's ribs.

'Should see the young gent who owns the place, real

handsome he is, brother or something to Mrs Hari Grenfell, so the rumour goes. *Duw*, he's a *cariad*.'

Eline smiled. 'I suppose you know everything about him, do you?'

'Right enough!' Carys agreed immediately. 'William Davies his name is and he's in his early twenties, I suppose. Just the age when a man is at his most vigorous, I'd say.'

Eline was silent; Joe had enough vigour to last her a lifetime even though he was twenty years older than she was.

'Aye,' Carys continued, 'I suppose you knew all about Hari Grenfell's shoemaking when you lived near the *town*.' Carys said the word 'town' with a turning down of her mouth as though it was something sinful.

Eline nodded. 'Mrs Grenfell's boots and shoes are known all over the country.' She looked at Carys drily. 'Not that I wore fine shoes to work the farm, mind, full of muck is a farmyard on a day like this and hard work enough for anyone.'

Carys rested a plump hand on Eline's shoulder. 'I know we tease you, *merchi*, and I suppose some of 'em round here think of you as soft, you not being a village girl but there's no malice intended, mind.'

'I know,' Eline said softly. She stepped from the beach on to the road and stared back at the sea. The skiffs were edging out into the bay, vying for position like children at play, sails bellying in the wind.

'Let's hope Skipper George is right and the wind drops soon,' Eline said worriedly. The boats that had appeared so solid and strong tied up at the moorings now seemed like corks, buoyant and frail, receding into the distance.

'Aye,' Carys said, 'he's always right is that one, don't you fret about your man. Joe has fished these waters since he was a boy, knows every inch of the bay from the Mixon to Sker Point and then some.'

11

'I know,' Eline said softly, 'and I'm not fretting, not really.'

'Of course you are, all we wives worry when our men go out to sea, it's only natural. But still,' she sighed, 'none of us would change our lives for all the money in the world.'

Eline was silent; she couldn't tell Carys that she was utterly disenchanted with her lot, pining for the life spent in the open air of the corn fields. She sorely missed the soft breezes and the lowing of the cattle at night, and mostly she missed herding in the cows for milking and staring across the hills on a sunny autumn day with the fruity scent of hay drifting around her.

'Why don't you have some little ones?' Carys said suddenly and Eline felt her heart lurch. 'Not that I've any right to speak, mind, being barren,' Carys added hastily, afraid she'd given offence.

Eline warmed to the woman's stark honesty. 'Come in my kitchen and have a cup of tea with me?' she asked tentatively and Carys smiled. It was a rare offer for Eline was known for keeping herself to herself.

'Aye, I'll do that,' Carys said. 'I've got to pickle a barrel of oysters for some townsfolk, but that can wait a while, I suppose.'

It was cosy in the kitchen with a good fire roaring in the grate, flames of yellow and blue leaping up the chimney. The brasses gleamed and the hob was black-leaded to within an inch of its life. The rag mats on the slate floor were bright and fresh and the white wood of the table was pale with much scrubbing.

'You keeps a nice house, mind,' Carys said almost grudgingly. She glanced through to the parlour where the good furniture gleamed, smelling of beeswax, and the walls were hung with a painting of Honey's Farm on a summer day.

'*Duw*, that's a fine picture,' Carys said pointing. She moved closer and peered upwards. 'The corn could almost be real and look there's your name in the corner, Emmeline, an outlandish name, mind, if you ask me,' Carys added with a good natured smile. 'Whoever drew it, though, was very clever. Was it a present?'

'I painted it as a present to myself,' Eline said shyly. Carys's eyebrows lifted.

'I'm good at painting, anything so long as it's the bottom of my Sam's boat!'

She sank into the old rocking-chair near the fire and watched as Eline made the tea. Carys edged close to the fire, hitching up her skirts and allowing the warmth of the flames to play on her plump knees.

'*Duw*, my bones are aching a bit today,' she said. 'I hope I don't end up like my mam, gnarled and knotted like an old tree.'

'I suppose it's just the coldness of the wind,' Eline said comfortingly. She sat at the table and put the cups on the scrubbed surface. Sighing she glanced around her. No wonder everything was neat and tidy, she had so much time on her hands now that she was married and it was strange after working all the hours the good Lord made on the farm.

'What about babbis?' Carys said, obviously inclined to pursue the subject. 'Haven't they come along or don't you want none?'

Eline sighed. 'I haven't been married a year yet, mind, and so far the babies haven't come along. I don't know why because Joe is so . . .' She broke off, the colour flooding into her cheeks.

'Don't blush, *merchi*,' Carys winked, 'there's many a woman in the village can testify to your Joe's energy.' She glanced quickly at Eline. 'Not since your marriage, mind, and what he did before carries no blame, him being a single man and all.'

Eline digested this in silence, it was a new and unwelcome idea that Joe had loved other women before she came into his life. But then he was a mature man and she could not have expected him to live like a monk all these years. And yet she felt a distinct throb of jealousy at the thought of her husband with another woman. She concealed her thoughts from Carys with a smile. 'I don't blame him,' she said softly and not quite truthfully.

'But then,' Carys continued relentlessly, 'I suppose living on a farm you are used to, well, nature. Males got to have their comforts, like, they won't go without at any rate.'

'Who are you doing the pickling for?' Eline changed the subject abruptly.

'Oh, just some townsfolk, don't know who exactly,' Carys said. 'My Sam's idea, it was. I don't hold with pickling fine oysters, mind, I like them baked between two pieces of beef or cooked in a pan with a bit of bacon. But then a sale is a sale, I suppose.'

'Joe is lucky,' Eline said thoughtfully. 'He's got a good trade with old Mr Lewis, buys all that Joe can catch he does.'

'Aye, well, Cal Lewis got the big place up in Swansea, mind, with a lovely oyster saloon at the back of his fish shop *and* he's got a smaller shop in the village. Old friend of your Joe's dad was Mr Lewis, mind, and loyal too. Don't see much of that these days.'

Carys drank some of her tea. 'But your Joe is going to have his work cut out running two skiffs, that's what I think at any rate. Did well with his old *Emmeline*, he did, but now he has to depend on another man to skipper his new boat.'

Eline glanced at her. 'Aye, and he's got no one in mind yet, looking around he is but in no hurry, wants to check that all is working well on the *Oyster Sunrise* before anyone takes her out.'

Carys put down her empty cup with a clink of finality and rubbed her chapped and reddened hands together. 'Well, I'd better get on with my work, can't sit around all day like some.' She smiled to soften her words. 'My Sam can't afford no help but me, and because I have no babbis he don't see why I shouldn't work.'

Eline saw her out with no comment and, when Carys had stepped into the cool of the street, closed the door gently behind her. Eline rested her head against the warm wooden planks of the door, smelling the smoke of Joe's old jacket on the hook, her eyes closed in an attitude of despair. What had she done, marrying a man she did not love and coming with him to live in this strange place? She must be mad.

She pulled herself upright and went to the sink and washed the cups in hot water from the kettle. When she had dried them and put them away she then set about making a pot of *cawl* for Joe. The soup was rich with mutton and vegetables and soon the smell rose invitingly and Eline realized she was hungry.

She ate a little bread and cheese and afterwards tidied away her dishes. She banked up the fire and stared around her, contemplating another long, empty day.

If only Joe would let her work with the oysters as did the other village women, she would at least have something to occupy her time. But Joe had a slick, well-run routine that had served him for years. Nina Parks worked the oyster perches for him, sorting and cleaning the catch ready for market. And sometimes, when the season was at its height, Nina's three daughters also worked on the oyster perches.

Eline, curious, had asked Joe about the Parks family once and had been given an unusually curt reply.

'Nina's husband was my best friend,' he said. 'He was drowned at sea and I decided to look after his widow and children, all right?'

Eline had warmed to Joe then, knowing him for a kind and good man, a man whose boots she wasn't fit to clean. She shook off her thoughts of the Parks family, not wanting to dwell on the suspicions about Nina that wormed into her mind, and moved suddenly to take her coat from the hook behind the door. She might as well get out into the fresh air, there was nothing to keep her here, tied to the kitchen all day long.

The wind was dropping now, just as Skipper George had predicted and the sea was calmer, washing the shore gently like the tongue of a friendly dog. The skiffs were gone from view but Joe and all the other men would be safe now that the weather was being kind.

She walked slowly. The village was small and all too soon she would reach the shops. Perhaps it would be interesting to look into the new boot and shoe shop that Carys had made such a fuss about.

The shop was situated near the end of the village street, just before the road turned to wind uphill and just before the mullion-windowed village inn. It was a double-fronted shop, the windows swathed in dark silk, the shoes set daintily apart as if to step out into a dance and Eline recognized the influence of Mrs Grenfell in the elegant display.

'Good morning.' The voice was close to her ear and Eline turned abruptly to look up at the man, a stranger, daring to speak to her. His eyes were full of laughter, his mouth smiling beneath the fine moustache There was a dimple in his chin and he smelled of fresh air and shaving soap.

'I'm William Davies,' he explained, 'proprietor of the new shop. May I count on your custom some time in the future?'

Eline tried to look away but something in his eyes held her still. She felt as if she knew this man, as though they had been together in the long distant past. She wanted to rest her head on his shoulder, feel his arms around her holding her tenderly. But that was absurd, she had never seen him before.

'I'm sorry if I startled you,' he said easily. 'Forgive me for staring, but I feel somehow as if we've met before.'

16

From the cultured tone of his voice, it was obvious that William Davies was a man of breeding and stature and the fine cut of his suit and the crisp white of his shirt confirmed her impression.

'No, you didn't startle me.' Eline felt awkward in her everyday coat and her heavy working boots. She swallowed hard.

'I'm sure I will buy my shoes at your shop, it looks very elegant. Reminds me of Mrs Grenfell's fine place in Swansea.'

'That's very perceptive of you,' William Davies said softly. 'Mrs Grenfell and I are old friends, I did my training with her.'

It was no surprise; Eline had known this man was different, a toff who mingled with gentry, the likes of the Grenfells. She tried to draw her gaze away from him, but his eyes seemed to bore into her as if seeking out her every thought and emotion.

'Not so perceptive,' she said drily, 'your shop is the talk of the village.' She hesitated a moment and then turned away from the temptation of his eyes and his smile.

'I'd better be going,' Eline said softly, but she glanced back at William Davies, breathing in the scents of him and feeling that somehow their lives were bound together.

'Would you like to come inside?' He spoke quickly. 'I would like to show you the interior of my shop, if you have time, that is.'

Almost against her will, Eline found herself following him inside, knowing with a sense of joy that he wanted to prolong the moment.

The shop was starkly furnished and the smell of leather permeated the long room. Curtains swathed the walls and William, seeing her glance, moved aside one of the drapes to reveal rows upon rows of boots and shoes in every style and shape.

17

'Anything you could wish for is here,' he said and his words, softly spoken, were imbued with hidden meaning. Eline sighed softly and moved to pick up a high laced-up boot from one of the stands. The leather was soft kid set against highly polished calf and the heel was elegant and well-shaped giving the boot flair.

'You like that style?' William asked. His hand, hovering over the boot, touched hers briefly and Eline felt a sudden shock of emotion running through her.

She couldn't speak, she turned and moved quickly towards the door as though a thousand devils were at her heels. In the chill of the street, she stopped, feeling suddenly foolish, and, turning, lifted a hand in a gesture of farewell.

William Davies was staring after her, a thoughtful look on his face. He inclined his head and turned away, obviously he had more important things to do than ponder over Eline's strange behaviour.

She returned home, struggling to find some sort of composure. Why was it, she asked herself, that contact with a stranger had set up such a vortex of emotions within her?

Eline paused at the edge of the sea, the tide on the ebb was never far out from the beach at Oystermouth unlike the wide sweeping bay of Swansea where the sand flats stretched for a mile at least.

Out there, on the restless seas was her husband, a good man, hard-working and a fine oyster fisherman. He had shown her nothing but kindness and for him, a certain sort of passion and yet here she was being unfaithful to him, if only in her mind.

'*Duw*, it's fine for some,' the voice of Carys Morgan interrupted Eline's thoughts. 'Day-dreaming your life away like a lady of leisure is what you have the time for now, is it?'

'I've just been to the shops.' Eline was flustered as

though Carys could look into her mind and see the wicked thoughts that were there.

'Haven't bought much.' Carys folded her big arms. 'Not going to make much dinner for your man with a handful of nothing, are you?'

Eline forced a smile. 'I was curious,' she thought it best to stick as closely to the truth as she dared, 'I wanted to see this new boot and shoe shop you talked about.'

'Aye and the handsome young owner, too, I suppose.' Carys laughed. 'Well, I don't blame you and isn't the man all I said he was?'

'Oh, he's handsome enough, I'll agree, but it was a pair of fine kid boots that really took my fancy.'

'Then you must be a fool or a liar!' Carys said in amusement. '*Duw*, I'm an old biddy alongside you and yet I felt a stirring inside me when I looked at that wonderful man.'

Eline felt some of her tension drain away. If a sensible woman like Carys could feel drawn to William Davies then Eline couldn't be at fault for simply agreeing with her.

'There is something fine about him, I must admit,' Eline said quietly. 'But perhaps he cultivates a way with women just to be a good salesman.'

'I doubt that,' Carys said. 'The man is just naturally charming without making any effort at all.'

Eline fidgeted uneasily. 'You're right, but I can't stand here talking all day, I've done enough time wasting as it is.'

She moved away. 'See you later, when the skiffs come in.'

She bought bread from the bakers, hardly noticing the hot, crusty smell of the fresh baked loaf and quickly retraced her steps towards home.

Once in her own kitchen, she hung up her coat and pushed the kettle on to the fire before sinking into a chair. In spite of her light-hearted conversation with

Carys, Eline knew that her meeting with William Davies was momentous to her. It wasn't just his charm or even his fine looks, there had been a rapport between them and Eline was sure he felt it too. The tension when his hand had brushed hers was clear in her memory as if it had just happened.

She allowed herself a few dreamy moments as she made the tea and set the pot on the hob to keep warm. She wanted to savour the experience of the morning because she knew it must never happen again. Her silly fancy for William Davies must be forgotten for she was a respectably married woman.

She poured the weak, glowing tea into her cup and sank down in the rocking-chair, the cup between her hands. She would forget William Davies and the riot of feelings he had woken in her but not just yet. No, not just yet.

CHAPTER TWO

'I think it will be a great success.' William smiled at Hari Grenfell across the table of Lewis's Oyster Saloon. 'The locals are already curious about the new shop. Indeed I had one potential customer in earlier today and took the trouble to show her round, though I'm not officially open yet, of course.'

He saw Hari smile and a feeling of affection for her washed over him. Hari was respected as the wife of one of Swansea's leading citizens, but was also accepted in her own right as a successful business woman. Over the past few years, Hari had become a household name in Swansea for finely fashioned, bespoke boots and shoes. And moreover, she was famous countrywide for her work on modified footwear for children born with deformities of the feet.

Her marriage to Craig Grenfell had been the talk of Swansea when it had taken place almost two years ago; the woman from the lower orders who had risen so high now had the unstinting admiration of her fellows. And yet she was still the same lovable, generous Hari he'd always admired.

'I don't know what I would have done without you, Hari,' William said softly. 'If you hadn't taken me from that hovel that was my home I would probably be begging on the streets of Swansea today.'

'I doubt it,' Hari said drily and changed the subject. 'From the way you speak about this customer' – there was a teasing note in her voice now – 'a certain light in your eyes, I'd say this "customer" was a very beautiful young woman.'

'Right as always,' William sighed. 'I never could keep any secrets from you, could I?'

Hari reached out and took his hand. 'Well, I should think not! Closer than brother and sister we've been to each other, Will.'

He gripped her hand. 'I know I don't often say it, but I've never ceased to be grateful for all you've done for me.' He spoke softly.

She leaned over and kissed his cheek. 'You have earned your success by your hard work and your talent and don't you forget it,' Hari said firmly. 'I'm very proud of you, Will, and I know you'll make a success of the shop at Oystermouth.'

William leaned back in his chair still holding Hari's hand. 'What shall I call the shop?' he asked thoughtfully. 'Shall I call Grenfell's after you, Hari?'

She shook her head firmly. 'No, the shop is yours as well as mine, we are partners, Will.' She smiled. 'What about THE WILLIAM DAVIES BOOT AND SHOE STORE?'

Will smiled. 'That sounds very good,' he said, excitement gripping him. 'And one day, if I meet the right woman, perhaps I can change the name to DAVIES AND SONS.'

Hari's eyebrows rose. 'I see, talking about offspring already then? This young woman you've met must be somebody very special.'

William sighed. 'I really think she could be. I don't know anything about her, I don't even know her name and yet there was a closenesss between us, I can't explain it, I felt I wanted to take her in my arms and hold her. It was as though she belonged to me.' He laughed self-consciously. 'Must be losing my mind, what do you think?'

'I think you were a bit slow, Will, to tell you the truth. Why didn't you find out more about this mysterious lady?' Hari said gently and William knew she was concerned for him. 'I mean you are so fluent with young ladies usually, I can't understand you not even learning her name.'

'I know,' Will confessed. 'I don't understand myself, but I didn't want to frighten her off by being too forward. She'll come to see me again, I know she will.'

Hari pushed away her plate. 'Those oysters were delicious, I must put in my order with Mr Lewis and have some delivered to Summer Lodge today.'

Will knew that she was deliberately changing the subject. Hari was not one to pry, her great gift was in showing her interest without intruding.

She picked up her bag. 'I'd better get back home, I'm not working today and I promised to take David to the park if the weather holds fine.'

David was Hari's young son, a handsome boy, the image of his father with the same dark hair and strong features. No one could mistake David for anyone else's child.

'And I'd better get back to Oystermouth,' he said, 'I've some hiring to do.'

Eline bit her lip, the incoming tide was bringing with it fresh storms. The rain clouds were heavy in the sky and the whipping of spray against the rocks was an ominous sight to the women waiting on the beach for their menfolk to come home.

'*Duw*, I hope Skipper George is bringing the boats in early' – Carys Morgan stood beside Eline, her plump arms folded over the fringes of her shawl – 'otherwise they'll all be caught in the gale that's coming. See the lowering clouds over the head? Always means a storm when the clouds gather above the rocks like that.'

Eline was used to looking for signs of weather changes, a storm could be just as bad on a farm as it was at sea. Lives could be wrecked, whole harvests lost but then she could not expect Carys to know that.

'They're coming in!' The call came from one of the

women waiting higher up the beach. 'I can see the sails just coming around the head now.'

Eline's heart missed a beat, the Mixon Sands just beyond the head were notorious for the strong currents that had brought many a sailor to grief.

Carys seemed to read her mind. 'Don't worry, *merchi*, the men know these seas like the back of their hands, mind; you won't catch the men of Oystermouth making any silly mistakes.'

But Carys was anxious in spite of her words; there was a feeling of tension about the way she tightened her arms over her plump breasts and her knuckles gleamed white as she clenched her hands into fists.

'Of course they'll be all right,' Eline agreed uncertainly. 'It doesn't do to worry.' She repeated Carys's words but there was a feeling of emptiness within her as she saw the pitifully frail boats battling against the rising tide.

The boats seemed to be huddled together as if for support but, as the first ones rounded the head, the women sent up a cheer.

'There we are,' Carys said triumphantly, 'once in the shelter of the bay the waters are calmer, the men will be safe now, please God.'

The *Emmeline* was one of the first boats to come in to anchor near the shore and Eline pushed the row boat quickly into the waves, preparing to greet her husband.

Inexperienced as she was, it was hard negotiating the stormy seas. She attempted to row but it seemed she was forced back on to the sand, her puny efforts to ride the waves thwarted at every dip of her oars.

Nina Parks appeared as though from nowhere and practically ordered Eline to leave the boat. Defeated, Eline complied and watched Nina steadily draw away from her towards the skiffs.

From where she stood, the spray cold in her face, Eline could see that Joe was not attempting to transfer the catch to the small boat. He climbed from the *Emmeline* and took the oars and with strong strokes pulled for the shore.

'Good trip?' Eline shouted above the wind, ignoring Nina.

'Good enough.' Joe leaped on to the beach and pulled on the line, drawing the boat on to the sand. The women came forward to help.

'Catch worth going out for Joe, *bach*?' Carys called to him and Joe glanced over his shoulder as he secured the boat.

'Aye, fair enough day's work, mind, but I'm glad to be home. There'll be the very devil of a storm tonight if I'm any judge.'

Even as he spoke it began to rain, huge torrents that washed down from the skies in a relentless sheet. The men and women laboured together to secure the small boats and when finally Eline led the way into the warmth of her kitchen, she was soaked to the skin.

'Get those wet things off,' Joe said, brushing the rain from her eyes with the pads of his thumbs. 'You look like a little girl there with your hair hanging loose down your back.'

Eline smiled. 'I don't care what I look like, not going to a grand ball or anything, am I?' She pushed the pot of stew on to the edge of the fire and hung her shawl over the peg on the door where it dripped rain that formed a shiny pool on the grey flagstones of the floor.

'I'm going to wash myself down at the pump in the yard,' Joe said. 'You see to yourself, love.'

Eline hurried upstairs and quickly undressed: her clothes dropped into a heap on the wooden boards which she kicked aside distastefully. There would be some hard work to do tomorrow, washing the stubborn sand from her petticoats.

As she reached out for a towel, Joe entered the bedroom. He was stripped to the waist, a tall, muscular man, a handsome man. He stood looking at her, his dark hair plastered against his forehead.

'*Duw*, there's lovely you are, Eline.' He came to her and took her in his arms, rubbing his hands against her spine. 'So pretty and frail, sometimes I can't believe my luck that you are really my wife.'

He kissed her neck. 'I waited so long for you, my love, so very long.' He kissed her mouth and held her close to him.

Eline pushed him away. 'Get dressed, Joe, or you'll be catching your death of cold,' she said, her heart thumping. She did not want Joe to make love to her, not now when she'd met the most wonderful man in all the world. It would be a betrayal. And yet wasn't that nonsense? Didn't she belong to Joe in every way? What right had she to refuse her husband?

His breathing became more ragged. Still holding her with one hand, he drew off his trews, dropping them alongside her clothes on the floor.

'My lovely, lovely girl.' He whispered the words in her ear as if they might be overheard. 'I want you so much, I'll always want you, my sweet Emmeline.'

He drew her down on to the bed and covered her with his body. 'Say you love me, just a little.' He rose above her, staring down at her as though he could read into her very soul.

'You are my husband, Joe,' Eline said desperately, 'of course I love you.' And it was true, she did love Joe, in a way. But it was not the way a woman loves her man, there was no passion in her love for him, no excitement. And perhaps her love was really gratitude for all he had done for her.

He touched her breasts with the tips of his fingers. 'So lovely,' he breathed. Eline closed her eyes as his mouth came down hot on her throat. Joe was crushing her to him, forcing a response from her in spite of herself. He was a strong, virile man and his appetites were great

26

and, she told herself sternly, if she didn't please him then there were other women in the village who would be only too happy to take her place.

Reluctantly, her arms closed around his broad shoulders. She gasped as he thrust against her, he was gripping her breasts so hard that his fingers, she knew, would bruise her pale skin. But he was lost now on a rising tide of passion, his eyes were closed, his breathing laboured. 'Emmeline!' he gasped and then it was over.

He rolled away and rested on his back, his broad chest rising and falling until gradually, his breathing became normal.

'I love you, Eline.' He reverted to the diminutive form of her name now that his passion was over. 'You are mine now and for always and I'd kill any man who tried to take you away from me.' He spoke with matter-of-fact calm and suddenly Eline felt a chill.

'No one is going to take me away from you,' she said quickly. She turned her face to the wall and there were tears in her eyes.

CHAPTER THREE

Eline scrubbed at the grey flags of the floor with an almost angry vigour; Joe walked sand and mud into the small kitchen with little thought for the work he was giving her.

She straightened, easing her back, aware that her knees were hurting from the cold hardness of the flags. And Eline recognized the need to punish herself for harbouring unworthy thoughts about the young man who had come to Oystermouth so recently.

William Davies had been on her mind constantly since the moment she had first met him; she even dreamed about him at night, erotic, passionate dreams that brought a flush to her cheeks when she remembered them in the morning.

She had caught sight of him from a distance several times. It was unavoidable that she should see him, Oystermouth being such a small village, but she had deliberately kept away from the boot and shoe shop that was now open for business and from all accounts doing very well. She knew that her feelings for the handsome young gentleman were misplaced, dangerous even. She belonged to Joe, she continually reminded herself, he was the man who had loved her ever since she was a child.

Eline rose to her feet. The floor was glistening with wetness, the flags given a transient sheen that would disappear as the floor dried to a dull, lifeless grey.

'*Bore da.*' The voice seemed to come out of the blue, startling her. 'Good heavens, Eline, you're looking like a thunder cloud, anything the matter?'

Eline turned, recognizing the squat shape of Carys Morgan outlined in the doorway where she stood squarely, blocking out the light.

'Come in, Carys,' Eline said quickly. 'Nothing's the matter, I just hate the way I have to scrub this floor to keep it clean after Joe's boots been on it.'

Carys sighed. 'All fishermen's wives have that trouble, *cariad*, you're not alone, mind.' Carys tiptoed over the wet floor to sprawl into the rocking-chair that creaked a protest under her weight.

'I know,' Eline said, suppressing her irritation as she carried the bucket to the door and tipped it into the street, watching the water wash down the pavement and into the cobbled roadway.

'Look,' Carys's voice carried to where Eline was staring dreamily along the roadway in the direction of William Davies's Boot and Shoe Store. 'I'm going to the market in Swansea this morning, what about coming with me?'

Eline turned eagerly. 'Oh, could I?' she said quickly, anything to get away from the boredom of the endless round of housework.

'Would I be asking if I didn't mean it?' Carys said reasonably. 'I want to do a bit of shopping in the market and if you could sell the oysters for me for an hour or so I'd be able to get it all done.'

Eline felt a qualm of dismay. 'But I don't know anything about selling oysters,' she said quickly.

'What's to know?' Carys asked, her dark eyebrows raised. 'You sits there with the sacks of shellfish and folk come up to you and buy some, nothing to it.'

Carys eyed Eline's slight figure. 'You won't be much use unloading the oysters from the cart, it's true, but then I'm used to doing that on my own anyway.' Carys put her head on one side. 'Don't mind a good walk, do you? Swansea's about five miles away, mind.'

'I'm used to walking,' Eline said defensively. 'When I

lived on the farm I walked more than five miles every day.'

'That's settled then. Get your shawl and don't wear anything tidy, mind, your clothes will smell of oysters by the end of the day.'

Eline wrapped a fresh, clean, white apron around her waist and took her old knitted shawl from the back of the door. She stood for a moment looking round her uncertainly.

'If the skiffs come back early, Joe will wonder where I am,' she said biting her lip. Carys tugged her towards the doorway.

'Don't worry about Joe,' she said reassuringly, 'I told my Sam before they sailed that I was going to ask you to come to Swansea with me, him and Joe will have chewed over the fat by now, they know everything that we women get up to, don't you worry.'

An ice-cold finger touched Eline's spine; Carys's words seemed to carry a warning and she shivered.

'What's the matter, *cariad*, a goose walked over your grave?'

Eline forced a laugh and drew the door of her cottage shut. 'Aye, something like that,' she said softly.

Outside Carys's house, the old mare stood patiently waiting between the shafts of the cart, head drooping to nuzzle the cobbles. Carys slapped the animal's rump good-naturedly.

'No oats down there for you, girl,' she laughed. 'Come on, Binnie, we're going to Swansea and I promise I'll let you chew some grass on the way.'

As the horse moved off, the cart jolted into motion and the sacks of oysters shifted, seeming to groan with life. Carys urged the animal forward holding the reins loosely in her plump hands as she led the horse out on to the roadway.

'Nice day for it,' she observed looking up at the clear skies. 'Hope the rain keeps off, though my Sam did say there's some coming later on today.' She smiled at Eline. 'We should be back by then.'

As the horse and cart jolted over the uneven ground, Eline glanced over to her left where the doorway of William Davies's shop stood welcomingly open. The window display had been changed, it was eye catching; a parade of boots seemed to be walking across a stage covered in black silk, bringing to mind an army marching to war.

'*Duw*, will you look at them boots,' Carys said enviously, drawing the animal to a halt. 'I'd love to see my Sam in something elegant like those high riding-boots.'

Handing the reins to Eline, she made her way across the road to peer in the window, hand against the glass.

Impatiently, Eline fidgeted, praying that William Davies wouldn't see her wearing her old skirt and a shabby knitted shawl.

He appeared in the doorway so suddenly that Eline gasped, his eyes were upon her, and he was smiling warmly. To her embarrassment, he came out of the store and lifted his hand to greet her.

'Good morning, fine day, isn't it?' He crossed the road and stood close, looking down at her. 'What's your name?' he said softly.

'Eline,' she said, almost afraid to look at him. Her colour was high and she wanted to back away from him so intensely did she feel the attraction between them.

'Eline, that's beautiful.' He spoke in a low tone and the words, ordinary in themselves, conveyed an intimacy that was unmistakable.

Unable to help herself, she looked up and her eyes met his. 'Mr Davies,' she began, knowing she must tell him she was married, that she was *Mrs* Eline Harries, but he stopped her with his hand raised in protest.

'Will, anyone who is important in my life calls me Will.' He thrust his hands into his pockets as though worried that he had been too familiar.

31

Eline heard his words in a flurry of excitement, he thought she was important, he wanted her to call him by his first name.

'I like your window,' she said in a voice she didn't recognize as her own, 'it's lovely.' How banal; why couldn't she think of something clever to say, something meaningful?

'Thank you, Eline.' He spoke her name lingeringly and it was like a caress.

The spell was broken by the return of Carys who took the reins of the horse from Eline's nerveless fingers.

'*Duw*, there's nice to see a toff like you talking to folks of our like,' Carys said robustly. 'And there's good it is to see a fine boot and shoe shop opening in the village. Could do with a bit of style like them town folk, we could.'

William Davies stepped back apace and smiled easily. 'I hope we'll see you as customers someday soon, both of you.'

With a last glance in Eline's direction, he returned to the other side of the road, his long legs covering the short distance easily. At the doorway of his shop, he turned and, though he didn't move, his eyes were on Eline as she fell into step beside Carys who was already walking along the street.

'There's a lovely young man,' Carys said. 'Seems to fancy you, mind.' There was laughter in her eyes. 'He don't know you're married to the finest man in the village.'

Her words were like a dousing of cold water and Eline gasped. 'I didn't think to tell him I was married,' she said and then added defensively, 'mind, we were only passing the time of day, didn't talk about anything personal.'

There had been no need for talk, the feelings transmitted between them had needed no words.

'Well, no harm in that,' Carys said good-naturedly,

'he wants customers. Anyway, he's got charm, just like I said before *and* he's a polite young man. More polite to you than to me, mind.'

'I suppose so,' Eline said but she knew that the attraction between Will and herself had been far more than politeness.

The sky had become overcast and grey and Carys looked upwards with a grimace. 'I hope the rain keeps away,' she said, 'otherwise we won't get many customers.'

Eline hardly heard Carys's words, she was thinking of Will standing so near her and yet not touching. His very words were a caress and the way he spoke her name made it sound romantic, golden and gleaming with sunlight.

He hadn't seemed to notice her old shawl or the faded skirt; he had looked into her face and into her eyes and he had touched some hidden spring within her that she had not known she possessed.

The roadway to Swansea seemed to be paved with feathers, the day seemed filled with sunshine and even the rattle of the cart-wheels against the hard ground sounded like the tinkling of bells.

The market as usual was vivid with life. Cockle women sat near the gate, baskets at their feet, scallop shells protruding from the beds of cockles waiting to be scooped, a halfpenny worth at a time, into jugs or dishes.

Farmers from Gower were there as usual with produce brought fresh from the rich earth. They called loudly to each other and to the shoppers passing by.

Looking at the earth-covered potatoes and the solid swedes and rich cabbages Eline felt a dart of home-sickness for her own farm up on the Town Hill. But it was not her farm now, she reminded herself sternly, Honey's Farm had been sold to strangers.

'Look, here's my pitch.' Carys lifted a folding table down from the cart and set it up, swiftly covering it with a snow-white cloth. 'I'll put the sacks at the side of you and here's my tin for taking the money.' She placed her measuring jug on the white cloth alongside the battered tin which contained some loose change.

'Will you be long?' Eline said uneasily. 'I'm not sure I'm cut out for this.'

'*Duw*, there's a worrier you are.' Carys hauled a sack down from the cart and the oysters rattled together noisily as though seeking an escape.

'What if I give the wrong change?' Eline persisted, glancing round with a feeling of panic.

'Don't worry,' Carys repeated, 'it wouldn't be the end of the world. Anyway, you'll find most people are honest and they'll put you right quick enough especially if you've done them out of a farthing or two.'

She drew her shawl round her big shoulders. 'I'm going to take Binnie out back to graze and then I'll go round the stalls. I want to buy some wool and some yards of cloth and a nice rich pie for our dinner and then I'll be back, all right?'

Eline watched Carys disappear into the crowd and bit her lip wondering why on earth she'd agreed to come in the first place.

Her first customer was a serving girl who bent over the sacks, her fingers raking the oysters diligently.

'Fresh, are they?' she said in an off-hand manner that put Eline on the defensive.

'Naturally,' she said, 'just out of the sea a few hours ago. If you want fresher you'll have to dredge them yourself.'

The girl looked at her sharply. 'No need to be huffy,' she said. 'If I give my master a bad belly, I'll feel the weight of his boot, mind.'

Eline softened. 'No need to worry, these oysters are fresh, I promise you.'

'All right then,' the girl said grudgingly, 'fill my dish up, to the top, mind.'

She watched as Eline scooped up the oysters in the measure, and tumbled them into the dish. The girl smiled.

'You gives a bit more than the other woman,' she said in satisfaction. 'Bit on the mean side, she is.'

The girl covered the dish with a cloth and dropped some money in the tin. 'See yer.'

Eline bit her lip, she must remember next time not to be so generous. She glanced into the tin and saw that the money the girl put in was short by a halfpenny. Well, that was her first lesson in selling, folk might not feel inclined to cheat the more experienced Carys, but Eline must count the money carefully from now on.

Eline looked round the market, a wash of women wandered past, servants from one of the big houses no doubt. Some had children with them, others carried loaded baskets over their arms, all of them were engaged in earnest gossip and suddenly Eline felt lonely.

'Hello again.' The voice was warm and low and Eline looked up to see William Davies standing over her. Strangely enough she wasn't surprised at his sudden appearance in Swansea, indeed she had the sneaking suspicion that he had come especially to see her.

'Hello.' Her voice trembled and her cheeks were warm, she felt tongue-tied and stupid, staring up at him, not knowing what to say.

A surge of customers arrived at once; they were pressing around her and flustered, Eline began to serve them.

'Good shellfish, these.' One of the women picked up an oyster and examined it. 'Fresh out of the sea if I'm any judge.'

Eline was caught up in a feeling of panic trying to serve everyone at once. Money was clanging into the tin and she had no idea if the customers were paying honestly or not.

She scooped up oysters from the nearest sack and

filled a variety of jugs and dishes, aware that her hair was tumbling out of the restraining ribbons, falling untidily over her face.

'*Duw*, there's a crowd you got by here.' Carys, solid and reassuring was at her side then, taking over the sale of the oysters with the ease of long practice. Soon the panic was over and Carys put her hand on Eline's shoulder.

'Take a breather, do a bit of shopping while you got the chance.'

Eline was only too glad to accept Carys's offer and, with a quick glance round, moved away from the small table.

She had seen at once that William Davies was still standing on the fringes of the crowd. He smiled as he came to her side.

'Well, that was rather a hectic few minutes,' he said. 'You looked as though you were terrified out of your wits.'

'I was,' she replied, pushing back her hair. 'I was never so glad to see Carys in all my life.'

'You are not a born oyster maiden then?' he asked, walking easily at her side as Eline made her way distractedly through stalls she didn't even see.

'No, I was raised on a farm.' She risked a glance at him and the colour flooded into her cheeks once more at the look in his eyes. 'I'm just an ordinary woman.'

'No, not ordinary,' Will said. 'You are so beautiful, Eline, and so vulnerable, I want to take you away and look after you.'

Eline lowered her head, now was the time to tell him she was married, that she had someone to take care of her, she had Joe. And yet the words would not pass her lips.

'There is something I can't explain,' Will continued, 'a feeling between us that I've never experienced before. You feel it too, don't you?'

Eline nodded, but she couldn't speak. They stood still in the middle of the crowded market and stared at each other as though each was trying to memorize the other's face.

Will held out his hand as though he would touch her and then he let it drop to his side. 'What is it, Eline? Is there something you are not telling me?'

Eline took a deep breath and knew that she couldn't tell him, she didn't want to break the magical, fragile bond that was growing between them.

'I must go,' she said. 'I have to think things out, please let me be.' She turned and hurried away from him and when she glanced over her shoulder, he had gone, swallowed up in the crowd.

The hours seemed to drag after that. Eline and Carys shared a pie, snatching the food between serving customers. Then, at last, the oyster sacks were empty, lying limply on the ground. Carys lifted her tin heavy with money and sighed contentedly.

'Time to fold up the table,' Carys said, 'there won't be any more customers today.'

Eline sighed with relief; she had been on edge, her eyes searching the crowds, seeing William Davies's build and bearing a hundred times, only to find out it wasn't him at all.

Carys transferred the money from the tin into a huge pocket beneath her apron and then folded the empty sacks and handed them to Eline. 'Let's pop round the back, fetch the horse and cart,' she said. 'We can ride a bit of the way back home, give our legs a rest.'

Binnie was contentedly chewing the grass at the edge of the roadway. Carys untied the reins from round the bark of a tree and stroked the animal's ears.

'Good girl, Binnie, come on, we're going home.' She threw the sacks on to the back of the cart and led the horse out on to the roadway.

'Jump up on the cart,' Carys said, lifting her skirts and

hauling herself on board. The cart swayed dangerously as Eline carefully climbed up beside her.

'Not a bad day's work,' Carys said, running her hands through the coins in her pocket. 'Hope my Sam got a good catch this trip out, got a special customer over at Caswell, a man that runs a tavern, been taking a lot of Sam's oysters lately, mind.'

The sky overhead was darkening, rain clouds seemed to be gathering over the entire bay, hovering over the craggy headland of Mumbles that was mistily visible from the Oystermouth Road.

Carys sighed. 'I spects I'll have a lot of work on the perches when Sam comes back, laying down them oysters is a back-breaking business.' She glanced at Eline.

'Your Joe don't let you do that though, do he?' she said, eyebrows raised. 'That's one mistake you should put right.' She sighed. 'Still, you don't know you're born having a man like Joe.'

Eline was scarcely listening but she made an effort to appear interested. 'I suppose I am lucky.' She glanced at Carys trying to give the conversation some of her attention. 'Why will you be laying down oysters this trip, then?'

'Well, I spects most of the big oysters have been dredged by now and the catch will be too small to sell, so the oysters will go on the perches to grow up a bit, see. Them oysters that are big enough to go to market tomorrow or the next day or perhaps next week they'll stay fresh and lively on the perches under the sea for a time.'

She glanced at Eline. 'Your Joe *should* let you work the perches and the plantations instead of having that hussy Nina Park and her girls to do it,' she said. 'Then you would be used to the ways of the village, you'd be a worker like the rest of us instead of keeping house like a little china doll.'

Eline looked up quickly wondering if Carys was criticizing her, but there was such a look of frankness on the woman's face that it was clear she was just speaking her mind with no malice intended.

'You're right, Carys, I must talk to Joe again, try to persuade him to let me do some of the work.' She paused. 'I know he feels a bit responsible for the Parks because Nina's husband was his friend.'

'Is that what he told you?' Carys said, her dark eyebrows raised. 'Well, it's not for me to tittle-tattle between husband and wife, but Nina's got a son at sea. He should come home and be responsible for her and the girls, not Joe. I'd keep an eye on things there if I was you.'

'What do you mean?' Eline asked quietly but Carys was clucking at Binnie, shaking up the reins and urging the horse to a trot.

Eline shrugged; there was so much that had happened in Joe's life before she was even born that it was pointless speculating about his past.

A salty breeze was coming in from the sea, lifting the untidy strands of hair from Eline's forehead, tugging at the ribbons, whipping them across her face. She glanced to her left where the tide was bringing in the rain and bit her lip worriedly.

'I wonder if the men will be in soon,' Eline said. 'I hope they won't stay out all night, it looks as if there might be a storm.'

'Those men know the sea in all her moods,' Carys answered. 'My Sam will never know my moods like he does those of the waters around Oystermouth.'

The horse was picking up speed now, trotting eagerly along the home stretch, sensing the nearness of home. The cart bucked over the hard cobbles and Eline felt the coldness of the wind against her face.

As the cart rolled along past the shops, Eline avoided looking at the boot and shoe shop fearful of seeing Will standing in the doorway. Why did she have to feel this way about a man who was a stranger to her? It was foolish and it was a sin against Joe and her marriage vows.

And yet, as the row of tiny cottages where she lived came into sight, Eline could not resist glancing back over her shoulder at the shops disappearing in the gloom. She thought she saw a lean figure of a man watching her from a doorway but she could not be sure it was William Davies. She saw an arm lift in greeting and responded at once and suddenly she was warm inside. It *was* Will and he had been looking out for her return.

'What's up with you, Eline?' Carys asked drily. 'You look as if you'd lost a farthing and found a shilling.'

'Just happy to be home,' Eline said quietly. She folded her arms around her breasts as if she was hugging a secret to herself and her eyes watched the figure in the shop doorway until it was no longer in sight.

CHAPTER FOUR

'You must never let our Tom know the truth.' Nina
Parks stood in the small kitchen, her hands folded across
her spotless apron, staring up defiantly at Joe. 'It would
bring shame on the boy to know he was born out of
wedlock.'

Joe felt a knot of anger within him; this was an
argument he'd had with Nina many times and, as usual,
she would not budge an inch.

'But I need my son,' he said, making an effort to be
reasonable. 'Can't you see he could have a fine future
sailing the *Oyster Sunrise* for me?'

'Tom may be your natural son,' Nina's lips trembled,
'but you have never given him your name, have you,
Joe?'

Joe looked away from her, guilt searing him. He
rubbed his hand over his eyes. 'I was young, frightened,
I couldn't face the thought of a wife and a child.'

'But I could?' Nina said, her voice rising. 'I could
manage the shame of it all, could I? *Duw!*' she went on,
'if it wasn't for that good man giving me his name I
would have been an outcast in the village and you know
it.'

'I know how good Kevin Parks was,' Joe said softly,
'he was my best friend, remember?'

'I know,' Nina's voice softened. 'He would do anything for you, even take on me and my bastard.'

'Don't say that!' Joe felt pain at her brutal words. 'I
let you down, but Tom is still *my* son and nothing will
ever change that.'

'Sit down, Joe,' Nina said, relaxing a little. 'Let me

talk to you while the girls are out and we have the chance.'

Joe seated himself at the kitchen table, big arms resting on the boards, waiting for the lecture that must surely come. He knew he'd been weak, he'd turned his back on her when twenty years ago Nina had come to him tremulously and told him she was with child. How could he, the man, excuse what the boy had done?

'Listen,' Nina reached out and rested her hand on his. He glanced down at the reddened, weathered hands, the hands of an honest working woman and felt pity wash over him.

'It's like this,' Nina continued. 'Tom never knew that you were his father, you know that. To him Kevin was his dad always.' She stared into his face earnestly. 'What would Tom think of you if he knew the truth?'

'I don't know,' Joe replied moodily. 'Perhaps now is the time to find out.'

'No!' Nina said. 'He would hate you. Tom is a young man with no tolerance, he would never forgive you for deserting us both, can't you see that?'

Joe sighed. 'But Nina, he can have a great future as my son, he can sail the *Oyster Sunrise*, take charge of the skiff and the crew, be his own man.'

'And when your young wife gives you other sons,' Nina asked softly, 'what will you do then?'

Joe sat back in his seat, confused; he had not thought that far ahead.

'It would be years before any such sons could sail for me,' he said.

'Agreed, but what about their inheritance? Would you take from Eline's son to give to mine?'

'Tom shall have what is just,' Joe said with less certainty.

'And how will you do that?' Nina said. 'You may have six sons in a few years' time. It's all in the hands of the good Lord, isn't it?'

'I need a son now!' Joe was growing impatient and more than a little uneasy at the turn the conversation had taken. Feelings he had kept hidden even from his self rose to the surface.

He had been married to Eline long enough to have filled her with child and God knows it wasn't from want of trying. With Nina, it had all happened so easily.

It had been summer, the scents of roses perfumed the air and the grass was sweet and lush. They had lain together in the soft darkness, hearing the call of the owl and clinging together as though they would never part. And then, a few weeks later, she had come to him whey-faced and tearful and he ran.

When he'd returned to the village, Nina was married to Kevin Parks and had given birth prematurely, so it was said, to a fine boy.

Nina touched his hand again, her eyes soft as if she, too, was remembering. 'It *was* good, wasn't it?' she said with a break in her voice. 'I loved you then, Joe, and I've loved you ever since, you know that.'

His hand closed around hers. 'And I've tried to make it up to you since Kevin died,' he said.

'I know,' Nina nodded, 'if it wasn't for you, Joe, I'd have been left with nothing but debts and four children to take into the workhouse.'

She leaned forward and rested her lips against his cheek. 'And I'd have been a lonely widow without you, Joe,' she said. 'It seemed that no sooner had Kevin fathered the girls than he was taken by the good Lord and you it was who helped me through the bad times.' She rose then and moved to the hob, pushing the kettle on to the flames.

'We're getting all sentimental and silly,' she sighed, 'but since you've been married, I've missed you, Joe.'

He looked at her, a woman of his own age who knew how to please a man. She was robust, experienced and knew what he liked.

43

Suddenly the memories overcame him and he rose and went to her, taking her in his arms. 'Nina!' He buried his face in the warmth of her neck and, at once, her hands were busy, familiar as they touched him intimately.

Joe stopped thinking and gave way to his senses. He wanted Nina, her strong body, her passionate responses like a thirsty man wanted water.

'Not here,' she whispered, 'come on upstairs.' She led the way and he followed, his hands round her body from behind, cupping her breasts.

The room was as familiar as his own, he drew her to the bed and helped Nina unfasten her bodice. Her breasts, full and round, sprung from the confines of the cotton and, greedily, he held them, his mouth finding the erect nipples.

Nina moaned; she always did respond most gratifyingly to his love making. He caressed her ardently, her eyes were closed, her cheeks flushed, she really was a lovely, earthy woman, his kind of woman, he thought in surprise.

'Come on, Joe, my love,' she whispered, 'give me your vigour like you used to, I've waited so long.'

When he came to her, she cried out in joy and he felt power surge through him. Joe was in charge, guiding Nina through the course of love and passion, bringing her to sobbing fulfilment.

And then the starburst came to him, searing him, drowning him. He was lost in the sweet sensation that he felt he could kill for. And later, as he rested beside Nina, he felt as though he had come home.

April was almost out, the blossoms were beginning to come to the trees. Hari Grenfell stared through the window of Summer Lodge and counted her blessings. She had achieved such wonderful things in her life and most dear was her happy marriage to Craig.

Behind her she could hear her son repeat his lessons in a bright intelligent voice. Mr Barnes was an excellent tutor and had been with the family for some time. David was a small boy eager to learn and when he was older, he would go away to school just as his father had done.

Hari shivered a little, not wanting to think of being parted from David, she needed him with her always at her side. But that was not the way the gentry lived and, even if she would never truly be one of them, Hari knew her son must be given every advantage so that he might live up to his father's expectations.

She moved from the window and went over to her son. David stared up at her, his dark eyes so like Craig's that love swept over her. She longed to kiss and hug him, but she knew that David, even at his tender age, would be mortified at such a display of affection in front of his tutor.

'I'll leave you now,' she said gently. 'I'm going to Oystermouth to see William, be good for Mr Barnes, David, learn your lesson well because your father will want to know what you've been doing today, mind.'

In the hallway, Jenny held her coat and gloves at the ready, the maid's good-natured young face wreathed in smiles.

'Shall I take some refreshment to Mr Barnes?' she said artlessly. 'And to young master David, of course.'

Hari hid a smile, Jenny's fascination with the serious young tutor was well known both below and above stairs.

'That would be very kind, Jenny.' Hari stared into the mirror and adjusted her hat, thrusting the long enamelled pin through the velvet to secure it. The spring winds could be wicked along the coast.

She stood still for a moment, staring at her reflection; her hair was dark and tamed now by good cutting, it no longer flared over her shoulders in an unruly cloud.

Hari was no longer the girl from the slums of World's

45

End, but the rich and successful Mrs Grenfell who had a string of boot and shoe shops to her credit. She had worked hard for them by the sweat of her brow and by using her initiative and her flair for design.

It was true that her husband was also a rich business man, for Craig owned the Grenfell and Briant Leather Company, but Craig's business was quite separate from Hari's. That way there was a mutual respect between them as well as a deep and abiding love.

Jenny, impatient to spend a few minutes with her idol, held open the large front door and Hari stepped outside into the brightness of the morning.

The carriage was waiting for her and the footman respectfully helped her inside. 'We're going to Oystermouth.' Hari eased on her gloves. 'Tell the driver not to travel too fast, I want to look at the scenery.'

The road winding from Swansea to Oystermouth was right on the edge of the sea. The bay curved in a golden sweep that culminated in the outcrop of rocks at Mumbles Head. It was a beautiful drive, especially on a morning such as this when the promise of blossoms budded on the trees and the scents of spring drifted in through the open carriage window.

Hari relaxed against the leather seat, her eyes closed as she breathed in the soft scents of spring. The clip-clop of the horses' hoofs against the road was soothing. She was so happy that sometimes that happiness frightened her. It seemed too good to last and yet hadn't she had her share of unhappiness in the past?

When Hari alighted outside the shop on the main street of Oystermouth Village, she gave her driver instructions to take some time off, once he had seen to the animals. He would be free to drink ale in one of the inns along the shore.

'Hari!' Will came forward, his hands held out to her, his smile wide and welcoming. 'What do you think of the window display? I did it myself.'

46

Hari stood back admiring the line of boots that appeared to be marching across the bed of silk. She nodded her head.

'Very impressive,' she squeezed his hand, 'but then I always did think you had many talents, Will.'

His eyes were warm as they rested on her and Hari felt once more that the two of them could not be closer had they been brother and sister.

'Anything I have achieved, I owe to you,' Will said softly. 'I'll always be grateful to you, Hari.'

'*Duw!* There's no need for gratitude.' Hari lapsed into her old way of talking; with Will she could be herself, the Hari who struggled her way to the top of her profession with sheer hard work and determination.

Inside, the shop was clean and sweet smelling, the few chairs artfully arranged to give the maximum comfort. Will led Hari forward.

'Look, I've got in a stock of men's working boots as well as some sensible boots for ladies. I've decided that this shop will be more practical than the ones in Swansea because this is essentially a working, seafaring village.' He smiled. 'The toffs will go to your place as they usually do.'

'Have you been busy?' Hari asked. She so wanted William to make a success of this, his first business venture. She herself had put up some of the funding for the shop, but, basically, it was Will's own enterprise and she wanted only the best for him.

'It's not been bad for the first few weeks,' he said, 'though much of the stuff is coming in for repair which is what I had anticipated.' He smiled. 'I've managed to get a damn good cobbler, an old chap from the village. Pendry doesn't say much but he's a good worker. I supply the leather and he does the cobbling at home, it should work very well.'

Hari sat on one of the chairs as the door opened and a stocky woman wrapped in a gleaming apron and wearing a woollen shawl came into the shop. 'Looks like you have a customer, Will,' she said lightly.

She watched as William smiled as warmly as though the woman was dressed in finest silk and marvelled at the charm he possessed. She felt a sense of pride; Will had more than proved himself worthy of faith in him and she felt sure he was destined for great things.

'Hello, Mr Davies, we met the other day, Carys Morgan.' The woman was used to the fresh salt air, Hari could tell by the ruddy glow to her cheeks and the weather-beaten arms that jutted from rolled-back sleeves.

'I remember, you were on your way to market with your oysters,' Will said pleasantly. 'What can I do for you, Mrs Morgan?'

'I need some new boots,' Carys Morgan said beaming widely. 'My Sam's been having good catches lately and now the dredging season is coming to an end I'd better get what I need before my husband complains there's no money.'

Hari was aware that the woman was regarding her with open curiosity and she found herself warming to the wide eyes and happy smile that seemed to be Carys Morgan's usual expression.

'*Bore da*,' she said in Welsh and Mrs Morgan's smile, if anything, grew wider.

'*Bore da*, madam.' She spoke almost shyly, overwhelmed by the fine clothes Hari was wearing. Little did she know that once Hari had been much poorer than ever Carys Morgan was.

William brought out a selection of boots and while he was fitting them kept up a pleasant conversation.

'These are the latest fashion, fine and smart, but very practical.' He smiled warmly. 'As you know we get a great deal of salt winds here at Oystermouth,' he continued, 'but these boots are stout enough to keep out even the worst of the elements.'

48

Carys was quite enchanted. She stood up and turned her ankle, admiring the buttoned boots with wide eyes. '*Duw*, they're lovely, but I don't suppose I can afford anything so fine.'

'These are not so expensive as you might think.' Will had lowered his tone confidentially. 'And for the first few weeks only I have a special price for my customers.'

Hari hid a smile. This was obviously an idea that had hit William on the spur of the moment, but it was a good ploy and perhaps he should expand on it a little, put a poster in the window to advertise his offer.

'I'll have them then,' Carys said excitedly. 'My Sam loves a bargain, not that he's mean, mind, but he's that careful with his money, his pocket's as hard to open as the oysters he dredges.' She rose to her feet looking wistfully at the boots. 'I'll call back later then and bring the money with me.' It was clear that the boots, though reasonable in price, were more expensive than Carys Morgan had anticipated.

'Please take the boots now, Mrs Morgan,' Will said in his most charming voice. That, Hari thought, was a very good move; Carys Morgan would be doubly grateful to him now.

When Will had wrapped the boots, Carys held them to her as though they were something precious. And so they were, Hari told herself. Had she so readily forgotten the thrill of having new boots and she a cobbler's daughter?

It was almost time for luncheon when Will decided to close the shop. 'Perhaps you would like to look at the books for me, Hari,' he said smiling, 'give me an insight about managing figures.'

Hari warmed with pride. She was happy that William wanted her to know all aspects of his business and she was certainly used to figures. She had coped well enough with all her own book work at the beginning of her career.

Hari walked along the street with William admiring the soft expanse of sea that washed in from Swansea Bay. His lodgings were situated in a tall, elegant building with gleaming windows and crisp, clean curtains. Mrs Marsh herself was a picture of an ideal landlady; she was neat and fresh-cheeked and she looked at Hari with blue, shrewd eyes before bobbing a curtsy and inviting her into the best parlour.

Hari took to the woman at once. 'I see you are looking after William as though he was a son,' she said gratefully and Mrs Marsh smiled, patting her already neat hair, embarrassed at the compliment.

Will brought her the books and Hari's experienced eyes took in the figures, seeing at once that William would not begin to make a profit for some months, but that was only to be expected with a new business.

'You have kept your outlay to a minimum,' she said approvingly, 'and as the rent for the premises has been paid in advance, you will have little further outlay for some time to come.'

She sighed. 'You know, Will, you are much better equipped than I was when I started out. How I had the courage to go to Mr Fisher that time and take on the building at World's End with no capital at all, I don't know.'

'It payed off though, didn't it?' Will spoke admiringly. 'You have guts, Hari, you always have had what it takes to succeed.'

'I didn't know that then,' Hari replied, 'it was one big leap in the dark. I took on the shop and the house without putting a penny down, but by the end of the month, I had enough to pay the rent, by some miracle.'

'No miracle, it was all due to your hard work and daring,' Will said.

'I had good friends to help me, mind.' Hari smiled. 'Cleg the Coal's wife brought me bedding she'd begged from the big houses and Meg and Charlie Briant had a hand in my success. I owe a lot of people a great deal, including you, Will.'

She closed the books and put them down on the sofa beside her, leaning forward eagerly. 'I want you to succeed too, Will, I know you can do it.'

'I hope so.' He moved to the door. 'Now, I'm going to get us some refreshment from Mrs Marsh, I think we both need some luncheon to sustain us. I have to return to the fray this afternoon, I haven't yet found a salesman, remember.'

The sun was high overhead when Hari and Will returned to the shop. The carriage was waiting for Hari outside the doors with the driver dozing in his seat.

With a sense of concern, Hari saw Carys Morgan leaning against the doorway, her face pale, an upturned basket of groceries at her feet.

William had seen at once that something was wrong and moved forward to support Carys, handing the keys of the shop to Hari. 'Let's get her inside,' he said urgently.

When Carys was seated in a chair, William brought her a glass of water and held it to her white lips. 'There you go, don't be frightened,' William said consolingly, 'you are going to be all right.'

Carys opened her eyes. '*Duw*,' her voice was faint, 'I feel so bad.' She rubbed her face. 'Bringing you the money for the boots, I was and I came over all funny, like.'

Hari gestured to Will. 'Tell the driver to get ready to take Mrs Morgan back to her home,' she said meaningfully.

When she was alone with Carys, Hari bent over her sympathetically. 'I'm sure there's nothing really wrong with you. Have you felt bad like this before?'

'A couple of mornings lately,' Carys said in bewilder-

51

ment. 'I've been that sickly when I first get up that it's a job to get to the beach to help my Sam with the oysters.'

Hari smiled. 'I expect you've missed your courses too, haven't you?'

Carys looked at her in amazement. 'How did you know that?' she said.

Hari sighed. 'Because I'm a mother, I've had a child myself and I think you're expecting a baby, Mrs Morgan.'

Carys shook her head at once. 'No, I'm barren, I can't have babbas.'

'Who told you that?' Hari asked. 'You've got a husband, haven't you?'

'Aye, I've got a man all right, but I've had him for three years and more and haven't caught for a child.' She rubbed at her cheek. 'Mind, no one *told* me I was barren, but my two older sisters have never had children and I thought I was going to be the same after all this time.'

'Three years isn't very long,' Hari said reasonably, 'and you're not very old, are you?'

Carys Morgan sighed. 'I feel old, I'm coming up to twenty-nine years of age now, mind.' A warmth came into her eyes. 'Could it be true, could I be with child? My Sam would be thrilled to bits if I was.'

'You will have to see the doctor I expect,' Hari said, 'but I don't think there's any doubt, there's a look, something about the eyes.'

William returned and Hari smiled at him and nodded. 'We are going to take you home in the carriage,' Hari said gently. 'I think you'd be better off by your own fireside now.'

'It's all right, madam,' Carys said. 'I only live a little bit further along the street, you could spit the distance from here.'

'Never mind that,' Hari said firmly. 'We can't have

one of our customers fainting away in the street, can we?'

Carys looked round in awe as she was helped inside the coach. '*Duw*, will you look at that fine leather then?' she said admiringly. 'There's lovely it is.'

To Hari's surprise, Will climbed into the coach beside Carys. 'Do you think I should ask your friend Eline to come in and take care of you until your husband comes home?' he asked hopefully and Hari bit her lip to hide her smile.

Carys looked doubtful but Will pressed home the point. 'I'm sure you'd like company just now, someone to have a cup of tea and a gossip with.'

'Aye, perhaps you're right,' she said, 'no one else in the street would think anything of having a babbi, they haves them all the time. Eline will likely be happy for me, she's such a nice girl.'

It took only a minute or two to reach the row of fishermen's cottages slanting up the steep hill leading from the main road and Hari was no longer surprised when Will jumped out of the carriage and carefully helped Carys Morgan into the street. Now he would find out where this dream girl of his lived.

When Hari saw Eline come out on to the step, her hair dishevelled into a cloud of curls around her shoulders, her small frame enveloped in an apron, she was reminded of herself as she had once been and a sense of nostalgia brought tears to her eyes.

She leaned out of the coach and watched as Eline took Carys's arm and led her gently indoors. When Will returned, he was glowing.

'Did you see her, Hari, isn't she lovely?' He sank down in the seat, his eyes staring wistfully towards the cottage.

'Yes,' Hari said softly, 'she is lovely.' She lowered her head. How could she tell William that on the girl's slender finger there had been a flash of gold. Eline, Will's dream girl, was married.

CHAPTER FIVE

An early sun streamed in through the window of the small, neat kitchen, dappling the still wet flagstones of the floor with patterns of pale light. Eline, seated in an upright, wooden kitchen chair, smiled across the scrubbed table at Carys whose face was wreathed in smiles.

'It's true then,' Eline said softly, 'you are going to have a baby?'

Carys clasped her hands together and nodded her head vigorously. 'Aye, Dr Thomas says I'm three months gone. I still can't believe it.'

Eline rose as the kettle hissed steam into the kitchen. 'I'll make us some tea.' She spoke absently, thinking of the moment a few days earlier when William Davies had brought Carys home. He had knocked on Eline's door and then stepped into her kitchen and for once Eline had been grateful for the hours she spent on her hands and knees cleaning the place.

William had stood close to Eline, telling her in soft words that he would be grateful if she came next door to stay with Carys, but all the time his eyes had been caressing her.

Eline had wanted to reach out for him, to hold him close, to kiss his strong mouth. She became aware that the kettle was still sending clouds of steam into her kitchen to run down the whitewashed walls like tears. Quickly, she made the tea.

'Have you told Sam yet?' she asked, bringing the cups to the table. Carys shook her head.

'I wanted to be sure as God made little oysters that I

was expecting. I didn't want to build up Sam's hopes if there was any doubt.'

'Talking about oysters,' Eline said, 'you shouldn't go lifting those sacks any more, Sam should get someone to help you.'

Carys laughed. 'You must be daft if you think Sam would spend a brass farthing on help for me! All men are not like your Joe, mind, ready to pay out hand over fist for another woman to do the work a wife should rightfully be doing.'

She put her hand over her mouth and looked sheepishly over her plump fingers at Eline. 'I'm sorry,' she said at last. 'I know it's not your doing that Joe pays Nina and her girls to work the plantations and perches. I didn't mean any harm.'

'I'm not a bit offended.' Eline drank some of her tea gladly for her mouth was suddenly dry.

'Carys,' she said slowly, 'is there anything I should know about Nina Parks?' She spoke softly, without anger, and yet Eline felt somehow that Carys was trying to warn her.

Carys's eyebrows jerked upward and then she composed herself.

'I don't know what you mean,' she said, but her eyes looked everywhere except at Eline.

'There's something going on,' Eline said. 'Joe seems preoccupied and when I asked him about a crew for the new boat he just shook his head and refused to say anything.'

'I expect Joe wants the boy to be the master of the *Oyster Sunrise*,' Carys said slowly and then stared down at her cup as though she'd said too much.

'The boy? Do you mean Nina Parks's son, Carys?' Of course she did and Eline didn't wait for confirmation. 'But I thought the Parks boy was out deep-sea fishing; why should he come home to work off shore?'

Carys didn't reply, but there was a look of acute embarrassment on her honest, open face.

'And why should Joe want him anyway when there are plenty of good men in Oystermouth just waiting for a chance to skipper a boat like the *Oyster Sunrise*?'

'Ask your husband.' Carys folded her lips into a prim line and it was clear she intended to say no more on the subject.

Eline sighed. 'I'm sorry, I shouldn't be trying to make you gossip about people, Carys, but you must admit that Nina Parks is a bit of a mystery woman.'

Carys drank her tea and placed the cup back in the saucer with a clink of finality. 'I'd better be getting some work done.' She rose to her feet. 'There's oysters to be washed ready for market and my Sam won't thank me for sitting about like Lady Muck while he's out in the bay working.'

Eline followed her to the door. 'You should be taking things easy,' she said softly. 'Perhaps I can help you wash the oysters; what do you think?'

Carys shook her head. 'No, you stay by here in your house where you belong.' It was clear that Carys had no wish to be put in a position where she might feel beholden.

Eline watched as Carys moved across the road and down on to the beach. The sun was warming the sea into a soft glints of azure and the sand was shading from palest gold to umber as the waves reached hungrily for the shore.

Soon it would be summer and the oyster season would be over until September.

Eline returned to the table and poured more tea from the pot, sighing heavily. She sank down into a chair and stared ahead of her knowing quite suddenly that she was no longer content to be Joe's pet, a little tame housewife washing and scrubbing and attending to Joe's needs. It simply wasn't enough for her. She must do something positive with her time or stultify.

Eline picked up her basket and moved towards the

56

door; she would go to the shops, perhaps some fresh air would clear her mind. There must be work for her somewhere, something she could do to make herself useful.

The air was clear and fresh and the salt scents of the sea drifted to where Eline walked along the village street. It was not a long street, it curved from where the oyster boats lay at off-season like a shoal of stranded fish to where the hill turned and rose upwards towards the ruins of the castle.

Taking her time, Eline nevertheless knew that she was making for the newly opened boot and shoe shop. She did not dare to question herself too deeply about her motives and yet the tingle of excitement as she neared the double-fronted building was unmistakable.

She stopped outside looking up at the newly painted sign overhead. WILLIAM DAVIES BOOT AND SHOE STORE. The very look of his name in golden paint on a black background made Eline tremble.

She allowed her eyes to rest on the merchandise within the windows; stout, solid boots rested on a bed of sprinkled sand with a starfish and some shells scattered around for effect. Then the handwritten vacancy notice caught her eye and she drew in a sharp breath. Her head seemed to spin, questions raced through her head. Dare she, did she have the courage to apply for the job and even if she did, what would Joe say?

'Good morning,' the voice was low and musical, 'come to apply for the vacancy, have you?' William stood smiling down at her and in the glow of the morning sunlight, he looked so appealing, so wonderful that, for a moment, Eline couldn't speak.

'The job,' he said softly, 'it's yours if you want it.' He stepped aside. 'Come indoors and we can discuss it.'

Eline followed him into the shop and, for a moment, the room was a long, dark abyss after the glare of the sunlight. She stumbled and William caught her arm and held on to her for a moment. Eline, looking up at him, felt a wash of emotion that was so strange that she almost gasped out loud.

'What would I have to do?' Eline found her voice. 'I've never worked in a shop, mind, I would probably make a fool of myself.'

'No, you wouldn't,' he said with conviction. 'I need a lady assistant and all you would have to do is help customers to make up their minds about what kind of footwear they want.'

'I don't know,' Eline said doubtfully, 'don't shop assistants have to live in?'

'In some cases it is appropriate,' Will agreed, 'but I want someone who lives locally who would go home at nights because I have no living accommodation on the premises.'

He smiled down at her, his eyes alight, as though he was more intent on drinking in her closeness than in what he was saying.

'I would be able to pay six shillings a week and, of course, the job would only be for a moderate few hours a day. I wouldn't expect you to work from dawn till dusk.'

It was so tempting. Eline looked up at William and smiled, resisting the urge to lean against him, to beg him to take her in his arms and ride away with her on a white horse. Such nonsense was not for a respectably married woman.

It was as if a bucketful of cold water had been thrown over her head. Eline gasped. What about Joe? What would he have to say about her mad idea of working in a shop? Then she became calmer. Joe could not keep her locked up like a doll in a case; she must be her own person like the rest of the women in Oystermouth. Not one of her neighbours lived the dull, restricted life she did.

'I'll take it,' she said quickly. 'Shall I start right away?'

William seemed taken aback by the suddenness of her decision. He thrust his hands into his pockets and looked around him.

'Yes, I suppose so.' He seemed to pull himself to-gether. 'If you could just take off your apron and put away your basket, I'll show you what I'd like you to do first of all.'

As carefully as if it was of the utmost importance to her, Eline folded her spotless apron, keeping the creases in place as she put the apron away in the empty basket.

Will led the way to the back of the shop. 'I'd like you to chose some ladies' shoes, anything you think appropriate, and then later, perhaps you'll set them out in the small window.'

'I don't think I'm clever enough to make up a window display,' Eline said doubtfully. She watched as William set up some boards, covering them with black silk.

'Of course you are,' Will said confidently. 'What do you think of the window with the boots in, effective, isn't it?'

'Very,' Eline agreed and William paused to look at her, his smile warming his eyes.

'I did that myself.' He spoke with an endearing air of boyish pride. 'I didn't think I was capable of such imagination but, you see, we all have a little bit of creativity in us.' His smile widened. 'And you, I'm sure, have more creativity in your little finger than I have in my entire body.'

He dropped the silk into place and turned to face her. Eline could smell the freshness of his skin and almost touch the streaks of light gleaming in his hair. She stepped back at once, her heart beating swiftly. Her emotions felt raw, she was like a foolish child adoring that which she could not have.

'Of course,' he said gently, 'if there are lady customers in the shop, leave everything and serve them.'

He led her to where the ladies' boots were stored and

soon Eline forgot herself in her preoccupation with the task in hand. She knew nothing about fashions, she was only too aware of that, but she knew just what footwear would appeal to the women of the village.

For some time Eline worked silently and then, looking up, she became aware that there were customers in the shop, four women gathered together like a flock of birds in their black skirts and white aprons. They were all staring at her, waiting to be served.

Eline moved tentatively forward. 'Can I help you in any way?' she asked and the women turned to stare at her in open curiosity.

Eline drew a deep breath as she faced Nina Parks whose eyes were suddenly filled with almost hostile glee.

'*Duw*, what you doing here then?' Nina Parks twitched her shawl into place and her three daughters gathered closer as if to watch some sort of contest.

'I work here,' Eline said evenly. She knew that Nina didn't like her, had never liked her and yet she had never reciprocated Nina's hostility.

'Do Joe know about this?' Nina's voice rose as though in disbelief and Eline, glancing over her shoulder, saw that Will Davies was out of earshot. She took a deep breath.

'I don't really see that it's any of your business,' she said quietly. 'Now, can I help you? Would you like to see some of our stock of boots and shoes?'

'Go on, Mam,' Gwyneth said, her beautiful dark eyes resting on Eline. 'Let her serve you, that would be a laugh, wouldn't it?'

Gwyneth was the eldest of Nina's three daughters, an attractive girl, but now her lower lip was thrust out as though in scorn. She tossed back her hair and with her chin raised looked at Eline as though daring her to say anything out of place.

'Make a change from us working for *her*, won't it?' she added, her words falling like stones into the silence.

When her mother stood uncertainly to one side, Gwyneth sat on one of the chairs provided for customers and lifted up her slim ankle.

'I'd like to try on a pair of nice soft pumps,' Gwyneth said quietly, 'something costing a lot of money.'

Eline hesitated; it was clear the girl was wasting her time. She moved then to the shelf of pigskin shoes and brought out a pair she judged to be the right size.

'Perhaps you would like to try these?' she asked, holding them out.

Gwyneth disregarded the shoes and looked up at her mother. 'Don't she talk posh, not like a village girl at all.' She looked back at Eline. 'Come on then, unbutton my boots for me.'

Eline was about to bend forward when William appeared at her side. 'Can I help?' he smiled warmly at the women and, at once, Gwyneth smiled up at him from under her long lashes. Shaking out her skirts, she still managed to show a little of her neat ankle.

It was Nina who broke the silence. 'We all want a pair of good boots,' she said, glancing round angrily at her daughters. 'Tidy boots, mind, not fancy things that cost the earth and will fall apart as soon as a bit of sand gets in them.' Her down-to-earth tone seemed to ease the air of tension in the shop and Eline felt herself relaxing.

With William's help, Eline managed to find the most practical boots in stock. She admired his smooth handling of the women and soon, Nina Parks was deferring to him, fluttering and blushing like a young girl.

When they finally left the shop, all of them were giggling, happily clutching their purchases. Eline watched with a feeling of relief as the Parks women walked along the street away from the shop.

'Why are they so hostile to you, Eline?' Willam was standing at her side and Eline felt protected and safe with him so close.

'I'm not a village girl born and bred,' she explained, 'and so I'm different. I'm what they call a "townie" even though I was born on farm.'

'I see.' William smiled down at her. 'Well, once they get used to you, I'm sure it will all sort itself out.' He paused, head on one side scrutinizing her.

'Of course I could see at once that you were different from the village women, but then you would stand out in any crowd.' He moved a fraction closer. 'Eline,' he said and she moved away from him quickly.

'I'd better get on with the window.' Her cheeks were flushed, her breathing uneven and Eline suddenly doubted the wisdom of being here alone in the shop with William Davies.

Eline worked industriously and in silence, but she was always aware of William's presence in the shop. After a few false starts, she found that she had a natural aptitude for creating an eye-catching window display and, as she worked the silk into small puffs like dark clouds around the array of ladies' boots and shoes, she felt a tremendous excitement fill her.

Eline had always liked painting pictures, she had handled paints ever since she was a child and now she found that to make up a window display was very much like composing a picture.

An idea struck her and she searched at the back of the shop for some other materials with which to enhance her display. Eventually, outside in the alleyway behind the shop, Eline found some discarded wooden crates and a length of rope and eagerly she took them back to the shop.

'Have you got any tools in here?' she asked William, her eyes avoiding his. 'Anything that will serve to pull the slats of the boxes apart?'

With a few twists of his strong wrists, William broke the boxes into tiny planks of wood, smiling indulgently as Eline carried them to the window.

Behind the clouds of silk, Eline began to construct a roughly tethered ladder of wood. She worked quickly, so absorbed in her task that she failed to notice that there were customers in the shop and that William was good-naturedly serving them himself.

When the ladder was fixed, Eline arranged some light slippers on the shallow steps, balancing them by the small heels so that the fronts of the shoes were facing the window.

At last, she stood back in satisfaction and admired the simplicity and effectiveness of her work.

She became aware that William was standing on the pavement, head on one side in a way she recognized as being characteristic of him, studying the display. After an agonizingly long wait, Eline saw him return to the shop.

'Do you like it?' she asked tentatively and bit her lip in anxiety.

'Excellent!' Will smiled down at her. 'I think even Hari Grenfell would be impressed with what you've done with a few bits of wood and a piece of rope. Well done, Eline!'

He raised his hand as though to touch her cheek and then let it fall to his side. Eline felt a thrill run through her; she knew it was absurd but she realized in that instant that she was in love with William Davies.

Something of her feeling must have shown in her eyes because William was about to speak when the door opened and a group of ladies came into the shop on a wave of chattering voices.

Eline could see at once that these were not village women but ladies of quality from the town. Their clothes were of good cloth, not made for working the oyster beds and the three of them wore expensive hats above well-groomed hair.

Eline moved forward and wondered if she should bob a curtsy to the obviously affluent customers. After a moment, she decided against it and, with her head high, moved forward.

'Can I be of any assistance?' she asked pleasantly and one of the women sank into a chair.

'Is this another of Mrs Grenfell's shops?' she asked setting down her large bag on the floor. 'I seem to recognize her touch in the beautiful window display.'

William stepped forward from the shadows and the woman's face was suddenly wreathed in smiles.

'Will! I wondered if I'd see you here, how lovely.' Her voice was smooth and cultured, that of a lady of refinement.

'Emily – Mrs Miller, didn't you see the name over the door and me so proud of it?' He took her hand and smiled ruefully.

'I saw the name, Will, and that's why I came in. But to be honest with you I'm so impressed with that wonderful window of ladies' boots and shoes, I thought that surely Hari must have done the display.'

William shook his head. 'As a matter of fact it was done by Eline here, my new assistant. Isn't she talented?'

Mrs Miller smiled at Eline. 'You are very clever, Eline, perhaps you should do some of the windows in my Swansea boot and shoe emporiums. You could easily make a career of window displays.'

'Don't entice her away!' William said. 'I've only just found her!'

He smiled and waved his arms around the shop. 'What can we do for you and your friends? Anything you want I'm sure Eline and I can find it for you, though I can't think of anything we'd have here that you haven't got in your own emporium.'

Mrs Miller smiled. 'I'll be honest, Will, my new shoes are killing me, the heels are too high for walking; pride must pinch, it seems,' she added ruefully.

Eline, warmed by the praise and by the way William

made her feel a valuable part of the team, was anxious to please.

'We have some lovely calf boots in stock, I could bring you those.'

Emily Miller nodded. 'I've come to buy something comfortable to wear for the rest of the day.' She looked up at Will. 'But while we are here, I'm sure my friends and I would be happy to patronize your shop, Will, get you off to a good start with a few orders.'

Eline served the ladies eagerly and when at last they left the shop, each of them was carrying several parcels of new shoes.

William smiled down at Eline. 'It was my lucky day when I first set eyes on you,' he said softly.

It was drawing near to closing time and Eline was just clearing up after the last of the customers had departed when the door was flung violently open. She looked up startled to see Joe standing in the doorway framed by the evening sunlight.

'What in God's name do you think you are doing, woman?' Joe stomped over the polished floor regardless of the clinging sand and mud on his boots.

William stepped forward at once. 'How can I help you, sir?' he asked and there was an edge of anger to his voice.

'There's nothing I want from you.' Joe stared past him at Eline. 'Come on home and don't you ever do this sort of thing to me again.' His voice rose. 'Do you think I'm not capable of earning a living for us now?'

'Joe,' Eline said anxiously, 'don't make a fuss, I'm not doing any harm.'

'Not doing any harm; do you think I want you working in a shop when I wasn't even willing for you to work on the oysters like the other women? Spoiled you've been, Eline. Ever since you were a child I've given in to you readily, but not in this, Eline, oh no! Get your things, we're going home.'

William turned to Eline. 'Who is this man?' he asked quietly. 'Is he your father, your elder brother, what?'

Joe's face reddened and Eline felt the breath leave her body as, shoulders hunched, he moved forward aggressively.

'I tell you who I am, you young whipper snapper, I'm her husband, that's who I am.' Joe caught Eline's arm and drew her towards the door.

Eline had time only to glance quickly over her shoulder, but that brief look was all she needed to tell her that Will was devastated by the news. With a mingling of joy and despair, she realized that William Davies had been drawn to her, perhaps was even beginning to fall a little in love with her. But at what cost? Her silence had made her a liar and now William could never ever trust her again.

CHAPTER SIX

'How could she do it to me, Hari?' William rubbed his hand through his hair so that it stood up on end. 'I was falling in love with her and all the time she was married to an *old* man!'

He looked at Hari, wondering why she was not agreeing with him, but she was staring silently down at her hands.

'You knew, didn't you?' he said accusingly. 'You *knew* she was married.'

Hari nodded miserably. 'I saw the gold ring on her finger, I'm sorry, Will.'

He sank down into a chair, and took Hari's hand in his own. 'How could you tell me? It wasn't your place to destroy my dreams, was it?'

'She could have been a widow, Will,' Hari said softly. 'Although she is very young, the fishermen risk their lives every day.' Hari shrugged. 'Anyway, I couldn't hurt you.'

William rose to his feet and thrust his hands into his pockets. 'I don't understand it, the way the man was talking, it was as though he'd known her since the day she was born. I thought she was his daughter or at least his young sister.'

He paced around the room. 'It must have been an arranged marriage, one of convenience. I expect Eline was more or less forced to marry the man – there's no other explanation.'

'Why couldn't she have told you about it?' Hari said softly. 'Then at least it wouldn't have been such a shock.'

Will rubbed his hand through his hair. 'I think she was embarrassed,' he said. 'I *know* she feels the same way about me as I do about her, so she must have had good reason for remaining silent.'

'Don't let a pretty face blind you to the truth, there's a good man,' Hari said rising and putting her hand on Will's arm. 'Eline is a sweet girl, but she's married and whatever the reason for her marriage, it is legally binding, nothing can change that.'

'I must see her.' Will felt the blood rush to his face at the memory of the way the man had dragged Eline unceremoniously from the shop. 'I must talk to her.'

'Look,' Hari spoke quietly, placatingly, 'find out all you can about the two of them but be discreet.' She looked up at him and Will could see her eyes imploring him to be careful.

A feeling of warmth washed over him. Hari was the one person in the world who loved him without reservation, she would do anything for him, he knew that, and her words to him now held a certain wisdom.

'It may be that your guess is right about Eline being pushed into the marriage and, on the other hand, perhaps she was very happy to be the wife of a self-sufficient fisherman, but whatever the truth, don't do anything reckless.'

The door opened and Craig Grenfell entered the drawing room, his dark hair sweeping back from his high, intelligent forehead.

'Good heavens! It's like winter out today with that easterly breeze coming in off the sea. Oh, hallo William, good to see you, how's the new store coming along?'

Will squared his shoulders, he had always been a little in awe of Hari's husband and never more so than now when the Grenfell and Briant Leather Company was a flourishing concern with branches all over the country. It made his venture in Oystermouth seem very small indeed.

'Fine, it seems to have started well enough, I've even been patronized by Emily Miller, though by accident rather than design.' He smiled down at Hari as she pouted in a pretence of anger.

'Didn't I tell you?' He smiled at Hari's raised eyebrows. 'It was only that her shoes pinched and the heels were too high, so she bought a pair of practical shoes made for comfort from me.'

Craig sank into a chair, his long legs stretched out before him, a big, handsome man with breeding in every line of his face and in the casual elegance of his body.

'Can't ask for a better patron than that.' He smiled broadly. 'The owner of the biggest emporium in Wales buying at William Davies's shop is an accolade not to be sniffed at.'

Craig looked at Hari and there was a world of love in his dark eyes. 'Where's that son of mine?' he asked softly and Hari reached out and touched her husband's hand.

'David is having a nap.' She spoke the ordinary words as though they were a caress and Will envied the couple their obvious happiness. That was just the sort of happiness he might have had with Eline.

'*Duw*,' Hari continued, 'the poor boy was worn out from running along the beach, that nanny of his is a great believer in fresh air!'

Will suddenly felt an outsider, looking in on a world of warm fires and even warmer emotions. He moved to the door. 'I'd better get back to Oystermouth,' he said, forcing a smile. 'Mrs Marsh will be sure to have a hot meal ready for me.'

Hari was on her feet in a moment. 'Oh Will,' she said catching his arm, 'I thought you might like to stay and have supper with us.'

Will covered her hand with his own, 'That's very generous of you, Hari, but I want to go over the books this evening. Another time?'

Hari rested her head against his shoulder for a brief moment. 'I love the way you talk, all posh-like. Have I ever told you, Will, how proud of you I am?'

'Then be proud of yourself,' William said gently. 'Craig too. Between the two of you I've become what I am today.' He laughed, suddenly rueful. 'A hybrid, half-gent half-working man.'

'Nonsense!' Hari said, 'you are a real gentleman in every sense of the word, my boy, and don't you forget it.'

As William strode away from Summer Lodge, he looked back at the large gracious house with its sweeping lawns and large wrought-iron gates and wondered that he, William Davies from the slums of Swansea, was welcome in such a place.

There must have been a star above him when he was born for, by rights, he should have spent his days in squalor and poverty in the hovel of a house at World's End. It was only through Hari's love and kindness and on the coat-tails of her vision and foresight that Will had been lifted out of all that and given a chance for a better life.

And yet he was not happy, well, not completely. He wanted a wife, a woman whom he could love and honour until the day he died, the way Craig Grenfell felt about Hari. In other words, Will wanted Eline Harries.

'I can't be held a prisoner like this, Joe.' Eline's voice was low and tears trembled on her lashes. 'Can't you see I'll pine away and die if I spend another day in this house with nothing to do but clean and cook for you?'

Joe turned on her. 'Well, have some children then.' His voice was rising with anger. 'Have sons for me so that they can grow and thrive and one day inherit my business.'

Eline hung her head, she didn't know why she hadn't conceived. It couldn't be Joe's fault; she must be responsible, she must somehow have failed, but she couldn't understand why.

She had come to be Joe's bride knowing nothing about

contact between men and women. Of course on the farm she had seen animals procreate, had taken it all for granted, but to translate those acts of nature into human terms had been beyond her.

It had been a terrible shock when Joe had come to her bed that first night. It had been a painful, almost bitter, experience. Even though Joe had tried to be kind, he had a passionate nature and his emotions had been roused to fever pitch because he had wanted and waited for her for so long and now he had her in his arms.

Eline had tried to understand that this was the way men were; she heard the village women talking often enough about preferring a tune on the fiddle to a night of passion and so she assumed they all felt as she did, that to give in to a husband was a duty rather than a pleasure.

And then Will Davies had come into her life and when he was near her, she experienced feelings and emotions that she had never known before. She wanted to be in his arms, to have him take possession of her body and yet such feelings could not be right.

'How could you expect me to let you work alone in a store with a strange man?' Joe seemed to pick up on her thoughts. 'Have you no shame, woman?'

'There would have been other assistants when Mr Davies had time to engage them,' Eline protested. 'In any case, the shop has two huge windows looking out on to the street, what could anyone make of that?'

'Don't argue with me,' Joe said sullenly. 'I am a plain man and I have spoken my last word, you are not to work for Davies or anyone else, so get that into your head right now.'

'Joe,' Eline said softly, 'I was born to be a working woman, couldn't I at least spend time on the oyster perches the way the other women do? I'm not a china doll, mind, to be stuck in a doll's house all day alone.'

'I have workers for the oysters as you well know,' Joe

said. 'I don't want you to work, Eline, are you deaf or stupid?'

Eline was suddenly stung to anger. 'No, I'm not deaf or stupid!' she said in a low voice. 'I know that something is going on between you and Nina Parks, *that's* how stupid I am.'

Joe jerked around to look at her. 'And who's been spreading vicious lies about me?' he thundered and, for a moment, Eline quailed before his anger.

'No one has been spreading anything,' she said, summoning her courage and lifting her head defiantly. 'I've always known there was something strange about the way you have kept going around there to *her* house every week.'

'Strange? What's strange in giving Nina and her girls the wages they have earned?' Joe demanded.

'The whole thing is odd,' Eline persisted, 'a debt to an old friend does not usually extend to keeping his entire family. If you ask me, Nina always was and still is your mistress, that's the debt you owe, conscience money and not an act of self-sacrificing goodness.'

Joe grasped her arm. 'Wash your mouth out!' he said and his face was red with anger. 'I love you, girl, I always have, but do not push me too far, do you hear?'

He shook her away from him and stormed to the door. 'I'm going out on the water now and by the time I come back I want you to have thought matters over. You will not work and you will not dare to question me on what is my own business, is that clear?'

When he had gone, Eline sat down in a chair and, resting her elbows on the scrubbed table-top, covered her face with her hands.

After a moment, she heard the door creak open and Eline dashed away her tears with her fingers.

'*Duw, cariad*, I couldn't help but hear your Joe shouting, going mad he was, what's wrong, lovely?'

Carys was looking well, her skin was glowing and there

was a light in her eyes, childbearing obviously suited her. Soon, she would no longer be required to pull out the row boats to the water's edge, the one concession to Carys's condition that her husband was prepared to make.

'He's angry because I wanted to work in the boot and shoe store,' Eline said flatly, knowing that Carys would doubtless have heard every word she and Joe had spoken.

'There, there, men are such fools,' Carys comforted softly. She took a seat opposite Eline and reached out her plump fingers to pat Eline awkwardly on the shoulder. 'He'll have forgotten his anger when he comes back, you'll see.' Carys smiled. 'If I know men, Joe will want to take you to bed and prove how good a husband he is, they always think that will solve any problems. Perhaps it will – for them,' she added drily.

Eline suppressed a shudder; she didn't want Joe to take her to bed. She had made a terrible mistake marrying him, she'd known that almost from the start, and yet it had taken the appearance of Will Davies to bring the fact home to her.

Perhaps she should leave him? But that was something unheard of, a woman didn't leave her lawful husband. In any case, Joe wouldn't let her go, he'd come after her wherever she went; he had waited seventeen years for her, he would never relinquish his hold on her not now, not ever.

'What am I to do, Carys?' Eline asked knowing that there was nothing she could do.

'Stick to your guns,' Carys said stoutly. 'Make Joe let you work if it's only on the oyster beds with us women.' She smiled. 'I don't blame him stopping you working with William Davies, mind, he's a handsome devil and would be a temptation to any woman.'

She banged her fist suddenly on the table. 'But insist you do something, keep on at him, deny him his rights, anything to get what you want, at least your days won't be so long if you're working the perches with us.'

She got to her feet and pushed the kettle on to the flames. 'I'll make us a nice cup of tea, shall I?' she said softly. 'And let me tell you, Eline, you are lucky to have tea in the house when it's so costly, most of us are not spoiled the way Joe spoils you, so just count your blessings now and again.'

'I know you're right,' Eline said, 'but I had a good life on the farm, mind, we were not short of anything there.' She paused, feeling disloyal to Joe. 'And he did benefit from the sale of the farm, remember, I didn't come to Joe empty handed.'

'I suppose not,' Carys conceded. 'Still, there's many a wife gets beaten and ill-treated, your only moan about Joe is that he's too kind.'

'I know,' Eline said again, 'but I'll go mad if I stay here alone in the house any longer.'

'Well, it's up to you,' Carys said, 'no one but you can do anything about it, see?'

When she was alone, Eline stood for a long time, staring out across the roadway to where the beach sloped down to the sea. Joe and the other men would doubtless be out all night making the most of the oyster season which was almost over.

For the short summer months, the oysters would be allowed to breed undisturbed. The spat would grow and metamorphose into tiny oysters, bedding themselves on any empty shell so long as the surface was clean.

By September, the older oysters would be maturing enough to cull and those that were too small would be thrown back to the sea. The fishermen had strict codes of practice; knowing that the oysters were their livelihood, they respected the off-season and the skiffs would be laid up on shore ready for repairs and repainting. Then the men of the village would grow restless and would be in a bad humour, wanting to get back to the sea.

Eline made a sudden decision, she must see William, explain to him what had happened, apologize for not telling him she was married.

She closed her door behind her and made her way along the winding street that traced the edge of the shoreline. The sun was up and the water sparkled like a thousand fallen stars. The air was fresh, clean and salt scented and Eline suddenly realized that being here in Oystermouth was the next best thing to being on Honey's Farm. If only, she thought ruefully, she was accepted by all the other villagers the way she was by Carys Morgan, life would be easier.

She made her way along the street, occasionally glancing behind her as though afraid she was being followed. Joe would be furious with her if he knew she was disobeying him. And yet he had not told her to keep away from the boot and shoe store, only that she shouldn't work there.

Her heart was beating so hard as she paused outside the newly painted front of the shop that Eline felt everyone would hear it and stop to look at her. She bit her lip, wondering if she had the courage to actually enter the shop after the scene Joe had made. Lifting her chin, she made her way into the leather-scented interior.

'Eline!' William was standing before her, framed in the entrance, the sun highlighting the planes of his face, his dear face.

'I'm sorry,' she said simply. She stared at him then in dumb misery and when he reached out his hand and rested it on her shoulder, she wanted to crumple into his arms.

'I should have told you about . . . Joe,' she began but he shook his head.

'Don't say anything more, Eline.' He drew her into the doorway. 'I've learned the circumstances of your marriage. You were just a child left alone in the world, what else could you do when protection was offered to you?'

The words were kind, forgiving, but a gulf was yawning between them and Eline could feel it as though it were tangible.

'You've been talking about me?' she asked in a small voice. He nodded.

'I had to know all about you,' he said, 'I couldn't help myself.'

'But why?' The words fell away as a woman appeared from the shadows behind Will.

'Eline,' Will said, his tone becoming brisk, 'this is my new assistant.' He smiled and drew the woman forward and with a sharp intake of breath, Eline looked into the beautiful, spiteful, dark eyes of Gwyneth Parks.

CHAPTER SEVEN

The sudden, unexpected easterly wind whipped up the waves sending flurries of spray to where the women worked, backs bent over the wooden-slatted trays of oysters.

'*Duw*, I spects you're sorry to be working now?' Carys said, easing her back with plump fingers pressed into her spine.

Eline looked up at her, fighting the urge to cry and shook her head wordlessly. The cold wind, combined with the icy-cold water had frozen her fingers so that she could scarcely handle the oysters she was supposed to be washing free of sand and grime.

Eline glanced at the sack beside her and bit her lip; it was almost empty, the folds hanging limply over the sand. In contrast, Carys's sack was bulging; satisfyingly full and her tray was almost clear.

Eline gasped as a jagged edge of a shell caught spitefully at her finger drawing blood. She straightened, tempted to give in and admit defeat, but she became aware of the other fishermen's wives, watching her, judging her.

Why on earth, she wondered, had she nagged Joe into letting her work? It had taken days of constantly arguing with him until at last in exasperation he had agreed to a trial period when she would work the oysters with the other women.

Clouds formed overhead and Eline bent to her task once again. She saw Carys's fingers nimble and swift in spite of the coldness of the day and envied the diminishing supply of oysters that still lay caked in wet sand on the tray.

One by one the women were finishing their work, tagging the full sacks with the name of their respective skiffs and dragging them up the beach out of the reach of the tide.

'Come on,' Carys said, throwing the last of her oysters into the sack and deftly tying up the neck with string, 'I'll give you a hand.'

'Soft, isn't she?' The strident tone of Nina Parks stopped the straggling group of women in their tracks and they turned to look in curiosity at Eline, wondering how she would react to Nina's words.

'Taking away an honest woman's work, you are, mind!' Nina continued in a loud voice. 'And anyone can see you are not up to it, been ruined like a child you have and now on a whim, you do me and mine out of work, proud of yourself, are you?'

'Go away, Nina,' Carys said evenly. 'Joe is *Eline*'s husband, he can have who he likes working for him, mind.'

'Shut your mouth, you.' Nina put her hands on her hips. 'And mind your own business, I've got no quarrel with you.'

'No,' Carys said, 'you know better than to tangle with me, Nina Parks, I knows too much about you. You'd rather pick on a girl young enough to be your daughter, wouldn't you?'

'It's all right,' Eline interrupted, 'I can speak for myself, Carys, but thanks anyway. Go on home, you've worked hard enough as it is in your condition.'

'I'll stay, if it's all right by you,' Carys said and Nina Parks walked past her and stared right into Eline's face.

'You are taking the bread and butter out of my mouth and you with a man to keep you,' she said loudly enough for the curious women on the beach to hear.

Eline was suddenly angry. This was the woman who had spitefully told Joe about her job in the boot and shoe shop, no doubt encouraging her daughter to take up the vacancy. Nina had always hated Eline and now she wanted to humiliate her before her neighbours.

Eline forgot the cold, forgot how her back ached and stood up, facing the older woman.

'And that's what you resent, isn't it?' Eline said equally loudly. 'I've got a man to keep me and you want that man, don't you, Mrs Parks?'

'Who do you think you are accusing me of the lord knows what?' Nina was blustering and Eline moved a step closer to her.

'I tell you what I'm accusing you of,' Eline was past discretion now, anger poured through her like wine, anger and frustration and some other emotion she didn't quite understand. 'I'm accusing you of lusting after my husband,' she said, 'of trying to take Joe away from me.' Eline flung back the hair that had fallen over her face. 'Well, you might get him into your bed now and then when he fancies pleasuring himself with an older woman, but I've got his ring on my finger and don't you forget it.'

Eline stopped speaking, appalled at the cruelty of her words. Nina had turned pale, her eyes glittered with anger and pain, and Eline knew that the woman had been badly hurt.

Nina leaned forward, her head jutting, her skin seemingly stretched tightly across her cheek-bones.

'Well, I had him first, Miss High and Mighty,' Nina said angrily, '*and* I've given him a son. That's something you'll never do by the look of you.'

Nina turned and walked through the ragged crowd of silent women, her head high, her shoulders stiff and Eline took a deep breath, trying to regain control.

'Go on home,' Eline said, shakily, staring at the village women, 'the show is over.'

In small, whispering groups, the women turned and left the beach and Eline stared blindly at the oysters piled up on the tray before her. So Joe had fathered Nina

Parks's son, had he? Anger and outrage poured through her; everyone must have known about it, everyone but Joe's own wife.

Eline stared down at the mud-caked oysters and she gritted her teeth. She would not be beaten, she would finish her task however long it took her; if Nina Parks could do it, then so could she.

It was almost dark by the time the last of the oysters had been washed. Wearily, Eline tied the top and sank to her knees in the wet sand. She rubbed at her eyes and they ached as though coated in grit.

After a moment, Eline got to her feet. It was time she dragged the sack to a higher part of the beach for the tide was coming in fast. But it was so heavy, weighed down by the plethora of oysters, it had become entrenched in the softness of the sand. Try as she might, Eline couldn't move it more than a few inches.

The waves were lapping spitefully round her feet now and desperately, Eline looked around for someone to help her. The beach was deserted, the sand stretching vast and empty towards Swansea where the lights of the town were beginning to come on like faint stars in the growing dark.

Eline tugged at the sack and some of the oysters spilled from its now-gaping mouth to disappear beneath the water. She felt the tears of mortification wet on her cheeks, but she still clung to the sack although the tide was sucking her in deeper, washing around her knees and she felt a sense of hopelessness rise within her.

Her hands were icy cold, they gripped the rough sacking so tightly that Eline felt she could never release her hold even if she wanted to. Eline flung back her head and cried out loud in her despair, 'Help me! Someone, help me!'

She hauled at the sack, perhaps the incoming sea would help lighten the load so that Eline could make it to higher ground. She paused, head sinking low as she stared in anger at the washing waves that threatened her. She was useless, Joe would be better off without her. Perhaps she should just let the sea take her.

Eline was so numb that she was unaware of a tall figure running along the sand towards her, urgently calling her name. She was ready to sink beneath the waves, she would not relinquish the oysters she'd slaved over for hours, they would not be given back to the sea.

Strong hands were dragging her backwards then and even though the water sucked at her, dragging her down, she was lifted upwards out of the coldness.

Numbly she saw that it was Will Davies holding her and wearily, she rested her head against his shoulder. It was so good to be in his arms, so right.

'The oysters,' she said and her voice was cracking with weariness.

'I've got them.' Carys's round face peered at her. 'Me and some of the other women saw the fix you were in and called for help. You got guts, love, hanging on to the catch like you did with the tide coming in fast.'

Dimly, Eline was aware of the women dragging the sack along the beach on to the high shoreline and safety. With a sigh, she resigned herself to the darkness that was pressing down on her.

When she opened her eyes, she was lying in her own bed and Carys was bending over her with a cup of steaming milk in her hand.

'Come on, girl, we all want you to get better, you got to work in the morning, mind.' Her voice was cheerful but there was sympathy in every line of her broad face. It was clear she felt that the oyster perches was the last place a girl like Eline should be.

Eline drank some of the milk and pushed herself up against the pillows. 'Will, Mr Davies, he got me out of the water, didn't he?' she asked, remembering the feel of his arms warm and protective around her.

'Aye, he did that,' Carys said admiringly. 'I called to

him to come and once he saw the trouble you were in, he was down the beach like a flash. Didn't give a fig for his best boots nor nothing, soaked his suit, he did, but he carried you out of the sea like a hero.' Carys's expression was rapturous. 'Lord, I wished I was you for a minute there.'

'The oysters, Carys, I didn't want to lose them.' Eline took another drink of the hot milk feeling the strength returning to her weary limbs.

'I know and much admired you are for your guts, mind. Once I started my bawling for help, the other women came out of the cottages, see, and I tell you, gone up a notch in their eyes you have.'

Eline sighed. 'I was a failure.' She took a deep breath. 'I nearly lost the lot, I think I'd should have left it all to Nina Parks and her girls after all.'

'Rubbish!' Carys said indignantly. 'And give that old crow more reason to gloat.'

Eline remembered then. Nina Parks had borne Joe a son, she had informed everyone on the beach about it, laid bare the matters that should have been kept private.

Eline looked up at Carys. 'Everyone knew about Joe and her, didn't they? Everyone but me, that is.'

'Aye, most of us suspected the truth anyway because Nina married in haste and gave birth to what she claimed was a premature baby boy.' Carys sighed. 'Now Nina has brought it all out into the open and I don't know what Joe is going to make of it when he gets in from the fishing, I'm sure.'

'Well, he must take what's coming to him,' Eline said acidly. 'He made his bed with the woman and he must face up to the consequences.'

It was no wonder Joe had always been so protective about Nina and her family, guilt must lie heavily on his shoulders, Eline thought angrily.

Carys gave her a strange look. 'Tolerance is a good thing in a marriage, mind,' she said softly. 'Remember what the good book says, "let them that are without sin cast the first stone"?'

Eline was silent; it was all very well for Carys to be forgiving, it wasn't her Sam who had fathered a son on another woman.

The fleet of skiffs came in with the morning tide and Eline, along with the other women, was on the beach to welcome the men home. The *Emmeline* was first to nose into the shelter of the harbour and before Eline could move, she saw Nina Parks push out the open row boat and head for where the skiff was dropping anchor.

Soon, a flotilla of small boats was heading like chicks towards a mother hen, the women rowing with the ease born of long practice towards the skiffs.

Impotently, Eline stood fuming on the beach, knowing that Nina was getting her version of the quarrel over to Joe before he landed.

It took some time to transfer the load of oysters from the skiff to the open boats and Eline grew chilled as she waited for Joe to row to the shore, the small boat low in the water, heavy with oysters.

He headed up the beach and caught Eline's arm, leading her towards the cottage, his face set and white.

'The catch,' Eline protested, 'I must get the oysters clean and packed.'

Joe didn't speak, he almost pushed her into the house and closed the door behind him. 'Sit down.' His voice was almost unrecognizable, with a hard edge of anger. 'I have something to say to you.'

Eline sat, staring in awe at this stranger who was her husband, this was a side of Joe she had never seen before. He'd flown into tempers and raised his voice now and again, but never had she seen this quiet, terrible anger on his face.

'I don't want you or anyone else going over my name in public, do you hear?' He leaned against the door and dragged off his cap, throwing it on to the table.

'What has Nina Parks been telling you?' Eline lifted her chin challengingly. 'A pack of lies, I suppose.'

'I don't want to discuss it,' Joe said, 'but I will say this, what happened in my life before you and me were married is none of your concern, understand?'

'So, having a baby by another woman is not my business?' Outrage caused Eline's voice to rise to an almost hysterical pitch.

'No, it is not!' Joe said. He sank down at the table and held out his booted foot. Eline stared at him without moving.

'Take your own boots off!' she said. 'Or else go to Nina Parks, she seems to have supplied most of your needs.'

Joe rose in a swift movement and his hand lashed out catching Eline's cheek. She reeled away almost falling to the ground.

Slowly she straightened and stared at her husband. 'Don't you dare do that, not *ever*!' she said in a low voice. 'I will leave you flat, Joe, if you ever lay a hand on me again, I mean it. I never had abuse from my father and I won't take it from you. I'll leave you, I swear I will.'

He rose to his feet and stared down at her almost disdainfully. 'And where would you go? You have no money and no skills, you wouldn't last five minutes without my protection.'

He moved to the door and opened it quietly. 'Don't bother going down to the beach,' he said. 'You almost lost me a full catch of oysters by your foolish ideas and it won't happen again.' He closed the door behind him before Eline could reply and she clenched her hands tightly wanting to run after him and hammer him with her fists.

She sank down into a chair. It was clear that Joe cared more about his oysters than about her safety; didn't it matter that she had almost lost her life saving his precious catch?

Common sense reasserted itself. Of course, Nina Parks wouldn't have recounted that part of the story, she would only have told Joe that Eline was slow and incompetent.

Wearily, Eline rose and stared out of the window, the beach stretched ahead of her alive with figures moving to and from the village, women busy with their work. Did they even notice that she was not among them this morning and that Nina Parks was back in her usual place, sorting and cleaning oysters for the skipper of the *Emmeline*?

Eline put her hands on her hips and lifted her chin in an attitude of defiance. Very well, if Joe would not have her work on the oysters, then he must accept the fact that she would find other employment and let him try to stop her a second time, just let him try.

Carefully, Eline washed her face placing a cold cloth on the burning cheek where Joe's big hand had struck her. Anger flared afresh, how dare he treat her so badly? Her own father had never raised a hand to her in anger and she wasn't going to take such treatment from Joe, especially when it wasn't called for.

She tied back her hair in a bright ribbon and pulled on her Sunday coat and skirt. For a moment, she paused at the door, almost losing her courage, then she straightened her shoulders. If she gave in to Joe now, she would never be anything more than his chattel.

Eline walked swiftly towards the terminus of the horse-drawn carriage of the Mumbles train determined to travel into Swansea to find work. She would have loved to find employment at William Davies's shop, but she knew that was an impossible dream; she would only cause trouble for him for Joe's wrath would be mighty.

As Eline climbed up the stairs to the top deck of the carriage, she settled herself in her seat and stared out to sea. Emily Miller had liked her work, had even invited her to come into town and dress the windows of her emporium and, though the words might have been spoken in jest, Eline hoped that there had been some hint of seriousness behind them.

Emily Miller was a fine lady; she and her husband owned many thriving concerns in Swansea. Even Joe would be reluctant to cross swords with such people, at least that's what Eline was hoping.

The carriage had not travelled far when a sudden noise exploded on the soft spring air. Eline stiffened in her seat, her hands gripping her bag were white to the knuckles. She and everyone else on board the Mumbles train knew the sound well; it was the distress signal to call out the Mumbles lifeboat crew. Something was wrong, some boat in trouble in the bay.

Eline was on her feet even before the train jolted to a halt. People around her were pushing forward, as anxious as she was to climb down from the top deck.

Once on the roadway, Eline stood for a moment, staring back towards Oystermouth. Everything seemed calm, no storm, no wrecked ships, could it have been a false alarm? Again the maroons sounded, lights flaring up into the sky. And Eline began to run.

CHAPTER EIGHT

William moved along the beach with swift strides, shading his eyes with his hand as he strained to see what was happening out in the bay. He had been unloading his van when the maroons, fired from the lifeboat station, had echoed around the village, alerting everyone to the knowledge that there was some disaster at sea.

The water running into the bay was calm, the skies overhead clear with just a few light clouds drifting lazily towards the horizon. And yet something was wrong.

Near the water's edge, the flotilla of small craft bobbed on the shoreline unattended. Further out, the fishing skiffs were at anchor and it was to one of these that the lifeboat was heading.

A group of fishermen's wives were gathered like anxious ragged birds, shawls lifting in the wind, poised at the edge of the tide and William recognized Carys Morgan's plump, squat figure as she stood a little apart from the others in an effort to see what was taking place.

'Mrs Morgan, what's wrong?' William stood beside Carys and stared down at her white, anxious face with a feeling of pity; he hadn't realized just how difficult it must be to have a loved one at the mercy of the ocean.

'I don't know very much,' Carys confessed, 'there's been some sort of accident on board one of the skiffs.'

'What sort of accident?' Will asked and Carys shook her head.

'*Duw*, I can only make a guess, see, some man slipped on a wet deck and broke a leg perhaps or even a drowning.' She glanced up at the sky. 'Though that's doubtful in this calm weather, please God.'

The lifeboat was heading towards the shore and a silence fell on the women on the beach as the boat came inland.

One of the crew of the lifeboat jumped into the shallow water and dragged the boat up on to the beach. The women surged forward and William heard a strong masculine voice call out above the noise.

'Stand back, ladies, give the poor bugger some air.'

'Thanks be to God,' Carys said, 'that's my Sam's voice, it's not him that's been hurt.'

William became conscious of someone behind him. He turned to see Eline running along the beach, her hair flying free, her cheeks flushed from her exertions and his heart seemed to melt.

Almost at the same moment, the crowd of women parted as two of the lifeboat crew, holding a limp figure of a man between them, made their way slowly up the beach.

'Joe!' Eline's voice was strong and clear; she gave William a quick glance and then moved towards her husband.

William could see that the man was badly injured, a blood-stained cloth covered his hand. His face was doughily white, drained of all colour and his half-drooping eyes revealed that he was only semi-conscious.

'We must get him to the hospital,' Eline's voice rang out clearly, 'otherwise he's going to bleed to death.'

William stepped forward. 'I'll get my van,' he said, 'we'll have him in Swansea in no time, don't worry.'

William hurried to the shop where the van stood, door still open, the horse half-asleep, head almost touching the cobbles.

William climbed into the driving seat, jerked the animal into movement and headed for the part of the beach where the crowd appeared like dark crows against the paleness of the sand. Before William had properly reined the horse to a standstill, the men were lifting Joe Harries into the back of the van and Eline crouched beside her husband, her face a white blur as she talked reassuringly to him.

The drive to the hospital was along a straight roadway that fortunately at this time of evening was not busy with traffic. William could hear Eline's voice, soothing, encouraging, and he felt a sharp pain inside him. Eline should have been his wife, he loved her as he never thought it possible to love any woman.

'How is he?' he called back over his shoulder and he heard Eline shift her position as the van jolted over some uneven cobbles.

'He's a strong man,' Eline said, 'he'll be all right if only we can get him some attention.'

William drove right up to the entrance to the hospital and whistled to the horse to stop. He climbed down from the driving seat and opened the doors for Eline, lifting her gently down into the courtyard.

There were people then, efficient doctors and nurses surrounding the injured man. Will fell silent, rubbing the ears of the horse absent-mindedly. His last sight of Eline was when she was ushered into a room with her husband and the doors swung shut, concealing her from his view.

William sat on the wall outside and waited; he could not leave her, she needed him and when she came out of the hospital, he would be there.

'We are keeping your husband in for the night, Mrs Harries, just as a precaution.' The doctor was fresh-faced and young, and, as Eline stared anxiously up at him, he smiled.

'Try not to worry too much. Your husband is as strong as an ox, he'll be himself again in a few days.'

'His injuries,' Eline heard herself asking, 'how bad are they?'

The doctor paused doubtfully and Eline shook back her hair. 'I want to know the truth, please.'

'He's lost three of his fingers,' the doctor said at last, 'caught them in the winch it seems. Very bad luck, but not fatal.' He smiled reassuringly. 'Give him a few days to replace the blood he's lost, feed him good liver and oxtail and he'll be as right as rain.' He was about to turn away when he spoke again.

'He won't be able to go back to sea for a few weeks though, make sure he rests, won't you?'

'Can I see him?' Eline asked, looking towards the door and the doctor nodded.

'Yes, but he'll be asleep, he won't be able to talk to you, not just now.'

Eline went into the long ward and saw at once the bed with screens around it and knew Joe was there. A nurse was just drawing the clothes up over Joe and she smiled as she saw Eline.

'Your dad will be just fine and dandy, *cariad*,' she said gently. 'Sit with him a bit if you like, but he won't be able to speak to you, mind.'

Eline thanked the nurse, not bothering to correct her misapprehension. What did it matter that Joe was taken to be her father? Eline leaned over Joe, seeing his pale face, usually so ruddy, with a dart of pain.

She had been about to go against all Joe's wishes, to flout her husband's authority and she didn't think she would ever get over the feeling of guilt that rested like a millstone on her shoulders now.

She stroked Joe's cheek; it was cold and clammy to touch. Eline edged the bedclothes closer round him, wanting instinctively to warm him. Tears blurred her eyes. 'Oh Joe,' she whispered, 'I'm sorry, my love.'

It was much later when she left the hospital and, as she made her way out into the fading evening light, she caught sight of William waiting for her near the gate. She felt grateful to him for his concern, the walk back alone to Oystermouth would have been the last straw. Eline felt she would have broken down and cried.

'Come and sit with me,' he said softly, holding out his hand and lifting her into the seat beside him. 'You look so pale and worried, I'm sure your . . . he'll be all right.'

Eline sensed that William could not bring himself to say the word 'husband' and she knew exactly how he felt. Sitting close to Will, she could feel her being soften with love for him; she wanted to belong to him, felt, in some strange way that she *did* belong to him.

Eline wished she could say the words, 'I love you', and have it over and done with, but guilt held her silent, though in the soft darkness, she felt William by her side and wanted him to be there always.

'I love you, Eline.' It was William who broke the silence. 'I know you're married, but I can't help it, I'll always love you and you love me too, I know it in my bones.'

She couldn't speak, but she gently rested her head against his shoulder, closing her eyes, breathing in the scent of him. Eline knew she couldn't be closer to him if she had known his physical love and for now it was enough that he cared.

It was nearly a week later when Joe was released from hospital. He was still pale and his hand was heavily bandaged. He stared down at Eline almost as though he didn't know her.

'Joe,' she said softly as she threaded her arm through his, 'come on, let's get back home.'

'I've made arrangements,' he said and he looked above her head to where, beneath the slender trees, stood the figure of a young man. 'My own flesh and blood,' he said unaware of his cruelty, 'has come to fetch me.'

Tom Parks came forward and stood for a moment staring at Joe as though uncertain what he should do. Joe reached out his good hand.

'I knew you wouldn't let me down – son,' he said quietly. After a moment's hesitation, the two men, as though on a given signal, moved together and embraced warmly.

'I shouldn't have let *you* down all those years ago,' Joe said hoarsely and Tom moving away smiled slightly.

'It made no difference, I think I always knew you were my father,' he said. 'I waited a long time though for you to acknowledge me, perhaps too long.'

'No, boy, bach,' Joe said quickly, 'it's surely never too late to make amends.'

The two men seemed unaware of Eline's presence; Joe leaned forward a little, his large frame drowning that of the younger man. But Tom Parks had dignity and a wry twist to his lips that told Eline a lot about him and she liked him, this son of her husband, as she had never liked his mother or his sisters.

'The *Oyster Sunrise*,' Joe said, 'she shall be yours, only prove to me that you are man enough to master her and you can have her for your very own, employ your own crew, do as you like with her.'

Tom's young face was suddenly illuminated. 'My own master, that's what I've always wanted to be,' he said, 'and I'm a good sailor. I'll prove it to you, don't you worry about that.'

Eline wanted to protest, the *Oyster Sunrise* was a boat bought with the money from the sale of Honey's Farm, it should rightfully belong to her own sons. But she had no sons, perhaps she would never have sons and, indeed, did she want any children at all by Joe Harries? That was a question to which she could find no answer. So Eline sat in silence in the back of the cart that Tom had provided, while her husband sat up on the driving seat talking softly to Tom, who guided the horse surely over the road to Mumbles. Making up for lost time they were, Eline guessed miserably.

That night Joe went to sleep at Eline's side without

once taking her in his arms. It seemed the accident had changed him and yet hadn't the change been apparent since the time when perhaps Nina Parks had managed to lure him once more to her bed?

Eline had only suspicions, but she knew instinctively that she was right about Joe's infidelity. Joe's attitude towards her had subtly altered ever since he had found her working in Will Davies's shop; it seemed he had turned to Nina for comfort and support and there wasn't much Eline could do about it.

It soon became the talk of the village how Joe Harries was training the young man reputed to be his son to master the *Oyster Sunrise*.

'I expect everyone is talking about me.' Eline was drinking tea with Carys in the small, neat kitchen while Carys knitted a tiny, white garment, her plump face wreathed in happiness.

'What do you mean, *cariad*?' Carys asked glancing up. 'Oh, the boy and the *Oyster Sunrise*. No, it's not you they are talking about, it's the way Nina Parks is setting her cap for your Joe, that's what folks are talking about, if you really want to know.'

It was clear to Eline that this was something Carys had wished to say for some time and had only been waiting for the right opportunity.

'Go on, I might as well know the truth, all of it,' Eline said softly. 'I already know that my husband spends more nights away from me than he does with me,' she added solemnly.

Carys sighed. 'I tried to warn you, girl.' Her voice was soft. 'I knew that Nina always loved your Joe and never would give up trying to win him back so long as she lived.'

'He's sleeping with her, in her bed,' Eline said wearily, wondering if she even cared.

'No!' Carys said sharply. 'Not with their son under the same roof. Not even your Joe would get away with

93

that, not with a fine, upstanding young man like Tom in the house.'

'What then?' Eline asked almost in disbelief. She could hardly credit that her lusty husband was abstaining from the pleasure of a woman's body for so long.

'He's like a man possessed,' Carys said. 'He wants young Tom to be the finest oyster fisherman on the whole of the Gower Coast.' She paused. 'Nothing wrong with that, mind,' she added hastily, 'but he's going to teach that boy everything except how to know where the oyster beds are and that sort of thing comes from instinct as much as experience.

'You can only teach so much by talking about things, then they have to be practised and how is young Tom to get his experience while the oysters are out of season and the boats laid up at Horseshoe Pool?'

Eline shook her head helplessly. 'I don't know what they do with their time, it's the women who take the oysters from the perches, pickle them or carry them to market. What can Joe and Tom find to talk about all day?'

The door opened and Joe himself stood framed against the brightness of the sunlight. Carys rose at once to her feet.

'*Duw*, home from the public, is it, Joe? I'd better go and make my man's dinner then.'

When Carys had gone, Eline rose and pushed the kettle on to the fire. Joe sat down at the scrubbed table and looked around him.

'I see there's no dinner for me, Eline.' His tone was accusing and suddenly, Eline was angry.

'How can I make you dinner when I don't know what day you'll be home, let alone what hour?' she said, her voice rising.

Joe stood and towered over her. 'A good woman has a stew pot on at all times,' he said, 'but then you are not wise in the village ways, are you, Eline?'

'No, I suppose I'm not.' Suddenly her anger left her to be replaced by a dull acceptance of her lot. She was Joe's wife, she was failing in her duty to him and duty was an all-important part of life. Hadn't her father taught her that?

'Go upstairs,' Joe said, undoing his belt. 'Perhaps you will prove more of a wife between the sheets than you do in the kitchen.'

Eline looked at Joe startled, tempted to refuse angrily, but after a moment's hesitation, she turned slowly towards the stairs. In the small bedroom, she pressed herself against the window and stared out at the sea. Was this to be her lot for ever more? A wife doing her duty without love or respect?

At least once Joe had loved her. He had bathed her in love, worshipping her. Surely all that couldn't have changed so suddenly?

Perhaps the change was not her fault; perhaps it was the longing for a son that drove Joe, the longing for a legitimate heir, the company of another man of his own flesh and blood to share with him the joys of the sea, was that what Joe wanted? Or was it simply that Joe had found more warmth in the arms of his old love, Nina Parks, than he could ever find in the arms of his wife?

So it was her fault then, in the end it must be. Eline undressed and crept between the sheets aware of the light of the day penetrating between the curtains. It seemed almost shameless for Joe to claim his conjugal rights in the brightness of the sun. And yet wasn't that when he made love to his paramour? He and Nina probably made love any time and anywhere.

Joe, when he came into bed, was eager for her. His abstinence from her bed had made him hungry, she realized that now. And yet when he put his hand on her small breasts, she knew instinctively that he would far rather be fondling the ample charms of Nina Parks.

She forced down her resentment as he threshed above

her, careless of her feelings, almost oblivious to her moans of pain as he thrust brutally against her unyielding flesh. He seemed to be punishing her and, at the same time, laying claim to her all over again. And when it was over and he had risen and gone out, Eline cried hot, bitter tears that did nothing to ease the ache within her.

The days seemed to pass in a haze of unhappiness for Eline. She saw little of Joe though now at least he came home each night to his own hearth. What did the gossips make of that? Eline wondered, though without much interest.

It was one morning when the summer sun spread shadows and bright patches of light on the grey slate floor that she realized that she had to do something with her life or go mad as she sat for endless hours before the window gazing out like a prisoner condemned to live for ever behind bars.

What Joe wanted was a doll, a plaything to amuse him when he was in the mood to be amused or when his paramour wasn't readily available to satisfy his needs. Eline knew, with a sudden sense of clarity, that she would come to hate Joe if she didn't do something that would change her life.

When Joe came in, she gave him his dinner in silence. She had made a special effort to cook a rich rabbit stew, his favourite meal, and to go with it, she had bought fresh crusty bread from the bakery.

As Joe ate, he, too, was silent, his blue eyes looking far away into the distance as though he was still at sea, straining to see an almost unrecognized horizon.

'I'm going to work in the quarry,' he spoke at last, pushing away his empty bowl. 'Clements are taking on casual labour and I want to earn a bit more money. It's always useful to have a ready supply of cash when the new season starts.'

'But, Joe, you don't have to work!' Eline protested.

'You are master of two oyster skiffs. Why do you want to work in the quarry?'

'I've told you,' Joe said reasonably, 'for money.' Eline poured his tea in silence though questions were throbbing through her mind, longing to be spoken. Surely there was enough money from the catches Joe had made in the spring, when the prices were up to ten shillings a thousand for oysters?

And there was the dowry she had brought him, the money from the farm, some of which had gone to buy the new boat, but some had surely been deposited safely in the bank?

'Is Tom going to work in the quarry, too?' she found herself asking and Joe gave her a look that would have frozen the sea.

He took a gulp of his tea and picked up his note book, making some rapid calculations in it without answering her question.

'I could work!' Eline said. 'If we really need money, let me take a job in Swansea, I know I could find work with Mrs Miller in her emporium. I would like it, really I would, Joe.'

'No.' He spoke uncompromisingly and it was clear he was not even going to consider her suggestion. 'I am not a man to shirk his duty to provide for his own,' he ended stiffly.

Suddenly Eline was angry. 'Indeed, the way you are pushing yourself to find extra work makes me wonder just how many are "your own",' she said quickly. 'I suppose you would count Nina Parks and her son Tom as "your own", wouldn't you, Joe?'

He looked at her coolly. 'What I do is my own business,' he said and returned to his calculations.

'But the *Oyster Sunrise* is only yours through marriage,' Eline said sharply. 'And did you even consult me before you handed it over to Tom Parks?' She stood before him. 'It's about time you realized that I am no longer a child, I'm a woman, Joe, with feelings and needs. And what about our own children? What will they have left to look forward to when they come along?'

He rose to his feet and took his coat and cap from the door. He stood poised for a moment, his hand on the latch.

'I've tried my best to give you a child,' he said coldly. 'I wanted nothing more than a son by you, Eline, but you have failed me.' He sighed heavily. 'The fault lies with you, Eline, for I know I am not lacking.'

He left then and Eline sank down into a chair and stared at the closed door. She tried to examine her feelings, but all she could recognize was that a host of conflicting emotions were sweeping through her. She wanted children, of course she did, but did she want them to be Joe's?

After a time, Eline rose and pulled on her light shawl beguiled by the sun streaming in through the window. She would walk to the shops, buy some fresh vegetables and a piece of lamb for Joe's tea. If there was no way of escape, then she must make the best of things; she could not go on living in disharmony with her husband otherwise she would lose even the last vestige of respect for him.

The sea was washing the gentle shore with small, white-flecked waves. The sand was golden in the bright light and the rocks of Mumbles stood out sharply against the sky. Soon it would rain, Eline decided, for the haze of heat had disappeared and there was a clarity of sea, sky and land that hinted at a storm.

The skiffs were laid up in the pool. Some of the men had already begun to white-lime the bottoms of the craft and they lay beached, like black-and-white fish, stranded above the shoreline.

There was a crowd of women standing around the grocer's shop and Eline recognized Carys's heavy figure and above a white-lace collar, the rotund face beamed broadly in welcome.

'*Duw*, there's nice to see you out and about, Eline. Have you been poorly then?'

'No,' Eline said cheerfully, 'just busy in the house.' It was a lie and they both knew it for Carys must have heard the rows that had been taking place between Eline and Joe.

'Well, I've come to get some greens, there's some lovely cabbages, look,' she said, 'fresh from the farm, they are.'

As Carys stopped speaking abruptly, Eline became aware of a sudden silence, the chattering of the women had ceased. She looked over her shoulder and saw Nina Parks smiling triumphantly as she moved through the throng.

'Well, if it isn't Mrs Harries,' Nina said with a show of outward respect, but with a sly smile in her eyes. 'How are you this fine day?'

Her eyes moved meaningfully over Eline's slim waistline. Eline felt herself flush but controlled her anger.

'I'm very well, thank you,' she said stiffly. 'And you, Widow Parks, how are you?' She knew the word 'widow' had hit home and suddenly Eline was ashamed of herself. She searched her mind for something conciliatory to say, but Nina Parks was suddenly confronting her, hands on her hips.

'What a pity you can't give your husband sons,' her voice was harsh, 'but never mind, we are not all barren, thank the Lord.' She turned away amid a wash of speculation and Eline was suddenly breathless.

'Take no notice of Nina Parks,' Carys said easily, 'she is full of wind and water, that one.'

'What did she mean?' Eline said in a whisper, 'she can't be having . . . ?' There was a gust of laughter from the other women and Eline's words trailed away into silence.

Colour stained her cheek and she felt she must turn and run. Then she became aware of the tall figure beside her and, looking up, she saw Will Davies looking down at her with compassion in his eyes. He took both Eline and Carys by the arm and led them towards his shop.

'Come along, ladies,' he said loudly, 'the new boots you wished to see have just been delivered.'

Will unlocked the door and once inside the coolness of his shop, Eline sank into a chair and stared up at Will. 'You heard everything?' she asked and her colour rose as he nodded.

'Take no notice of that one.' Carys had seated herself on one of the absurdly small chairs, her broad legs spread apart to accommodate her large stomach. 'Nina's *old*, got to be getting up to forty years of age, she has, can't be having no babbi at her age, surely?'

Will brought two glasses of iced tea from the back of the shop and Eline sipped the drink gratefully. 'If this is true, it's the end for Joe and me,' she said. 'I can't go on living in the same house as a man who has no scruples.'

'Men are men,' Carys shrugged and glanced up quickly at Will, 'present company excepted, Mr Davies, but when the husband gets restless, as they do, they will find what they want in another woman's arms.'

Eline finished her drink and set the glass down on the counter. She rose to her feet and stood before Will. 'Thank you for your kindness,' she said softly. She could not meet his eyes, she felt ashamed and degraded, wondering how Will must see her now. What must he think of a woman who couldn't even keep the loyalty of her husband?

The door sprung open and Gwyneth Parks entered the shop. 'Am I late, Mr Davies?' she asked coyly. 'There's sorry I am.'

'Don't apologize, I'm a little early.' He spoke absently and at his side, Eline stiffened. Carys sniffed and walked past Gwyneth and after a moment, Eline followed her.

'There's sorry I am for poor Eline,' Gwyneth's voice

carried into the street, 'she must feel so bad that she can't have little ones, not that it's right for her husband to stray, mind, I don't agree with that.' There was a pause before Gwyneth spoke again. 'Mind, I suppose you can't blame a man for straying if his wife is found wanting, can you?'

Eline didn't wait to hear if Will made any reply, her cheeks were burning, her humiliation was complete.

CHAPTER NINE

Joe sat beside the *Emmeline* and stared out towards the placid sea that for days now had lain quietly against the sun-bleached land in shades of turquoise and azure. The sand was honey coloured, hot to the bare feet of the children who romped and played among the rock pools that sparkled like gemstones in the haze of heat.

The brush containing white-lime and tallow rested against the rock where it had fallen for Joe had forgotten all about painting the boards of his boat in an attempt to prevent them separating in the summer sun and was rubbing the beads of sweat from his forehead. How, he wondered, had he managed to make such an ungodly mess of his life?

His young wife, Eline, whom he loved with a desperation that verged on the obsessional, was drifting away from him, alienated by his fecklessness and his philandering with a woman old enough to be Emmeline's mother.

And yet Nina was like a part of him, a woman of warmth and sensuousness and more; a woman who was so fertile that he only had to plant his seed once and a child sprang up within her. He had lain with her only a few times before his conscience and the return of Tom to the family home had put a stop to the affair.

And now Nina was with child by him again. What was he to do? He could not marry Nina and give her child a name. All he could honourably do was to support her financially.

He thought suddenly of Tom, his son whom Joe was only just winning over. What would he say when he learned that his mother had been betrayed yet again?

'Damn and blast!' Joe picked up the brush and slapped it against the underside of the boat in an explosive gesture that sent the lime flying around him like snow. He began work again like a man possessed and all the time his mind was going around like a rat in a trap, trying to sort out his muddled thoughts.

'Joe!' The voice was soft, cajoling, and he looked up with sudden gladness to see Eline standing above him, the breeze moulding her bodice against her small breasts so that she looked like a young nymph from another world. She slid down on to the rocks and sat beside him, her young arms gleaming softly golden in the sunlight, the sweet rise of her breasts revealed now by the opening of the calico of her bodice.

'Joe,' Eline looked at him beseechingly, 'I must ask you something.'

He leaned towards her, his coldness vanishing. How could he blame her for anything, this sweet child he'd loved since she'd been in her cradle? It wasn't her fault that she had not caught for a baby, she was still so small, so vulnerable, little more than a girl herself. He should give her a chance to mature and fill out a little and then she would be ready for motherhood.

He put his arm around her shoulder. 'Ask me for whatever you want, my little one.' He smelled the sunlight in her hair and the freshness of newly washed skin, young skin, and his senses were aroused. He wanted to drown himself in her warmth and innocence; women of experience like Nina were around in abundance. It was only rarely that a man had the good fortune to find himself an innocent to love.

'I want to know the truth about Nina Parks, Joe.' Her words fell softly against the sudden wild beating of his heart. He heard the laughter of children and the barking of a dog as though they were in another world, a faraway

103

world that had nothing to do with Joe Harries and the mess he had made of his life.

'Is she having your baby, Joe?' Her voice was low, that of a little girl, a trusting child and he could not see her thin face twist into lines of pain.

'What is this nonsense?' he found himself protesting. 'Nina Parks is a woman almost forty. Why should she be having a child and in any case, what makes you think it would be mine?'

Eline's eyes were steady, so blue that they outdid the sea in splendour. 'She almost said as much today in the grocer's.'

Joe got to his feet angrily. 'I have told you before not to go over my name in public.' He was suddenly incensed. Why should the women in his life act as though he was God with all the virtues and all the answers to their infernal questions?

He put his brush down carefully in the pot of tallow and lime and wiped his hands on an old rag, rubbing vigorously at the white-lime that had become ingrained in the creases of his fingers as though the task was the most important thing in the world to him right then.

'Joe?' Eline's voice was soft but insistent. He looked down at her, his anger washing away as suddenly as it had come.

'I am a man, Eline,' he said slowly, 'and when a man is not welcome in his wife's bed he must find a woman who wants him.'

'That's not fair, Joe!' Eline said swiftly. 'I've never denied you.'

'But neither have you welcomed me with open arms, Emmeline.'

He sighed heavily and sat down beside her, deciding he must end the lies and deceit once and for all, face up to what he had done like a man.

'I went to her, it's true,' he said, 'and if Nina is with child, then the fault *is* mine.' He took Eline's small hand

104

in his. 'I can only ask you to try to understand and forgive me for what was one lapse on my part.'

He saw her eyes darken like the waters of the sea covered by clouds. She bent her head and her unpinned hair swept forward hiding her face.

'I am at fault, too, Joe,' she said at last. 'I am not woman enough for you, I haven't given you sons.'

He felt pierced by guilt, he had cruelly taunted her with her lack of children and his thrusts had gone home hurting her badly.

'There is time for that,' he said gently, 'I forget how young you are, Eline, there is time aplenty for us to have a family.' He sighed heavily. 'The problem now is Nina, what am I to do about her?'

Eline bent towards him, her hand on his shoulder. 'If there's a problem, we'll face it together, Joe, like man and wife should.'

She rose and smoothed down her skirts and, as he watched her, Joe felt himself melt with love for her. 'Come on, *cariad*,' he said thickly, 'let me take you home.'

Nina sat in her kitchen, aware that the sickly feeling that gripped her now every morning was abating. She closed her eyes and leaned back in her chair, relief bringing the beads of perspiration to her forehead.

She got up and stared at herself in the mirror, she was very pale, with deep lines running from her nose to the sides of her mouth. 'You are an old woman, Nina Parks,' she said, 'and this is your last chance to land your man.'

Of course Nina knew she could not expect marriage, Joe was tied to that young silly girl, legally at least, but the two of them could go away, somewhere far from Swansea where no one knew them. They could live as man and wife and bring up their child in peace with no wagging tongues to bother them.

She was well aware that Joe enjoyed her passion, the

way he'd fallen into her arms so gratefully betrayed his lack of the love of a proper woman these past years. And what's more his pale-faced wife had not given him chick nor child to care for, while she, Nina, had provided him with a fine son in Tom.

She rested her hand on her stomach with a sense of sudden misgivings. Tom had gone on a trip and what would he say when he came home from the deep sea and found his mother with child? He was only just beginning to forgive Joe for abandoning him when he was a baby. He was coming round to the idea that he could be master of the *Oyster Sunrise* when the season began in September and instead of just being a hand on board a big ship, he would have another man and a boy to crew with him. If he proved as good an oyster fisherman as his father, he would make a fine living for himself.

'Oh, *duw*!' She sank once more into a chair. Why was she fooling herself? It was all a terrible mess. Joe would never leave his wife or his boats, he would never leave the shores of Oystermouth where he had made his living since he was a boy following in the footsteps of his father and his grandfather before him.

She put her head into her hands and felt the hot tears; why had she conceived of a child so easily and after so many years? Irfonwy, Fon, as she was affectionately called, was almost sixteen, the sweetest daughter any woman could wish for, and as for the twins, Sal and Gwyneth, they were women grown and ready for marriage. Sal was already walking out with a young man she'd met at the house where she was in service and Gwyneth, well, Gwyneth had her pick of all the young men in Oystermouth, she was so pretty and full of spirit.

Nina sighed and rose to her feet; perhaps she should try to eat a little breakfast now, keep up her strength for she felt fit for nothing and her with all the washing to do before supper time.

Nina managed to eat some thin porridge and, after she had cleared away, she dragged the bath out into the yard. It was an effort to lift it on to the bricks that Tom had placed strategically near the wall but at least when it was in place, she would not have to bend so far to do the washing.

Her thoughts wandered as Nina filled and refilled the kettle and the big potato pot, boiling up the water on the fire and carrying it to the yard, hearing it drum against the ridged bottom of the bath and feeling the steam cloud her vision. Or could the moisture be tears? But that was absurd, she was Nina Parks, Widow Parks, always willing and able to fight her own battles and she would not be defeated now. She would find a way out of this mess, she would, if it was the last thing she did.

It was much later that Nina sank exhausted into her chair near the fire. Her back ached and her arms felt as though they were being torn from their sockets, but it was satisfying to see the line of clean sheets flapping on the line, billowing like the sails of a ship as the wind caught them.

The door opened and Gwyneth came into the kitchen, her face wreathed in smiles.

'What's up with you?' Nina asked. 'Found a gold sovereign have you?'

'No,' Gwyneth said, 'but I'm going to have a bit more money at the end of the week.' She rubbed her hands together gleefully. 'Mr Davies is putting me in charge of the boot and shoe store when he goes into Swansea tomorrow. He's a fine handsome man, mind.' Her eyes were alight.

'Don't you go getting no fancy ideas about that Mr Davies now,' Nina said sharply. 'I know these gents, they have one thing in mind and that's to have their way with you.'

'Don't be daft, Mam,' Gwyneth said scathingly, 'don't you think I know that?' She laughed as she pushed the

107

kettle on to the fire. 'I might let him have his way, too, but only if he offers me a gold ring.'

'Aye, go on you, girl, be clever, but Mother Nature got a way of making you want a man, don't make no mistake about it, that's how babbis gets born.'

'Well, you should know, Mam,' Gwyneth said cheekily. 'What's for supper?'

'I made a pot of stew yesterday, we'll have to make do with that. I been washing all day, mind, up to my elbows in sheets and bolster cases. 'Bout time you did your own things now, Gwyneth, you're not a child any more.'

'Aw, but Mam, I'm working all day on my feet in the shop.' Gwyneth slipped off her boots and began to rub her ankles. 'You don't realize how hard it is.'

'Huh! And I suppose I've been doing nothing all day, just sitting about enjoying myself, is it?'

'What time is our Fon coming in from the beds?' Gwyneth said adroitly changing the subject. She leaned back in her chair still rubbing at her feet. 'Funny, a few weeks ago we were all working the oysters and now it's only Fon left on them.'

'Well,' Nina said, 'Sal wanted to go into service because of that nice boy she got an eye for and I don't see any harm in it, at least she has her keep and a nice room to herself and so long as she stays respectable, the work is steady all the year around.'

'And me,' Gwyneth said smiling, 'I wanted something better than Joe's charity and the cold days of winter spent freezing to death on the beach seeing to those damn oysters. Ruining my life they was.' She looked archly at her mother.

'Now I got the company of a real gent, he's showing me ropes, like, how to keep the shop nice and how to speak to the posh customers who come in.' She sighed. 'Not that we get many of those, mind, it's mostly folks like that fat Carys Morgan who wants barges to put her big feet into. God! You'd think she was the only one having a baby in this village. But she's not, is she, Mam?'

Gwyneth's smile had vanished and she looked anxiously at her mother. Nina felt her colour rising.

'Look girl, I've never hidden nothing from you. I had Joe to my bed it's true, I couldn't help it, like I told you, nature got a way of making you want a man.' She smiled ruefully. 'I've always been Joe Harries's woman at heart, see?'

She paused, giving herself time to think. 'I suppose I might as well tell you, I've missed my courses for three months now and I get sick of a morning.' Nina shrugged. 'There's no doubt about it really.'

'Well, I think you were a bit quick taunting Eline with the good news,' Gwyneth said drily. 'Now all the village is talking about you.'

Nina lifted her head defiantly. 'So? What's different about that? Haven't they always had a good go at Nina Parks then? Why should I care about the villagers, they don't keep me in bread, do they?'

'All right, Mam, only saying.' Gwyneth rose and fetched the pot of cold stew from the pantry, pushing the heavy black pot on to the fire. 'Sit by there, you, I'll see to the supper.'

Nina felt tears sting her eyes, it wasn't often any of her children showed her such consideration. Spoiled them she had, trying to make up for being both Mam and Dad to them, she supposed.

'I'm going out after,' Gwyneth said as later, mother and daughter sat together at the table. 'Mr Davies has asked me to help him take stock of the boots and shoes.' She smiled impishly. 'And don't worry, I'm not going to give him so much as an inch, I'm not going to make the same mistakes as you, Mam.'

Nina flinched, her daughter sometimes could be too outspoken for her own good. She was about to remonstrate with her when the door opened and Fon came into the room, her white apron smeared with sand, her curly hair falling from its ribbons.

'*Duw*, there's a lovely smell.' She sank down at the table and pulled off her heavy, sand-encrusted boots.

'Get a bowl, *cariad*,' Nina said, 'and help yourself from the pot. There's plenty of bread cut and there's a bottle of dandelion beer in the pantry on the floor.'

Fon smiled, her tawny eyes full of warmth. 'Thanks, Mam, I'm that starving I could eat a whole loaf by myself.'

Gwyneth pushed away her bowl and rose to her feet. 'I'm going to have a quick wash and then I'll be off back to the shop, Mam,' she said. 'Fon, don't you go leaving all the washing up to Mam, now, and fetch the sheets in from the line for her before it gets dark.'

'Been washing today have you, Mam? No wonder you look tired out.' Fon fetched her soup and returned to the table and began eating daintily.

Nina, watching her, wondered as she often did if this, her youngest daughter, was a changeling; she was so different to the other girls, so small and dainty, with a bush of chestnut hair and fine, expressive eyes. And she was so good-natured and kind while Gwyneth and Sal both were sharp-tongued enough to cut through the toughest leather.

'Why are you going back to work, Gwyn?' Fon asked, her large amber eyes resting on her sister with curiosity. It wasn't like Gwyneth to be over enthusiastic about work.

'Like I was telling Mam, I'm going to help with the stock taking,' Gwyneth said importantly. 'I mean to make myself so useful to Mr Davies that he won't be able to do without me.' She smiled wickedly and watching her, Nina thought how like herself was this, her daughter.

Gwyneth had a sort of earthy quality about her; she was dimpled and rounded, her thick hair dark like Nina's own, her eyes green as the sea on a stormy day. Nina feared for her, for if Gwyneth were to fall in love with this Mr Davies, then she would be lost for she had the same senuous nature as her mother, whatever claims she might make to having too much common sense to stray.

Nina wanted to say something, to warn Gwyneth, but the girl was on her way out through the door. In any event, she wouldn't have listened; like all young people she was so certain of herself, so sure that she could handle her emotions under any circumstances.

'Well now then, Fon, tell me, how did you get on today on the perches?' Nina rested her chin in her hands and looked at her youngest daughter.

'Took up a few sackfuls for Joe,' she said, 'he's delivering them tonight, oh and Mam, he said he'd call over and see you, wanted to talk to you about something or other.' She paused. 'Isn't our Tom's ship due in dock later tonight?'

Nina's heart dipped in fear; had Fon put two and two together at last? Did her youngest one know that Joe had become Nina's lover once more and had filled her with child? But the look in her eyes was free of all guile.

'Perhaps,' Nina answered, shakily, 'but you never know with Tom, he's like will-o'-the-wisp.'

She attempted to speak casually. 'Did Joe say what he wanted to see me about?' In spite of herself, Nina's voice cracked with anxiety and Fon looked at her thoughtfully.

'No, Mam, but then he wouldn't tell me anything, would he?' She smiled. 'I saw him and Eline together, sitting on the rocks they were, so close together, kissing they were. They looked so lovely, mind.'

She had no idea how much her words were hurting her mother, but then why should she? Fon never listened to gossip, her head was always too full of the lovely music she made up and played on her old accordion.

Anyway, because she was so young, the women usually

111

watched their tongues where Fon was concerned. She was a little ethereal, always lifting her eyes to the heavens, touching the silver cross around her neck and looking so saintly that it would be a shame to make her aware of worldly matters.

What Fon would make of the fact that her mother was going to have an illegitimate child, Nina dreaded to think, but she would have to be told sooner or later.

Fon washed up after supper and then went out into the back yard and brought the washing in from the line.

'The sheets are bone dry, Mam,' she said. 'Come on I'll help you to fold them.'

Nina loved the fresh scent of linen that had dried in the sun and, as she flapped the sheets into neat folds, she smiled at her youngest daughter.

'There's a good girl you are, Fon, I don't know what I'd do without you.' She paused a moment. 'But do me a favour, when Joe comes over, leave us alone to talk private like, will you?'

Fon nodded agreeably, suspecting nothing. 'That's all right, Mam, I'm going over to the church for their choir practice after anyway.'

Nina sank into a chair and brushed a hand across her forehead. She felt hot and weary and not a little apprehensive about Joe's visit. What was he going to say to her? Would he want to take her to bed again, to hold her in his arms? She hoped so if only to give herself some comfort in the knowledge that she was not alone with her worry.

When Fon had left the house, Nina washed herself over with some hot water from the kettle and a good flannel cloth and then changed into fresh clothes. She wanted to look her best for Joe, but when she stared at her reflection in the mirror, she saw a woman with fading hair and a tired expression around her eyes.

'Nina Parks, you are too old to be a mistress, you need to be a wife to some man who'll take care of you.'

The words fell into a hollow silence and Nina felt tears burn her eyes; there would be no kindly man like her first husband to come along and save her from shame a second time.

When Joe knocked on the door, Nina opened it with a smile. 'Come inside, Joe, my lovely,' she said, 'I've been waiting for you.'

He sank into the chair and removed his cap, pushing back his thick curls.

'Leave the door open a bit, love,' he said, 'I could do with a breath of fresh air.'

Nina sat near the table, her hands twisting nervously in her lap. Joe didn't look like a man best pleased with his lot. His long silence was ominous especially after what Fon had said about him sitting on the rocks with Eline.

'What is it, Joe?' Nina said softly. 'What have you come to tell me?'

'Just that I feel bad about what happened.' Joe sighed heavily. 'How is it that I make you with child whenever we come together?'

'I don't know, love,' Nina said, 'I suppose it's nature, the signs must be right for us making children, I expect.'

'I'll support you,' Joe said and Nina knew then she'd lost, there would be no getting Joe to come away with her to make a new life together.

'Must I face the shame of having a babbi alone then?' Her voice rose more in fear than anger. 'Joe, how could you desert me a second time, leaving me like this?'

Nina was so overcome that she didn't hear a sound at the door or see the figure standing against the light.

'Joe, for God's sake, what can I do? I can't have this babbi by myself, I just can't.'

The door was flung open with a resounding crash and Tom strode into the kitchen, his face red with anger.

'Mam,' he said in a strangled voice, 'have you let this bastard bed you again and get you with child?'

Tom looked at Joe as if he hated him and Nina rose to her feet, her breath catching in her throat.

'Get out of this house!' Tom directed his anger towards Joe. 'I don't want you or your lousy hand-outs, do you hear?'

Nina found her breath. 'Tom, don't you speak to Joe like that,' she said quickly. 'Please, try to understand how things are between Joe and me.'

'Oh, I understand all right,' Tom said, 'you are his part-time whore whenever he wants a change from his little wife.'

Nina reached out and her hand connected with her son's cheek so hard that the imprint of her fingers showed up redly on his face. 'How dare you!' she said quietly. 'I am no whore, but I am a woman with flesh and blood feelings all the same.'

'Right then,' Tom said, 'go with him, get out of my sight before I kill you.' He raised his fist and smashed it against the mirror which shattered into pieces so that for a moment Nina had a crazy image of her son's maddened eyes and her own fear.

'Come with me.' Joe caught her arm and took her out of the house. 'We can talk to the boy when he has cooled down.'

Nina fought to suppress her tears as she saw the curtains twitch as she walked along the road beside Joe. No doubt her neighbours had heard everything and she would once again be the talk of the village.

But she had more to worry about than that now. She swayed a little and Joe put his arm around her.

'Steady on, girl,' he said softly, 'you are going to be all right.'

'Where are you taking me?' Nina asked faintly, her arm clinging to his for support.

'I'm taking you home, where else can I take you?' Joe said quietly.

Nina didn't reply, but suddenly she wanted to burst

out into hysterical laughter. Joe was taking her to his home, where she had always wanted to be. But in his home waited his lawful wife and Eline was not going to be very happy to see her husband walk in with his mistress.

CHAPTER TEN

The garden was drenched with hot July sunshine, the roses, heavy with rich, creamy petals, had a glorious perfume which drifted to where Hari sat in a chair, beside the open window, fanning herself with her hat.

She smiled at her old friend, happy to see Meg looking so well. 'What a beautiful day to be alive.'

'Yes, it's lovely here, this house is always so peaceful.' Meg Briant was leaning back in her chair, smiling dreamily. She was older than Hari, but was still a lovely, attractive woman. She had been widowed for several years now, but it was clear that at times she still pined for her husband, Sir Charles Briant.

Charlie had been a big, handsome man, a fine eccentric character and one loved by many of his friends including Hari. After his death, Meg had thrown in her lot with Hari and Craig and had become a partner in the leather business.

Looking at her now, Hari thought Meg had a delicate quality about her that was rather touching. Though her face was rather too thin and there were shadows beneath her eyes, she appeared to have a fragile beauty that owed more to an inner peace than simply to facial structure.

Hari sighed. 'The house has a certain air about it, hasn't it? I'm very lucky, I know, and I never cease to count my blessings.'

'I don't feel settled yet in my house,' Meg said. 'I know the house is beautiful but I don't feel at home there, not really. I still miss Charlie, I suppose, even after all this time.' Meg bit the edge of her nail and, watching her,

Hari felt her heart contract with pain. She leaned forward and held out her hand.

'I can understand that; Charlie was always such a live wire, I miss him, too.'

Meg smiled suddenly. 'He would have approved of me going into business with you and Craig and I've never had to worry about money, not since the Briant name was added to that of the Grenfells.' Her smile vanished. 'But money can't make up for love and companionship.'

'You are still young,' Hari protested, 'don't talk as though you've given up on life, you may meet a man who could make you happy, though I realize no one will ever take Charlie's place.'

'No,' Meg bit her lip, 'no one ever will fill the gap he left in my life.'

The door opened and the new, young maid bobbed a curtsy. 'Excuse me, madam,' she said in a small voice and Hari smiled at her, sensing the girl's nervousness.

'What is it, Avril?' she asked kindly. 'Speak up, I'm not going to eat you.'

'It's a gentleman, madam, a Mr Davies, he wants to see you.'

'Will!' Hari rose to her feet, smiling in delight as Will appeared in the doorway behind the maid. 'Come in, love, it's good to see you.'

He looked tanned and handsome, Hari thought, as Will seated himself beside her on the plump-cushioned sofa.

'How's the business going?' Hari asked, leaning forward and her smile included Meg who was relaxing now against the cushions, her mood of low spirits temporarily forgotten.

'Very well,' Will replied. 'I've got a new shop assistant and I'm looking for another one because I seem to get busier by the day.'

'That's what I like to hear,' Hari said warmly wondering if she dare enquire about Eline Harries. William saved her the trouble.

'There was almost a tragedy down at the beach, a few weeks ago,' he said. 'Eline was picking oysters from the perches when the tide came in and caught her unawares. Good thing the other women called me to the beach before it was too late. That man Joe Harries should be shot for allowing a delicate young girl like Eline to do such work.' He paused. 'And according to the gossip of some of my customers, he's not even the faithful sort.'

Hari concealed a frown, rubbing at her forehead, head bent. 'I'm sorry,' she said quietly. 'I hope Eline's all right now.'

'I hope so, too,' Will said in a low voice. 'I haven't seen her since then.'

'Who is this Eline?' Meg said in open curiosity. 'A new sweetheart perhaps?'

Will shook his head. 'I wish she was,' he said fervently and Meg tapped his hand.

'Don't be faint-hearted, Will, any girl would love to be wooed by a good-looking man like you.' She turned to Hari. 'Do you know I was in Will's shop the other day and I swear that the little assistant has set her bonnet at him? She can't take her eyes off him and who can blame her?'

There was an embarrassed silence and after a moment Meg rose and picked up her bag. 'Well, my dear Hari, I must be going, I have to change for supper which I am having with some very boring business people.' She drew on her gloves while Will stood politely, ready to open the door for her.

'The Gardeners are thinking of taking over the theatre, you know. They have asked me to sell out to them.' She looked directly at Hari and sighed heavily.

'And are you going to let them have the building?' Hari said, taking Meg's arm. 'It might be just as well.'

'I don't know, I suppose I will have to sell up some

118

time and the place might as well be in use. Though to me it will always be Charlie's theatre; I suppose it's seen its best days now.'

Hari saw Meg to the door and the two women embraced warmly before Meg climbed into her carriage. Hari watched as the carriage rolled away down the drive of Summer Lodge and then she returned to where Will was still on his feet, staring out of the window.

Hari moved to him and rested her head on his shoulder. 'Will,' she said softly, 'you'll get over her.'

He looked down at her and after a moment kissed her forehead. 'Maybe, Hari, but I can't stop thinking about her; in the morning I wake with Eline Harries on my mind and in the night I dream about her.'

'What about this girl who works for you?' Hari changed the subject; it was pointless warning Will yet again that Eline was a married woman. 'Is she really falling in love with you?'

'Gwyneth Parks?' Will said quickly. 'No, that's just a bit of fancy on Meg's part.'

Hari looked down at her hands. 'I do hope you'll meet some suitable young lady soon,' she said and then smiled at the pomposity of her words. 'Listen to me!' she said. 'I sound like a snob and me coming from the slums of World's End, I should be ashamed of myself.'

Hari sank into a chair and Will settled himself opposite her. 'No,' he said gently, 'I know you want only the very best for me. Don't worry, Hari, I am wise enough to realize that Eline is a married woman and not for me and I won't do anything silly like falling into the arms of any pretty lady who happens along.'

Hari smiled and touched Will's cheek. 'I suppose you've done your share of flirting like most young men, but you've just never met the right woman. I must start organizing musical evenings or perhaps a ball. Snob or not, I want you to meet a suitable kind of young lady.'

'Hari!' Will chided gently. 'I'm a man now, you

needn't think of matchmaking. When I want a wife I shall find one, don't you worry your pretty little head about that.'

'Don't bother to protest,' Hari said smiling. 'Craig and I are having supper with the Millers and some of their friends tonight and I'll ask Emily if she knows of anyone suitable for you to meet.'

'Don't you dare,' Will said with mock indignation and then he smiled. 'And if you do, I'll probably hate the girl on sight.'

He stretched his long legs out before him. 'I think you've forgotten that too many of Swansea's high society remember my humble origins, Emily included, even though she married a man from what she would call "the lower orders".'

'Aye,' Hari said ruefully, 'just as they remember my humble beginnings. Oh, most people are polite and sometimes even quite friendly, but I know I'm only accepted because of Craig's influence in the town.' She stared at Will earnestly. 'But I don't care, I'm happy to be Craig's wife, he loves me for what I am and the poverty of my background doesn't concern him in the least.'

She saw Will smile and shook his arm playfully. 'What are you laughing at? Come on, tell me!'

'You, Hari, you think I'm such an eligible bachelor, but I have no great wealth and I haven't got one quarter of your talent either.'

'Nonsense!' Hari protested. 'You are young and handsome with excellent prospects, anyone who catches you will be very fortunate.'

'I suppose that's why the society women are flocking around me?' Will said drily. 'But as I said, don't worry about me, I made my big mistake when I was younger. I was taken in by Sara Miller's pretty face, I even believed for a time that I was the father of her child.' He smiled ruefully. 'I must have been a fool in those

120

days' – he straightened – 'but no more, Hari, I assure you.'

He rose abruptly to his feet. 'I must go, I've work to do.' He kissed her cheek and then smiled down at her. 'Now remember what I said, no matchmaking.'

When Will had gone, Hari sat for a little while staring into the garden. She didn't see the roses or the lush grass, she was seeing instead the shabby workshop in World's End where she had sat with her father learning her trade as a boot and shoe maker.

In spite of their lack of wealth, the Morgans had been a happy family. Dewi Morgan had made a meagre enough living mostly tapping working boots that should long ago have been put on the fire, but at least he provided food and shelter for his sick wife and his daughter. He had taught Hari all he knew so that when eventually she was left alone in the world she was able to continue with the trade that had been her father's and grandfather's before her.

Hari rubbed at her eyes, talking about the past had brought back disturbing memories, memories of Sarah Miller and her Sam Payton snatching David and holding him to ransom. How Hari had feared for her son in those dark days when he had been kept hidden in an old shed on a hilltop.

But Craig had succeeded in rescuing their son and Hari remembered how her fear turned to relief when she saw Craig come through the dust with David safe in his arms.

In the confusion Sarah Miller and Sam Payton had disappeared as though from the face of the earth.

'Good riddance to them!' Hari's voice startled her. At once she was back in the present and she saw the softness of the garden and breathed in the scent of roses through the open window with a feeling of thankfulness. The past was over and done with; Sarah Miller would never have the nerve to return to her father's home in Swansea.

She sighed and turned towards the door. David would have had his afternoon rest by now and his nanny would be getting him ready for tea in the nursery. A warmth filled Hari and suddenly she wanted to hold David in her arms and reassure herself that he was all right.

Emily Miller stood in the dining room surveying the exquisitely set table with satisfaction. The silver gleamed and the napkins were starched and white, twisted into fan-like shapes against the gleaming mahogany of the table.

'Looks excellent.' John had come up behind her unawares and now, he put his arms around her waist, drawing her back against him.

'I hope we are having some interesting people to dinner?' he said. 'I'm fed up of being looked down on by some of the folks you have here.' He turned her to face him and Emily placed her hands against his cheeks.

'You are my husband, John, and I love you more than life itself, you come first always, you know that.'

He sighed. 'I know, but I'm not really accepted, am I? John Miller, one-time cobbler, now sitting at table with the élite of the town, it doesn't go down well.'

'It's only a few snobs who have recently made money and think they are a cut above anyone else,' Emily protested. 'The real gentry of Swansea are far too nice and polite to make you feel anything but one of them.'

'I know,' John kissed her lightly, 'most of the time I don't think about it, but now and again I realize that I'm not really good enough for you, my darling.'

'Hush!' Emily said softly. 'What would I do without you at my side? I would rather be dirt poor and have you, John, than be rich and alone.'

'Well, you have both, my love,' John said, 'and you can be proud of your achievements. You were left with a pile of debts when your father died and you fought

122

your way to the top again.' He kissed her again, more deeply this time.

'You are a remarkable woman, Mrs Miller,' he said softly.

Both of them looked up as the sound of a child's voice echoed down the hallway and Emily smiled in delight. 'Pammy is awake,' she said catching John's hand. 'Come on, let's go and keep her company for a little while.'

The little girl was holding her nurse's hand, but when she saw Emily, she held out her arms at once.

'Mamma,' she said in her light voice, 'Pammy wants to come to you, Mamma.'

Emily hugged her. 'It's all right, Mrs Caldwell, I'll take her for a while.' Emily nodded to the nurse, dismissing her and, sweeping Pammy up into her arms, carried the child into the sitting room.

John sat down opposite his wife and watched her with the child, a shadow of pain falling across his heart. If only the child was his and Emily's how happy he would be. But every time he looked at Pammy's lovely, dimpled face he was reminded of her mother.

Sarah was his only daughter, she had been headstrong, easily led. She had allowed herself to become captivated by Sam Payton who was nothing but a villain. Payton had pursuaded Sarah not only to abandon her own newly born child, but to kidnap the son of Craig and Hari Grenfell and hold the boy for ransom, almost killing them all in the process. It was only Grenfell's courage that saved them from certain death when the hillside, where Sarah and that man were hiding the child, was blasted to make way for a new road.

'What is it, John?' Emily asked and he smiled ruefully, she could always read him well.

'Nothing really, just thinking about old times,' he said. 'Now, tell me, who am I going to put up with at dinner tonight?'

Emily smiled. John might think he was fooling her into

changing the subject but she knew, she always knew, when he was thinking about his daughter and it hurt.

'Wait and see,' she said gently, trying to infuse a teasing note into her voice, but suddenly she was beset by the old fears and worries. 'Come on,' she said rising to her feet, 'let's take Pammy to the park.'

Later that evening, Emily sat looking round the dining table with mixed feelings. It was good to have Craig and Hari with her again and Will Davies appeared to be making headway with the youngest daughter of the ever-pompous Lady Caroline, but the memories raked up that afternoon continued to haunt her.

Emily met Hari's eyes and there she saw reflected the same darkening of the spirit that mirrored her own fear. Emily leaned over and spoke quietly to Hari.

'Have you been thinking over the past, too?' she asked softly. 'I have and it always makes me feel nervous.'

Nervous – that was an understatement. The past made Emily feel fearful of losing everything she had, it made her tremble with dread.

'I've been thinking about that awful time when I almost lost David, yes,' Hari said.

Emily sighed. 'I don't know what it is, the time of the year perhaps, but I can't seem to get the feeling of apprehension out of my mind. I suppose the real fear is that Sarah will one day come back and claim Pammy. I think I'd die if that happened.'

The knock on the door startled them all and Emily exchanged a quick, fearful glance with Hari. The butler entered the room and bent over Emily and John.

'Excuse me, there's a young – er – lady wishes to see you, I tried to put her off but she was most insistent. I thought I'd better let you know.'

Emily stared fearfully towards the open doorway and suddenly her heart was beating so swiftly, she thought she would swoon.

CHAPTER ELEVEN

Eline stood near the table, her hands resting on the scrubbed surface. She stared at her husband with his mistress at his side and she could scarcely believe the words he was speaking.

'So, for the time being Nina will have to sleep in the spare room.'

Eline's legs were trembling, she wanted to scream at Joe, tell him to get his harlot out of her house. How dare he bring Nina Parks into their home?

But Joe's expression made the words die on her lips. He was frowning, red with embarrassment but determined to be the master in his own house; it was his home, Eline realized with sudden clarity and not *her* home. Well, he could do what he liked with it, but not with her.

'I see.' Her voice was surprisingly controlled. 'And how long do you expect this *arrangement* to continue?'

Joe shrugged, not reading the warning signs in the colour of Eline's cheeks and the tautness of her shoulders.

'Until I sort things out,' he said. 'I'll soon find Nina rooms in the village, don't you worry.'

'So you are accepting responsibility for her?' Eline asked quietly. 'In other words you are admitting you are the father of her child?'

Joe looked uncomfortable. 'Now look here, Eline, I've had enough of argy-bargying with Nina's family. In my own house I expect a bit of respect.'

Eline folded her arms so that Joe would not see her hands shaking. 'And me, don't I warrant respect as your

125

wife? Am I supposed to sleep in the next room while you spend your time with *her*?' The sarcasm in her voice finally got through to Joe and his colour rose.

'You will do as I say!' He spoke loudly now as though to a stupid child. 'You are my wife or have you forgotten that little fact?'

'I can't believe this,' Eline said. 'Have *I* forgotten that I'm your wife? That's rich when you are bringing a pregnant paramour to my door wanting me to take her in.'

'I'm not *wanting* you to take her in,' Joe said, 'I'm *telling* you to take her in, is that clear?'

'Oh yes,' Eline said bitterly, 'that's clear all right.' She moved to the door and ran quickly up the stairs and began frantically to throw some clothes into a bag. How dare Joe treat her this way? Well, he could not have both of them, he would have to choose between Nina and his wife.

The enormity of what she was doing washed over Eline; in a small village like Oystermouth women did not walk out on their men. But then neither did husbands inflict such humiliation on their wives. No one would blame her for leaving Joe in the circumstances.

She returned more slowly to the kitchen where Nina was sitting in Eline's chair rubbing her hands over her face as though she were the wronged one.

'And what do you think you are doing?' Joe's voice was dangerously quiet.

'I'm leaving, what did you expect?' Eline asked. 'Joe, it's about time you grew up. You are old enough to be my father and you are behaving like a child wanting your cake and eating it. Well, the answer is no, I won't have it, I'm going.'

Nina Parks spoke for the first time. 'Aye go, you, a woman who has no respect for her husband don't deserve a good home like the one Joe has given you here.'

126

Eline didn't even look at her, she moved towards the door and Joe reached out and caught her arm, a haunted look on his face.

'You walk out of that door now and you don't come back,' he said, but his eyes were pleading with her. Suddenly Eline felt a deep sadness.

'Joe, if you think I'd trust you ever again after this you must be more stupid than I took you for.'

Joe's hand caught her across the face but Eline didn't flinch. 'That's just one more nail in your coffin,' she said and, opening the door, let herself out into the growing darkness.

Joe didn't come after her and Eline could imagine the sharp tongue of Nina Parks telling him he was better off without an ungrateful wife like Eline.

She stared around her, wondering where she was going. She had no money, nothing but a bag of clothes. She forced back the tears, she would not cry, she was a woman now not a child and she would fend for herself, as many others did.

She caught the last train to Swansea and the coach, as it rattled along the rim of the bay, was almost empty. She could hear the sound of the horses' hoofs echoing in the darkness, she heard the wash of the waves against the shore and suddenly, feeling unutterably alone, she hunched down into her seat as though she could make herself disappear.

When Eline alighted in the town, there were the bright lights spilling from public bars and the singing of men happy in drink and the sights and sounds only made her more aware of her vulnerability.

She saw a priest walking along the roadway and suddenly making up her mind what she would do, approached him to ask for directions to Emily Miller's house. He stared at her suspiciously for a moment and then seeing she was respectable, he smiled.

'And what, my dear child, are you doing out alone like

127

this? Are you in any sort of trouble? If so, I may be able to help.'

Eline shook her head. 'I'm a chapel girl, I'm not a Catholic,' she said. 'Why should you want to help me?'

'Because we are all God's creatures, child,' his voice was gentle, 'and all worthy of his love. Come, I will walk with you myself to the house of Mrs Miller and sure doesn't everyone in Swansea know where she lives.' He fell into step beside her.

'Which is to ask,' he said drily, 'where have you come from?'

'Oystermouth Village, about five miles along the coast,' Eline said softly, warming to the old priest's kindness.

'Is there anything I can help you with, my child? You seem troubled,' he said, glancing at her as though trying to read her expression in the darkness.

'I don't think anyone can help me,' Eline said softly, but suddenly wanting to confide in this wise man. 'My husband has brought home another woman, she is expecting his baby and he wanted her to stay with us in our home.' She looked up at the priest. 'I suppose I should turn the other cheek?' she said.

The priest shrugged. 'We are all human and can only take so much damage to our pride, for that's what it is, isn't it, child, it's your pride that is most hurt.'

'I suppose so, sir,' Eline said doubtfully. The priest chuckled.

'Just call me father, Father O'Brian, and I'm not so wise, just observant. If it was more than your pride that was hurt, you'd have stayed and fought this woman tooth and nail, would you not?'

'Perhaps,' Eline said with some surprise. Was he right, was it just stubborn pride that made her walk out on Joe? Was there even some feeling of relief that now no one would blame her for leaving her husband?

Father O'Brian stopped walking. 'Here it is, the

home of Mrs Miller, a lovely old house, wouldn't you say?'

Eline was taken aback at the grandeur of the building, the house towered above her, with elegant gables and fine big windows. For a moment, her courage wavered.

'Where is your church, father?' she asked urgently and without hesitation he told her.

'St David's. It is in the middle of the town and the door will be open should you need me.'

'Than you, Father O'Brian,' Eline said gratefully.

She watched him walk away back down hill towards the lights of the town, then the darkness stretched around her and she shivered suddenly.

She rang the bell with trembling fingers, seeing the big, curved doorway with a sense of wonder that Emily Miller, the woman who had offered a job when they'd met that day in William Davies's shop, should live in such splendour.

The man who opened the door looked down at her in surprise, his sharp eyes taking in her working clothes and heavy boots with a sniff of disdain.

'Tradespeople usually call at a convenient hour and go to the back of the house,' he said pointedly and made to close the door.

'Wait!' Eline said quickly. 'You don't understand, I must see Mrs Miller tonight, it's urgent.'

Something in her tone made him hesitate, she didn't seem the usual run-of-the-mill girl asking for skivvies' work.

'All right, come into the hall and I'll speak to Mrs Miller when I have the chance,' he said at last.

Eline stood in the hallway and stared around her in wonder; the carpet was rich and deep underfoot and beside her stood a magnificent clock, taller than she was by some inches.

The stairway wound upward in an elegant curve to a well-lit gallery from which many doors seemed to lead off. Eline sighed, what would Mrs Miller think of her intruding in this way? She would hardly wish to employ her.

Then Mrs Miller was coming from a large doorway, her face pinched and anxious, her eyes narrowed. She stopped in her tracks when she saw Eline, there was no light of recognition in her eyes, no smile of welcome. She seemed upset as she put her hand out towards the man at her side.

'Oh, John,' she said in a breathless voice, 'for a moment I thought Sarah had come back.'

'You go back to our guests,' he spoke with such a wealth of love in his voice that Eline realized he was Mr Miller and that he cared about his wife very deeply.

'Yes?' He came towards her, eyebrows raised. 'What can I do for you?' He sounded edgy and Eline stumbled over her words, feeling foolish at having bothered these people at such an hour.

'I'm sorry if I've caused any upset,' she said quickly, 'Mrs Miller asked me to call on her some time with a view to giving me a job, I'm sorry if it's inconvenient now, I suppose I didn't realize how late it was.'

'Well, I'm sure if Mrs Miller said there would be a job for you then there is one, but if you could call back tomorrow sometime,' he gestured towards the dining room. 'We have guests visiting at the moment.'

'Yes, I see.' Eline was already backing towards the door feeling very silly, her colour high. She could not bring herself to tell this man, however kindly, that she had nowhere to stay.

As she stood outside in the darkness, she looked back and saw the lights from the windows shining like beacons into the darkness and she felt an ache of loneliness within her.

She walked down the drive, tears brimming in her eyes, she was alone in the darkness with nowhere to turn. But it was her own fault, she should never have travelled to Swansea at this time of night, she should have waited until morning. But then, how could she have remained in the same house as Joe and his mistress? It would have been condoning what they had done.

'Eline!' The voice rang out through the darkness, strong and urgent. 'Eline, wait, it's me, Will Davies.' He caught up with her and took her arm. 'I've been having supper with Emily and I recognized your voice in the hallway, so I came after you.' He looked down at her, his face handsome in the moonlight.

'What on earth is wrong? Why are you out alone at such an hour?'

'I just couldn't stay.' Eline was reluctant to speak about her humiliation even to Will. 'Please don't ask me any more, I had to get away from the house, that's all there is to it.'

'You must stay with me,' Will said quickly. 'I'll take you to my lodgings and ask Mrs Marsh to put you up, at least for tonight.'

Eline shook her head. 'I can't do that, I have no money and I won't be beholden to you, Mr Davies.'

'For heaven's sake!' Will sounded exasperated. 'I'm not expecting anything in return, I just want to help, call it a loan if you like.' When she remained silent Will looked down at her, a rueful smile curving his mouth.

'All right, if you don't accept my offer, what will you do? Return home?'

Eline shook her head. 'No! I won't do that.' She sighed, feeling suddenly helpless. 'I could always spend the night in St David's Church; the doors there are always open, the father told me that himself.'

'To vagrants and gin drinkers and the like,' Will said reasonably. 'I dare say the father is a kind man, but you can't expect him to keep you company all night, can you?'

Eline suddenly felt her spurt of independence had

131

vanished; she needed help badly and Will Davies was offering it.

'If you're sure I won't be a burden, I'll come to your lodgings with you,' she said in a low voice. Will's face lit up.

'Good girl!' He said softly. 'Now where is the cab I ordered? I asked the driver to pick me up at just about this time. It should be meeting me at the gate about now.'

He led Eline down the drive and there indeed was the cab, the lights gleaming, the horses moving edgily on the cobbles.

Will helped Eline up into the coldness of the leather seat and she sank back, suddenly grateful to have all decisions taken out of her hands. She closed her eyes, seeing again the triumph on the face of Nina Parks, Joe's old love who was still young enough to get with child by him.

Was it, as the old priest had said, just pride on her part that had made her walk out? But no, what woman would accept the presence of a rival in her home? It was asking too much of even the most forbearing of women.

'What happened?' Will said gently. 'I know it must have been something dreadful to make you leave your home at this time of night.'

Eline opened her eyes and tried to see Will's face but it was too dark. And yet she knew that his expression would be one of concern. He wasn't asking questions from mere curiosity, he cared about her.

'Joe brought home his mistress,' she said in a flat voice. 'She is going to have his child and yet she is old enough to be my mother. I have failed Joe, I realize that, I can't work the oyster beds like Nina Parks and I can't even give Joe children.' She shook back her hair. 'But whatever I have done to fail him, I just can't put up with his mistress being under the same roof, I just can't.'

Will was silent, but his hand found hers in the darkness

and held it gently. Eline felt a rush of mixed emotions, if only she was free, she would curl her hand into his, snuggle against him, close her eyes and feel his mouth on hers.

She stopped herself abruptly; whatever Joe had done he was her husband and she had no right to be thinking such wicked thoughts about another man.

'I wish I'd been at home to look after you,' he said quietly. 'What made you come into Swansea to see Emily Miller?'

'Desperation, I suppose,' Eline replied. 'Emily Miller promised me a job,' Eline explained, 'remember when I was in your shop that time? I suppose I thought she could take me in there and then.' She bit her lip. 'I don't really know what I thought, I was clutching at straws.' She swallowed hard.

'Am I doing the right thing coming with you, Will? You know how angry Joe was to find me working in your shop that time.' She rubbed at her eyes tiredly. 'I don't think I've thought clearly since the moment Joe walked into the house with Nina Parks clinging to his arm.'

'Forget it all for now,' Will urged, 'things will look different after a good night's sleep.' The drive into Oystermouth was over very quickly and, as Eline alighted from the cab, she glanced around her nervously. Joe might well be making his way home from one of the public bars at any time and the last thing she wanted was a confrontation with him right now.

Will paid the cab driver, then unlocked the door and led the way into the house. It was silent and dark with just one gas lamp shining on top of the stairs.

'It looks as if Mrs Marsh is in bed,' Will said. 'Come on, you can have my room for tonight and I'll sleep in the sitting room.'

Eline was too tired to argue, in any case, what alternative did she have? She certainly couldn't go home.

Will led her through his small sitting room and showed

her the bedroom and he stood there for a moment, pushing his fingers through his hair.

'Is there anything you need?' he said quietly and Eline shook her head. He moved to the door and she spoke his name softly.

'Will, I can't ever tell you how much your help means to me.'

He held up his hand. 'Think nothing of it, rest now, you look worn out. Good night, Eline, we'll talk in the morning.'

She sank on to the bed and stared at her small bag of belongings; a few clothes and a hairbrush was all she had to show for her marriage to Joe.

Suddenly, Eline was crying, unable to suppress the sound of her bitter sobbing. And even though she knew her tears were selfish and self-indulgent, she couldn't stop them from running salt and bitter down her face.

The door opened and William hurried across the room and, without a word, he took her in his arms, cradling her as though she was a child, smoothing the hair from her hot, flushed face.

'There, there, it won't look so bad in the morning, I promise you,' he said soothingly.

He was so good and kind, Eline thought abstractedly, how could Will know that his very touch set her alight with love and desire?

She moved away from him and poured water from the jug on the table into the matching bowl and splashed her hot face with the cooling drops.

'I'll be all right now,' she said and her voice was muffled. 'Please go.'

She didn't turn as she heard his footsteps cross the room and then the sound of the door closing because if she had looked into his dear face she would have thrown herself into his arms and begged him to stay with her all night.

She undressed and climbed in between the sheets

breathing in the sweet scent of William; she buried her face in his pillow and squeezed her eyes tightly shut. It took all her control not to go to him in the other room.

But she was a fool, William was a fine gentleman, he needed a wife who could live up to his sort of life-style. In any case, even if William wanted her, Eline was not free, would never be free.

She seemed to toss and turn for hours and at last she gave up all attempts to sleep and glanced towards the window where the moonlight lingered in fragmentary shards. She watched until, at last, the blue darkness gave way to the pale morning light.

In the little house at the other end of the village Joe would be rising from bed, the bed he had no doubt shared with Nina Parks. Eline sighed heavily, what an awful mess her life had become. Would she ever find a way out of it?

At last she slept and she wasn't aware of William putting a note on the table beside the bed or of him staring down at her with love naked in his eyes. But in her dreams she was in his arms, clinging to him, loving him and when she awoke, her pillow was wet with tears.

CHAPTER TWELVE

The sun was hot overhead, the sky a cloudless blue and the sea, spread out below on the edge of the town, shimmered in the summer heat.

From her vantage point up on the hill, Fon Parks looked down at the scene before her. She breathed deeply of the crystalline air and leaned against the dry-stone wall, fanning her face with her small, slender hand.

What was she doing? She had asked herself that a hundred or more times since she left Oystermouth earlier that morning. What did she know about farm life? All she knew was the sea and the oyster beds. But the oyster season was over and would not start again until September and that was two long months away. In any case, Fon felt she could not remain in Oystermouth and suffer the spiteful gossip of the neighbours who had blackened her mother's name.

The gossip had spread swiftly enough round the small village and, in the telling, the story had been embroidered and exaggerated. Still, the facts were indisputable: Nina Parks was installed in Joe Harries's house, expecting his baby while his lawful, wedded wife had been driven from her own hearth.

Fon felt the heat in her face intensify with the shame of it all and now her brother Tom was threatening violence, telling all and sundry that he would kill Joe Harries once he got his hands on the man.

Fon's sisters seemed relatively unaffected by it all; Sal was happy living in at the Pascoe household and Gwyneth, who was spending more and more time at the boot and shoe store, didn't give a fig for the gossips. It was she, Fon, who was left at home with nothing to do, no more oysters to bag or take to market, and Fon, it was, who had to contend with Tom's nightly drinking bouts after which he made all sorts of vile threats against the man who was his father.

Fon had seen the advertisement by accident, the newspaper had been wrapped around some cockles she'd bought in Swansea Market. It sounded easy enough, a young lady needed to look after a baby; it was something she could do, wasn't it?

Fon had carefully written down the address, Jamie O'Conner, Honey's Farm, Townhill. It sounded so pretty, so peaceful that Fon had written to Mr O'Conner at once, carefully scripting the note with her fine hand-writing and for once, she was glad that she had taken the lessons at the free school that her mother had insisted upon.

The reply had come within a few days asking Fon to come for an interview. She picked out several spelling mistakes but the tone of the letter was friendly and open and Fon, who liked to think well of people, imagined an old man, tongue in cheek, laboriously composing his reply.

And so here she was, on the top of the world, it seemed, staring out over the sprawling streets of Swansea, breathing in the soft hillside air and feeling the heat of the sun through her crisp, clean, calico dress.

The farm was quite a small one with low buildings mellow in the sunlight and sheep grazing contentedly in the lush grass. Fon heard the plaintive sound of cattle from somewhere behind the house and she felt a flutter of apprehension, she knew nothing about farms or farming and she knew she would faint with fright if a cow came anywhere near her.

A dog ran barking towards her, tail wagging furiously and Fon instinctively backed away.

137

'Sure there's no need to be afraid of Duffy,' a strong masculine voice said kindly. 'He's an old softie, he wouldn't hurt a fly.'

The man was bare headed, his face tanned by the weather, his eyes startlingly blue. He smiled down at her.

'You must be the young lady who answered my advertisement,' he said gently. 'I'm Jamie O'Conner. Do you know much about babies?'

Fon shook back her hair nervously. 'I don't know anything, really,' she confessed, 'but I love children and I'm willing to learn.'

'Well, you seem to be the only one in the whole of Swansea that my dear wife Katherine will consider now, though many a young lady has had a try at the job.' His smile widened. 'Come and meet my son.'

He led the way into the farmhouse and the coolness of the kitchen struck a pleasant contrast to the heat outside.

'The boy is having a sleep,' Mr O'Conner said at once, 'and his mammy is resting too. Mrs O'Conner is not very strong, not since she had the baby and that's why we need help here.'

The infant was lying on his stomach, his dark hair clinging in curls around his forehead.

'He's lovely!' Fon said in genuine delight and Mr O'Conner nodded, accepting the accolade as his right.

'Aye, Patrick is a fine boy for a two year old, full of mischief so he is and wearing his mammy out.' He looked at Fon's slight figure doubtfully.

'Can't say that you look too robust, my girl, seems you need feeding up.'

'Oh, I'm stronger than I look,' Fon protested, 'I used to work the oyster beds and that's no job for a weakling.'

'Jamie,' the voice came from the other room light and breathless, 'who is it, Jamie, is it the new girl?'

138

Mr O'Conner gestured for Fon to follow him across the landing. He seemed suddenly tense, his big shoulders hunched.

His wife was a faded woman, faded blue eyes stared out from beneath sandy lashes and pale lips stretched a little into a half-smile.

'*Bore da*,' Fon moved forward in sympathy at once with the woman in the bed who seemed too weak to lift her head.

'Good-morning, Fon, is it? What a funny name to be sure. I'm Katherine, I'm glad to see that you look respectable and tidy, like.'

Fon realized that Mrs O'Conner had a poor opinion of the other girls she'd seen and must have proved a hard taskmaster. She wondered how many young ladies had come and gone from Honey's Farm in the short life of Patrick O'Conner.

'Sit down and talk to me,' Katherine said easily. 'Jamie, you are forgetting your manners. Bring us a couple of glasses of iced lemon, if you please.'

A look of surprise passed quickly over Jamie O'Conner's face to be replaced by an expression of relief. He had been expecting opposition, it seemed, and was glad not to have found it.

'Now, tell me about yourself,' Katherine said in her dry, light voice. 'I could see from your letter that you are nicely educated not like most girls these days.'

This Fon could agree to without hesitation. 'Oh, yes, my mother made sure I went to school, I can read and write and work at figures quite well enough.'

'Good and I'm sure your family is most respectable.' Katherine fortunately did not wait for confirmation. 'I know a tidy girl when I see one and I'll be happy to leave the care of my little boy in your hands, my dear.' She sat up a little straighter.

'Now I'm sure you would like to know what your duties are?' She saw Fon's brief nod without pausing and it was clear that whatever it was that ailed her did not prevent her using her voice to full benefit.

'You will rise early but then I'm sure you are used to that. You must make breakfast for Mr O'Conner, he likes a bit of haddock and a poached egg most mornings and as for me, I shall take, as usual, nothing but a piece of dry, toasted bread. The baby has porridge but only after his bath.' Katherine drew a breath but Fon could think of nothing to say so the silence lasted only a few moments before Katherine broke into conversation once more.

'Patrick is well trained, he rarely has a little accident at night and providing you take him to the privy immediately upon rising you will have no problems with him.'

She smiled kindly. 'Don't look so worried, you'll soon get used to our little ways.'

Jamie O'Conner entered the room with a tray bearing two glasses of lemon and Fon kept her eyes lowered as she took her glass. She felt suddenly shy as the realized the kindly man with the handsome, open-air ruggedness would be paying her wages.

'You will, of course, have the benefit of a room of your own, something most young girls find a luxury.' Katherine sipped her lemon and made a face. 'To be sure you could have put in a little more sugar, Jamie! The drink is as bitter as vinegar.'

The distraction saved Fon from replying, though she would have had to agree with Katherine O'Conner, a room to herself would be a luxury. Up until the time Sal went into service the three girls had slept in the same bedroom, Tom having one bedroom and Mam having the main front bedroom that looked out over the sea.

She would miss the sea, Fon realized with a sudden dart of homesickness; she would miss the wash of the waves on the shore and the sound of fog horns mourning through the mists. She swallowed hard reminding herself that she would also be missing the spiteful gossip and the continuing shame of seeing Mam grow bigger with child and her not married.

'When shall I start?' she asked quickly. 'That is if you find me satisfactory.'

'As soon as you like,' Katherine said. 'If you take Patrick with you, Jamie will drive you in the cart to fetch your things, save you another long walk today.'

'That's very kind of you, Mrs O'Conner,' Fon said earnestly. 'I will work very hard and I will make up for your kindness to me.'

'I know,' Katherine said, 'and don't call me Mrs O'Conner, please call me Katherine. I'm not like the rich snobs who live around here, I'm an Irish woman with no side.' She smiled and for a moment she looked almost pretty. 'I want us to be friends.'

When she stood once more in the kitchen of the farmhouse, Fon looked round her feeling as though the tide had come in and snatched her off her feet. This was to be her home; tonight she would be under a strange roof and events suddenly seemed to be moving too fast for her.

Nina sat in the kitchen staring into the flames of the fire, it was so hot, too hot with the sun streaming in through the open door and windows, but she needed the fire to cook Joe a fine meal when he got home.

She knew he would be down at the pool, white-liming his boat, the *Emmeline*. The skiff was old and needed care and she knew that even though Joe now owned the brand-new *Oyster Sunrise*, he would never love the new skiff as much as he loved his old one.

She smiled wryly; perhaps he would never love Nina Parks the way he loved his wife. Nina patted her hot face, but now that Eline had chosen to run off, Nina would make a damn good job of making Joe happy. It couldn't have worked out better, she mused, here she was safely ensconced in Joe's house, his wife in all but name. It was only the bitter anger of her son that cast a shadow over her happiness.

There was talk of course, talk enough about Nina and Joe living openly together as man and wife. Furthermore it was quite obvious now that Nina was once again with child and she a woman rising forty.

Nina's lips curved in gratification as there was also talk about sweet little Eline who, it seemed, had spent the night with Will Davies, owner of the boot and shoe emporium. The crafty little bitch had not been so clever because she had been seen leaving Will Davies's lodgings in the early hours of the morning.

Joe didn't know anything about that and it was something Nina intended to keep up her sleeve. A weapon to use against Eline, should she ever need it.

Nina sighed; if only Tom would come to terms with the fact that she loved Joe and needed him. After her son's threats, she wondered why he had not confronted Joe face to face; perhaps, she thought uneasily, Tom was biding his time and would pounce when Joe least expected it.

A dark shadow fell on to the clean slate floor and Nina looked up smiling to see Joe entering the kitchen. He smelled of tallow and white-lime and there was about him an air of dejection that Nina could not ignore.

'What is it, Joe?' she asked, rising to push the pot of stew on to the fire. He slumped into a chair and pushed back his thick hair.

'She's in Swansea, my wife, working for that Mrs Emily Miller,' he said bluntly. He thumped the table with his fist. 'I told her I didn't want her working, I told her!'

'Joe,' Nina said softly, sensing she was on dangerous ground. 'Don't fret about her, she's nothing but a headstrong girl who wants her own way.' She put her arms around his neck and wriggled herself on to his knee.

'Forget Eline, Joe, put her out of your mind. She'll come running home when she sees how hard it is living in the outside world alone.'

Nina knew that this was not the time to put in her barb about Eline staying the night with Will Davies; let Joe become used to the difference in his life-style, let him see how good it was to be looked after by a mature, loving woman and he'd soon stop missing Eline or worrying about what she was doing. But for the time being, Nina knew she must play the game very carefully.

'Don't you think that she's wishing right now to be home in Oystermouth with you, Joe? Any woman who would exchange a job in Swansea for a life with a fine man like you must be out of her mind. She'll be back, Joe, give her time.'

She bent to kiss his mouth. 'In the mean time, Joe, let's enjoy what we have here, we're getting the bad name, so let's earn it, right?'

She put his hand on her full breast and heard with pleasure the sudden deepening of his breathing. Appeal to what a man hides in his trousers and you had him cold. She pressed closer to him, darting her tongue into his mouth.

'Come on, Joe, take me to bed,' she whispered softly. 'I want you so much, my lovely, you are a real man and you know how to make a woman feel good.'

He took her in his arms and carried her up the stairs. On the landing she put her head against his shoulder, her eyes closed.

'It'll have to be your room, Joe,' she said softly, 'I've taken all the sheets off the bed in the spare room and they're still on the line.'

He seemed to hesitate and Nina held her breath; would Joe resist this last bastion, breach the code that so far had prevented him taking Nina to his marriage bed?

143

'You don't need anyone but me, Joe.' She kissed his mouth. 'We'll show the world, won't we, my lovely?'

He kicked open the door to the bedroom and set her down on the wide bed, his marriage bed. Nina felt a moment of pure triumph, she felt that now she was truly mistress of Joe Harries's house.

Fon found the baby a delight to care for; Patrick was good-natured and adapted well to the routine she had set him. During the afternoons, Patrick had a nap and afterwards, Fon would take him round the farm, holding his hand, guiding his stumbling feet across the fields, telling him baby stories about oysters and fishing boats.

There had been a few tricky moments when Jamie had taken her back to Oystermouth and Tom had been sitting in the kitchen, a bottle of gin on the table before him.

'Who's he?' Tom had demanded. 'You're not going the same way as your mother, are you, Irfonwy?'

The situation had been taken out of Fon's hands when Jamie stepped forward. 'I'm James O'Conner,' he said easily. 'My wife and me have employed Fon here to take care of our son. Are there any objections I should know about?'

Tom had thought for a moment and then his shoulders had slumped. 'No, I suppose she might as well be out of all this.' He'd reached up and pulled Fon towards him.

'Look after yourself, girl' – his eyes seemed misty – 'a good name is all you got so keep it.' He turned his back on her then. 'Choose a husband well when the time comes or you could end up like poor Emmeline, out on the street with no one to care for you.'

There had been silence on the drive back to Townhill until Jamie drew the horse up outside the low farmhouse.

'We won't say nothing about this to Katherine, she doesn't hold with folks drinking' – Jamie smiled mischievously – 'though I manage one myself from time to time.' He lifted down her bag.

'This Emmeline your brother talked of, would it be Eline Harries, Eline Powell as was?'

Fon looked at him in surprise. 'Why, yes, do you know her then?' Her mouth was dry; what if Jamie and Katherine were friends of Eline's? How would they feel about employing the daughter of the woman who'd stolen Eline's husband away from her?

'Not know her exactly,' Jamie said. 'It's just we bought the farm from her or rather from her husband. Bit of gossip about the family, is there?'

Fon sighed heavily. 'Aye, gossip enough,' she said, 'Joe and Eline have gone their separate ways, so it seems.' Fon hoped she wouldn't be asked to enlarge on what she'd said.

Jamie helped her down from the cart and then lifted the sleeping Patrick on to his shoulder. 'I always thought that Joe Harries looked old enough to be Eline's father, so I did,' Jamie said thoughtfully. 'Spring and autumn don't make good bedfellows.'

To Fon's relief he had left it at that and moved inside the house and now, as Fon sat at the table, spooning porridge into Patrick's eager mouth, she looked around her, wondering that Eline had been brought up within these walls; it was a small world as her mam was fond of saying.

She sighed and glanced out of the window at the rolling fields outside. Eline must have loved this land, the place where she had been born, but give Fon the open seas any time. Suddenly, Fon felt very close to Eline, both of them had lost their homes and suddenly Fon's eyes were misted with tears.

CHAPTER THIRTEEN

Eline's first impression of Mrs Miller had been confirmed when William had taken her to the grand emporium up on the hill in Swansea to talk with the elegant owner of the boot and shoe emporium. Emily Miller was beautiful, with a serene expression in her eyes that must come, Eline decided, from being secure in her husband's love because it was plain for anyone to see that Mr Miller adored his wife. The way his eyes followed her when she moved and the gentleness with which his hand brushed hers whenever they were near each other was touching to see. Mrs Miller was a very fortunate woman, Eline thought enviously.

She and Will could have that sort of love, Eline mused, if only things had been different. Will had been so kind to her; after putting her up at his lodgings for the night he had arranged for her to have an interview with Mrs Miller almost straight away. Eline knew that Will must have intervened on her behalf, because it was clear that the job had been hers before she even set foot into the splendid emporium that dominated the entire length of College Street.

To Eline's surprise, she had quickly learnt that the emporium was not only for boots and shoes, but housed a clothing department as well as a floor that sold furniture and carpets. It was incredible to consider the money that must pour into the tills every day; Mr and Mrs Miller must be very rich indeed.

And now that Eline was settled in her job, she realized that although she was a very small cog in the smooth-running emporium, she was quickly accepted by the rest of the staff.

The lady assistants lived in, the rooms on the top floor of the emporium having been converted into bedrooms and one large, communal sitting room. There was a large kitchen equipped with the latest stove for cooking and an elegant bathroom which was so ornate that Eline felt she scarcely dare touch anything. And she was almost happy.

This morning she had been asked to decorate one of the large windows and tentatively she had begun to assemble a few items that she thought might make a tempting picture.

She had spent quite a long time in thought, sizing up the window and studying the sort of people who stopped to look into the store. It seemed to Eline that the folk who patronized Mrs Miller's emporium were mostly the well-off residents of Swansea, ladies who would put high fashion before comfort and gentlemen who took to whatever their wives told them.

Eline was hesitant at first, asking diffidently if she might have a carpet laid in the shop window, but once Mrs Miller gave her approval, Eline grew more confident and soon, a small suite of furniture, discreet in colour, was set around the window as if it were a drawing room.

So engrossed was she that she was entirely unaware of the audience that was gathering both inside the shop and outside the large window.

At the foot of one of the soft chairs, she set a pair of ladies' shoes, high heeled and elegant, something an older lady might wear and in the chair opposite a pair of fine gentlemen's boots of polished calf. At the base of the sofa, a pair of soft pumps, decorated with amethyst, nestled against fashionable boots, tooled with intricate design, as though the wearers were lovers, sitting close together. Finally, near what would have been the fireplace had the room been real, Eline set out several pairs of children's shoes in an apparently untidy huddle, but the entire effect was of a family together as though spending an evening at home.

She stood back to admire the scene but something was lacking and she knew suddenly just what it was. Carried away with enthusiasm, she asked for curtains to be brought and hung at the front of the window display and at last she was satisfied. The effect was of a scene on stage with the actors invisible except for their shoes.

When she had finished, there was a burst of spontaneous clapping and Eline looked up in surprise, her colour rising as she saw the crowd of people watching her. She retired to the back of the shop and rubbed at her temples with dusty fingers, realizing she had been at work for hours without noticing it.

Later, Mrs Miller sent for Eline and she wondered if she was going to be reprimanded for what could be seen as her arrogance in ordering so much stock and causing a great deal of work, but Mrs Miller was smiling.

'Sit down, please,' she said and Eline perched on the edge of a leather chair, awed by the sumptuousness of the office.

'I congratulate you on your display,' she said gently. 'The only other person who could better what you have done today is Hari Grenfell herself.'

This was praise indeed and Eline warmed to it. 'Thank you, Mrs Miller,' she said humbly. She waited, hands folded in her lap, for her employer to go on. There was clearly more to come and Eline was a little apprehensive as to what it might be.

'How would you like to make a career out of window dressing?' Mrs Miller said at last. 'You seem so sure of yourself that you must have had some sort of training.'

Eline shook her head. 'No, my father was a farmer, he owned Honey's Farm over at Townhill.' Mrs Miller seemed a little disappointed so Eline added quickly, 'I always liked painting pictures, though.'

'Well, no matter,' Mrs Miller said, 'Hari Grenfell had no training either; I expect this sort of talent must be a gift more than anything.'

She smiled suddenly. 'How would you like to go to a ladies' college and further your education?' She spoke as though on a sudden inspiration. 'I know you can write beautifully, I've seen the requests you made for your window dressing today.'

Eline shook her head. 'I was sent to the free school for girls in Goat Street when I was young and I liked my lessons well enough, but I would be out of place in a college, Mrs Miller. Perhaps you are forgetting I'm an old married woman,' she said, ruefully aware that Mrs Miller was looking at her thoughtfully.

'Married maybe, old you certainly are not,' Mrs Miller replied. 'I don't want to pry, but it's quite obvious you're separated from your husband; would he be in a position to object to your education being advanced?'

'It's not that,' Eline answered, 'it's just that I'd be out of place. In any case, I wouldn't be willing to take charity, but thank you for the offer all the same.'

Mrs Miller wasn't going to drop the subject easily. 'We could treat it all as an apprenticeship,' she said evenly. 'I don't want to see your talent wasted, Eline, that's all.' She rose to her feet signalling that the interview was over and Eline bobbed a curtsy before leaving the room.

Outside the door, she expelled her breath in relief. Mrs Miller was a formidable woman and for a moment there, Eline imagined she would be forcibly sent away to college. It was strange really, the effect Mrs Miller had on her; she was perhaps a woman in her twenties, certainly not more than four or five years older than Eline, but she had such poise and character that it was difficult to say no to her.

It was growing dark now and as Eline made her way upstairs to her room, she found herself wondering what it would be like to be taught by a real artist, someone who could tell her how to tackle difficult perspectives, how to mix colours to the best advantage and the proper use of light and shade. She sighed heavily; she was far too old for that sort of dreaming, she was a woman separated from her husband, a woman who had been betrayed, a figure of scorn perhaps.

As she reached the door of the sitting room, she saw a tall figure unwind from one of the comfortable chairs.

'Will – Mr Davies,' she corrected herself hastily, 'what are you doing here?' She was aware her words were abrupt, rude even and the colour rushed to her cheeks.

'I came to see you,' he said simply, taking her hand and leading her to a seat. 'I have to talk to you, Eline.' He smoothed her wrist and Eline felt desire for him flow through her like a potent wine. She was well used to the attentions of a man for Joe had always been vigorous in the marriage bed, but never had Eline felt this over-bearing urge to be loved, to be crushed like a petal, to be pierced so that the sensations racing through her demanding release were satiated.

She sat down, her legs trembling. 'What is it? Is there anything wrong?'

He kept hold of her hand. 'I don't know but I think you should be aware of the gossip that's sweeping Oystermouth.'

Eline sighed heavily. 'I'm sure there's gossip, Will.' She spoke his name easily now, her self-consciousness vanished beneath the weight of his words. 'There was bound to be gossip with me leaving Joe and him taking Nina Parks into the house.'

'It's not only that,' Will said, still smoothing her wrist as if to quiet a nervous animal. 'It's us, me and you, they say we spent the night together.'

Eline felt her cheeks flush with hot, angry colour.

'The devils!' she said. 'How dare they talk about us and we doing nothing wrong?'

'You were seen leaving my lodgings in the early morning,' he said, 'that seems to be enough meat for the gossips to get their tongues around.'

Eline sank back in her chair feeling suddenly exhausted. 'And Joe, how is he taking all this?' She wondered that her husband hadn't gone for Will with a pickaxe by now for Joe was the sort who laid down one law for himself and another for his wife. 'He can be violent, you know.'

Will shrugged. 'I don't know, I haven't seen him.' He leaned towards her. 'Don't worry about that, I can take care of myself.'

'What an awful mess!' Eline said softly, tears burning her eyes. Will gripped her hand more tightly and would have drawn her close, but she extricated her fingers from his grasp.

'No,' she said, 'we mustn't do anything that would fuel the flames.' How could she tell Will that she feared for his life? If Joe were to believe the gossip he would feel that honour must be satisfied and in his book that would mean giving Will and possibly Eline herself a good hiding.

'Perhaps I should have listened to Mrs Miller and gone away to college,' she said softly, knowing even as she spoke that it would be impossible.

'Is that what Emily wants you to do?' Will asked anxiously. Eline smiled at his tone and looked down at her hands to conceal her delight at his reaction.

'It is, but there's no fear of me going to college, I don't want to leave Swansea.' Or you, she added silently.

'Well, I've been talking to Emily myself as it happens and between us we've come up with a great idea.' Will took her hands impulsively. 'So great I wonder why didn't I think of it before.'

'What idea?' Eline asked quickly, her cheeks blushing hotly as Will's hands closed strong and firm around hers.

151

Oh Will, she thought, looking at his dear face so close to her own, if only, if only.

'We thought you could spend one or two days a week with Hari Grenfell, she would teach you all she knows about window dressing and about shoes; no one understands leather like Hari.'

'Why should she want to spend time teaching me anything?' Eline asked reasonably and Will smiled down at her.

'Hari loves her work,' he said, 'she can teach you design and drawing; it would all be of help to you if you want to get on in this life.' He warmed to his subject. 'Hari was poor once, very poor, she's got where she is by sheer talent and hard work.'

'She wasn't married to Joe Harries,' Eline said ruefully. 'She was lucky enough to marry a Grenfell.'

'Hari made her own way in life,' Will said gravely. 'She was a woman alone with a child, she married Craig after she had made her own mark in the shoe business.' His words were like a reprimand and Eline drew her hands away.

'I'm sorry,' she said. 'I shouldn't make comments about people I don't know.'

Will rose to his feet. 'I'd better be going,' he smiled and Eline longed to go into his arms. 'I shouldn't be here, really,' he said, 'gentlemen followers are definitely not encouraged.'

If only he was her follower, Eline thought wistfully, at this moment anything seemed possible but soon, the dream must end, and she would find herself back in Oystermouth with Joe. She stood in the back doorway of the emporium long after the sound of Will's footsteps had died away. The lamplight was casting soft pools of gold on the cobbled roadway and suddenly the light swam before the tears that were suddenly burning Eline's eyes.

It was a week later when Eline met Hari Grenfell at

Summer Lodge, her beautiful home on the soft hills outside the town. Hari looked at her with interest, her eyes alight with welcome and everything about her spoke of success from her neatly pinned dark hair to the tips of her satin pumps.

On the table were spread drawings, designs for shoes and even the cursory glance she allowed herself told Eline that they were good, very good.

'Sit down and make yourself at home,' Hari said, 'there's no need to stand on ceremony with me, mind.'

Eline took in the elegantly furnished sitting room and the long windows that showed to advantage the splendid views of the golden beach with the sea slipping timidly into the curve of the bay.

'It's lovely here,' she said impulsively and she saw Hari smile.

'I know, I never get tired of looking out of the windows. The sea is never the same, sometimes it's racing in against the rocks and other times, like now, it's so soft and gentle.'

Hari signed. 'Everyone keeps telling me I'm a very fortunate woman, I know that only too well, sometimes I'm afraid of losing it all.' She smiled suddenly at Eline.

'But now to business, I've heard so many glowing reports about you from Emily that I'm half-afraid to work with you. What if you know more than I do?'

Eline warmed to Hari's modesty. 'I don't know anything about shoes,' she said truthfully, 'but I'd like to learn.'

'Well, you seem to have a flair for window dressing, I've seen your stage set and I think it's brilliant.'

Eline felt her colour rising. 'It's very kind of you to say so, Mrs Grenfell.'

'Call me Hari, it's going to be so cumbersome otherwise and you'll make me feel about a hundred years old if you keep calling me Mrs Grenfell.'

Hari sifted through the drawings. 'See this one,' she

said, selecting a piece of paper, 'it's a lady's side-spring boot. I've been working on the design for my own version, but I can't seem to get the elastic vent quite right.'

Eline took the drawing and studied it for a moment and automatically reached out for a pen. With a few strokes she altered the drawing and then set it down on the table.

'That's excellent!' Hari said warmly. 'Where did you learn to draw?'

Eline looked up a little embarrassed at her own temerity in altering the drawing of the great Hari Grenfell.

'I painted a great deal when I lived on the farm,' she said almost apologetically, 'no one taught me, I just did it.'

'Well, you are far more talented than I am at artwork,' Hari said, 'perhaps we will be able to teach each other a great deal. In any case, I'm going to look forward to us working together.'

She leaned forward. 'I can teach you about cutting leather, tapping boots and building up shoes for children with foot defects but, as for window dressing and design, I don't think you've got much to learn, it's just a case of practising as much as you can.'

Hari searched among her folders and brought out a picture and showed it to Eline.

'This is a design by William Stephens Clark,' she said. 'You've heard of the Clark's factory in Somerset?'

Elaine nodded slowly. 'I think so.' She twisted her hands in her lap wondering how suddenly her life had been transformed from working in her small cottage scrubbing the unyielding stone floor to sitting in a plushly carpeted room talking to Hari Grenfell like an equal.

'This little shoe here,' Hari pointed to the picture, 'is a child's dress anklet in black enamel seal and it is still worn by children today even though it was designed by Mr Clark more than twenty years ago.' She sighed. 'I wish I could come up with a design that would become so famous.' She smiled at Eline. 'Perhaps between us, we will. Now let's get some work done.'

Eline spent the next few days at Hari Grenfell's store, feeling she was in a world of wonderful dreams from which she must surely awake. She watched the cobblers at work and saw, to her amazement, Hari Grenfell cut and mould leather with the best of them. She might be a small woman, but Hari had strength in her wrists that was only matched by her strength of character and Eline found herself admiring the woman greatly.

Eline tried her hand at sewing shoes on the machine, accepted tips from Hari on designing and window dressing and the days seem to fly.

At nights, it was true, she was lonely. She lay awake thinking of Joe and Nina and the mess the three of them had made of their lives. And then, inevitably, her thoughts would turn to William Davies and his very name brought a warm feeling to her heart.

But it was all so hopeless, she was still married to Joe and Eline knew he would never let her go. What she must do, she decided, was to forget love and turn her energies towards her career. And yet as the soft summer nights pressed down on her, the sweet urges of the flesh were very hard to subdue.

It was a fine, crisp, sunny morning and William Davies left his lodgings with a feeling of energy running through him. He breathed in deeply the salt air and looked out towards Mumbles Head where the sails of a pilot ship billowed like a wedding veil in the soft breeze. And he thought of Eline.

She was never far from his thoughts; he wanted her with every fibre of his being, but he would only be content to have her as his wife.

He turned the corner and his footsteps faltered to a halt. The salty wind ruffled his hair but he no longer felt its balmy touch, his attention was focused on the front of his shop.

He moved forward in dismay to see the windows smashed, the boots and shoes covered with what appeared to be white-lime and he knew at once who was to blame.

'Bastard!' he said through clenched teeth as he moved forward and pushed open the door that was hanging on its hinges.

'*Duw*, Mr Davies, what's happened here?' Gwyneth Parks was standing in the doorway behind him staring round her in horror, her hands to her cheeks, her eyes wide.

In the centre of the shop was a mound of boots and shoes still smouldering, the smell of burnt leather permeating the shop.

Will clenched his teeth in anger; only one man hated him enough to try to destroy his stock. 'Joe Harries,' he said. 'I'm going round there to see him and have this out right now.'

Gwyneth caught his arm. 'Don't be hasty, Mr Davies, begging your pardon, sir, but you got no proof.' She sighed. 'My mam is besotted by Joe, she'll swear he was there with her all the time even if he wasn't.'

Will took a few deep breaths and then nodded. 'You're right, Gwyneth, but I can't let him get away with it.' He rubbed his fingers through his hair in an angry gesture.

Gwyneth was rolling up her sleeves. 'I know what I'm going to do, get this mess cleaned up, that's the first thing.' She seemed to have taken charge. 'You get the constable, Mr Davies, let him see what's happened here and that will be a start.'

Will looked at her gratefully. 'You're a gem, Gwyneth,' he said warmly, 'I'll be back soon and then we'll both get to work on the shop. We'll clean up the mess even if it takes us all day and all night, right?'

As he left the shop, Gwyneth watched him and around her mouth there was a self-satisfied smile; she was getting on the right side of Mr Davies and that is just where she wanted to be.

CHAPTER FOURTEEN

Joe sat with his head in his hands not hearing the mournful sound of a tug edging shorewards in the direction of the docks or the lonely cry of the seagulls overhead. Sitting on the top of Mumbles Head, the mist swirling around him virtually concealing him from anyone on the beach, Joe felt suitably isolated, he wanted to be alone with his misery.

It seemed to Joe that he had exchanged the harmony and joy of his life with Eline for one of discord and worry with Nina. He felt the pain of his loss very deeply, he wanted Eline, longed for her virginal ways, even her lack of enthusiasm in the marriage bed seemed desirable after a surfeit of Nina's overt sexuality.

He was also ashamed, ashamed of his attack on William Davies's shop, what had his hour of wanton destruction achieved? He had come away from the ruined store without even feeling self-satisfied.

He had heard the rumours, they had stirred up his anger, but, even as he heard that Eline had been seen leaving Davies's lodgings in the early hours of the morning, he knew Eline would never be unfaithful to him; it simply wasn't in her nature.

He thumped his fist into his hands, he wanted to hate Will Davies for his interference and yet he didn't. In some strange way he was grateful to the man for looking after Eline, for finding her honest work.

Joe knew he had no one to blame but himself for the mess he was in. Nina, safely ensconced in his house, was growing fatter by the day, the sound of her feet slopping about the floor irritated Joe and he missed the light, swift footsteps of his wife.

'Eline,' he whispered into his hands, 'Eline, my child bride, my love.' He groaned inwardly, he could not see any way out of the situation he was in; he had taken home another woman, pregnant by him, how could any wife be expected to stand for that?

He rose to his feet and stared down at the misty sea, rushing against the rocks below; he only had to move forward, lean out over the abyss and it would be over, he would be at peace.

'Joe!' The voice called to him frantically and looking over his shoulder, he saw that the fog had lifted somewhat. 'Joe, come home, Mam needs you.'

Gwyneth was white-faced and Joe knew that something was badly wrong. He hurried back down the hillside, his feet slipping on the muddy surface and when he gained the roadway, he caught Gwyneth's arm.

'What's wrong? What is it, is Nina sick?' He frowned, knowing that he wanted Nina well and strong, he still loved her in some strange part of his being.

'It's Tom, his ship is drifting off Port Eynon, in danger of going on the rocks. Mam's in a terrible state, upsetting herself and threatening to take the horse and cart down the coast on her own.'

'Damn and blast!' Joe gave vent to his pent-up frustration; would things ever get better or would they go on getting worse and worse?

Nina was in the kitchen, her face red with crying, her eyes swollen. Joe knelt beside her and took her hands in his.

'Now what's happening? How do you know that it's Tom's ship off the rocks at Port Eynon?'

'Skipper George was down there this morning, he just got back an hour ago, he came to see you, Joe, but as you wasn't here, he had to tell me that Tom's ship, *The Red Dragon*, was coming in and that there was danger

159

of her going on to the rocks.' She grasped his hands. 'You will take me there, won't you, Joe?'

He felt guilt sear him; there he'd been feeling sorry for himself, wallowing in self-pity, blaming Nina for what, after all, was his own fault and her wanting his support so badly. Was he any use to anyone?

'Aye, I'll take you, girl,' he said. 'You wrap yourself up good and warm and I'll get the horse and cart from Carys next door.'

Half an hour later, he was driving over the common land towards Port Eynon, a silent Nina beside him, her face drawn and white. The wind seemed to increase in strength the further over the common land he drove and Joe bit his lip; the waters round Port Eynon were studded with rocks and more than one ship had floundered there.

He felt the pull of paternal love for Tom was his child, flesh of his flesh, perhaps the only son he would ever have and he wanted him safe.

Joe was well aware of Tom's anger and even his hate, the boy had felt his mother was betrayed, but surely now that Tom could see Joe was doing right by her all would be forgiven?

It was as though Nina read his thoughts. She put her hand on his shoulder, leaning against him and somehow her warm nearness was comforting.

'He respects you, really, mind,' she said softly. 'I know Tom was bitter and angry, but he'll get over it and remember, Joe, there are quarrels in every family, but it doesn't drive them apart for long, not if they really love each other, it don't.'

The hill down to Port Eynon was steep and the horse slipped a little on the rutted surface. Joe climbed down and led the animal carefully forward.

The sweep of the bay came into sight and the thunder of the waves seemed to hit Joe along with the rushing of the wind; conditions really were bad, he realized with a sinking heart.

The beach was crowded with people and Joe led Nina to the shelter of the ruined salt house. 'The lifeboat is out there,' Joe said. 'Stay by here, Nina, I'll go and see if there's been anyone brought ashore.'

He made his way along the broad beach and grit stung his face as the wind whipped up the sand in spiteful gusts. He put his hand above his eyes and stared out to sea and could just make out the stern of the ship as she dipped into a trough of waves.

'Any men been brought off yet?' Joe asked one of the fishermen who lined the beach waiting to help survivors ashore. The man shook his head.

'The lifeboat can't get near her, she's bucking like a frightened mule; my bet is her cargo's shifted and she's off balance.'

The men stood in silence, watching helplessly and Joe looked up at the sky aware that it was growing darker. He could hardly leave Nina sitting in the salt house for what might be hours.

'Any rooms to let round here?' he asked and when the fisherman looked at him in surprise he felt some explanation was necessary. 'Got my wife with me, she insisted on coming because our son's on board.' He made a rueful face. 'My wife is with child again so I have to look after her.'

The man grinned. 'Looked after her well enough if you ask me!' he said and Joe warmed to the grudging admiration in the fisherman's face. 'Up by there,' he jerked his thumb, 'Mrs Adams, the house behind the Ship Inn, she'll give you a room.'

'Thanks,' Joe said and, as he made his way back across the sand to where Nina was waiting, he squared his shoulders, he had new responsibilities now, there must be no more self-pity, no more time wasted on crying for the moon. He must face up to life like the mature man he was.

*　　*　　*

161

It was quiet in the shop, almost closing-time, when Eline packed away her pins and pieces of paper and looked round at the latest window display, hoping that Mrs Miller would be pleased with her efforts. Eline sighed, she was enjoying spending her time moving between Mrs Miller's emporium and Hari Grenfell's home where she was being taught so many new and interesting things. And yet there were so many loose ends to her life and she could see no way of resolving them.

Outside, the wind howled around the corners sending papers flying and forcing ladies to hold on to their bonnets. It was more like winter than late summer, Eline thought sadly.

Soon it would be September, the oyster season would begin again and the men would go to sea in the skiffs and make their living in the way they loved best. For a moment, nostalgia flooded over her, she wondered how Carys Morgan was feeling, her time must be near, soon she would be a mother, her greatest dream fulfilled and Eline would not be there to rejoice with her.

Still, Joe had made his decision, he had chosen Nina Parks and though Eline still felt slighted and somehow cheapened by his act in bringing his mistress home, she knew that most of all she was relieved to be out of a situation that had daily become more intolerable.

She made her way upstairs to the living quarters above the emporium knowing that she was privileged to have the freedom that was denied to the other shop assistants. But then she was no longer classed as a shop assistant, Mrs Miller had made that quite plain. Eline had been given her own suite of rooms with a private sitting room where she could work on designs to her heart's delight.

Eline liked living the way she did now, private and yet not alone. She enjoyed window dressing as much as ever, but the part of her job she enjoyed most was the days she spent with Hari Grenfell over at Summer Lodge. And then, of course, there was Will.

Eline sank into a chair and looked down at her dusty hands without seeing them. Will Davies loved her, she was sure of it, though he never spoke of it. How could he when she was still a married woman? That she loved him, she could not doubt; she longed for him, had an urgent need to be in his arms but more than that, she wanted him near her always.

She bowed her head in pain as she tried to picture the face of her husband. Joe, who had loved her all his life, had taken care of her, made her his wife, and now she could not recall his face or his touch after only a few weeks apart from him.

She rose and stood at the window looking down at the town spread out below, the long streets, the women bustling about their business, skirts awry, tugged by the ever-strengthening wind.

She thought of the oyster boats and was glad that they were laid up in the pool for the summer, in a gale like this many a man could lose his life as well as his livelihood.

Later, as Eline sat beneath the oil lamp reading a book, she heard a knock on the door and suddenly, she was tinglingly alive.

'Come in,' she said softly and was not surprised to see Will enter the room for he visited her often. He sat down opposite her and she saw that his face was troubled.

'What is it?' she asked, a small quiver of fear in her voice.

'It's the shop,' he said, 'I've had to close it for a few days, a fire has burnt most of my stock.'

Her eyes were wide, questioning. 'How?' she asked and yet she knew the answer.

Will shrugged. 'Who knows?' he said gently, but Eline got to her feet and faced him, her hands brushing at her skirts nervously.

'It was Joe, wasn't it?' she said flatly. 'Joe heard the gossip about you and me and this is his revenge.' She felt a chill sweep over her.

'Let's not jump to conclusions,' Will said. 'In theory it could have been anyone who had a grudge against me. All I know is that the fire was deliberately set.

'Sit down,' he said gently, 'there's more news and it doesn't look good.'

Eline sank into a chair; what more could be wrong? Will shrugged apologetically.

'It isn't any of our concern, really, but I thought you'd want to know.'

'What?' she asked, her throat tight. 'Tell me, Will, I might as well know everything.'

'It's Joe, he's taken Mrs Parks down to Port Eynon, the ship, *The Red Dragon*, is running aground there and it seems that Tom Parks may be on board.'

Eline bit her lip. 'Joe, he wouldn't do anything silly, would he, like trying to rescue Tom by putting out to sea himself?'

'I should think the lifeboat will have everything under control,' Will said reassuringly. 'It's just that it's all over the village, you were bound to hear about it sooner or later and I wanted to be the one to tell you.'

Eline sighed and looked away quickly as her eyes met Will's and she saw the desire in the way his pupils darkened.

'Thanks for coming,' she said stiffly, wanting to fall into his arms. 'I must go to Oystermouth, see if there's anything I can do.'

'You're going back there, tonight?' Will asked in surprise. 'But what *can* you do and where will you stay?'

Eline sighed. 'I must go home, it still *is* my home, you know. I must find out if Joe is all right.' Her words hurt him, she knew by the sudden lines around Will's mouth, but she must drive a wedge between them somehow, she would not forget her marriage vows and anyway, she cared for Joe, not in the way a woman should care about her husband but she loved him all the same.

'Very well, let me take you,' Will said reasonably. 'I

164

have to go back to my lodgings and it's just foolish for us to travel separately.'

After a moment, Eline nodded. 'But would you please tell Mrs Miller I have to take some time off,' she said. 'Explain things to her while I pack a small bag.'

Will looked at her in a way that brought tears to her eyes.

'I'll be back in just a minute,' Will said gently.

The cab driver was reluctant to drive the five miles along the coast road with such a gale blowing, but the generous payment Will offered convinced him. It did not prevent him from grumbling, however, especially when spitful darts of rain began to fall.

Inside the cab, Eline was very conscious of Will's nearness, the scent of soap and spice emanated from him and it was with great effort that she sat in apparent calmness at his side, her hands folded in her lap.

'Eline . . .' Will's voice was strange in the darkness; she knew instinctively that he was going to make some declaration of his feelings and she couldn't bear it.

'No!' Her voice was surprisingly strong. 'No, Will,' she said more gently, 'don't say anything.'

She glanced up at him, his profile was lit up briefly by lamplight as the cab drove along the street and he looked somehow lost and alone.

'If only things were different,' Eline said softly, 'but they aren't. I'm married, I made my vows to Joe and nothing will ever change that.'

'I know,' Will said softly, 'and I wouldn't expect anything less of you.' His hand reached out and covered hers and Eline impulsively curled her fingers in his. They sat thus, unspeaking, fingers entwined for the rest of the journey to Oystermouth and Eline was almost sorry when the cab jolted to a halt outside the small house where Joe had taken her on their marriage.

'Will you be all right?' Will asked as he helped her down into the coldness of the street. Over the other side of the road, the beach stretched out darkly, the wind sending the waves booming shoreward. The moon appeared for a moment between the racing clouds and a swath of light was cut across the restless water.

'I'll be fine,' Eline said though her legs felt as though they would not carry her the short distance to her door. She didn't look back as she let herself into the house and for a moment she stood in the low glow from the dying fire staring around her as though she had never seen the small kitchen with its grey slate floor and sparse furnishings before.

How quickly she had become accustomed to carpets and fine furniture and the ease of a life where there was no sheer grind of scrubbing floors, lighting fires, carrying water or cooking meals to think about.

Eline lit the lamps and then started rebuilding the fire. She stared down at her hands, grimy with coal dust and wondered that only this morning, they had held a pen and made drawings on pristine paper. She sank into a chair and wondered if she could ever become readjusted to this sort of life.

Restlessly, she wondered upstairs and saw that the bed in the spare room was covered in a dust sheet. In the main bedroom, the one she'd shared with Joe, there were signs of Nina Parks's presence in the softly coloured gown over the chair and the small bunch of flowers dying in a glass vase.

Eline turned her back and retraced her steps until she stood in the kitchen once more. This was no longer her home but Nina Parks's and pray the good Lord, Eline thought anxiously, she would never have to accept this life again. Suddenly, inexplicably, Eline was weeping.

CHAPTER FIFTEEN

It was still dark when Eline heard a knock on the door in the early hours of the next morning. She roused herself stiffly from the chair where she had spent a restless night and tried to respond to the cheery voice of Carys Morgan calling her.

'Eline, I thought it was you in here last night, but I didn't want to disturb you. However, I am so excited, I want to show you my little boy.' Carys's broad face beamed a welcome and a warmth filled Eline as she saw the baby nestling in a Welsh shawl, held securely against Carys's ample breast.

'You've had your baby!' Eline said. 'Let me see him. What have you called him?'

'We've named him after his father, look, isn't he the handsomest thing?' Carys smiled ruefully. 'But he don't sleep much, mind. Oh, once he's woken me up and got me up out of bed, he settles down then!' Her proud smile belied her words.

The child was sound asleep now, his tiny eyelashes resting on rounded cheeks. Looking down at him, Eline was filled with a warm glow, but in that moment, she felt an inner sense of gratitude that she had not borne a child by Joe Harries. A child was a precious thing, to be born into a household of love and security, not into a marriage as rocky as hers.

'Sit down, Carys, I'll make us some tea.' Eline had kept the fire going in the long, dark hours of the night unwilling to sleep in the bed that Joe and Nina were occupying together. Joe, Eline thought, have you no loyalty, no conscience at all?

She had been on tenterhooks all night expecting Joe to return at any moment from Port Eynon. She had dreaded the moment when she would come face to face with her husband again and yet now that he wasn't there, she had the dreadful fear that something might have happened to him or to his son.

'Heard anything from Port Eynon?' Carys said as though reading her thoughts.

Eline sighed. 'No, and it doesn't sound as though the storm has blown itself out, does it? I shouldn't think the crew will have been brought ashore from the stricken ship yet, do you?'

Carys shook her head. 'My old man has gone down the coast along with Skipper George. All the fishermen of Oystermouth have gone to offer their help, because we've had enough tragedies at sea ourselves.'

Carys took the cup and sipped at the tea gratefully. 'Lovely, not much tea left in our house, mind, I'll be glad when the season starts again and there's money coming in.' She shuddered. 'Though this sort of summer weather makes you wonder what the winter will be like this year.'

The two women sat quietly for a moment and then Carys coughed as though she was unnerved by the silence that was broken only by the falling of the coals inside the kitchen and the booming wind outside.

'Will you be coming home?' Carys said softly. 'I do miss you, mind. That Nina Parks, she's not a good neighbour like you, too wrapped up in herself she is, mind.'

'I don't suppose the women are very kind to her,' Eline said drily, feeling that the attitude of the villagers was bound to be hostile towards one they would see as a fallen woman, but she was wrong.

'Folks have been all right to Nina,' Carys said slowly. 'She's one of us, after all. I've tried to be friendly, not wanting to be disloyal to you, mind,' she added hastily,

168

'but the woman is with child and could do with a friend close by.'

'She has her daughters,' Eline said a little coldly. 'I don't suppose she needs anyone else.'

'Perhaps not,' Carys agreed, 'but then Gwyneth is working and Sal is in service and not much bothered with her mam and the other one, the youngest one, Fon, she's gone to work up on Townhill on a farm somewhere.'

Eline looked up suddenly interested. 'A farm, do you mean Honey's Farm?'

Carys shrugged. 'Aye, that sounds right. Tom Parks was telling my Sam about it, glad he was that little Fon was out of it, away from the nasty gossip 'bout his mam living tally with your Joe.'

Eline sighed feeling suddenly homesick for the open land where the green fields rolled downhill towards the rushing stream and where it felt as though she lived on the very top of the world. There her life had been uncomplicated; she had been young and innocent and had lived for the peacefulness of the countryside. In that moment she envied Fon.

'That Gwyneth is a strange one,' Carys continued, 'she's a good girl to her mam, mind, looks out for her well enough, but her head is full of dreams.' Carys paused for a moment and Eline looked at her, anxious about the guarded look that came over Carys's face.

'What do you mean?' she asked. It was unlike Carys to be fanciful and Eline waited, suddenly apprehensive about the explanation.

'You know she works for Mr Davies in the boot shop, don't you?' Carys said softly. 'Well, it's common knowledge she's set her cap at him so to speak. Above her in station he is, mind, but they are together a lot in that store and her sleeves were rolled up helping him clean up after the fire. Strange thing that fire, no one knows how it got started. Anyway, getting in good there, Gwyneth is, looking after number one.'

Eline felt as though she had been doused in cold water, she swallowed hard and willed herself to speak naturally.

'Well, why not?' she said and her voice, to her surprise, sounded almost normal. 'She's a single girl and he is a free man, nothing really to stand between them.'

She felt suddenly sick and ill and, although Eline told herself it was simply the weariness of a night without sleep, she wanted to cry out her pain and frustration.

Instead she invited Carys to have another cup of tea and looked in the pantry for something to eat. Perhaps with food inside her she could better cope with whatever would happen that day.

'I must go,' Carys said shaking her head at the offer of hot buttered toast, 'there's the washing to be done for the baby and food to get ready for my Sam, though God knows what time he'll be home from Port Eynon.'

When Carys had left, Eline stared around the small kitchen, knowing that whatever happened, this could never be part of her life again. Even if Nina Parks should leave Joe for good, choosing her son over her lover, then Joe would have to remain alone.

She rose to her feet; why should she even wait here for him? Did it matter to her if he lived or died? He had betrayed her, taken another woman to their marriage bed and Eline no longer owed him any loyalty.

Yet, even as she picked up her things and made for the door, she sighed heavily; she would have to wait, she could not go back to Swansea without knowing that Joe was safe, she owed him that much.

She returned to her chair and sank down into it burying her face in her hands. Her tears were not for Joe, but for herself because she feared that Will Davies just might be falling in love with Nina Parks's daughter. Blast the Parks family! Eline thought bitterly, what more pain were they to bring her?

Nina woke up feeling that something was wrong. She stared around the strange room and remembered where she was and what had happened. Tom, her son, was caught at sea in a storm and by now might have drowned – how could she have allowed herself to sleep?

Suddenly the pain struck. Nina grasped her stomach where the pain was growing stronger until it seemed to be tearing her in two.

'Joe,' she called out, 'the baby, it's coming early, I'm not going to lose it, am I?' She sank back against the pillows and stared round the unfamiliar room wondering why all this tragedy should be happening to her.

Joe came into the room; he smelled of sea, salt and cold wind. 'Hush now,' he said softly, 'I heard you moaning in your sleep and I've sent for the midwife. She'll be here before you know it.'

He sat silently by the bed, staring out at the storm-tossed sea beyond the railings of the garden and Nina could see by the tenseness of his neck that he was worried.

'The ship, is she brought into shore yet?' Nina forced her mind above the pain that was wrenching at her body. She knew by Joe's silence that Tom was still in danger. 'The men can't hold out any longer, they'll be exhausted, swept out to sea, oh Joe, I can't stand it!'

Her voice rose in spite of herself and immediately, Nina felt ashamed. She had borne four children without a murmur, suffered the pangs of childbirth with fortitude as any woman should, for it did no good to scream and protest; a child would only come when it was ready. But this one, this one that was to bind her to Joe once and for all, was coming too soon, six weeks too soon.

'When the midwife comes, I'll go down to the beach,' Joe said placatingly, 'I'll find out what's happening, don't you worry, the storm is running itself out now.'

'Please God,' Nina said softly. The storm within herself was growing stronger, she knew now that nothing could stop the child from coming into the world, the pains were too fierce to be resisted. She groaned softly just as the door opened and a tall, elegant young woman entered the room.

'Out you go,' she said briskly to Joe, 'I'm Mrs Morris, the midwife around here, I'll see to things now.'

Nina wished fervently that she was home in Oystermouth, with kindly old Mrs Flynn who was gnarled and grey but whose hands were deftness itself and whose wisdom in matters of childbirth was legendary. How could she trust herself to this young chit of a girl who looked down at her so dispassionately?

'How long have you been having pains?' Mrs Morris asked, lifting the sheets and carefully pressing Nina's swollen belly.

'For hours, nurse,' Nina said, 'but the child isn't due for some time yet. I won't lose it, will I? I'm too old to be having a baby really.'

Mrs Morris smiled for the first time and her face was transformed into a picture of reassurance.

'I shouldn't think so, not a woman of your strong stock. In any case, what I always say is never look for trouble till trouble looks for you, Mrs Harries.'

Nina didn't attempt to correct the midwife's misapprehension; let her think that Nina and Joe were lawfully married, it was one comfort at least not to have to bear the woman's scorn or worse, her pity.

As the midwife examined her, Nina pondered over her words. She had been comforting about the chances of the baby being born all right, hadn't she? And Tom, he would be brought off the ship quite soon now, surely, it seemed that the strength had gone out of the wind. She tried to calm her fears, everything was going to be all right.

'Right then, the contractions are coming strong and

172

hard and you are near enough fully dilated. Only a few hours more now, Mrs Harries.'

'How many more hours?' Nina asked fretfully. 'Enough time for me to get home to Oystermouth?'

'I wouldn't advise moving you at this stage,' Mrs Morris said tartly. 'I'm quite capable of looking after you, don't you worry about that.' She came and stood beside the bed.

'I can see I'm going to have to be honest with you, the baby is not in a good position; it's going to be a breach birth, difficult at the best of times.'

Nina looked up at her, her eyes steady even though her nerves were suddenly screaming. 'And this isn't the best of times, that's what you're saying, isn't it?'

Mrs Morris nodded. 'The baby is not full term, otherwise it would probably have righted itself by now and would appear head first. And then there's your age . . . no, I wouldn't advise a journey right now.'

There was a sudden if faint cheer from the beach outside the house and Mrs Morris moved quickly to the window. 'Good,' she said, 'it looks as if the crew have been landed on the beach, just in time, too, because the ship is listing badly. Once the tide comes in, she'll go right over more than likely.'

Nina struggled to sit up. 'Tom, my son, he was on board, I pray to God that he's all right.' And if Tom was safe, how would he react to Joe being on the scene and Nina brought to bed with child?

'Your husband is coming towards the house and there's a handsome young man with him,' Mrs Morris said softly. She didn't add that the pair of them seemed to be quarrelling furiously. She let herself out into the sun-warmed day and Nina fell back against her pillows, knowing in her heart that the midwife was issuing a warning against any upsets to her patient. Nina felt relieved, at least now the men would have to be civil to each other.

173

When her son entered the room, he was drawn and tired and there was a bruise around his temple, but otherwise he looked his usual self.

'Tom!' Nina wanted to tell her son how much she loved him, but the words wouldn't come. Instead she held out her arms and he embraced her.

She hugged him close for a few moments and then brushed aside the damp hair from his forehead. 'You're wet through, son,' she said, 'but are you all right?'

'Aye,' Tom said, 'but are you, Mam? You look right bad to me.'

'Go now,' Nina felt a pain coming and pushed her son aside, 'get into dry clothes, Joe brought a pile of stuff with us. See you don't catch your death of cold and leave me to get on with my business.'

As soon as her son was out of the room, Nina pushed her fist into her mouth and bit hard. The pain seemed to encompass her, not the natural, ebbing pain of childbirth, but a tearing that left her gagging and weak.

Mrs Morris stared down at her patient and frowned. She moved to the door and through her mist of pain, Nina saw Joe standing outside, his face strained, harsh lines running from nose to mouth. His eyes met Nina's and, for a moment, he smiled.

'Hang on there, *cariad*,' he said hoarsely, 'everything is going to be all right.' He turned away as Mrs Morris pushed the door shut and Nina felt suddenly bereft. She groaned low in her throat as the pain hurled her into a pit from which she felt she would never rise again.

'The doctor is on his way,' Mrs Morris sounded falsely cheerful. 'He'll give you something to ease the pain.'

She laid a sympathetic hand on Nina's forehead and them, lifting the sheets from Nina's tortured body, put into place a sheet of brown paper that crackled with a life of its own.

Nina was dimly aware of the doctor coming in, looking

down at her, talking, endlessly talking. Why didn't he do something?

A spoon was pushed between her gritted teeth and Nina gulped at the bitter medicine, hoping it would bring her release from the agony that was wearing her down. She was a strong woman, God only knew how she'd managed alone all these years, bringing up her three girls and her son, but this awful torture, she could not bear it.

'The mother or the child?' the doctor was asking a question of someone unseen, the answer was unintelligible and then Nina felt herself falling into the welcome blackness of an abyss.

'Two days!' Eline said softly as she stared into the fire. 'Two days I've been here waiting for what the good Lord only knows. I must be out of my mind.'

She had scrubbed and cleaned the small house from top to bottom, almost as though she could erase any presence of Nina Parks from her home. But Eline knew it wasn't any longer her home and now never would be regardless of what she did.

She had seen a very little of Carys in those two days, although she had popped in for a few minutes to relate that the crew had all been safely brought ashore from the stricken ship at Port Eynon. She had been uneasy and had not stayed long and Eline had the definite feeling that Carys had been instructed by her husband not to get involved in her neighbour's affairs.

At least Eline had learned that there had been no fatalities during the sea rescue though one or two men had been injured. No names had been mentioned and Eline had been afraid to leave Oystermouth until she knew if Joe was safe.

Eline had seen little of Will; it was as though both of them through a tacit, unspoken agreement had kept out of each other's way.

Eline heard the loud ticking of the clock on the mantelpiece and the coals shifting in the grate and on impulse, she rose to her feet. She had remained here long enough, there had been no further news from Port Eynon, no one had come to the cottage to volunteer any information and it was almost as though she had ceased to exist.

She was busy taking off the sheets from the spare bed where she had slept the previous night when she heard the door open and the sound of voices downstairs.

Reluctantly, Eline went down to the kitchen in time to see Joe lower Nina into a chair. Beside her was her son and all three turned to look at Eline as she entered the room, her arms full of sheets.

Eline could not fail to see the way Joe's face lit up for a moment before falling once again into lines of worry as he stared down at Nina.

It was Tom who spoke. 'Have you come to claim what is yours, Eline?' he said and there was something resembling sympathy in his eyes.

She shook her head. 'No, but I wanted to be sure everything was all right . . .' Her voice trailed away; it was clear that nothing was right. Nina's face was almost yellow, her eyes shadowed by black circles, her skin hanging like discarded linen on the big bones of her face.

'I've lost my baby,' Nina said almost distantly and it was as though she didn't recognize Eline. 'It was coming too early, see, and breach birth and I was too old, too old to be carrying.'

'It's all right, Mam,' Tom put his hand on her shoulder, 'you must get strong now, we'll build you up, you'll see.'

For a moment, there was silence in the kitchen and Eline felt it was up to her to take the initiative.

'I'll just put these sheets in the bath out the back and then I'll take my leave.' She spoke as though she was a visitor, a cleaning woman perhaps, come to help out at times of crisis. And that is just how she felt, removed from it all, from Joe's pain and Nina's weakness, and although she was sorry, she also was relieved. It felt as though somehow she had been freed from a heavy burden.

'I'm sorry,' she said softly, 'I hope you'll be well again soon, Mrs Parks.' The title sounded foolish in the circumstances and yet Eline could not address the older woman as Nina, she never had and this didn't seem a propitious moment for familiarity. She looked first at Joe who was staring down at his boots and then at Tom.

'If there's anything I can do,' she said, 'just ask.'

As she moved to the door, Tom followed her and stood outside on the step, looking down at her. 'Go to our Gwyneth, tell her Mam needs her.' He was almost begging. 'Mam's nearly out of her mind with the pain of it all.'

'I'm sorry,' Eline said again though the word was futile, inadequate. 'I'll tell Gwyneth at once.'

Eline hurried along the street and paused for a moment outside Will's shop. Taking a deep breath, she pushed open the door and went inside and, as her eyes became accustomed to the gloom, she saw Will standing near the counter, staring at her with such a look of happiness that she felt the colour rise to her cheeks.

'I must see Gwyneth,' she explained quickly in case he misunderstood her presence in his shop. 'Her mam is sick, she needs her to come at once.'

'What is it?' Gwyneth came out of the shadow of the shelves. 'What's this about my mam?' She sounded suspicious almost as though she thought Eline was playing some trick on her. 'I thought she was down at Port Eynon.'

'She's back,' Eline said softly, 'Joe and Tom are with her, she's very ill, she needs you.'

Gwyneth looked from Eline to Will uncertainly as though she couldn't make up her mind what to do.

'She's lost the baby,' Eline said reluctantly, knowing that nothing else would convince Gwyneth that she was needed.

'Oh, my God!' Gwyneth said quietly, 'poor Mam.' She pulled on her shawl and moved quickly to the door.

'I'm sorry, Mr Davies, I'll have to go,' she said breathlessly.

'That's all right,' Will said, 'I'll come with you, see if there's anything I can do to help.' He turned to look at Eline, holding the door open as though bidding her goodbye. 'I'm sorry, I have to go,' he said quietly and she wondered if she had imagined the happiness in his eyes.

Eline looked up and, seeing Will's polite expression, suddenly felt very tired. 'That's all right,' she said, 'I'm going now, my home is not in Oystermouth, perhaps it never was.'

As she walked away from the shop and towards the train terminus, Eline felt she never wanted to set foot in Oystermouth ever again.

CHAPTER SIXTEEN

Fon sat in the warmth of the garden that backed on to the whitewashed walls of Honey's Farm. Above her head arched a trellis of roses and the heavy scents drifted towards her as she cradled the sleeping child on her knee. Patrick lay in the crook of her slim arms and there was a contented smile on the little boy's face as his chubby fingers curled around Fon's hand.

Fon smiled down at him; in the few weeks she had been here on Honey's Farm, she had grown to love Patrick dearly. She spent most of her time with him except for the evenings when he was in bed and then she sat with Katherine and stitched the holes in Patrick's linen.

Katherine had come to depend on Fon's company until about nine o'clock, when she would settle down to sleep, issuing firm instruction that Fon was to help Jamie with the books for he could not be relied upon to balance the figures correctly or order fresh supplies.

A sudden heaviness came over Fon, like a shadow passing over the sunlit garden, and she shivered. She had come to love the time she spent with Jamie, that hour before sleep took her, the hour when the cattle had settled for the night and the farm was silent. Then they sat together in the lamp-lit kitchen, working over the books. On occasions, she felt that she and Jamie were meant to be together, to be close, but that was an area of her feelings that she must not, would not, explore.

Sometimes she almost thought that Katherine was pushing them together, encouraging some sort of relationship between then, but that feeling must surely be attributed to Fon's own fevered imagination.

She lifted up Patrick's small body, heavy now in sleep, knowing she must put him in his bed where he would be more comfortable. She took her time over the task, enjoying the sound of soft, contented breathing and the feel of smooth baby skin against her cheek. When she'd settled him down, covering him with only the lightest of sheets, Fon made her way to Katherine's bedroom.

'Come in, there's a good girl, I want to talk to you.' Katherine looked paler than ever, even her hands on the bedclothes were as white as if they had never seen sunshine. Fon looked down at her own hands, they were golden with a sprinkling of freckles and she knew her face, too, would be freckled, something that she had always hated.

'Would you like an iced drink?' Fon asked quietly, still a little in awe of the woman in bed. Despite the fact that she was pale and suffering ill-health, Katherine had an indomitable spirit, a strength of will that Fon sometimes found intimidating.

'Not now,' Katherine said. 'Come in and close the door, Fon, there's a good girl. This is woman's talk and I don't want Jamie to hear.'

Puzzled, Fon moved towards the bed and sat on the edge of the armchair, hands clasped in her lap. 'What is it, Katherine, are you feeling bad?'

Katherine sighed. 'No worse than usual but I have to confide in you, Fon, and I think that now the time is right.'

Fon was suddenly cold in spite of the sun slanting over the gardens outside and the soft breeze bringing the scent of the roses into the room.

Katherine smiled. 'Don't look so frightened, love, it's all right, it really is, I've had a long time to prepare for what I have to face.'

She sat up a little straighter and suddenly Fon noticed

how hollow Katherine's cheeks had become in the last few weeks.

'You do want to stay on here, don't you?' she asked intently. 'I can see you love my son and Patrick loves you, but are you sure there's no follower who will come and sweep you off your feet?'

'No,' Fon said in bewilderment, 'there's no one. And yes, I do want to stay on here, I couldn't think of any other life, not now.'

Katherine sighed as though content. 'I have only a very short time left.' Katherine spoke so matter of factly that Fon wasn't quite sure she understood her correctly.

'What do you mean?' Fon knew she must sound foolish but a feeling of dread was beginning to develop within her.

'Look, Fon, don't waste time feeling sorry for me, I'm leaving this life, but I have no regrets.' She rushed on before Fon could think of anything to say.

'My only concerns were my son and my husband and this is why I tried a great many girls before I took you on. You will be a wonderful mother to my little Patrick.' Katherine's voice faltered but only for an instant. 'And as for Jamie, so long as you help him with the books and the stocks he will be all right, too.' She smiled softly. 'He's a good man is Jamie, just needs a little leading, that's all.'

Fon found her voice at last. 'Katherine, how do you know? I mean the doctors, surely they can . . . ?'

'There's nothing to be done,' Katherine said positively, 'it's a condition of the blood, incurable.'

She smiled. 'Will you promise me, Fon, that you will stay here for as long as you are needed?'

'Yes, of course I will.' Fon felt tears mist her eyes at the courage of the woman in bed who could face death and think only of her husband and child.

Katherine handed her an envelope sealed shut. 'I want you to open it . . . afterwards, is that clear?'

181

Fon nodded. 'How long?' she asked tentatively and Katherine shook her head.

'I don't know.' There was real regret in her voice. 'It's too hard to predict but I hope I live to see Christmas once more.'

Fon rose to her feet and Katherine looked up at her. 'Now how about that iced drink?' she said in that matter-of-fact way of hers and Fon knew the conversation would not be referred to again.

'I'll fetch it straight away,' she said taking her cue from Katherine, 'and then shall I get on with sewing up Jamie's working trousers? He's torn the hem again.'

'Good idea,' Katherine said and sighing wearily, she fell back against her pillows. 'Bring the sewing in here,' she said, 'I could do with some company.'

Fon lay awake that night staring up at the moon-splashed ceiling. In the corner near the open window a spider's web shimmered like gossimer, as light and insubstantial as Katherine's hold on life, Fon thought painfully. She wanted to cry for the bravery of the woman she had known for only a few weeks, but the tears seemed to have formed a hard lump in her throat and it was a long time before she slept.

She woke late the next morning and washed in the cold water in the basin in her room and dressed hurriedly before tiptoeing into Patrick's room. 'Bless us!' Fon said in relief, 'he's still asleep.'

She hurried downstairs to the kitchen knowing that Jamie would want his breakfast but, to her surprise, Jamie was already up and was making a pot of tea. At the table sat a young man, his unruly hair falling over his forehead and with a dart of apprehension, Fon looked into the face of her brother.

'Tom!' Fon kissed her brother's cheek. 'Is anything wrong at home?' She poured a cup of tea for herself and held it between her fingers, feeling suddenly cold and strangely insecure. She hoped he hadn't come with bad news, she didn't think she could take any more.

'It's Mam,' Tom said, 'she's lost the baby. I think she's going out of her mind with it all. I came to ask you to come home and look after her.'

Fon sank into a chair and sipped her tea, giving herself time to think. 'Is Mam in any danger?' she asked anxiously.

Tom shook his head. 'No, not in any physical danger, anyway. She's over the worst and she's strong, she'll get well but she needs someone with her all the time, see.'

'And you think it ought to be me?' Fon said bitterly. 'You don't understand, Tom, I can't leave my job here. I'm needed, Katherine is not well enough to look after Patrick.' She paused, feeling as though she was a traitor to her mother, but Fon had made a vow to Katherine and she would keep it at all costs.

'Ask our Sal, let her come home, or Gwyneth, she's only working down the road, let her see to Mam.'

Tom looked shocked almost as if Fon had slapped him. 'You're not coming?' he said in disbelief.

Fon shook her head. 'I'm not coming,' she repeated. 'I wasn't consulted about all this baby business, was I? I was left in the dark, little Fon who couldn't be told the truth. Well, I'm sorry, Tom, I can't help, not this time.

'Anyway, if you think I could live in the same house as that Joe Harries, the man who caused all this trouble, you can think again.' She breathed deeply.

'I've got my place here now, Tom, and I'm happy. I'm treated like a grown woman for the first time in my life. I'm sorry to upset you, Tom, but there it is.'

Tom rose to his feet. 'Will you at least come to visit then?' He spoke so anxiously that Fon relented a little. She glanced at Jamie and he smiled and nodded.

'Go on you, you're due a day off anyway. I'll manage here for a few hours, don't worry.'

Fon slipped into Katherine's room and leaned over the bed. 'Katherine,' she said softly, 'are you awake?'

Katherine opened her eyes and smiled. 'I'm hardly ever asleep,' she said ruefully. 'What is it? I heard a strange voice in the kitchen, didn't I?'

'It's my brother, Tom, he's taking me home for a few hours. Mam isn't very well, but I'll be back, you needn't worry about that.'

Katherine's thin dry hand grasped Fon's. 'I have your word on it?' she said anxiously and Fon smiled.

'I'm not leaving here, I give you my word before God that I will look after Patrick and Jamie as I promised.'

She straightened. 'Mam's feeling sickly but I have two sisters who can care for her and then there's Joe, it was his child Mam lost so she's his responsibility.' Fon moved to the door.

'If I sound hard, I'm sorry but it's too long a tale to go into now, I'll tell you all about it one day.'

'It will have to be soon,' Katherine said softly, but Fon was closing the door and didn't hear her.

Joe rubbed his hands against the oily rag as he tried futilely to get the white lime from the cracks in his skin. He stared down at Fon Parks, his brow creased as he attempted to understand her hostility to him. He was doing his best by her mam, wasn't he?

'She's a bit mixed up, like,' he said, 'your mam hasn't got over the loss of the babbi yet, not in her mind at any rate.'

'Where is she?' Fon faced him, a small, red-headed freckled creature looking much as Nina had done when she was young, Joe suddenly thought with a searing pain of nostalgia.

'Out back, hiding herself away, as usual,' Joe said suddenly feeling alone, unable to cope with Nina's attitude of despair.

'I'm not staying, mind,' Fon said quickly. 'I've only come on a visit, Tom is coming back for me in about an hour.'

184

Joe sighed heavily, Tom had wanted to beat the living daylights out of him, his intention had been clear to see from the moment he was brought off the ship in Port Eynon. But the boy had been saved from danger himself only to find his mam fighting for her life and the knowledge seemed to serve to make him more bitter.

He had turned on Joe, his face red with the beating he'd taken from the sea and the gales, but the anger in his eyes had nothing to do with his ordeal on board the floundering ship.

'Why did you bring her here in that condition?' He spat out the words, his big fists clenching as though he was holding himself back. 'You must be out of your mind, man.'

Joe had no spirit to fight his son's anger. 'She insisted on coming,' he said dully, 'I had to come with her or watch her travel alone, there was no stopping her. And no one was to know the baby would come this early.'

It was Joe's attitude of total submission that prevented Tom from venting his anger on him there and then.

'I'll go see Mam then, shall I?' Fon's voice cut into Joe's thoughts; he flung down the rag he'd been holding and nodded briskly.

'Aye, go on you, I'll shove the kettle on the fire, a cup of tea always helps things along.'

He stood in the window and watched as Fon went out of the back door. Nina was sitting in the old rocking-chair, a crumpled heap of clothing, a far cry from the lusty woman she had been only a few weeks ago.

'Mam.' Fon's voice drifted to where Joe stood watching. 'Mam, are you feeling better?'

He saw Nina look up indifferently and nod her head. 'I'm as right as I'll ever be, girl. Not that anyone round here gives a damn about me, mind.' Her voice was thin, thread-like, as though it was too much of an effort to speak.

He saw Fon stand up straight and look down at her

mother almost angrily. 'That's not true, Mam, and you know it,' she said sharply.

Joe looked at the girl as though seeing her for the first time, no one else had dared to speak to Nina in that tone of voice, everyone was too busy humouring her, trying to jolly her out of her torpor.

'Well, Gwyneth won't give up her job.' Nina's voice had taken on the whining quality which Joe had learned to dread. 'And Sal, she's so wrapped up in herself that she scarcely bothers to call to see me.' She stared up mutinously at her daughter.

'And you, Fon, my youngest, this is the first time I've seen you since I was took ill.'

Fon put her hands on her hips and her pale skin was suddenly flushed.

'For goodness' sake, Mam, pull yourself together!' Fon spoke angrily. 'You chose to live with Joe, you didn't give two figs for me then, or for Gwyneth and Sal, did you?'

'Well!' Nina was speechless for a moment and then her voice rose to something like its normal pitch. 'How dare you speak to me like that, girl, I'm your mother, remember?'

'Aye, I can't be allowed to forget it, can I?' Fon said in a hard voice. 'The minute you need someone, send for Fon, well, it won't work, Mam, so you might as well get up off your backside and sort yourself and your home out before you lose everything.' Fon carried on speaking in spite of her mother's gasp of disbelieving anger.

'Have you seen that kitchen? It's filthy! And Joe, he looks as though he's worn the same clothes for weeks, you'll be having him run back to his little wifey if you don't watch it.'

Joe held his breath, wanting to walk away from what was, after all, a private conversation between mother and daughter, but he was fascinated by the transformation that was coming over Nina.

'How could you be so cruel?' she said and there was a touch of hysteria in her voice. 'You know I could have died down there in Port Eynon, don't you?'

Fon softened now, kneeling beside her mother's chair, taking her hands gently.

'I know, Mam, but you didn't. You can get well, you can live a full life again, there are those who can't.'

'What do you mean?' Nina asked and Joe wondered that for the first time in weeks Nina seemed interested in something other than her own well-being.

'The lady I work for, she's young, Mam, not much older than me. She is dying, there's nothing can be done for her and she is leaving her baby and her husband and she is facing what future she's got left with such courage, Mam. I have vowed to be there to look after her family when she goes and I can't, I won't, let her down.'

Suddenly Nina was crying, real tears that were for once not for herself. Joe made to move towards the back door but he saw that Fon was crying, too.

Mother and daughter clung together drawing comfort from each other and Joe turned away knowing he was not needed.

It was late afternoon when Tom came for Fon; he had a young lady with him but she remained in the trap, her hands folded modestly in her lap.

'Is Fon ready?' Tom asked gruffly and Joe beckoned him to come inside.

'She's done wonders with your mam,' Joe said softly and together, they stood in the kitchen watching as Fon said something and Nina smiled, a smile that warmed her eyes as well as her mouth.

'What happened?' Tom forgot his hostility in his surprise and Joe felt relief run through him.

'I don't know what it was that did the trick, but I do know Fon went for her mother hammer and tongs. It's brought Nina out of her fit of the vapours, thank God!'

Joe and Tom went into the garden and Nina, looking up at them, smiled a little hesitantly. 'I hope you two are going to let past quarrels rest?' she said. 'Otherwise I can see myself sinking into a decline again, mind.'

Joe, searching her face, saw that Nina's threat was made more in anger than in earnest.

Joe looked at his son and Tom shrugged; both men accepted the prospect of an uneasy alliance between them as the pattern for the future.

'I'm glad you brought Fon to see me,' Nina said, as she rose to her feet and clutched Joe's arm, heading through the back door into the kitchen. 'She's grown up, mind, there's more sense in her young head than many an older one, believe me.' She stood and looked out of the window and saw the young woman waiting for Tom and grimaced ruefully.

'I realize that you all have your own lives to lead,' Nina said, 'I've been a selfish woman these past weeks, haven't I, Joe, but I think I'm going to get over it a bit now.'

'Well,' Tom said in a falsely hearty voice, 'we'd better be going if we're to get you back to Honey's Farm this side of nightfall.' Tom addressed his remarks to Fon, but at the same time he was glancing over his shoulder at the young woman who was lightly holding the reins of the horse as she sat waiting in the trap.

'Bye then, Mam,' Fon hugged Nina and Joe, seeing the genuine love in the girl's eyes, guessed how hard it must have been for her to talk as sharply as she had done to her mother.

'Come and see me soon, Fon,' Nina said softly, 'and God go with you and give you strength, my lovely, you are surely going to need it.'

Joe watched as Fon followed her brother out on to the road. Tom lifted Fon into the trap and the two young women seemed to be exchanging pleasantries. There was something about Tom's lady friend that seemed familiar and yet Joe couldn't quite place her.

He turned to Nina and put his arm around her shoulders. 'Come on, love, let's go out and watch them drive away,' he said gently.

'Aye, don't I know the girl from somewhere?' Nina said puzzled. She clung to Joe's arm as they stood in the doorway and waved until the trap had bowled away along the street in the direction of Swansea.

Joe turned Nina's face to him. 'Have you come back to me now, Nina?'

'Aye love, thanks to my daughter,' Nina said softly. 'I feel as though I've been asleep for a long time but now I'm awake again.'

Joe felt hope surge through him as Nina closed the door behind them and stared round the kitchen. 'Fon is quite right, the place is a mess,' she said sinking into a chair. 'I'll make a start on it tomorrow, you'll see, Joe, I'll soon be as right as I ever was.'

Joe bent and kissed her. 'Thank God for that, my girl, I couldn't have gone on like we were for much longer, blaming myself and watching you fall more and more into a world of your own.'

Nina touched his cheek. 'It's over now, love, all I must do is get strong again, then you can all look out, you'll feel the edge of my tongue, believe me!'

Joe had just stepped outside to fetch some coal when he heard Nina calling him.

'Joe!' Her voice was urgent and he dropped the scuttle and hurried back into the kitchen.

'What is it? What's wrong?' he asked anxiously and Nina stared up at him, with an expression of concern.

'I've just remembered where I've seen Tom's girl-friend before. She's the one who all the scandal was about, the one who stole Hari Grenfell's son and nearly got him killed. That girl with my son is that no good hussy, Sarah Miller!'

CHAPTER SEVENTEEN

The sun shone in through the long windows of Eline's room and dappled the deep green carpet so that in the confusion of light and shade it resembled a field of rich grass. Eline was reminded of her life on the farm; of the ragged fallow fields, the brook running at the bottom of the hill and the smell of the corn; she wondered at the quirk of fate that had taken her away from it all so finally. First to live the life of a fisherman's wife and then to land in the strange and wonderful position she was in now, working for Mrs Emily Miller.

She had been glad to leave Oystermouth, but she still could see the pain in Joe's eyes as he had looked at her. And Nina, crouched in a chair, weak and pale as though any movement might shatter her thinly held composure. Eline had turned her back on them and returned to Swansea, putting all thoughts of the past behind her, including her foolish longing for Will Davies – especially, she emphasized to herself, her longing for Will Davies.

Eline had found comfort in the solitude of her suite of rooms and had been gratified at the warmth extended to her by Mrs Miller. And slowly, over the days, her life had fallen into a pattern once more and Eline was grateful.

As it transpired, Eline's own modification for the side-spring boot had been sold to a big boot and shoe company and both Hari Grenfell and Mrs Miller had given Eline full credit for it, talking about the achievement to anyone who would listen.

'You have a wonderful future before you if you only

work hard and dedicate yourself to the business.' Mrs Miller had smiled and some of her natural reserve had melted. 'I knew you were destined for success, there was something I recognized in you straight away. Welcome back to where you belong, Eline.'

A knock on her door startled Eline from the warm glow that filled her whenever she comforted herself with those words of praise and, even before she rose to open it, she knew that Will would be standing outside. He would be waiting on the beeswax-scented landing, his hair falling across his wide forehead, his eyes, as penetrating as ever, would be looking right into her being.

Eline hesitated, her hands clenched into small fists, torn between joy and despair. Why couldn't he leave her alone and stop torturing them both in this way?

'Who is it?' She scarcely recognized her own voice and then the door was opening and he was there, so much more handsome, so much more dear than in her imagining.

'Will, Mr Davies, what can I do for you?' She forced herself to speak formally, as though he was a stranger. He paused, looking down at her, and then he had entered the room and was holding her arms almost roughly.

'Don't shut me out like that,' he said in a quiet anger. 'I don't deserve that from you.' He sighed, released her and thrust his hands into his pockets, while Eline closed the door. There was no point in letting everyone in the building know her business.

'I shouldn't have let you go like that,' Will said. 'When you came to my shop to fetch Gwyneth Parks I could see how upset you were. Don't you think I needed to know what was wrong?'

Eline stared at him steadily, resisting the urge to accuse him of paying too much attention to Gwyneth Parks. It really was not her business to interfere, Will must make his life elsewhere; he had no future with Eline that was sure.

'It's kind of you to worry,' she said sitting down and clasping her hands in her lap, 'I *was* upset.' She shrugged. 'But who wouldn't be? It wasn't pleasant seeing Nina so ill and Joe, my husband,' she smiled wryly, 'sick with worry. Perhaps I'm a coward but I just had to get out of there.'

'No woman could be expected to cope with a situation like that,' Will said reasonably, 'no one could blame you for leaving.' He looked down at her but didn't touch her.

'I don't understand why you went to see *him* in the first place. There was really no need for you to go back to Oystermouth at all, was there?'

There was a reproof in his words and Eline spoke up defensively. 'Whatever he's done, Joe is still my husband, I had to make sure he was all right.' When Will didn't reply she rushed on. 'I've known Joe ever since I was a child, he was always there for me, a strong presence when everything else had gone and Joe loved me, still loves me come to that.'

'Why did you make way for another woman then?' Will asked sharply. 'Why didn't you fight for what was yours?'

Eline felt a pain deep within her but she would not show Will how much his words hurt her.

'I think that is my business,' she said coldly, 'I don't have to make any excuses to you.'

'You're right,' he said and moved towards the door. 'I'm sorry I bothered you, I see it was a mistake.'

Her voice stopped him. 'Will,' she said softly and when he turned to look at her she held her hands up in despair. 'There's no future for us, can't you see that? Go on and live your own life because I'll never be free of Joe, never.'

Without a word, Will went out and closed the door.

After a moment, Eline moved to the table and stared down at her drawings determined to work. But the patterns swam before her eyes and her brain could think of nothing but Will and at last, Eline collapsed into a chair and, covering her eyes with her hands, gave herself up to despair.

Emily was in the nursery, having just settled Pammy down for the night, when she heard a commotion in the hallway. She moved out on to the landing, her skirts swirling around her slippered feet, her heart thumping so loudly she thought it would burst through her flesh.

'I have every right to be here, I'm your daughter after all.' The voice was raised an octave. 'And you've got my baby or have you forgotten that?'

'Sarah!' Emily felt the blood draining from her face, she clung to the ornate banister and stared down at the girl standing with her hands on hips, her eyes staring upwards in what appeared to be fiendish delight.

John caught Sarah's arm and hustled her into the sitting room while Emily hurried down the stairs to join them. What could it mean? Surely Sarah wasn't coming to claim Pammy after all this time? It couldn't be, the little girl was Emily's life, she had brought her up from the day she was born, loved her as though she had carried her herself. Sarah had abandoned her child, she couldn't want her back now.

None of the turmoil Emily was feeling showed itself in her voice when she greeted her step-daughter. 'So, you've come back to Swansea, Sarah, do you think that was wise?'

'It's my home,' Sarah answered petulantly, 'you've no right to keep me out of it.'

'I have every right to call the police and have you arrested, madam!' Emily said sharply, aware that John was looking at her beseechingly but she did not soften her tone. Sarah might be John's daughter but she was a disruptive influence, a wicked girl who would stop at nothing to get her own way.

'You haven't forgotten that you and your boyfriend abducted Hari Grenfell's child and held him for ransom, almost getting yourself killed into the bargain, have you? Because you can be sure none of us have forgotten and never will.'

Sarah subsided into a chair and Emily sat down opposite her. 'You were lucky that Craig Grenfell saved you and your precious Sam from the explosion. Lucky, too, that you were quick enough to get away from here before you faced prosecution for your crime.'

Sarah didn't answer but stared moodily down at her hands.

'I suppose Sam Payton has at last run out on you,' Emily said cruelly. 'You didn't expect a man like that to stay faithful, did you?'

Sarah glared at her for a moment and then smiled. 'I give Sam the push, so there, and anyway, I got fed up of living in Port Eynon, one-eyed hole that it is. I've got a new boyfriend now, Tom Parks is handsome and honest and he was good enough to bring me back to Swansea with him.'

'Port Eynon?' Emily was incredulous, she had believed that Sarah would have fled abroad or at least to England. Who would have though she would be hiding away in a small seaside village not more than sixteen miles from Swansea?

'Well,' Emily tried to compose herself, 'what do you expect of us now, madam? Why shouldn't we turn you over to the police constable right away?'

'Now then, Emily,' John intervened, 'I think Sarah has suffered enough and it was Sam Payton who instigated that whole thing, you know.'

Emily was momentarily irritated by her husband's blindness. Couldn't he see his daughter was a bad lot and that nothing would change her?

'I only want a job,' Sarah said coaxingly, looking up at her father, 'and somewhere to live.' She glanced at Emily slyly. 'I won't interfere with the way you bring up *my* baby, honest.'

Emily forced down the feeling of anger and sickness that threatened to engulf her. 'Well, you are not living here!' she said positively. Sarah had manipulated her once before, forcing herself on Emily and John, disrupting their lives and Emily wasn't going to have that again.

'You can stay at the emporium for the time being at least,' she said, 'and if you don't like it there, you can get out of my life and stay out, understand?'

Emily turned to John. 'Take your daughter down to town and let her share Eline's rooms for now. We'll talk more about it in the morning.' Her voice brooked no refusal and John, after a moment, nodded.

'Come on, Sarah, you'll be comfortable enough and we can talk everything out when we are all much calmer.'

Emily clasped her hands together aware they were trembling. 'And Sarah,' she said firmly, 'try not to upset my staff too much.'

She stood rigidly still until she heard the door close behind John and his daughter and then Emily sank into a chair and sighed with relief. She had got rid of Sarah for the moment but what sort of havoc was the girl going to cause this time?

Emily chewed her lip, thinking about Hari and Craig. What would their reaction be when they knew that Sarah was back in Swansea? Would they wish to prosecute the girl for her part in the abduction of their son? If so, she couldn't blame them. And in a small corner of her heart, Emily wished it would work out that way, because with Sarah imprisoned, her own worries and fears would be over.

Emily went upstairs and stared down at the little girl she had come to think of as her own, the child she had taken into her arms at birth when her mother had rejected her so brutally.

'Don't worry, Pammy,' she whispered, 'I won't let anything happen to you.'

Eline was not happy with the arrangement, not happy at all. From the first moment she had met Sarah Miller she had disliked the girl and now, a week after that first introduction, her dislike had hardened into a feeling of contempt.

Sarah made no secret of her past, she even boasted about her many conquests and it seemed that she was leading poor Tom Parks around like a bull with a ring through its nose.

Sarah did very little work but worse she disrupted Eline when she wanted to sit over her drawings and had ruined the precious sanctuary in the little suite of rooms above the emporium. The only respite Eline had was when Sarah went out walking with Tom and often returned smelling of gin. Eline didn't think of herself as a prude but it was clear that Sarah held virtue very lightly indeed.

Then one night, Eline was awakened by the sound of laughter and loud voices and startled, she sat up in bed, staring around her, feeling for a moment disorientated. Her eyes grew accustomed to the dark and she pushed back her heavy plaits of hair, rubbing her eyes tiredly.

Another shriek of laughter from the direction of Sarah's room brought a feeling of anger rushing over Eline. She slid out of bed and drew on her robe, tying it firmly around her waist with sharp movements of her fingers.

She crossed the small hallway and knocked on the door but it was not latched and swung open at her touch. The scene before her was one of complete abandonment and Eline recoiled in embarrassed fury. There on the bed with her stays undone and her legs wrapped around the naked body of a red-faced Tom Parks was Sarah.

She was not at all abashed when she saw Eline but shrieked with laughter once more, her head flung back, her hair loose around her white shoulders.

'Come in, Miss Poe Face,' she laughed, 'you might learn a bit about real life and how a woman keeps her man interested!'

Eline started to close the door but Sarah's voice continued remorselessly. 'Lost your husband to Tom's mam, I hear, what a scream! But then there's no red blood in your veins from what I hear, you're so cold and barren that no man would want you anyway!'

Eline returned to her room and sank down on to the bed, her whole body trembling. Was there any truth in Sarah's words? Was Eline cold and barren? The accusations had stung and Eline climbed into bed, her robe still wrapped around her because, suddenly, she was shivering.

The sun was shining the next morning but the brightness of the day did nothing to dispel Eline's feelings of dejection. One thing she knew, she could not continue to live in the same building as Sarah Miller.

'Thank heavens it's my day off!' Eline said aloud. It would be good to get outdoors into the freshness of the day, to walk beside the sweetly rolling tide that crept into the crescent of Swansea Harbour. Eline would forget work, forget the emptiness of her marriage and forget the hurtful words spoken in derision by a woman little better than a whore. Bur first she must speak to Mrs Miller.

Emily was entirely sympathetic; she welcomed Eline into her sitting room as though she was an honoured guest and instructed the maid to bring some cordial. When they were alone, she turned to Eline and there was a patient smile on her handsome face.

'I know it is a difficult situation and I intended it only

to be a temporary solution,' she said at once when Eline complained as politely as she could about Sarah's disruptive presence in the emporium. 'Indeed,' Emily added, 'I have taken the precaution of finding my step-daughter some lodgings with a Mrs Marsh, a very respectable landlady, living a little way out of Swansea.'

Her tone implied that the further away the better. 'You are a hard-working girl, Eline,' Emily continued, 'a special sort of person just as Hari Grenfell was when I first met her.' She smiled ruefully. 'I didn't treat Hari's talent with enough respect – that's a mistake I don't intend to make with you.

'Mrs Marsh's boarding house?' Eline repeated. 'Isn't that where, Will, Mr Davies, lodges?'

'You are right, I never thought of that,' Emily said, 'but I think he'll steer well clear of her type these days.'

Emily Miller smiled, speaking again before Eline had time to ponder on her words. 'I believe Sarah's new follower lives in the vicinity, perhaps his attentions will be enough to keep her occupied for most of the time. Who knows, this Tom may even marry her one day.' Her tone indicated that it would be a great relief to have Sarah safely off her hands.

Emily rose from her chair and Eline knew that the meeting was over. Outside, Eline began to walk towards the bay thinking how peaceful her life would be with Sarah out of the way. Oystermouth would suffer from Sarah's disruptive presence but Eline could not see the villagers putting up with any nonsense from her.

She pushed a curl of hair from her forehead. Poor Will, he would not appreciate the loudness of a woman like Sarah under the same roof as him but, by all accounts, Mrs Marsh would be a strict landlady and would keep Sarah in check.

It was warm on the edge of the sand with the coarse grass shooting between the golden grains like pointing fingers reaching for the sky. Out in the bay, small ships bobbed on the restless waters but not oyster skiffs, they would be beached for another few weeks yet before the season began again.

Eline seated herself on a flat piece of stone and felt the warm breeze fan her cheeks with an almost sensuous pleasure. As she lay there self-indulgently, she was struck by the idea that perhaps she was being foolish in remaining faithful to her husband while Joe was so obviously unfaithful to her.

Perhaps she should allow herself to yield to Will's embraces; she knew she loved him so could it be wrong? She wanted to prove to herself that the harsh words spoken by Sarah were untrue. Eline was not cold, she was a woman with hot blood singing in her veins and she wanted Will with more passion than she could begin to express.

'Hallo.' He was beside her so suddenly that Eline blushed scarlet, expecting him to have read her thoughts. 'I've had a devil of a job finding you,' he continued, 'I wanted to apologize for my rudeness the other day.'

'William, you startled me!' She said, excusing the rich colour by fanning herself as though it was the sun that had brought a blush to her cheeks.

He sat beside her and she was aware of the scent of him, the male, animal attraction of him and she wondered at her own determination to resist him. For how long? For ever? Was that possible?

Eline looked down at her hands; was she to go through life not knowing what it was like to lie with the man she loved? To know only the coldness of duty to a husband many years older than her?

Questions flared through her mind, turning and twisting until she thought she would go mad. She looked up at Will and somehow she was leaning towards him, her mouth turned to him in open invitation. Without speaking, he took her face in his hands and drew her mouth

199

close to his, her very skin tingling with anticipation as his lips hovered above hers.

When his mouth touched hers, it was as though her senses were swamped with a rush of desire so spontaneous and so compelling that if she had not been in the open air with the sound of children's voices ringing in the distance she would have clung to him and begged for his love.

The kiss went on and on, Eline felt his arm accidentally brush her breast and she felt she would swoon with her need for him. She had not known such passion existed and a thought swam through her drunken senses, steadying her, was she so much different from Sarah Miller, after all?

She drew away from Will and brushed at her hair with shaking fingers. He sat looking down at her and his eyes were pleading.

'I love you, Eline, and this can't go on or I'll go mad with the feelings I have for you.'

'I know,' she said, reaching out and touching his hand lightly but the caress of her fingers was redolent with promise. 'I do not want to resist any longer, we must meet, Will, my *cariad*, we must be private.' She stumbled over the words, not knowing what to say, how to put into plain speech her decision to consummate their love. But he understood and his hand turning, gripped her fingers.

'I love you, Eline, and we will be as man and wife, I promise you that, I won't look at another woman as long as I live. We will go away, if you want,' he continued, 'make a new life abroad where no one knows us, I'll be good to you always, I give you my word of honour.'

She put a finger to his lips and hushed him. 'I won't allow you to give up everything you've worked for in Swansea,' she said firmly, 'our love will be a secret, just between you and me.'

She rose to her feet then and twitched her skirts into

200

place. 'I have made up my mind,' she said, 'I shall follow my career and you yours but we will be together whenever we can.'

She looked up at him and then rested her head against his shoulder, closing her eyes with the joy of his nearness. It would not be easy conducting an illicit liaison with Will, there would have to be arrangements made, lies told, but it would be worth it, she told herself stoutly. And when he bent to kiss her again, she melted against him, clinging to him, holding him so close as though she would never let him go again.

CHAPTER EIGHTEEN

'I don't see why I should be pushed out for the sake of some shop girl!' Sarah's mouth was set in an obstinate line and she glared at her step-mother, resenting her high-handed attitude.

'You seem to forget that you've got *my* baby,' she flung at her knowing her words would hurt, 'why shouldn't I take her away right now?'

She saw Emily straighten her shoulders as if she bore a great burden but her composure was unruffled. 'Because,' Emily spoke with infuriating reasonableness, 'you don't want to be saddled with a child, you just couldn't take the responsibility of it all, could you?' Before Sarah could think of a reply, Emily was speaking again.

'In any event, I would fight you through the courts and I don't think your past exploits would go unnoticed, do you? Abduction and demanding money are not inconsiderable crimes; you might well be put in prison, and at the very least you would be found to be an unfit mother. No, Sarah, don't threaten me, instead accept with gratitude what I am offering you, comfortable accommodation and a more than generous allowance.'

Sarah was silent. Emily would keep throwing the past up at her but there was a great deal of truth in what Emily said, most of all in her assumption that Sarah would not wish to be saddled with a child; a kid around the place would be the last thing Sarah wanted and Emily knew it, damn her!

'All right,' Sarah said at last, 'I'll see how I go on down at this Oystermouth place, it can't be as outlandish as Port Eynon anyway.'

'There is a coach waiting outside to take you there,' Emily said softly, 'and remember, you will live comfortably enough on your allowance, you will not have to work for a living but if you step out of line, the allowance will be stopped and not even your father would be inclined to forgive you another scandal.'

'You've got it all worked out, haven't you?' Sarah said bitterly. 'Get rid of me; out of sight, out of mind, is that it?'

Emily rose to her feet and opened the door. 'Be thankful for what you have, Sarah,' she said gravely, 'the opportunity to make a new start, find a respectable husband and set yourself up in a nice home. Don't throw it all away by being foolish, again.'

Sarah left the house and climbed into the waiting cab, leaning back against the cold leather seat. She scarcely saw the streets of Swansea as the coach clattered along the cobbles, scattering a flurry of chickens that had been pecking at a fallen crust of bread. Driving away from the town and along the coast road, Sarah brightened up considerably as she thought of Emily's words. Emily was quite right. Sarah had the world at her feet now, a generous allowance, nice rooms in lodgings where she would have to do no work but be waited on like a lady and perhaps there might be a rich husband in the offing. Tom Parks was all right as a temporary lover but Sarah wanted far more from life than to be tied to a lowly seaman all her life.

She was glad she had come back to Swansea, at least Emily was offering her a comfortable living. It was all a far cry from the years she'd spent with Sam Payton. It would not be easy to forget the times when she had lived from hand to mouth, with Sam carping and complaining and she tired and beaten down with weariness. Then Sarah had worked in all sorts of places from the beer-soaked public bars of shabby inns to being a lowly maid in service at one big house or another.

Sarah had hated her enforced servility, she bitterly resented carrying coal and water up endless flights of stairs, bobbing curtsys to those who thought they were her betters, who saw her as nothing but a servant put on earth to slave for them. The humiliation was often too hard to bear and Sarah cried herself to sleep on many a night.

And then Sam left her, running off with the owner of the Brighton Hotel on the west coast of Devon and Sarah had been left with nothing but the clothes she stood up in. For a few days, she had become a hermit, closeted in the small room which Sam had rented. It was only when the landlord, an elderly, lecherous man, had tried to coerce her into submission that she had roused herself from the torpor into which she had sunk.

Sarah had been desperate, she had gone to the docks in Bristol and used her wits and her body to secure a passage on a ship that was crossing the channel to the Welsh coast. She had made her way to Port Eynon where she had worked in the one and only inn in the place and though she had thought often of returning to Swansea, she feared the reception that might await her there and lacked the energy to make the move.

Then she had met Tom Parks. It was clear he had never heard of her or of Sam Payton and his obvious adoration had supplied the necessary impetus to bring her back to Swansea.

Now, sitting in comfort in the leather seat of the cab, wearing good, clean clothes and with money in her bag, she told herself she was well off, ripe for a new start in life. She could be even better off if she met the right man, someone in trade perhaps, a man who would keep her in comfort and security. But for now, Tom Parks would do very well, he was handsome and well set up and full of energy beneath the sheets.

The cab jerked to a stop outside a tall, substantially built house that stood just a short way uphill from the sea front. Sarah didn't see the sweep of the bay below her or the soft clouds scudding across the sky, she was far too busy sizing up the heavy curtains on the window of the Marsh household, noticing how cleanly the windows shone and the gleaming brass of the door fittings.

She was met by a motherly woman whom Sarah presumed was Mrs Marsh herself and wanting to make a good impression, Sarah smiled politely.

'I'm Sarah Miller,' she said allowing the older woman to take her bag. 'What a lovely house you have here, I compliment you, Mrs Marsh, on your fine home.'

The woman warmed to her, it was clear from the way she bobbed a curtsy that she considered Sarah to be well born, one of the gentry, and Sarah was well pleased.

Mrs Marsh led Sarah to her rooms on the first floor of the tall building and flung open the door, standing back to allow Sarah entry.

'I hope you will be comfortable, Miss Miller,' she said respectfully, 'as instructed I have made my best rooms available for you. I think you will like it here in Oyster-mouth.'

'I'm sure I will,' Sarah lied, knowing already that the long street strung along the bay was going to be far too quiet for entertainment. But then, the theatre at Swansea was only a coach ride away and now that Sarah was a lady of leisure she would make sure she enjoyed it to the full.

'Supper will be at eight,' Mrs Marsh was saying. 'You can have it in your room if you wish or come down to the dining room and meet my other guests.'

Sarah brightened. 'Other guests, how many are there?' she asked in apparent unconcern.

'Five, no six including you,' Mrs Marsh replied. 'An old gent, Mr Frogmore, and his grandson who occupy the top floor and then there's the two Misses Grace who are very quiet and respectable and are just across the landing from you and then there's young Mr Davies who owns the boot and shoe shop in the village. A fine man is Mr Davies, a real gentleman.'

Sarah looked up with interest. 'William Davies?' she asked and Mrs Marsh nodded her head, her lips close together and Sarah thought better of questioning the woman any further. It wasn't ladylike to be too interested in a young man and for the moment, Sarah was content to play the lady.

'I shall come down to supper and meet them all,' she said as though bestowing a great honour. 'I might have something in common with your Mr Davies because my father owns Miller's Boot and Shoe Emporium in Swansea.'

The woman was probably well aware that Sarah was one of *the* Millers, Sarah thought, but it didn't harm to make certain. When she was alone, Sarah stood before the mirror and stared at her reflection. She hadn't changed much over the years, her skin was still blooming and her hair was fine and curly; she looked little more than the girl she had been when she had left Swansea under a cloud two years previously.

Yes, she mused with a smile, she might have a great deal in common with Mr Davies and supper promised to be an interesting event – she could hardly wait.

Will was feeling happier than he had done for some time, Eline had warmed to him, there had been a promise in her eyes when she had left him and he knew that she did not make promises lightly.

He wanted Eline like he'd never wanted any woman before, he loved her and desired her and even though she was married, he knew he must possess her.

Will considered that Joe Harries had forfeited any rights to Eline by his faithless ways, not only had he slept with another woman but he had the effrontery to take her into Eline's home. No woman could be expected to suffer such humiliation, certainly not Eline with her fine spirit of independence.

He fastened his shirt collar with the stud and adjusted his tie, it was almost supper time and Mrs Marsh liked her guests to be punctual.

He hurried down the stairs and into the hallway and the low murmur of voices from the dining room reached out to him like a welcome. It was good to be part of a family even a family made up of strangers. Will craved for family life, he wanted a home of his own, a house full of children and a wife to come home to every evening.

Well, Eline could never be his wife in name but she would soon be his wife in the real, meaningful sense of the word and he could not wait.

He opened the dining room door and the voices rose to a swell of good natured chatter, he saw the Grace sisters, grey heads bobbing vigorously as they took it in turns to talk, each of them waiting as though on the edge of the seat for the other to finish speaking.

Will smiled, he was fond of the sisters, they gossiped a great deal but they were never to be heard speaking ill of anyone.

Jack Frogmore was sitting back in his chair looking as though he could do with a puff of his pipe but good manners forbade him to smoke in the presence of the ladies. His son Geoffrey was leaning forward talking to a lady who must be the new guest Mrs Marsh had told him about earlier. Geoffrey's shoulder was blocking the way so that Will saw only a glimpse of a rounded arm and a surprisingly work-roughened hand.

Then he saw her. Will took a deep breath as Geoffrey leaned back in his chair revealing in full the face of the new boarder.

'Sarah!' the name escaped Will's lips almost silently like a sigh. She looked up at him and smiled, as though nothing had ever happened between them, as though they had never lain together and learned the joys of the flesh and as though she had never betrayed him.

'Mr Davies, please come and meet our new guest,' Mrs Marsh smiled, extending her hand as though she was a dowager at a great ball introducing a lady of distinction.

'This is Sarah, Miss Miller, I hope you will take the seat next to her and tell her all about your business venture in the village.'

Will took his seat without protest, it was clear that Sarah did not intend to acknowledge their past in any way but to treat him as if he was a stranger.

He looked at her hard, she had changed very little from the Sarah whose virginity he had taken in a moment of lust mistaken for love. She was as fresh and young as ever, except for her hands. Her nails were short and uneven, her fingers rough and red. He felt a momentary sense of satisfaction, it seemed life had not been so easy for her as she had anticipated.

The past seemed to flash before him in a series of images, Sarah naked in his arms, thugs standing before him beating him to within an inch of his life because of her and worse than all that, Sarah trying to fool him that he was the father of her child. Betrayal was too slight a word for what she had done to him.

'Vegetables, Mr Davies?' Sarah's full lips were moving but it took a few seconds for him to take in the words she was saying.

'Thank you,' he could not keep the iciness out of his voice though no one seemed to notice. Will glanced around the table, everything seemed normal, the two elderly Grace sisters were still bobbing gray heads in animated conversation and old Jack Frogmore was saying something to his son. Geoffrey, however, had eyes only for Sarah and Will knew the young man was falling for her obvious charms as he himself had once done.

'I hear you are in business, Mr Davies.' Sarah's voice had lost much of its Welsh lilt, she seemed composed as though acting the lady came easily to her. 'The same sort of business as my father and step-mother.'

Will inclined his head, acknowledging her words, smiling to himself at the irony of the situation. By a quirk of fate, Sarah's father, a humble cobbler, had married one of the richest women in Swansea and Sarah, it seemed, was out to use her new background to full effect.

Will became aware that Mrs Marsh was looking expectantly at him, waiting for him to reply to Sarah's question. For a wild moment, Will was tempted to call Sarah's bluff, to expose her disguise as a lady but then he realized it would be a pointless exercise, one of spite and malice. And what did Sarah matter to him now? Soon, he would be with Eline, they would find a place to meet, away from curious, prying eyes.

'I can't claim that my shop is in the same league as that of Mrs Emily Miller,' he said pointedly, 'but I hope I may be of assistance to you some time?'

If there was irony in Will's voice, it was lost on all but Sarah and she was impervious to it. She lifted her head and smiled coquettishly, turning to the already enslaved Geoffrey.

'And you Mr Frogmore, what is your calling in life?' He looked at her, his eyebrows raised apologetically.

'I am a mere accountant, Miss Miller,' he said softly, 'nothing very interesting, I'm afraid.'

Will sat back, inwardly cursing Sarah and all the memories she brought with her. Memories of Sam Payton who had put Will in hospital, had almost killed him, not single handed in man to man combat but like a thief at night, creeping up on Will in the darkness and with the aid of several of his cronies. Payton, the real father of Sarah's bastard.

Bitterness that he thought long forgotten engulfed him

and as soon as the seemingly endless meal was finished, Will made his excuses and retired to his room.

He sat at the window, staring out into the night trying to come to terms with the anger that overwhelmed him. It was a fruitless emotion, the past was over and done with, he had his future to think of now and that future included Eline.

Will became aware of his door opening quietly and he was not surprised to see Sarah slip into the room and carefully close the door behind her.

'What do you want?' he asked, his voice conveying his complete lack of interest in her. Sarah was nothing if not thick skinned and she came to where he was sitting and rested her arm across his shoulder.

'What are you doing?' he asked coldly, shrugging her away. She leaned towards him, her mouth half open, her tongue darting across white teeth. Her breast full and round as he remembered pressed against him and he was angered and disgusted by his involuntary response to her nearness.

'You found me attractive enough once,' she whispered, 'remember how we loved each other when we were both so young and innocent, wasn't it sweet?'

'It was until you turned the whole thing sour,' Will said rising to his feet and drawing away from her. She immediately came closer and wound her arms around his neck, pressing herself against him, her pelvis tilting towards his. She laughed softly.

'You can't pretend you don't fancy me,' she said triumphantly, 'your body tells me otherwise.'

'I fancy you, as you so delicately put it, as much as I would fancy any tuppeny whore plying her trade in Wind Street. As a dog chases after a bitch,' he added cruelly.

'That's all right,' Sarah said thickly, her mouth against his neck, 'I'm not after love, mind.'

For a wild moment, Will wanted to throw her back on the bed, tear off her clothes, thrust into her with cruel force, punishing her for all the wrongs she had done him in the past. But then reason asserted itself, Sarah would enjoy her power over him and then she would doubtless cry rape, that was her style.

He propelled her towards the door and flung it wide dragging her out onto the landing.

'I'm sorry I can't be of any further help to you, Miss Miller,' he said loudly, 'but if you'd care to come to the shop sometime tomorrow I'll show you our latest fashions.'

He closed his door with a ringing bang and slid the bolt home noisily and he smiled as he imagined Sarah going off sulkily to her own rooms, angry at herself for being defeated.

He sank down onto his bed, his arms behind his head. He was still roused, he needed a woman badly. But now he had found that just any woman wouldn't do, it must be Eline, she was his love, his darling. She was pure and honest, trusting and child like, so far removed from Sarah as to be from another world.

With a groan, he rose from the bed and let himself out of his room, hurrying down the stairs and into the night. He would walk away his frustrations, forget Sarah and all the emotions she had roused within him, try to forget the urgent needs of his healthy young body. But it would not be easy.

CHAPTER NINETEEN

Fon sat in the small kitchen stitching at the fine garment even though the light was poor and her eyes burned with weariness. Jamie was bent over the books, and Fon, glancing up, saw with a dart of pain the way his dark hair curled against the column of his neck. How dear he had become to her though not by a look or a touch had she intimated as much. As for Jamie, he saw her as nothing but a helpmate for Katherine and a nursemaid for Patrick. He was an honourable man and Fon would have had it no other way.

Katherine was asleep now, soothed by the medicine the doctor had given her. She still clung to life by some unknown strength of character and Fon loved her for it.

The women had become very close over the past weeks, Fon spent a great deal of time in the sick room, arranging it so that when Patrick was asleep, she was free to read to Katherine from the Bible that stood at the side of her bed.

Fon somehow understood that the ancient rhythms of the words soothed Katherine as much as the message behind them. And Katherine could do with all the comfort she could get for the illness was slowly and inexorably taking its toll.

Jamie sighed as though reading her thoughts and ever attuned to his moods, Fon looked up at him and smiled.

'Like some tea?' She put the sewing aside and rubbed at her weary eyes. 'I'll put the kettle on and then go and check on Katherine.'

'No,' Jamie said softly, 'I'll go, you bide here and make the brew and not too much of the tea leaves, mind, I'm not a rich man.'

Fon smiled to herself. Jamie kept up the pretence of being a thrifty, almost mean, man and yet he was generous of spirit, willing to give to the beggars who came almost daily to his door. There would be a few eggs, a jug of milk or if there was a meal cooking, some potatoes. He was sometimes too generous but Fon loved him for it.

Jamie returned after a few moments and his face seemed long with the misery that darkened his eyes.

'She's asleep, Fon,' he said slumping into a chair and putting his hand over his eyes. 'She's getting worse, isn't she?'

Fon moved to crouch beside his chair, touching the hands that covered his face almost timidly.

'She's a fine fighter, mind,' she comforted, 'Katherine will not give in an inch to the sickness.'

'But it's going to beat her in the end.' Jamie sounded broken. 'My Katherine will be gone and I can't bear the thought of it.'

Fon rose to her feet and impulsively put her arms around him and, like a child, he leaned against her breast. She smoothed back his hair, talking softly to him as though he was Patrick.

'It's going to be all right, don't fret now, it will be all right.' But she lied. How could it be all right when Katherine was fading away before her eyes?

He looked up at her as though she could work miracles. 'Will it, Fon, will it be all right?' he pleaded and she kissed his forehead gently.

'It's in the hands of the Lord,' she said softly. 'I don't know any other way but to make Katherine happy while we can.'

'But I don't want to live without her.' Jamie protested as though Fon could make things right for him. 'She's

213

the love of my life, my bride from the time she was just about your age, Fon.'

'I know, I know.' She cradled him, rocking him to and fro. 'I know Jamie love, I know.'

He cried then, the first tears she would ever see him shed and the last. The sobs wracked him so that he shuddered in her arms and she held him, feeling his pain, knowing she could do little to lessen it. After a time, he was quiet and still against her and she reluctantly released him.

'Right,' she said with forced cheerfulness, 'we'll have that cup of tea and then I'll go over the books for you, you're so tired you've probably got it all wrong anyway.'

He took the cup from her and moved to the door. 'I'm going up to bed now,' he looked beaten, 'but I'll see to the boy first, make sure he's all right.' At the door he paused. 'Thank you Fon,' he said simply, 'I don't know what I'd do without you.'

She hurriedly placed her cup on the table and leaned over the books. 'That's all right.' Her voice was muffled, she didn't dare look up because her eyes were filled with tears and after a moment, Fon heard the door close behind him.

She spent some time correcting the mistakes Jamie had made as she found them. They were small mistakes, made from tiredness and worry, but they would prevent the books from balancing come the end of the month.

She lifted her head hearing a small sound from Katherine's room and she moved swiftly across the hall, opening the door a crack to peer inside.

'Come in, Fon,' Katherine said, 'I'd like to talk for a little while if you are not too tired.'

'No,' Fon lied, 'I don't feel sleepy at all.' She sat beside the bed and Katherine pointed to the Bible. 'Read me a bit of Matthew,' she said, 'you know that part.'

Fon moved the lamp nearer and opened the Bible,

trying to see the words that blurred beneath her tired eyes.

'*Come unto me all ye that labour and are heavy laden and I will give you rest,*' she read softly.

Katherine looked up from her pillows, her face grey with pain. 'I long for rest, Fon,' she said softly, 'I pray for it to come. Is that sinful of me?'

Fon felt suddenly inadequate to cope with the pain of the woman in the bed, or of Jamie her husband. Fon watched to fling down the Bible and run from the house and from the responsibilities that were suddenly hers.

She closed the Bible softly and laid it on the table. 'No,' her voice was steady, 'it's not sinful, you could never be sinful, Katherine, so don't torture yourself.'

Katherine's eyes closed and her lids were blue almost transparent. 'Don't leave me, Fon,' she whispered, 'don't leave any of us.' She struggled for breath. 'I know this is hard on you and I'm sorry but you are my only hope for the future for my husband and my son, I so want them to be happy.' She reached out and grasped Fon's hand and her grip was surprisingly strong.

Fon was suddenly filled with strength, it seemed to flow from the thin fingers holding hers into her veins. She bent and kissed Katherine's cheek.

'I won't leave,' she said, 'I'll never leave.' She sat back into the chair and waited until Katherine had sunk into a weary sleep and then, with renewed determination, Fon made her way to her own bed knowing she must rest to prepare herself for the ordeal ahead.

Eline had waited for what seemed days for Will to come to her, she knew that he would make arrangements for them to be together sometime, somewhere. In the mean time, she was content to get back to her work free from the disturbing influence of Sarah Miller.

She wondered what Will would make of the girl; would he find her amusing, attractive even? A small snake of jealousy wound itself round her heart and then Eline told herself not to be absurd. If Will had wanted any other woman why would he take up with someone like her who was married and until now had denied him?

'Eline,' Mrs Miller came up behind her as she sat at her table, pencil poised over the paper, 'I'm sorry to disturb you at your work but I wanted to talk to you.'

'That's all right, Mrs Miller, I wasn't working,' Eline admitted, 'I was lost in thought.'

Mrs Miller smiled. 'Well, isn't that the way most creative work is done?'

She seated herself opposite Eline, her full skirts spreading out around her. She was a beautiful woman, in a graceful elegant way, Eline realized.

'I know you love working with Hari Grenfell and that's the best training anyone could have, better than any college, but I would like you to go to Somerset for a few days.'

She paused. 'I want you to see the factory belonging to Mr Clark of Street, I think it would interest you greatly.'

Eline bit her lip uncertainly. 'I've never travelled very far alone,' she said, 'I'm a bit of a baby, I suppose.'

'That's all right,' Mrs Miller said quickly, 'I will be travelling there with you.' She lifted her eyebrow quizzically. 'Not for the first time, mind you. Once I went there alone, not a ladylike thing to do I might tell you, but it was necessary at the time.'

Eline looked at Mrs Miller with admiration, no wonder she was a success, she was brave and would not shirk any task however delicate or dangerous.

'When will we go?' Eline asked, suddenly excited at the prospect of visiting the greatest boot and shoe maker in the country.

'Within the next few days,' Mrs Miller said rising to her feet, 'I think you will enjoy the experience, Eline, and I'm sure you will benefit greatly from the visit.'

When she was alone, Eline dropped her pencil. She couldn't concentrate, excitement filled her mingled with a feeling of regret, regret that her love pact with Will would have to be postponed.

She felt a surge of love and desire for him and bit her lip. Why postpone what she wanted above all else? What was to prevent her from going to him in Oystermouth?

She stared down at her hands, thinking of Joe, cosily ensconced with Nina Parks in the home that had once been Eline's. Surely she didn't owe them any consideration?

Eline bit her lip as she admitted to herself that she was more than a little worried that she hadn't seen Will for some days. Had he regretted his words of love?

She rose and picked up her coat and fastened the buttons with a feeling of determination. At least she could talk to Will and even if they had no time or opportunity to be alone, she could tell him she was going away for a few days.

She caught the Mumbles train at the terminus and as she climbed aboard, she felt the breeze from the sea lift her hair from her face. Eline settled herself on the top deck of the coach and stared out to sea, anticipating her meeting with Will, scarcely feeling the jolt as the horses moved forward between the tracks. She tingled with excitement, soon she would be with him, she would see his dear face, touch his crisp hair, feel his mouth on hers.

The rich colour came to her cheeks at the daring thoughts and she caught her breath sharply. Doubts assailed her; was she doing the right thing? Would Will think her a fast woman for coming to find him?

The coach jolted onward, past Black Pill and round the curve of the bay to face Mumbles Head. The scene was one of breathtaking beauty, the sea and sky merged on the horizon and closer to land, the waves were white tipped, rushing shoreward and retreating on the chatter of shells dragged by the ebb.

217

On the hard, skiffs were lying drunkenly, white-limed along the bottoms to keep the boards from opening during the enforced rest. But soon the season would start again and the rich harvest of the oysters would be ready for dredging.

For a moment, Eline felt a nostalgia for the simplicity of her life as she'd lived it in Oystermouth. She had spent her days cleaning the little house, washing the grey slate floors, scrubbing the wooden table until it gleamed, blackleading the grate and using ash and water to clean the brass fenders.

She straightened her shoulders, knowing that she could never go back to that life now; she had moved on, she had become a window dresser for Emily Miller, she had spent days working with the great Hari Grenfell learning at her feet like a disciple of old. It was easy to remember the uncomplicated existence she once had with rose-coloured thoughts, but she did not wish for it again.

She knew that she was considered odd by the people of Oystermouth Village. Always an outsider, she was now a woman who had left her husband's hearth and bed, a poor, betrayed, rejected figure, an unwanted wife. The only one who would bother with her was Carys and now she was busy with her own family life.

Eline alighted at the end of the line and stared around her, breathing in the familiar air of Oystermouth. It was a lovely place, a place of serenity and beauty and quiet lives, and she had no place in it.

Will Davies's Boot and Shoe Store was open for business as usual and for a moment, Eline hesitated on the threshold, wondering what she would say to Will. Now that the moment had come, she felt weak and uncertain of her feelings and her mouth was dry as she went into the dimness of the interior.

'Yes, can I help you? Oh, it's you, Eline Harries, what do you want?'

218

Gwyneth Parks stood before her, nicely gowned in a dark dress with long sleeves and an elegantly nipped waist. She looked very different from the girl who had hauled oysters into a sack and carried them to market.

'I would like to speak with Mr Davies. Is he here?' Eline forced herself to speak politely though she felt like running from the shop and returning to Swansea on the next train.

'No, he's not here, you can see that for yourself, can't you?' Gwyneth's tone was insolent and Eline was suddenly angry.

'How is your mother getting along in *my* home and with *my* husband?' She spoke loudly just as two well-dressed ladies entered the shop. Gwyneth looked around in embarrassment and spoke more politely.

'Mr Davies is at home, he's not been feeling very well and I don't think he wants any visitors.'

'What you think is of no interest to me,' Eline said flatly. She turned on her heel and left the shop and once out in the brightness of the day, she released her breath.

Why had she come here? She should have known that it would be upsetting. She clenched her hands into fists and stared across the bay longing to be back in Swansea, safe in her rooms, respected and valued for herself alone.

Then she thought anxiously of Will; what was wrong with him, might it be something serious? Eline walked the hundred yards or so to Mrs Marsh's lodging house and, taking her courage in both hands, she knocked on the door.

The young girl who helped Mrs Marsh in the house stood in the small hallway and stared at Eline curiously. 'Mrs Marsh isn't here,' she said, 'and if it's a room you want, I think we're full up.'

'No, I don't want a room,' Eline said, 'I would like to see Mr Davies. I'm a friend and I understand he hasn't been very well.'

The girl stepped aside at once. 'Come in, miss, he's

had a right nasty fever, real bad he was for a day or two, but over the worst now, so the doctor says. Wait by here, I'll ask him can he see you.'

Eline looked round the hallway, at the leafy green plant in the large pot and the well-polished tiles on the floor, at least Will would have been well cared for but she could not help feeling that she should have come sooner.

Suddenly a voice interrupted her thoughts. 'I don't think Will is up to seeing you today.' Sarah Miller was coming down the stairs behind the young maid and she was smiling in a superior way that made Eline suddenly go cold.

'Is it up to you to make that decision?' she asked acidly, staring at Sarah with a hostility she was unable to conceal.

'Yes, I would say so,' Sarah retorted, smiling, her teeth showing like those of a cat about to pounce on a helpless prey.

'I think not.' Eline made to move past her but Sarah blocked her way, catching her arm in a none-too-gentle hold. 'I have every right to speak for Will,' she said quietly, 'after all, he and I were lovers before I left Swansea.'

'Liar!' The word was wrenched from between Eline's numb lips, something in Sarah's eyes, in the triumphant line of her neck, told Eline she was speaking the truth.

'You mean you didn't know that Will was the father of my child, the child that my dear step-mother Emily is rearing?' Sarah's tone was mocking. 'And now I'm back, Will and I will have to sort things out, settle our future and that of our daughter.'

'I don't believe what you are saying about Will and in any case you were walking out with Tom Parks.' Eline was clutching at straws and she knew it. What did a small matter like walking out with one man while bearing a child by another mean to a woman like Sarah Miller?

Sarah seemed to read something of her thoughts. 'In any case,' she said spitefully, 'from what I hear, you are a married woman, I should think that to Will you were just a convenience. Who misses a bite out of a bruised apple?'

Eline felt herself flush with anger, she opened her mouth to protest, but how could she? It was true that she and Will had never been lovers but the intention was there and after all, she *was* a married woman.

She turned to leave and then heard from the landing above Will's voice calling to her, 'Eline!' The urgency in his tone held her still as he hurried down the stairs and came to her side.

'Eline, why were you going to leave without seeing me?' he asked, his eyes bright as though he still had a fever. Eline looked into his dear face and longed to cling to him.

'I've been telling Eline about us,' Sarah said sweetly. 'I think she should know how we almost renewed our acquaintance in the most intimate of ways. Don't you think she had the right to know?'

Will looked at Eline. 'I'm denying nothing, everything that happened was before I met you, you can't hold it against me.'

'But Will,' Sarah interrupted, 'what about the other night when we were alone together we almost gave in to temptation, didn't we?' She rushed on without waiting for a reply. 'And there's our child. We haven't discussed her future, have we?'

Will glanced back at Sarah in exasperation and Sarah met his gaze challengingly.

'Will,' Eline spoke softly, 'is the child yours?'

Will shook his head. 'Sarah has told so many lies I can deny nothing. *I* don't even know whose child Sarah gave birth to.'

Eline felt as though a stone was hanging heavily in her breast. Without a word, she moved out into the freshness of the air, breathing deeply, trying to calm herself. In the space of a few minutes everything seemed to have changed; Will was not the free man she had believed him to be, he had loved Sarah once and might be the father of her child.

Eline became aware that Will had followed her. 'I'm going to Somerset for a few days,' she said softly as Will closed the door on Sarah's prying eyes. 'When I come back we will talk again.'

'Eline,' Will said softly, 'I have never held your marriage against you, please don't hold the words of a spiteful girl against me.'

Eline put her hand on his arm. 'Go back indoors, Will, you still look a little feverish. We'll talk again when I get back, really we will, I'll have had time to think things out then.'

'Eline, I nearly had you, so nearly.' Will traced the outline of her cheek with his finger. 'Never have I wanted anyone the way I want you.'

'Goodbye, Will.' Eline almost ran along the road, her eyes were filled with tears and there was a heaviness that weighed her down so that her footsteps seemed to drag. She longed to be alone in her own rooms where she could fling herself on the bed and let the hot angry tears that ached in her throat have full release.

She thought of Will and how he might have been in Sarah's arms and then she thought of Joe, her husband who had vowed to love only her. Were all men faithless, driven only by their own needs?

She climbed aboard the Mumbles train and huddled in a seat in the warmth of the lower deck. She didn't want to look out at the passing beauty of the sea, or of the darkening skies over Mumbles Head. She was so low in spirits that nothing seemed to matter any more. She felt beaten, rejected and betrayed and all she wanted now was the sanctuary of her own room.

CHAPTER TWENTY

Somerset was a sweet, red-earthed country with late roses flowering around thatch-roofed country cottages and Eline felt at home there from the first day she had set foot in the place. Mrs Miller had booked them both into a small inn on the outskirts of Street and from the window beneath the sloping roof of her room, Eline could see along the main roadway of the town.

Eline had never been used to luxury before she had her own suite of rooms above Emily's emporium and so she accepted the small bedroom with its varnished wooden floor and the sagging bed covered in a patch-work quilt with equanimity. She was filled with anticipation as she stood now at the small-paned window, staring out at the soft countryside, glad to be far away from Swansea and from Will. She could not help but wonder what he would be doing now; could he be wrapped in the arms of Sarah Miller, putting Eline completely out of his thoughts?

It troubled Eline how nearly she had betrayed all her instincts and gone to Will's bed, it was foolishness, she saw that now, no good could come of being unfaithful to her marriage vows. Two wrongs didn't make a right and it was about time she realized that.

Eline forced her thoughts to return to the business in hand, the visiting of Clark's Boot and Shoe Emporium. The visit was mainly social, Emily Miller had made that clear, but Eline guessed that a foretaste of what the famous Clark's factory was planning would be of enormous help in the progress of Emily's own business.

When she had passed the Clark's factory on her

arrival, Eline had been surprised at the remoteness of the buildings. The factory could have been a large private dwelling, turretted, with many windows, that stared out into pleasant tree-lined grounds. Somerset was unlike Swansea through its purity of air and the undamaged richness of the countryside.

Swansea had the copper smoke from the Hafod and the White Rose factories as well as the coal dust from small mines to contend with and yet Swansea was dear to Eline, the ugliness mitigated by the golden curve of the bay and by the slopes of the soft hills rising above the town.

Eline heard Emily Miller's voice outside on the landing, so she drew on her coat and did up the buttons, ready and waiting to visit the Clark factory.

'Ah, there you are, Eline, punctual I'm happy to see.' Emily was pulling on her soft kids gloves. 'We have a cab waiting outside, what a pity it's begun to rain.'

The roadway outside the inn was quickly turning to mud, the wheels of a passing cart churning channels into the softness sending up a flurry of damp earth in all directions.

Mrs Miller clicked her tongue in annoyance as a few spots clung to the hem of her skirt and her back was as straight as a poker as she climbed into the cab.

Eline followed her and sank into the creaking seat, shivering a little at the coldness of the leather upholstery.

'Not a very pleasant day, is it?' Mrs Miller remarked looking through the window and Eline agreed dutifully.

She still felt a little in awe of Mrs Miller who wore an air of remoteness, her tone of voice, when she spoke, always brisk and businesslike. She had been more than kind to Eline and yet there seemed no warmth in Mrs Miller. Except, Eline conceded, when her husband was around.

Emily and John Miller seemed the perfect couple,

there was an unspoken regard for each other's opinions and the love that flowed between them when they touched was almost tangible.

It was Mrs Miller who had sent Sarah to live in Oystermouth, Eline reflected with some irony. Perhaps if Eline hadn't complained about Sarah she might still be living at the emporium and probably Eline and William would have been lovers by now.

And yet, wasn't it better to know now about Will's past than to find out later that he had a child?

Why was it that the men in her life seemed to have found some other woman to give them an heir? Perhaps it was just as well, Eline thought dismally, she was barren, unable to bear a child. In any case, it hardly mattered now, she had made up her mind to abide by her marriage vows come what may.

'You are very quiet, Eline,' Mrs Miller said, 'not homesick already, are you?'

Was she? Eline considered for a moment and then shook her head. 'No, I'm enjoying the change. I want to see and do new things, I want to learn all I can about, about everything.'

Mrs Miller smiled. 'I remember well when I was like that myself, now I'm inclined to settle for some peace in my life, I could do without disruptions like the appearance of my step-daughter.'

Eline was surprised, it wasn't like Mrs Miller to speak of personal matters. She bit her lip, she didn't think it polite to agree with Mrs Miller and yet she couldn't in all honesty speak in Sarah's defence, Sarah *was* disruptive if not to say dangerous.

Mrs Miller looked directly at Eline. 'You know about the baby, don't you?'

Eline nodded slowly. 'Yes, Will Davies's child, I believe.'

'What?' Mrs Miller said in surprise. 'No, the baby wasn't Will's, would that she were, at least I'd know she

225

came from honest stock. No, it was not Will but Sam Payton who was Pammy's father.'

Eline looked up and met Emily Miller's direct gaze realizing she saw more and was far wiser than she allowed anyone to know.

'But, Sarah told me that Will was the father of her baby and when I asked him point blank if it was true, he didn't know what to say.'

'I'm not surprised,' Mrs Miller said drily. 'In the beginning, Sarah told so many lies, I seriously wonder if the girl would know the truth if it got up and bit her. In any case, she treated Will Davies most shabbily, I shouldn't think he'd want any more to do with her.' She looked out through the window, apparently having lost interest in the conversation but Eline knew that in her way, Emily wanted to set the record straight.

'Ah, we're here.' Emily's tone indicated in no uncertain terms that the subject was closed and then Mrs Miller was stepping down from the cab, treading gingerly across the muddy roadway.

It was Francis Clark who welcomed them into the building, a genial man with a pleasant smile on his face. He was smartly dressed and his beard and moustache were neatly clipped.

'Mrs Miller, I'm sorry my brother isn't here today, pressing business at Northover.' He smiled and indicated that the ladies should take a seat.

'You know we've moved our sheepskin side of the business over there under the management of John Morland. Here in Street we are concentrating more than ever on boots and shoes.'

He sat at the desk and smiled warmly at Eline, as though he sensed her shyness. 'I've ordered some tea,' he said, 'and then perhaps you can tell me how I can be of service, Mrs Miller.'

'I'll be honest with you,' Emily leaned forward. 'I wish to know all that is the latest in the shoe business and who better to consult than the famous Clark family of Street in Somerset?'

Francis Clark nodded. 'Always willing to give advice to such a successful lady as yourself, Mrs Miller.' His face broadened into a smile. 'I've heard much about the time you came here and made a deal to have boots and shoes delivered to Swansea without a penny changing hands.' His smile widened. 'I think it was your spirit of independence that impressed everyone at Clark's, my brother most of all.'

'My cheek, you mean,' Mrs Miller said quickly. She turned to Eline. 'This young lady here is very talented, I would like her to see how your process works, I think with a bit of training she'll have a great future as a designer, perhaps as great as that of Hari Grenfell.'

'That is praise indeed,' Francis acknowledged softly, 'Hari Grenfell's name is renowned for expertise, design and innovation. You must be very good indeed, madam.'

Eline was silent not knowing what to say. She was pleased when the door opened and a maid entered the room bearing a silver tray.

When the tea was served, Francis leaned back in his chair and regarded Eline steadily. 'I wish you the very best of good fortune, with your work,' he said. 'May the good Lord go with you.'

'Thank you,' Eline replied feeling totally inadequate as she sipped her tea and breathed in the smell of leather.

'We mean to introduce a new line later on,' Francis mused, his gaze including both Eline and Emily. 'We are calling the line Hygienic Boots and Shoes and we intend the footwear to be designed on anatomical principles following the shape of the foot more accurately than before.'

He placed his fingertips together and after a moment, continued speaking, 'The actual formula is a secret at the moment, but I'm sure your Hari Grenfell has worked in this line along with her remedial footwear.'

'I'm sure,' Emily agreed. 'This is all very interesting.' Her eyes revealed what her voice did not that she really was fascinated by the idea of anatomically designed footwear. 'I'm sure you will have great success with such an imaginative and worthy idea.'

Eline leaned forward. 'I have done some work of that nature myself,' she said in a quiet voice and Francis nodded thoughtfully.

'You are indeed a talented lady and I congratulate you.'

After tea was finished, Eline followed Francis Clark and Mrs Miller in silence as they walked through the factory. The noise of the sewing machines was like the continuous humming of giant birds interspersed with the clacking sound of the cutting machine.

Eline was not interested in this side of the shoe-making process, she wanted only to draw and modify, correcting weaknesses in patterns and bringing the footwear to a more realistically designed shape. Indeed, from what she could see, she had begun to draw the anatomically practical shoe already.

The noise gave her a headache and Eline was glad when they left the factory behind and moved out into the roadway once more. The rain had ceased and there was a freshness to the air that soothed Eline's throbbing head. She watched as Emily said her thanks and her goodbyes and was relieved to turn once more to the coach.

The drive back to the inn was silent except for the rolling of the wheels on cobbles and the creaking of the leather seats. It was only when Mrs Miller led the way to her rooms indicating that Eline should follow her that it became clear what the visit was really all about.

'Francis is a kindly gentleman,' Mrs Miller said thoughtfully, 'but then the Clarks are Quakers, religious and so very nice.' She changed the direction of her thinking so abruptly that Eline had difficulty in keeping up with her.

'Did you take notice of the new designs that were being made in the factory?' Mrs Miller asked, discarding her gloves. 'See the broader shape of the heel and the way that more room was being allowed to accommodate the toes?'

Eline smiled. 'I could have saved you the trip,' she said with great daring, 'I meant it when I said I'd been working on those lines myself for some time.'

Mrs Miller seemed for once at a loss for words. She sank down into a chair and drew off her hat, shaking the rain from it thoughtfully.

'I see, then I should have been paying more attention to your work, shouldn't I?' She unlaced her boots. 'Still it's been an experience for you, Eline, has it not? And now I know what the Clarks are calling their new footwear, I can avoid using the same description.'

'Of course,' Eline pointed out, 'the Clarks are not ready to go into production of their new line, not just yet. What they were making on some of the machines were simply prototypes. They manufacture boots and shoes in such great quantities that it will take months to build up enough stock to go on to the market.'

'You are a bright girl,' Mrs Miller praised softly. 'Pack up your belongings, Eline, our work here is finished. We are going home.'

Nina Parks stared at her reflection in the spotted mirror hanging over the sink; she looked well, she decided, better than she'd done for some time.

She smiled to herself. Joe had come to her bed last night, the first time since she'd lost the baby. Nina had been worried by his abstinence, she knew that a man like Joe needed to satisfy his appetites and if not with her then he would find someone else.

But he had been as passionate as ever and much more loving; it seemed that the loss of their child had brought them closer together.

She moved to the kitchen and peered into the pot of stew simmering nicely on the edge of the fire; Joe would be hungry when he came home, he'd been working all day at the quarry and would be hungry, tired and dusty. Very soon the oyster season would begin again, and then Nina would be happier because a man like Joe needed the freedom of the open sea. There, he was at his best, doing the job he loved, bringing in the oysters.

A figure appeared suddenly in the open back door and, looking up, Nine smiled a welcome. 'Gwyneth! What are you doing here? Mr Davies give you the day off, did he?'

Gwyneth sat down in one of the wooden kitchen chairs and brushed her hair back from her forehead. She looked distinctly ruffled and there was a downward tilt to her mouth that betrayed her ill-humour.

'That cow! How I hate her,' Gwyneth burst out, her eyes hot and angry.

Nina folded her arms. 'Well, that's a nice way to come into my kitchen, no greeting, no "how are you feeling, Mam", nothing but a show of temper. Who has got on the wrong side of you today?'

'It's that Sarah Miller,' Gwyneth said, rising and kissing her mother's cheek in a perfunctory gesture of greeting. 'Makes trouble wherever she goes, she does. Been in the shop this morning, cornering poor Will Davies and him not recovered from his fever yet.'

'A nip of beetroot wine will make you feel better, girl,' Nina said, sighing inwardly. Why Gwyneth made such a drama out of things she couldn't imagine, she certainly didn't follow her mother for moods; it must be poor Kev coming out in her.

'Got some hold over him she has, I swear,' Gwyneth continued, taking the mug of wine her mother handed her. 'Don't know what it is but it must be something big or he would send her away with a flea in her ear.'

'What do you care?' Nina asked, seating herself

opposite her daughter across the kitchen table. She rested her elbows on the scrubbed wood and stared at her daughter thoughtfully. 'You are in love with Mr Davies, is that it?' The words were spoken like an accusation and Nina recognized it as soon as they were uttered, but it was too late to take them back.

'So?' Gwyneth demanded. 'Is that something to be ashamed of?'

'No, love,' Nina reached across the table and touched her daughter's clenched fist in sympathy. 'But it's not wise, is it? I mean he's not our kind, he's a boss.'

'Bosses are still men underneath their trews!' Gwyneth said coarsely. 'And that Sarah Miller is after him, it's clear as daylight.'

'What about Mr Davies?' Nina asked. 'Is he interested in this Sarah?'

Gwyneth shook her head. 'I don't think so, he never looks pleased to see her but she's living in the same lodgings as him, she's got every chance to get her claws into him.'

'Men don't like that,' Nina volunteered, 'they don't like to be chased, or at least they like to think it was all their own idea. Cunning is better than brazenness any day.'

'What do you mean?' Gwyneth was all attention and Nina felt flattered, well, why shouldn't she be proud? She'd got her man away from a much younger woman and a wife at that.

'Be friends with Mr Davies, side with him, flatter him, tell him you're feeling faint and you need him to walk you home. You have the cottage to yourself days, so use your brains, girl.'

'Aye, perhaps you're right,' Gwyneth agreed softly. She sipped at the wine and then replaced the mug on the table where a ring of red etched itself around the bottom of the mug.

'Our Tom is mad, too,' Gwyneth said. 'He brought

231

Sarah Miller back to Swansea from Port Eynon with him and now she seems to have forgotten all about him.'

Nina felt a dart of anger and pain that Tom should be thwarted in love. She felt a sudden virulent anger against Sarah Miller for using Tom and then apparently discarding him.

'Well, she's probably realized that Tom isn't very well off and Mr Davies is,' Nina countered bitterly. 'Women like her are out for what they can get.'

Nina didn't see that the sentiments she'd just expressed could be applied to herself. She knew she loved Joe but the gossips would say that she'd stolen him from his wife because he owned the cottage he was living in as well as owning two oyster boats.

'I shan't let her get Will,' Gwyneth said sulkily, 'I love him and not for his money and position but for himself.'

'Aye, it's easy to fall in love and it always pays to fall in love with the rich man rather than the poor one,' Nina responded drily.

She poured more wine and changed the subject quite deliberately. 'I haven't seen hide nor hair of our Sal,' she said, 'not since I lost the baby. You'd think she'd have come to see me by now, wouldn't you?'

Gwyneth nodded abstractedly. 'Aye, but Sal is feathering her own nest, mind, wouldn't be surprised if she married that fellow of hers before long.'

Gwyneth looked at her mother. 'You've seen our Fon though, haven't you? She's fallen on her feet up there on Honey's Farm, hasn't she?'

'I don't know,' Nina said, 'it can't be a bed of roses working for those people. From what Fon tells me, that poor woman is sick unto death and depending on Fon more than she does on her own husband. Mind, that shouldn't surprise me, men are no good at all when it comes to sickness and it can't be easy caring for a man and a child who are not your own.'

Gwyneth rose to her feet. 'Well, I'll get back now,

Mam, and thanks for the advice, perhaps I'll take it, some of it anyway.'

'And perhaps you won't,' Nina said sighing. 'But you children must live your own lives now, I can't stop you what ever you want to do.'

Nina watched as Gwyneth walked away from the house and along the street without so much as a glance at the beauty of the bay or the softness of the breeze drifting over the calm waters.

Nina returned to her kitchen and took a freshly baked loaf from the pantry, holding it against her and slicing the bread thickly the way Joe liked it. She smiled as she thought of Joe, he was a fine man, her man and she would hold on to him for the rest of her life.

CHAPTER TWENTY-ONE

He had lost her, she had slipped away from him, William felt it in his bones, Eline would never be his now. It was the silly gossiping words of Sarah Miller that had put an end to his dreams, Sarah who, in her bitterness and sheer cussedness, had thrust in the knife and turned it. And Will had wanted Eline to be his more than he had ever wanted anything in his whole life.

She had left town, gone to Somerset with Emily Miller, having a taste of the world beyond the boundaries of Swansea and he feared she would come home much changed by her experience. Eline was so sweet, so trusting and he loved her so much that the thought of her being far away from Swansea where he could not reach her hurt.

She was right though, he could see it in her eyes that she still considered herself a married woman. In spite of all the indignities Joe Harries had heaped on her, Eline felt she should be faithful to her vows. To have come to his bed would probably have served to make Eline feel guilty and ashamed, Will should not have expected it.

And yet he knew himself well enough, if Sarah had not intervened and Eline had come to him willingly, he would have accepted the gift of herself with open arms.

'*Duw*, you're lost in a world of your own, Will.' Hari Grenfell smiled warmly and leaned towards him, her slender fingers pushing back his hair as she'd done when he was nine years old and her apprentice. 'What's wrong, boy, anything I can help with?'

They were sitting in the comfortable drawing room at Summer Lodge, the late sun dying away into the hillsides, the sky streaked with red, but Will saw none of it as he shook his head.

'I was just thinking about Sarah Miller and how even after all this time she is able to cast a blight over my life.'

Hari frowned. 'Why what has the little hussy done now?' Her tone was indignant and Will smiled.

'Oh, nothing really, just inflicting petty irritations on me, nothing I can't manage. The worst of it is, she's living in the same boarding house as me, I wish Emily had shown more foresight when palming the girl off the way she did.'

Hari sighed. 'Emily meant only to get rid of Sarah, for all our sakes – the girl is a threat to *my* peace of mind. I know that I can never forgive her for what she did to me when she took my son.' Hari paused. 'I suppose Emily wanted to push Sarah into the arms of the poor unsuspecting Tom Parks, the man who brought her back here from Port Eynon. It seemed reasonable enough to Emily to select Mrs Marsh's boarding house, it's one of the best in Oystermouth. I don't think she even connected the place with you.'

'Well, it's just unfortunate for me,' Will said, 'but I wish Sarah would go away again, do anything but leave me alone. I'll lose my temper with her one of these days and tell her what I think of her.' He sighed. 'She really isn't worth it, though.'

'What is really worrying you, Will? It's got to be more than Sarah Miller's proximity that's getting you down.'

Will smiled; Hari knew him well but he could not even confide to her that he had almost possessed Eline Harries. If it hadn't been for Sarah's interference, Eline and he would be lovers by now.

He rose to his feet abruptly. 'I'd best be getting back home.' He stretched his arms above his head and yawned hugely. 'Forgive me, Hari, it's very rude of me to act like this but I'm so tired.'

Hari stared at him unblinkingly. 'All right, don't tell me, if that's what you want. But take my advice, get yourself a house of your own, install a housekeeper, get out of harm's way, because I don't trust Sarah Miller an inch. She'll cause havoc wherever she goes and I'd rather you were out of her path.'

'You may be right, Hari.' Will smiled, but how could he afford a house of his own on the small profit he was making from the shop? Hari had become so used to getting just what she wanted from life that she didn't realize not everyone had her gifts.

'I understand Emily is on her way back from Somerset,' Hari said casually and Will smiled.

'Thanks for the information.' They both knew what he meant and Hari, rising to her feet, kissed his cheek. 'I don't know how it can all work out for you, Will, but I wish you luck, I know your heart is set on having Eline Harries for your own.'

Will looked down at her, he loved Hari fiercely, he loved her as a sister and he would lay down his life for her, but how could he talk over with her his confusion of thoughts and feelings?

He wanted Eline; he would have taken her to his bed because he was a man and he wanted to possess the one he loved and yet he wanted Eline as a wife, not simply as a mistress.

'It's a mess,' he said softly, 'one that can't ever be resolved.'

Hari squeezed his arm comfortingly. 'What is meant to be will be whatever we do,' she said softly.

He left her then and strode down towards the town, surprised at the force of the night breeze sharp against his skin. Across the bay the oyster skiffs were out, the season under way once more. The elegant crafts were cutting through the waters, sails billowing, dredges dragging the ocean floor as the fishermen laboured for their livelihood.

Joe Harries would be amongst them in his boat ironically named the *Emmeline*. Will took a deep breath, his hands clenched into fists, it was hard to swallow the idea that Joe Harries had possessed Eline and had given her up for an older woman – the man must be mad.

Will decided to walk to Oystermouth, he was restless, his longing for Eline almost unbearable. Even if he couldn't possess her physically, the knowledge that she was not even in Swansea was painful to him, her very nearness would be enough. If only he could see her, speak to her, look into her lovely face.

The wind was whipping up sharply, lifting his hair away from his face and looking up at the sky Will saw that storm clouds were gathering. It would be a poor lookout for the men of the oyster fleet if they didn't return to shore before the rain struck and the winds became too rough. The waters around the Mixon could be treacherous and the rocks of the head protruded out to sea in a way that could catch out the unwary.

Will sighed. The men of the oyster fleet were all experienced sailors, used to the vagueries of the weather and with the seas about the coastline well charted, they would not be in too much danger.

He reached the door of Mrs Marsh's house breathless and windblown after his long walk and saw that the waves were whipping against the rocks, rushing shoreward in angry tumult. He paused for a moment to wonder about Joe Harries out in such weather aboard the *Emmeline* and then turning his back on the restless ocean, he went inside.

'*Duw*, I haven't seen a storm like this for years, mind.' Nina was on her doorstep along with the other women of the village, their eyes straining to see into the rain-swept darkness. Tonight she was not Nina Parks, paramour to a married man but a woman like them all in Oystermouth in fear for the safety of their menfolk.

'They'll be pulling in to the moorings, any time now, don't fret,' Carys Morgan said quickly, her plump body jigging to and fro as she unthinkingly rocked her baby who was already fast asleep beneath the stout Welsh shawl. 'Won't bother even unloading the catch into the small boats, not in a sea like this vixen!'

'It's my Tom that worries me,' Nina said, 'my boy isn't used to handling a skiff, deep-sea fisherman he is, see, and not an oyster boat, man.'

'Got a good crew with him, hasn't he?' Carys said shortly. 'Skipper George's two youngsters know the ropes, mind, they'll guide your Tom all right.'

Nina held her tongue, she didn't want to offend her neighbours for it was a good feeling to be accepted by them. It was only the imminent danger of their menfolk that made her for tonight, at least, one with them.

Nina bit her lip, it would be her fault if anything happened to her Tom; it had taken a great deal of persuasion to get him to accept the skippering of the *Oyster Sunrise* and she had kept on to him day and night about it. Nina had talked and talked telling her son that it was his right to own a boat. Wasn't his father responsible for seeing him set up for the future? He would be a fool to throw it all away because of pride.

Tom had agreed at last but declared that nothing would make him forgive Joe Harries for all he had done though he conceded that now, set up in Joe's home, Nina was as near respectable as Joe could make her, and at least now Joe was trying to make amends.

Still, Nina consoled herself, Tom's decision to take on the *Oyster Sunrise* owed more to her son's attempt to make Sarah Miller notice him than anything she had said.

'I can see a sail!' Carys was straining forward as though to pierce the gloom with her eyes. 'Yes, there's a boat coming in, no, there's at least four of them, look, they're in the calmer waters of the bay now, well away from the rocks of the head.'

A cheer went up from the women waiting on the shore and then they fell silent as the boats drew nearer and each woman tried to identify her husband's skiff, willing the boats into safety.

An explosion of thunder resounded round the silent street and one of the women cried out in fear. Nina remained rigid, eyes straining as she tried to see through the pelting rain. 'Please let them be safe,' she murmured, clasping her hands against the rain-soaked bodice of her dress.

One by one the men made the shore, weary and bedraggled, limbs aching from the strain of fighting the storm. Nina watched as Carys, clinging to the arms of her Sam, face radiant with relief, disappeared into her house.

It seemed the fleet had all come home with the exceptions only of the *Oyster Sunrise* and the *Emmeline*.

'Oh, dear God, save us!' Nina felt herself alone in the world, her heart beating in a crazy rhyme of fear. She almost screamed out loud and then she became aware that Skipper George had come to stand beside her.

'They'll be in, give them time,' he said reassuringly, 'my boys were born to the ocean, they know the tides and they know the pitfalls of the seas from Sker Point to Porthcawl and then some.'

He looked down with something akin to pity in his eyes. 'Go indoors, missis,' he said, 'stoke up the fire and push the pot on the flames because your men will want cheering when they get back.'

Nina took a deep breath. 'But will they come back?' Her voice sounded strangled and Skipper George put a kindly hand on her shoulder.

'I can't answer that, missis, you'll have to talk to the good Lord about it. But hope is a good thing, mind,' he continued, 'don't give up hope whatever you do. I want

my sons back as much as you want your menfolk, so
we'll watch and pray, right?'

Nina stood for a long time staring through the darkness, unable to see anything because the rain was coming down like a curtain now, obscuring the crags of
Mumbles Head and the waters beyond. At last, she
turned and went into the silent house and stood watching
the pools of water drip from her clothing on to the cold
grey slate of the floor turning blue with moisture.

She lifted her head and looked around her; this was
only an empty house when all was said and done. It was
never her home, never would be because the shadow of
Eline was everywhere. Much as Nina tried to erase all
evidence of Joe's wife from the rooms, Eline's presence
was still there, haunting her.

When the cold light of morning dawned, Nina was
seated in the chair before the window, her eyes red and
dry from the sleepless hours she'd spent keeping watch,
waiting for the maroons to be fired, waiting for the
lifeboat to be called out. At least then she would know
that the oyster skiffs were within striking distance of the
shore. But all had remained silent, even the rain and the
wind given way to the calm after the storm.

And yet tragedy was about to strike, she knew it in
her bones and nothing, not all the prayers she'd said,
would alter what destiny decreed. Her men were gone,
lost to her for ever, drowned in the violent sea that could
be cruel and unrelenting. The ocean had almost taken
her son once, had the cold waters of the night come to
claim him?

Nina rose and rebuilt the fire, going through the
motions of living even though she knew nothing would
ever be the same again. She made herself some weak tea
and drank it gratefully and then returned to her vigil at
the window. The skiffs bobbed gently now on the calm,
almost timid, waters of the bay. The men were out there,
unloading the catch on to the small boats. Some of the

oysters would be left on the perches and later, the women would pack them in bags or baskets, ready to make the first sales of the new season. All seemed bright and normal, life went on but not for her, Nina thought despairingly.

There was a knock on the door and it was opened by Skipper George who looked into the kitchen, his pale blue eyes far seeing and wise. 'A boat's been sighted,' he said kindly, 'I thought you'd want to know.'

'Which one?' Nina pulled her shawl so roughly from the hook on the door that she tore a hole in it. 'The *Sunrise* or the *Emmeline*, which is it?'

'I don't know yet,' George admitted and it was clear he was making an effort to speak calmly. Nina put her hand on his arm.

'I'm sorry, I keep forgetting that your sons are out there, you must be as worried as I am.'

Nina followed the skipper to the edge of the water and glancing around, she saw that the hill above her was crowded with people. It seemed the whole village had turned out to watch the single boat coming in.

The waiting was interminable and then, limping, like a bird with a broken wing, came a skiff edging around the rocks, making for the safety of the moorings.

Nina strained her eyes, trying to see which skiff it was but, in the early morning sunlight, it was difficult to make out the shape of the vessel. The amber sails were torn, hanging useless like washing dangling from a line.

'I think she's holed,' Skipper George said, his voice rough with emotion, 'see how she's listing?'

Oh God, Nina thought, who do I want it to be, my son or my lover? It was a question she could not answer, did not want to answer.

The boat crept inward, dipping into the shallow waves as though never to rise again. Nina held her breath as the skiff lurched and leaned crazily over, the bedraggled sails almost in the water.

'Don't worry,' Skipper George said, 'from this distance, the men could swim ashore.'

'Not if they were hurt,' Nina replied desperately. 'Oh, God, which one is it?'

She felt as though her head was about to burst, she was to be punished for her faithless ways, that was it, she had sinned and now came the moment of retribution.

'Bear up, missis.' Skipper George grasped her arm. 'It won't do to go all weak and wobbly now, whoever is in that boat needs your strength. Come on, show 'em all what you're made of, *cariad*.'

Gratefully, Nina looked into the weatherbeaten face of the old man, he smiled, his mouth stretched into a falsely hearty grin beneath the flowing white moustache.

'That's the way,' he said as she straightened her back, 'stand tall and face what's to come.'

But what exactly was to come? Nina saw the crippled boat edging painfully nearer. Soon now, she would know the worst, she would know if it was Tom's boat that was lost or if it was Joe who had failed to come home.

From the hillside came a cry, arms were waving, a roar of voices were calling, calling out the name of a skiff.

In blind panic, Nina covered her ears, she could not bear to know, not just yet, she pressed her hands to her head and then all she could hear was the deafening sound of her own fear.

CHAPTER TWENTY-TWO

Eline had been happy to be back in Swansea. Much as she had enjoyed her experience in Somerset she was relieved to return to the safety of her own rooms in Mrs Miller's emporium working on her designs as if she had never been away.

And then the news had come of the disaster in Oystermouth, a sudden storm last night, a freak wave and one of the boats had failed to return from a dredging trip. But no one seemed sure which one. The only information that was clear was that the lost ship belonged to Joe Harries.

Eline was travelling towards Oystermouth now on top of the Mumbles train, her hands twisted in her lap; the *Emmeline* or the *Oyster Sunrise*, which one was it?

In any case, she must be there, the loss of a ship was a disaster, even to a man like Joe who owned two vessels, the financial cost could mean ruin. And casualties, no one seemed clear about that. Even now she could be a widow and Eline felt her heart contract. Much had passed between her and Joe, he had humiliated her by bringing home his pregnant woman and yet he was dear to Eline in some unfathomable way.

Joe had always been there, an old family friend, a strong shoulder to lean on. He had been such a great support when Eline's father had died that she didn't know what she would have done without him.

She had married Joe blindly, unthinkingly, feeling it the only way forward. She had known love for him and it was only much later that she realized the love was not that of a woman for her man.

The horses pulling the train came to a halt and Eline stumbled to her feet. She climbed down from the carriage and stood in the roadway for a moment, trying to pull her shattered thoughts into some semblance of order.

To one side, the sea, innocent enough now, lapped the shore gently. The oyster boats were still fixed to the moorings, a sure sign that Oystermouth was in mourning.

Taking a deep breath, Eline crossed the road and walked the short distance to Joe's house. She could not think of it as *her* house any longer, it belonged to Nina and Joe, they had taken possession of it and suddenly, Eline realized that it didn't matter to her at all.

The door was closed, the curtains drawn against the morning sunlight. Hesitating, Eline pushed open the door, it seemed fatuous to knock, a foolish act of politeness in the circumstances.

Nina was seated near the fire, dressed in black, her hair scraped back from the angular planes of her face. Huge shadows etched lines beneath her eyes, she was clearly a woman in mourning. She looked up at Eline uncomprehendingly for a moment and then recognition followed.

'It's bad,' she said and her tone revealed her hostility towards Eline and yet they were in this tragedy together, they had to talk and Eline's heart started to beat furiously.

'Joe?' she said, hardly able to breathe. Nina looked up at her and bit her lip.

'He's alive,' she said as though realizing Eline didn't know. 'He's broke his back but he's alive.' Once she started to speak it was as though Nina had burst a dam within her and a torrent of words gushed forth.

'Tried to save my Tom, see,' she said in anguish, 'knew the *Oyster Sunrise* was foundering, did Joe.' Her shoulders sagged. 'But it was useless, my boy couldn't survive, not in seas like that.'

244

Eline tried to digest the information Nina was imparting so haphazardly. Tom was dead, young healthy Tom, Nina's son, was dead.

'Joe, where is he?' Eline said softly, pushing the kettle on the fire, Nina looked as if she could do with some comfort.

'In the hospital,' Nina answered. 'Nothing they can do for him, mind, anyone could see his spine has gone, finished he is.' Suddenly she looked heavenward. 'Oh God, what have I done to deserve all this punishment? I loved a man too much that was all.'

'Hush now,' Eline said firmly, 'it's not your fault, none of it, accidents happen at sea, you know that as well as I do.' But she was trembling inside. Joe, big strong Joe with his back broken, it didn't bear thinking about.

She made the tea quickly and stirred a spoonful of honey into Nina's cup.

'Anyone else hurt?' she asked, her mind racing over what Nina had said. Eline tried to picture her husband as an invalid but she just couldn't believe it.

'Skipper George's boys drowned at sea like my Tom. Brought in early this morning they were, the three young men in the prime of their lives, God rest their souls. Put them in the church they have, laid them out in their last resting place.' Her voice trailed off and tears ran silently down her face.

'Do you know what it's like to lose your son?' she asked abruptly. 'Flesh of your flesh born in pain and anguish?'

'I'm so sorry,' Eline said, the enormity of the tragedy sweeping over her. She sank into a chair and drank her tea, her hands trembling as she lifted the cup to her lips.

'Course you don't know,' Nina said dully, 'how could you? You're just a bit of a girl yourself.'

She looked into Eline's face intently. 'I've wronged you,' she said urgently, 'I've wronged you and I must

245

pay for it, but I didn't expect the reckoning to be so high.'

'It was an accident,' Eline repeated her earlier words, 'nothing you did could make it happen or prevent it. What did Skipper George do to lose both his sons then? Ask yourself that, Nina.'

But Nina wasn't listening, she put her head in her hands and her shoulders were shaking with the depths of her distress.

After a moment's hesitation, Eline went to her and held Nina in her arms, rocking her to and fro. There were no words she could say, no comfort she could offer for Nina's life seemed in ruins, her son dead, her lover laid low in hospital, his livelihood gone. Nina must be wondering what more could happen to her.

The door opened and Gwyneth Parks entered the room, but it was not the girl Eline saw. Behind her was Will, his hat held respectfully in his hands, his face sombre. And yet his eyes lit up when he saw Eline, or did she imagine it?

'Mam, you're to come home with me,' Gwyneth ignored Eline and spoke directly to Nina. 'There's nothing for you here now, you come back to our house where I can keep an eye on you.'

Nina made an effort to pull herself together. She shook her head and wiped away her tears with her fingers.

'How can I go?' she asked pitiously. 'I must look after Joe when he comes home.'

Gwyneth caught her mother's arm. 'You are not his *wife*,' she said fiercely, 'let *her* see to him, she's tied by her vows, you are not tied by anything, Mam.'

Eline was suddenly filled with fear, to come back here, to nurse Joe for the rest of his life, to give up her hopes of a bright future in the shoemaking business, how could she bear it? And then shame engulfed her, how could she think such selfish thoughts at a time like this?

'I hardly think that's fair.' Will was speaking, looking

down at Gwyneth, his brows drawn together in a frown. 'Joe preferred your mother, took her into his home, she can't desert him now.'

Gwyneth glanced up at him. 'You don't understand our ways, Mr Davies, here in Oystermouth, we look after our own. My mam isn't well, she hasn't got over losing Joe's babbi yet and I don't know how her nerves will stand losing Tom as well. No, Joe is not Mam's responsibility, that's his wife, her over there.'

She nodded to where Eline was standing. 'She's here, isn't she, laying her claim in case she's going to become a widow? What would my mam do if Joe died? She'd have to get out of here then, wouldn't she, and no thanks to her.'

In a sudden sense of clarity, Eline knew that Gwyneth, hard as her words might be, was right. If Joe died, Nina would have nothing, be nothing, not in the eyes of the law.

'Go on home, Nina,' Eline said softly, 'your daughter speaks sense. I'll look after Joe, it's my duty.'

Will made to speak again, but Eline shook her head slightly and he fell silent.

'Let me go to see him at least,' Nina was saying, 'let me speak to Joe, explain things to him.'

'No,' Gwyneth shook her head, 'what is there to explain, Mam? Come on, we're going home. We've got our dead to bury, mind, and if it wasn't for Joe Harries our Tom would be alive now.'

She drew her mother towards the door and glanced back over her shoulder for a moment. 'Anything of Mam's you can send over later, right?' She paused and there was a look almost of pity in her eyes. 'I got to look out for my mam, you understand?'

Eline nodded without replying and then she was staring at Gwyneth's back. Will moved towards her and stood looking down at her without touching her.

'If there's anything I can do, just let me know,' he said

247

softly. Eline lifted her head and took a deep breath. 'I've got to work,' she said in a rush, 'I have to earn a living if I'm to look after Joe. And yet Swansea is five miles away. Oh Lord, how am I going to manage?'

She sat down in a chair, her legs trembling and, after a moment, Will came and crouched down beside her.

'You are welcome to work for me,' he comforted her. 'I can't pay much, you know that, but I'll help you all I can.' Gently he touched her face.

'Are you sure this is the right thing to do, Eline, why should you give up everything for a man who betrayed you?'

'He's my husband,' Eline said simply, 'there's nothing else I can do.'

Will rose to his feet and nodded. 'When you are ready to start work just come along to the shop. Take care, Eline, my love.' The last words were almost a whisper and then Will was gone and the silence of the kitchen pressed down heavily on Eline as she looked around her.

Emily Miller sat in the window of Summer Lodge looking towards the sea, remembering the days when she lived in the house as a young carefree girl, the apple of her father's eye. She had been so easily pleased then, so shallow, so intolerant. Who would have thought that she would be sitting here now as a guest of the very girl she'd looked down on, almost despised?

'What are you thinking about Emily?' said Hari Grenfell, rich and successful now, elegantly attired, beloved wife of Craig Grenfell, Emily's cousin.

'The old days,' Emily replied. 'I was such a heartless little snob then.'

'Oh, I don't know,' Hari smiled, 'I suppose you were a bit of a snob but no more than anyone else of your station.'

'I was insufferable,' Emily argued, 'I think I looked down on you always, even when you were obviously so much more talented than me.' She paused and sighed. 'It was only when you saved my life that time I fell sick with yellow fever that I realized we were all cast from the same mould, none of us immortal.'

'Deep thoughts, Emily,' Hari mused, 'what's brought this on?'

'Oh, I'm so sorry for Eline Harries, I suppose that's what it is,' Emily said. 'Her husband has been badly injured, you know, and won't work again, ever.'

'I know,' Hari said softly, 'Will told me.'

'She reminds me of you.' Emily continued, 'so young, so talented, what a waste it's going to be her leaving the emporium.'

'It needn't be,' Hari said and Emily looked at her curiously.

'What do you mean?' Emily leaned forward in her chair, her eyes alight, wondering what Hari had in mind. Hari had a fertile imagination but also the courage to put her imaginings into practice.

'We could let her work from home,' Hari said. 'She can make designs just as well on her kitchen table as seated at an elegant desk in your place.'

Emily smiled. 'Trust you to come up with a practical solution to the problem.'

'Well, like you, I think it a pity if Eline Harries doesn't get the chance she deserves.' She looked down at her hands. 'According to William, Eline is taking on far too much.'

'In what way?' Emily's curiosity was aroused, Eline spoke little of her private life but it was clear she had parted from her husband which in itself showed great strength, coming from the sort of background she did.

'Her husband had taken in a woman, a woman who was pregnant by him. Sadly, she lost the baby but decided to remain where she was, with Eline's husband. But when he was so badly injured, the woman couldn't cope and so she returned to her own home.'

249

Emily nodded. 'That's just what I had gathered from the little Eline told me. I think Eline felt it was no more than her duty to look after the man, he is still her husband, after all.'

'But she needn't let her talent go to waste, all the same,' Hari said firmly. 'I mean to help her all I can.'

Emily smiled. 'No one helped you,' she said drily, 'you made the grade all on your own.'

'Not quite,' Hari returned her smile, 'I had good friends.'

Emily rose to her feet. 'I must get back. I've the pleasure of the company of John's daughter tonight.' She shrugged. 'How Sarah dare show her face around here after what she did, I don't know, but she has the hide of an elephant.'

Emily saw Hari's face darken. 'I know she's no good,' she said quickly, 'and she hurt you badly but I have to make an effort for John's sake. She's bringing home a young man, a Mr Frogmore, I hope she might marry him and have done with it, at least she'd be out of my hair then.' Emily sighed as she moved towards the door.

'The trouble is she's still John's daughter, he loves her and like most men he's blind to her faults. He firmly believes she was led astray by Sam Payton that time . . .' Emily's voice trailed away as she looked at Hari's set expression.

'Anyway,' she said, 'I'll sit politely through dinner, be charming to this young man and pray that he takes Sarah off my hands.' She brushed back a stray curl of hair.

'I still fear that one day she might take Pammy away from me,' she said in a small voice.

'Don't worry about that!' Hari spoke reassuringly. 'Not if she has a young man in tow, she won't want him to know she's got an illegitimate child, will she?'

'I suppose not,' Emily bit her lip. 'I'll see you soon, Hari, and we'll talk again.'

She left Summer Lodge and climbed into her carriage

and, as she turned and looked back at the old house mellow in the sunshine, Emily wondered at the store she'd once set by it. All she'd longed for was to own Summer Lodge once more, how bitter she'd been when her cousin had inherited the house. Now she didn't give a fig, a house was just a building. She had John, she loved him dearly and she would forgive him anything, even his blind spot where his daughter was concerned.

Later, as Emily presided over the dinner table, she looked at the rather thin young man Sarah had brought to her home and wondered what the girl saw in him. Geoffrey Frogmore was an intelligent young man but then Sarah's needs were more physical than cerebral.

'More fish, Mr Frogmore?' Emily said politely, but the young man declined with a shake of his head. He was nice, Emily decided, too nice by far for a hussy like Sarah. And yet selfishly, Emily couldn't help hoping that the liaison would be serious. She wasn't disappointed.

After dinner, John retired to the drawing room with young Mr Frogmore and Sarah leaned forward excitedly.

'He's asking Dad for my hand in marriage,' she said brightly. 'What do you think of him, Emily?'

'He seems very nice,' Emily spoke guardedly, 'but what of his prospects? That's the sort of question your father will be asking.' Privately Emily thought Mr Frogmore couldn't be of great means if he was lodging at Mrs Marsh's house in Oystermouth. But it seemed she was wrong.

'He's very rich,' she said, 'he and his father have been looking for property in the area, they want to buy a fine house, especially now that Geoffrey wishes to be married.'

Sarah spoke quite well, Emily realized suddenly, her travels around various parts of the country before she had settled in Port Eynon had mellowed her accent, softened it so that she sounded quite genteel.

'Do you love him?' Emily regretted the question almost as soon as it was spoken; it was the question of

251

a concerned mama not of a step-mother who wanted nothing more than to be rid of the girl.

'Love! That's got nothing to do with it.' The scorn in Sarah's voice made Emily aware that Sarah had not changed one iota from the heartless little whore she had always been. She smothered the bitter thoughts. Sarah was John's daughter, surely she could not be all bad?

In the past Sarah had had a difficult time, had been used by Sam Payton, a man who was older and more ruthless than she was. She'd thrown away the love of William Davies for the privilege of being with a villain of the first order and where was he now? Would Payton ever return to Swansea and pose a threat to Emily's peace of mind?

When the ladies went into the drawing room, John was smiling and it was clear he approved of Geoffrey Frogmore and his intention to marry Sarah.

Later, he took Emily aside. 'This is a fine chance for my girl,' he said, 'she can make an honest wife to a good man, wipe out the past and perhaps in time be accepted in Swansea.'

Emily doubted that but she kept her own counsel and joined in the celebratory drink that John pressed on her.

'To my dear daughter and her new fiancé,' he said raising his glass and smiling happily around him.

Men were so simple sometimes, Emily thought indulgently, John believed that now everything would be all right, Sarah would reform and behave herself as a daughter should. Well, time would tell. In the mean time, Emily was content that Sarah no longer wanted to accept Pammy as her own, she had other concerns now, the most important one was to convince her husband that she was a model of virtue.

Feeling almost happy for the first time since Sarah had returned to Swansea, Emily accepted another drink from John and sipped it slowly, her eyes resting with hope on the happy couple.

CHAPTER TWENTY-THREE

Eline was prepared, at least in practical terms, for Joe's homecoming. With help from Carys and Sam, she had brought the bed down into the little-used parlour and set it up against the far wall so that Joe could look out into the garden and the sea beyond.

Was it cruel, she wondered, to allow him to look at that which he couldn't have? Let him watch the sea in all her moods never to sail on her again? Eline could not be sure of anything with Joe, not in the long days since the accident.

He blamed himself for Tom's death, a reaction, thought Eline, that was to be expected but the bitterness and anger with which he treated Nina's failure to come to the hospital and her apparent rejection of him was something Eline had not bargained for.

She made her way purposefully upstairs to the large bedroom at the front of the house. The floorboards were bare except for a few rag mats and the only furniture was a table and chair placed before the window to capture the light. Eline intended to work here in the little spare time she had from serving in Will's shop.

The shop. The taut lines of her young face softened as she thought of her days spent with William. She could almost be happy when she was serving customers or, better still, changing the window display. Will's nearness, too, was a comfort, though honourably, he never gave so much as a hint that he wanted their relationship to be anything more intimate than employer and employee.

The presence of Gwyneth Parks was the one flaw in

an otherwise happy working arrangement. She had resented Eline from the first moment and made her hate of Joe Harries painfully obvious.

Eline sighed in apprehension; she had taken the day off because today, Joe was coming home. Eline glanced down from her window and saw that the van bearing the name of William Davies Boot and Shoe Store stood outside the house. The moment had come: from now on her life would be harder than it had ever been before.

She hurried downstairs and saw Sam Morgan standing beside the van, smiling at her encouragingly. Sam had volunteered to drive the van loaned by Will and rigged out with a comfortable couch to the hospital.

'Ready for the great day then, missis?' Sam was bluff and short of small talk but he was kindly and Eline knew she was going to be glad of his presence before the morning was out.

Carys came to stand in the doorway, her baby in her arms. 'Good luck,' she mouthed the words, knowing more than her husband about Joe's moods, having shared Eline's confidences. Eline rushed over and hugged Carys in an uncharacteristic gesture of affection. If it wasn't for Carys who had agreed to keep an eye on Joe during the daytime, Eline would have been unable to work. She and Joe would have been penniless.

There was the *Emmeline* of course; the boat, though old, was seaworthy and would fetch quite a bit of money if Joe would only agree to part with her. Up until now he had been obdurate on the matter, the *Emmeline* was his, he would not give her up.

Eline climbed into the van and, as Sam flicked the reins and set the horse jerking forward between the shafts, she took a deep breath. Joe was coming home and her life would be dedicated to caring for him, and, she vowed, there would be no looking back now.

★   ★   ★

Nina Parks stared out of the window watching the van that was going to bring Joe home and her body seemed to ache with the pain of it all. She should be sitting up in front with the driver bringing her man home to care for him. What must the neighbours be thinking of her?

Nina looked round the spotless kitchen; it seemed alien to her now, a strange place that was no longer her home. There was no Tom to come in making a mess on the clean floor with his dirty boots, no sound of happy laughter round the table. Sal was a rare visitor these days and Fon had enough to contend with up on Honey's Farm. And as for Gwyneth, she had her job in the shop to keep her occupied.

Nina dragged herself away from the window and went over to the fire, stoking it up, moving the coals about with the poker. She felt cold, the weather had turned chilly, September was nearly out and the days were drawing in, the evenings dark and dismal now.

Nina wondered for the hundredth time if she'd made the right decision giving up her place in Joe's home. There she would have been useful, needed, there she would have a purpose in life. What purpose did she serve sitting looking at these four walls?

Damn Gwyneth for acting so hastily, dragging Nina away home without giving her time to think things out. 'Joe, my lovely boy what have I done?' Nina covered her face with her hands and pressed back the hot tears.

Gwyneth, she knew, blamed Joe for Tom's death but Nina understood her man well enough to realize Joe would have fought tooth and nail to save their son.

Nina made herself a cup of tea and then let it cool untouched on the table. She had nothing, a woman alone and scorned, a woman who couldn't even do her duty by her man but run out on him the minute the going got tough. How she hated herself.

She hurried upstairs and quickly made the beds, smoothing down the patchwork quilts with unnecessary care for no one else would see them but Gwyneth. No man would ever lie beneath the quilts again, holding her close whispering words of love.

At last, Nina heard the rumble of the van outside the house and she rushed to the door, pulling on her shawl with hasty careless fingers.

It seemed the whole of the village had turned out to see Joe come home. Nina remained on the fringe of the crowd, a sick feeling in the pit of her stomach.

A cheer went up as Joe was lifted on a stretcher and carried from the van into the house. Nina knew she had no right to be there, she was an intruder, a nobody. Joe must despise her now, deserting him when he most needed her.

Nina thought of the comfort they could have shared, each buoying up the other with memories of Tom – memories that would, in time, have been all good with the bitterness wiped away. She became aware that heads were turning to look at her and she felt a flash of her old spirit, so, placing her hands on her hips, she confronted the curious stares.

'What are you all gawping at?' she demanded and slowly, the crowd began to disperse. The door to Joe's house closed suddenly and Nina felt as though she had been slapped in the face. No one closed their doors, not in Oystermouth Village.

'Go home, Nina, girl.' Skipper George stood beside her, the only kindly face in a sea of hostility. Nina put out her hand remembering that he, too, had suffered a loss.

Nina was suddenly gripped by an overwhelming urge to be near her son. 'Come with me to the grave, for pity's sake.' The words were whispered but Skipper George heard them. He took her arm and guided her away from Joe's house and along the street to the gentle hill leading to the graveyard.

The graves were planted with a few late roses, the

fresh earth like a scar on the land. There were no headstones yet for stones cost time and money.

Nina sank to her knees; she was not a religious woman, never went to the services, never listened to the bells calling the faithful to prayer, and yet how many times had she prayed for her menfolk when storms pounded the coast or when ice threatened to weigh down a boat so that nothing would work on board?

She saw the skipper doff his hat and his thick white hair lifted in the cold wind that blew in from the sea. He was a good man and there were lines of suffering on his face as he stood, head bowed, before the graves of his sons.

Nina felt in that moment that somehow she must make amends for all the wrong she had done in her life. She had sinned so much, could she ever find salvation?

She felt she needed forgiveness initially from the living; she would go to see Joe and beg to be allowed to help in whatever way she could. She rose from her knees feeling a new resolve; she would shake off the past and try in future to be worthy of respect. She glanced up at the skipper and met his far-seeing blue eyes.

'Can someone like me, who has taken another woman's husband, ever find forgiveness, George?' she asked humbly.

George smiled. '*Duw*, you're asking a bright spark about forgiveness, my love. But the worst of sinners can repent, if the good book means what it says.'

Nina sighed. 'All I can do is try,' she said softly. 'That's all anyone can do.'

Eline watched anxiously as Joe was carried into the parlour and carefully lowered on to the bed. He groaned a little and Eline bit her lip seeing the pain etched on his face.

She carefully drew the blankets up over his broken body and smoothed back a lock of hair that had fallen

257

over his forehead. His hair felt dry, full of salt and Eline wondered just how she would set about washing it.

There were so many little tasks that she would have to master, she realized with a sickening lurch of uncertainty. Could she cope with Joe's needs and with a job? In that moment of almost blind panic, she doubted it.

There was a sudden sound of voices as some of the neighbours came to welcome Joe home. Eline let them in and they crowded around Joe, wishing him well. He smiled and nodded though he spoke little and all the time Eline could see that the strain was telling on him.

'I think it's time Joe had a little rest now,' she said at last and Carys was the first to nod her head approvingly.

'Aye, Eline is right,' she raised her voice, 'come on friends, give the man a chance, is it?'

The well-meaning visitors began to disperse and Sam Morgan was the last to leave.

'I'll take the van back, shall I?' he asked and Eline nodded in gratitude.

'If you can spare the time, Sam, it would be a great help,' she said, 'and give our thanks to Will – Mr Davies, won't you?'

'I'll do that.' He left the house and led the horse towards the roadway and Eline watched until the clip-clop of the animal's hoofs faded into silence.

Glancing across the street, Eline caught a glimpse of Nina Parks, hugging her shawl around her shoulders. There was something in the woman's eyes that Eline didn't understand and in a sudden spurt of anger, Eline slammed the door shut.

'Well, Joe,' she said brightly, 'glad to be home, are you, love?'

'Don't talk daft, woman,' Joe said sourly. 'Why should I be glad about anything when I'm lying here on my back unable to move? Unfeeling as the planks on a deck you are.'

Eline took a deep breath, she had not expected gratitude, neither had she expected this blast of criticism. She was doing all she could for Joe and that was a fat lot more than Nina Parks was doing.

'Are you hungry?' She forced herself to speak pleasantly. 'I've got some soup ready, nice and thin it is with carrots and parsnips and . . .'

'For God's sake shut up, woman!' Joe said irritably, 'I don't want you blathering on, treating me like a child or an idiot. If I'm hungry I've got a tongue in my head, I'll ask, right?'

'Right, Joe.' Eline felt her patience slipping but she tried again. 'I hope the journey home wasn't too awful for you.'

'You had to go and get *his* van, didn't you?' Joe said sharply. 'Rubbing it in that you got Will Davies breathing all over you just waiting to get his hands on you. Well, you needn't think you are going to carry on working for him because you're not, understand?'

Eline drew a chair up beside the bed and took one of Joe's calloused hands in hers. 'Listen to me, love,' she said and her tone was gentle but firm. 'Let there be no lies between us, we'll start as we mean to go on.'

'Oh aye, going to tell me how lucky I am now that you are standing by me, is that it?' Joe turned his face away from her.

'I'm going to tell you the facts of our life together as I see them,' Eline said. 'You can like it or lump it but I've got to work, otherwise we'll starve. No one but Will Davies has offered me a job and in any case it wouldn't be convenient for me to work anywhere else.'

'Well, you would say that,' Joe growled. 'Could clean and cook in one of the big houses, couldn't you?'

'And live in?' Eline asked. 'Who would look after you then? As it is, I am only a few hundred yards away down the road, I can come home and give you food at dinner

259

time and when the shop closes, I'll be home in just a few minutes.'

'So, I'm to stay alone all day?' Joe's voice faltered and Eline felt pity for her husband sweep over her. It occurred to her suddenly that Joe was afraid of being alone.

'No love, not alone, not entirely anyway. Carys is going to pop in from time to time make sure you're all right.' She rose and moved away from the bed wondering if she had the strength to carry on with what seemed such a grinding, difficult routine. Every day would be the same; she would spend her days in the shop and her evenings cleaning the house and washing Joe's sheets. She squared her shoulders.

'It's the best I can do, Joe.' Her voice quivered in spite of herself and she bit her lip not wanting Joe to realize how very frightened she was, too.

'We'll work it out, *cariad*.' His voice was softer now, less hostile. 'Give it time and I'll be on my feet again, you'll see.'

Eline doubted that; the doctors had not been at all optimistic about a recovery but then doctors could be wrong and in any case she couldn't take away Joe's feelings of hope.

Eline slept badly that night. She had made up her bed in the spare room away from the sounds of the roadway. And yet she was tense, listening for any signs of restlessness from Joe and, when she did sleep, nightmares haunted her.

She woke unrefreshed and heavy-eyed and as she made her way downstairs, she tried her best to feel cheerful for Joe's sake. She would light the fire, make his breakfast and then get off to work. The thought of work and Will had the effect of lightening her spirits so that when Eline went into the parlour she could smile with genuine good humour.

Joe, however, was not smiling. 'Get me to the privvy,

for God's sake.' The words harshly spoken greeted Eline and blushing, she realized that her husband's needs were going to be of a far more intimate nature than she'd anticipated. It was impossible, she would never get Joe out to the back where the privvy stood, she would have to carry him bodily and she simply wasn't capable of such a feat.

She stood for a moment in bleak despair, wondering if she should go next door and ask for Sam Morgan's help but would Joe put up with the lack of privacy that bringing in the neighbours would entail?

She glanced around her in panic and then her eyes lit upon the old, dusty commode that had stood in the corner of the parlour for years, looking as innocent as an ordinary chair.

'I'll fetch the commode,' she said with relief and hurriedly dragged the heavy chair nearer to the bed. She lifted the seat to reveal the old chamber-pot, which had never been used as far as Eline knew unless by Joe's long-dead parents.

The effort of getting him out of bed was almost beyond her; Eline caught Joe around the waist and half-lifted, half-pulled him into place on the commode.

She turned her face away from him, knowing how awful he must feel.

'Christ!' he said bitterly. 'I'm a grown man and I am to live my life as a child. I'm to be fed and potted and washed and dried – I might as well be dead.'

'Don't say that, Joe.' Eline saw to him with as little fuss as possible. At last, making sure Joe was comfortable, she took the chamber-pot outside.

Later, when she had lit the fire, she cooked Joe a breakfast of bacon and eggs and set it on a tray with a fresh pot of tea on the side.

'I've got to get off to work now, Joe,' she said quickly. 'I'll be back at dinner time and Carys will be in later to see if you want anything.'

Joe didn't reply, he turned his back to her and after a moment, Eline left the house. As she walked along the road she was already bone weary; lack of sleep and the sheer hard effort of lifting Joe had made her spirits sink to an all-time low. How could she go on living such an existence? It surely was asking too much of her.

At the door of the boot and shoe store, she turned and looked back along the roadway, her hand to her throat, her heart beating swiftly. Someone was entering the house, a woman and from where she was standing, Eline had the definite impression that the woman was Nina Parks.

CHAPTER TWENTY-FOUR

Nina Parks walked right into Joe's house without hesitating; she didn't feel like an intruder, after all, she had lived there as mistress for some time, it was her home too. And in any case, the time had come for her to make amends with Joe for deserting him when he needed her. She must look after Joe, see to his bodily needs, it was her duty. His wife had gone out and left him alone, hadn't she? Eline didn't give a fig for Joe's comfort or his state of mind.

She had watched from her window as Eline passed on her way to work in Will Davies's shop and bitterness overwhelmed her. Nina had had everything in the palm of her hand and now she had given Joe back to his dear little wife. Well, Eline would have no chance to deny her, everything would be settled before Eline came home, Nina would be back in her rightful place once more.

Nina stood beside Joe's bed and smiled down at him, affection rising within her for the man he had once been. It hurt her to see him brought low, like a wounded animal, earthbound and with much of the spirit knocked out of him.

'Hallo, love,' she said, rolling up her sleeves, 'I've come to help out.'

Joe glowered at her. 'So you've come, have you? How good of you.'

'Don't be like that, Joe.' Nina knelt beside him. 'I know I should never have gone away from here but I thought it was what you and *she* wanted.'

'Is that why you never came to see me in the hospital?' he demanded angrily.

'I'm sorry about that, Joe, but I'm not your wife, mind, I had no rights to come to the hospital to see you, they all made sure I knew that, too.'

'Who do you mean by "they"?' Joe asked and Nina shrugged. 'A lot of the villagers, Eline herself, you know how it is, Joe. Anyway, I'm here now, now that *she* is out of the way. Come on, what would you like me to do, give you a lovely wash down first, is it?'

Joe's relief at Nina's presence overcame his bad humour and she could see that he was glad that she'd come.

'Aye, whatever you like.' He paused. 'I've been going mad lying here thinking all sorts of thoughts. I don't want to be alone all day and every day, that's no sort of life for any man, I'd rather be out of it.'

'And what do you mean by that sort of nonsense?' But Nina knew Joe, lying abed helpless and hopeless was not for him. He would want watching, otherwise he would be tempted to find a way out of his pain, for good.

'Well, never mind all that, you are here now,' Joe said. 'I can bear it so long as I'm not alone.'

'That's right, cheer up, show the guts you've always shown,' Nina replied and there was a break in her voice. She made an effort to gain control of herself before she spoke again.

'I've brought some nice chicken for you,' Nina said changing the subject. 'Cooked it already I have, I'll soon knock up a lovely crusty pie, you'll see.'

Nina went to the pantry and brought out some flour, she knew just where to put her hand on things. Wasn't this her kitchen more than it had ever been Eline's?

'I'll make you a nice meat pie for your supper,' she called through to the parlour, banging the rolling-pin against the scrubbed table-top in the kitchen. 'I know just how you like it, Joe, and as for your Eline, she will have to like it or lump it.'

She was setting out the rules; Nina was telling Joe that

she was here to help but not to take second place to his wife. Nina would come and go as it pleased her.

Joe understood her and swallowed his disappointment. He could do with Nina around him all the time now, a grown woman who knew how to nurse a man not a young untried girl who put her work first. It was as though Nina, wise as usual, read his thoughts. 'Got some guts that wife of yours,' she smiled to herself as she rubbed the fat into the flour, 'got herself a job, didn't she?'

'How come you are so nice about Eline, all of a sudden?' Joe's voice drifted to where Nina worked at the dough, moulding it with strong fingers.

'I don't say I like her taking over here, Joe,' Nina spoke bitterly, 'but she can earn money to keep you and it seems I can't. Tried for work on the perches I have, but no one wants me, see. Too old I spects.'

She lined the enamel dish with pastry and placed the chicken pieces inside. Deftly, Nina made a gravy from onions and chicken fat and added it to the meat. Lastly, she placed a funnel in the middle of the meat and covered the dish with a pastry cap.

'I'll just brush this over with some milk,' she called, 'then how about a nice cup of tea, Joe?'

She was sitting down beside his bed sipping from one of the cups she herself had brought to Joe's house when the door was pushed open and Carys Morgan came into the parlour, a look of surprise crossing her plump, good-natured face.

Nina smiled at her. 'Don't worry, Carys, I'm not here to cause mischief, I'm going to help out all I can until Joe is better, I owe him that much.'

Carys rubbed her hands on her apron. 'I was just going to make a cup of tea, the baby is fast asleep and I've got a spare few minutes. Promised Eline I did that I'd watch out for Joe, see?'

'No need,' Nina said positively, 'I know you're busy

what with your baby and your own house to keep, I'll talk to Eline when she gets home, she'll be right glad that I'm able to help, you'll see.'

'I'm glad enough of the company, mind,' Joe spoke for the first time. 'I know you're a good neighbour, Carys, but I'll go mad if I'm alone most of the day, you can see that, can't you?'

'Aye, I can see that,' Carys said. 'But will Eline see it that way?' Carys had clearly made up her mind to speak bluntly. 'Nina has been living with you, sharing your bed, isn't it going to be hard for Eline to have her here now taking charge of things?'

'We'll see about it when she comes home from work,' Nina said soothingly. 'And if she don't like it, I'll go away and leave her be.'

'Right then,' Carys retorted stiffly, 'I'll leave you to it.' She went out and Nina grimaced at Joe. 'Don't approve, does she?' she smiled. 'Neither will Eline at first but I'm sure she'll see the sense of it after a bit of thought.'

Joe's eyes were closing in weariness and Nina took the cup away from his big, clumsy hands.

'Have a sleep, you, I'll peel a few potatoes and then see what green vegetables you got here.'

'Nina,' Joe's voice stopped her as she made to leave the room, 'if it gets too much for you, looking after me, you'll help me out of my misery, won't you? You know what I mean.'

Nina knew exactly what he meant and after a moment, she replied, 'No need for any of that talk, I'm going to do my best to make you better, Joe, but I give you my word that if I can't make you better I'll help you out.'

In the kitchen, she knelt on the square, multi-coloured rag mat and put her hands together in prayer.

'Dear Lord, I know it's a sin to take a life but you must understand, I can't see Joe helpless and hopeless like this. If it is your will then make him right again and if not . . .' She shrugged eloquently knowing she would be understood by Him above.

By the time Eline came home at dinner time, Nina had prepared a meal of bread and cheese. The pie she would keep for Joe's supper, all Eline would have to do was to put it out on to plates.

If Eline was angry, she concealed it well until she and Nina were alone in the kitchen with the doors closed.

'Now, what do you think you are doing in *my* house, creeping in behind my back?' Eline said with soft, controlled fury.

'I'm keeping Joe company, looking after him properly, because he needs it.' Nina replied defiantly. 'Do you know he was talking about doing away with himself? Is that what you want? Because that's what will happen if he's left alone too long.'

Eline sank into a chair and put her hands over her face and for a moment, Nina almost felt sorry for her. Then common sense reasserted itself; Eline didn't love Joe and didn't really want him, she was offering him only cold charity and he knew it.

'Let's leave things as they are for now, is it?' Nina suggested. 'At least until Joe is more himself.'

Eline remained silent and she accepted the meal Nina put before her without looking up. 'I'll take it into the parlour and sit with Joe,' she said stiffly and Nina could only admire the girl's control.

Nina watched as Eline bent and kissed Joe but the kiss was not the salute of a lover, but rather the affectionate kiss of a dutiful daughter.

'I need Nina, do you understand, girl?' Joe asked, his eyes anxious. 'Nina is such a comfort, she cares, see, and with all the best will in the world you can't expect me to be alone all day, how am I going to manage . . . things?' He looked away. 'Well, things I couldn't ask a neighbour to see to, you know.'

Eline's eyes sought Nina's. 'All right,' she said simply,

'if you can take care of Joe then I've got nothing more to say on the subject.'

Nina suppressed the sudden rush of triumphant tears. 'That's all right then,' she said briskly, 'it's settled.'

Joe laughed suddenly, a real hearty sound. 'Who would have thought it,' he said, 'my wife and my mistress breaking bread together?'

'Don't push your luck now, Joe,' Nina said angrily, 'we will never see eye to eye, mind, but it's you who comes first right now.'

Nina regarded Eline surreptitiously, the girl looked so very young and vulnerable that pity tugged briefly at her heart. Eline's eyes were shadowed with blue and she was far too thin for her own good. But then why pity Eline? She had everything.

With a pang, Nina thought of her own daughter Fon, Fon who was fey and mystical, dipping into her Bible at odd hours of the day. She would need her faith now to endure the future ordeal for when the lady of the house passed away, Fon would be the mainstay of the family. Were her shoulders too small to bear the load?

And yet Fon, like Eline, had a built-in strength beneath that delicate exterior; it was big hefty women like Nina herself who needed love and guidance.

Nina began to clear away the dishes, leaving Joe alone with his wife. There was nothing between them, Nina realized that. Eline and Joe were ill-matched, he following an obsession that he called love and she looking for a father.

Well now the roles had reversed because Eline was the bread-winner and Joe the hapless dependent. How would he live with that kettle of fish? Badly, Nina thought dejectedly.

'I'm going back to the shop now.' Eline came out of the parlour, pulling her good coat on to her slim shoulders. 'Nina, I want to talk to you.' She stood head held high.

'I confess I was angry at first, I saw you coming in here as I went off to work this morning and I felt sick inside. But now I see how good you are for Joe and so I will put up with things as they are. But don't think you can walk in here and take over again because you can't.'

Nina wanted to strike out at the girl; who did she think she was, her with such airs and graces? 'I can do just what I want to do,' she said defiantly.

She watched as Eline turned away and let herself out of the house. Walking quickly, Eline made her way along the Oystermouth Road towards Davies's store and still watching her, Nina wondered if Gwyneth would be giving Eline a hard time. Nina sighed, there was a lot of herself in Gwyneth, a lot that was bad. Well, her daughter would learn life the hard way as she had done.

'Right then Joe, boy,' she said stepping briskly into the parlour, 'let's have a look at them bad legs, see what can be done.'

Eline was happy while she was working in the shop. The hours slipped by so quickly that she had no time to brood on Joe's sickness or the fact that she alone was responsible for keeping the roof over his head and the bread in his mouth.

With Will she kept up an air of formality which at first he had tried to break down but then, defeated, Will accepted that Eline could only work with certain barriers between them.

As the weeks went by Gwyneth was a constant source of irritation to Eline, and she made no secret of the fact that she found William attractive. Indeed her adoration of him must have been a balm to his feelings of hurt and rejection because his attitude to her had become distinctly warmer of late.

Eline deliberately turned her thoughts away from the jealousy that beat at her like dark wings whenever she saw Gwyneth and Will in close conversation; sternly, she told herself it was none of her business.

Eline was pleased and surprised when one morning Mrs Hari Grenfell paid a visit to the shop and asked Will's permission to 'borrow' Eline's services for a day or two.

'I have some designs that I would like you to work on for me.' Hari smiled warmly at Eline. 'I have made children's and men's corrective footwear but haven't ever attempted built-up shoes for ladies. I can't solve the problem of how to conceal the platform and incorporate a decent heel so that the footwear at least looks fashionable.'

Eline looked up at Will who was smiling benevolently at Hari Grenfell. He shrugged and draped a casual arm around Hari's shoulder.

'Who am I to stand in the way of genius?' he asked leaning his head for a moment against hers.

Eline envied the close friendship the two so obviously enjoyed. She could never be like that, not with William, but then their senses were so heightened when they were near each other, awareness crackled between them like dry tinder beneath a match.

'Right then,' Hari Grenfell said confidently, 'if you don't mind, Eline, we'll go back to Summer Lodge and I'll show you what I've done so far.'

Eline had time to glance quickly at Will and then she found herself climbing into Hari's coach. She sank back into the leather seat and rubbed her hand over her eyes.

'I'll have to be home by supper time,' Eline said apologetically and Hari, leaning back against the leather seat, adjusted her full skirts and sighed heavily.

'I know your predicament and I'm sorry about your husband, Eline, but you have even more need to think about your future now.'

Eline bit her lip. 'I *must* make a success of things for Joe's sake,' she said. 'I don't mind hard work, I'll work from morning till night if need be, anything so that I can take care of him.'

'That's the spirit,' Hari replied. She put her hand over Eline's. 'I know I look very rich and successful now, but I had to fight tooth and nail for it.' She paused and looked directly at Eline.

'I was poorer than you can imagine,' she continued, 'in debt and fighting all the odds but I was determined to do it and I can see the same quality in you, Eline. But you shall start off with more than I had because I mean to give you all the help I can and fortunately I have a lot of influence.'

Eline was silent not knowing what to say. She felt humble and grateful but couldn't put her feelings into words.

'You have your talent,' Hari said, 'a great talent and I'm selfish enough to want to nurture that talent so that I can say I had a hand in the career of Eline Harries.'

Eline smiled; she didn't need words, Hari could read her thoughts in her expression.

The design for ladies' shoes was in the throes of construction, drawings lay on the table, discarded designs of all sorts of shoes.

'You see?' Hari sat down on a chair and gestured towards the untidy papers spread over the table. 'I just can't get it right.'

Eline sat down and studied the drawings, then picked up a pencil and a fresh piece of paper. She worked in silence, her brow furrowed while Hari watched her, a contented smile on her face.

Later, Eline sat up straight and stretched her arms above her head. 'I think I've got it.' There was a subdued excitement in her voice that was not lost on Hari.

'Look, you've been working on a high-heeled slipper where it is impossible to hide a built-up sole, but what if you make a ladies' boot with what would almost be a gentleman's heel, large and curved? Add to it a great fold-back cuff from the top of the boot, sweeping round the back to the instep which will effectively conceal the built-up sole.'

'That's fine!' Hari seemed delighted. 'I could make the cuff out of soft pigskin so that it appears almost like a skirt.'

'And if you fringed the edges it would be a ladies' boot with a sort of cloak around it.'

'That's what we'll call it,' Hari said quickly, 'the Eline Cloak Boot. Excellent!'

Eline laughed in joyous amazement, the ideas had bounced off from Hari to herself and back again with great success. 'The Eline Cloak Boot,' she repeated, 'it sounds wonderful.'

'Right, we shall make it all legal, so that you have the financial rewards as well as the credit,' Hari said decisively. 'And we shall go into production immediately.

'You deserve a rest and some refreshment and then, Eline, you must take your rough drawing home and work the design out properly, add a few embellishments, decorate the cuff if you like, but leave a space for my own hand-tooled daffodil which I use as my trade mark on all prototypes.'

Eline was almost too excited to drink the hot sweet tea and as for the tiny cakes, she knew she would never force one down, her throat was dry, constricted with the feverish wish to get on with the drawing as soon as possible.

'I'll see if I can think of variations on the design,' Eline said, 'something suitable for the men as well as the ladies.'

'What a good idea!' Hari agreed. 'I don't see why we shouldn't make as much out of this pattern as we can.'

Later, as Eline sat in the carriage that was taking her home to Oystermouth, she pondered on her good fortune in finding people like Hari Grenfell to take an interest in her work. But she must broaden her horizons;

Eline knew she must not depend entirely on help from Hari, she must begin to make her own way, perhaps design shoes for other businesses and make use of her gift for window dressing into the bargain.

Perhaps the time had come to go it alone, leave the safety and the temptation of working with Will in his shop and be entirely independent. And yet, could she bear to lose touch with him altogether?

When she climbed out of the coach outside her home, Nina Parks was just leaving. 'The supper is ready,' she said, shortly, nodding her head. 'Joe is resting comfortably, I've seen that he's got everything he wants.' Eline went indoors and closed the door on the world but now, there seemed to be a glimmer of hope ahead.

After a few weeks, Joe began to look brighter. He was able to sit up, his back injuries seemed to be less drastic than they had first appeareed. He was still unable to walk but Nina had got someone to make a chair with wheels so that Joe could leave his bed whenever he chose and at least Joe himself seemed more content, less bitter with his lot.

'Good day, love?' he said as Eline came in from work and shrugged off her coat. 'I'm just putting out the plates for our supper. Nina's made us a chicken pie and some baked potatoes to go with it. Have you had a good day?'

'I've had a very good day,' Eline said softly and as she took a cloth and lifted the pie, brown-crusted and succulent, out of the oven on to the table, she smiled to herself. Today she had seen the first of the Eline Cloak Boots go into production and it looked as though the line was going to be a great success.

CHAPTER TWENTY-FIVE

Fon was up all night; between Patrick's frantic cries as he cut his teeth and Katherine's soft moans of pain, she was constantly leaving her bed. And so morning found her heavy-eyed and weary, feeling ill-equipped to face another day.

Fon wondered if she could plead a headache and find the rest she craved but that would leave Jamie in charge and she didn't honestly believe he could cope.

'You're looking pale this morning,' he said as later, Fon handed him his breakfast. Patrick mercifully was still asleep, giving Fon enough time to drink a cup of tea before getting him up and boiling the water for his bath.

'I'm tired,' She didn't see any point in prevaricating. 'I was up most of the night. Poor little Patrick was cutting another tooth and Katherine needed so much attention I hardly had any sleep.'

'You should have called me,' Jamie said guilty at having slept like a log through it all. 'I could have helped a bit.'

'I did think of it,' Fon confessed, 'but you've so much work to do on the farm, what with the early milking and bringing in the last of the hay, I knew you'd have your hands full.'

'Well, you must have a rest this afternoon.' Jamie said earnestly, 'I can't have you falling sick. I would be lost without you.' There was an element of panic in Jamie's voice that Fon recognized, she had felt it herself very often over these last few days. She smiled reassuringly. 'I'm all right, I'm young and strong, remember?'

Jamie looked at her doubtfully, wanting to believe her. 'Well, if I can get back in from the fields, I'll take over and you can go to bed for an hour, right?'

'Right,' Fon said, more to please Jamie than because she had any confidence that he would remember to come in and give her a rest.

When Jamie left, the house fell silent and Fon stood for a moment, drinking in the feeling of peace, steeling herself for the moment when her day would begin in earnest. She decided she would see to Katherine first, while Patrick slept.

Katherine would need to be washed; although her thin frame shrank in pain from the touch of the flannel, she would nevertheless be grateful for the cleansing feel of the water on her skin.

Fon closed her eyes for a moment; never had she known such a terrible, overwhelming feeling of pity for anyone in her life. Katherine was racked with pain but she clung on to life, wanting, she said, to see Christmas with her son before she relinquished herself to the inevitable.

Galvanizing herself into action, Fon poured water from the kettle into a bowl and let it stand while she fetched a fresh towel from the line above the fireplace. Warmth seemed to comfort Katherine and she could do with all the comfort Fon could provide.

'Morning.' Katherine's voice was thread-like but with a note of cheerfulness that belied the transparently taut look on her face.

'Morning,' Fon forced a smile, 'wash time, I'll be as careful as possible, I promise.'

'Just my face and hands for now,' Katherine said softly, 'leave anything else until I'm feeling stronger.' It was an unusual request. Katherine was meticulous about herself, she must be feeling ill, Fon thought in apprehension.

'You had a bad night,' Fon said. 'What if I get

the doctor out, he might give you something to ease you?'

She held Katherine's skeletal fingers and washed them gently.

'Yes, all right,' Katherine said, her voice little more than a gasp of pain. Fon glanced up at her face.

'Worse today, is it?' she asked and Katherine closed her eyes for a moment as if the effort of replying was too much for her. Slowly, she nodded her head.

'I don't think I can hold out for Christmas after all,' she said wearily.

Fon completed her task as rapidly as she could and then smiled reassuringly. 'I'll get Patrick and take him down to the doctor's with me,' she said, 'I won't be long, I promise you.'

With Patrick wrapped in a Welsh shawl, Fon set out for the huddle of houses that clung to the hillside far below Honey's Farm. Patrick was chewing with enjoyment on a crust dipped in honey, for Fon felt there was no time to stop and feed him properly.

The doctor's house stood on its own, a high, mellow, stone building with many windows that gleamed in the pale sunshine.

His wife came to the door. 'The doctor is out on his rounds,' she said, 'but I know he's planning to call on Katherine today some time.'

Fon sighed. 'She's real bad,' she said pleadingly, 'isn't there anywhere I could find Dr Haney, get him to come to Katherine at once?'

'He's gone in the pony and trap, I don't know where to start to look for him. I'm sorry.'

Fon watched, as the doctor's wife moved indoors; she might be sorry but by the look on her face she was used to requests like Fon's. No doubt the doctor's wife had seen a good many people die and learned to take it in her stride.

Fon returned home and set down Patrick to play in

the garden. The small grass patch was fenced in and Patrick would come to no harm playing in the fresh air for a time.

Fon went back into Katherine's room and saw with a dart of anguish that she had tears on her thin cheeks. 'I know I'm weak,' Katherine said in her thread-like voice, 'but I don't think I can stand it any more. Fon, will you help me?'

'I don't know how to,' Fon said desperately. She wished Jamie would come in or that the doctor would call, anyone who could take the responsibility from her, for she knew full well what Katherine was asking.

'The bottle of medicine, in the drawer over there, fetch it for me, Fon, just put it beside me. And water, a glass of water, please, Fon.'

Fon hesitated and then looking into Katherine's haunted, beseeching eyes, she moved across the room and opened the drawer taking out a dark green bottle, staring at it with horrified fascination.

'I'll get you some water,' Fon said, unable to recognize her own voice, 'I won't be a minute.'

She hurried into the kitchen and stood for a moment staring wildly around her. From outside, she could hear Patrick babbling nonsense to himself. She glanced through the window and saw the baby, rounded, plump and healthy, and she shuddered as she thought of the woman in the room across the passageway, dying in pain, wanting only release.

It was against all the good book said, Fon knew that, but she knew, too, that God was merciful, he would not want any one of his creatures to suffer under such a burden.

At last, she plucked up the courage to take the glass of water through to the bedroom and stopped short in her tracks. As though in a dream, Fon saw that the small green bottle was empty, it had fallen from Katherine's fingers and was lying on the quilted cover. She picked

277

it up and stood it on the chest at the bedside, then bit her lip as she looked down at the woman in the bed.

'It's all right,' Katherine whispered, 'it's going to be peaceful now, just look after Jamie and Pat as you promised.'

'I will,' Fon said earnestly, 'I'll never leave them, I give you my word of honour as God is my judge.'

Fon heard the back door open and then the sound of Jamie banging the mud from his boots on the step.

'He's just in time.' Katherine forced a smile, her pain seemed to have gone and the lines of her thin face had eased.

Jamie came in, his stockinged feet making no sound on the boards. He looked eagerly towards the bed and sat down, leaning over his wife.

'I had to come back home,' he said, 'I just felt, strange, I can't explain it.' A variety of expressions fleeted across his face, anxiety, hope, bewilderment and a dawning realization that made his big shoulders slump.

'It's the end, my love,' Katherine whispered, 'but don't be sad, I'm glad to go, so I am.'

Jamie looked up at Fon frantically, as if somehow she could perform a miracle. 'She looks better, doesn't she look better, Fon?' he said pleadingly.

Fon hung her head, her tongue felt as though it had swollen to fill her mouth. Her eyes ached with unshed tears, but she knew it would do no good to break down now, no good at all.

'Katherine, my beautiful girl, you can't leave me,' Jamie said hoarsely. 'Fon,' he turned, 'fetch the doctor, he'll know what to do.'

Katherine was shaking her head. 'Don't fret so,' she whispered, 'the time has come, don't grieve for me, Jamie, love, I'll be looking down on you wishing you all the happiness in the world.'

'How can you say that?' Jamie asked. 'I can't be happy without you, Katherine, you must know that.' He looked over his shoulder at Fon, more desperately this time. 'Fon, the doctor.'

'I've been to fetch him,' she said and her voice sounded distant, odd. 'He'll come as soon as he can, don't you worry, now.'

Katherine looked up at Fon. 'The baby,' she mouthed the words, 'bring him.'

Fon hurried out into the garden, the sun was still shining, a pale, wintery sun but the sun nevertheless. The birds were singing in the chestnut trees that bordered the farm, it might have been a normal November day except that within the farmhouse walls a fine, brave woman lay dying.

Fon picked Patrick up in her arms and he clung to her, nuzzling his head against her shoulder, ready to sleep again like the baby he was.

She took him in to the bedroom and although Katherine's eyes devoured the little boy, Fon knew she would not be strong enough to hold him.

Fon sat on the bed, as close as she dared to Katherine without hurting her. Katherine took her son's hand and smoothed the plump skin, her pale eyes alight with love.

It seemed incongruous to Fon, the whole strange picture: Jamie big, healthy, his skin ruddy from the fresh air; the baby round, bouncing with health; and in the bed, the very picture of death lay Katherine, struggling to breathe her last.

Fon tried to take her mind above the room, above the woman in the bed and her pain; she felt Patrick's plump body heavy in her lap and clung on to the baby as though he could keep her sane.

'The doctor,' Jamie said hoarsely, 'go look for him, Fon, bring him back, *please*.'

Fon handed the baby to Jamie and, with a swift glance at the woman in the bed, moved out of the room. The doctor, however good he might be, could do nothing for Katherine now.

*   *   *

'She seemed frantic,' the doctor's wife said calmly, 'only a young girl she was, too, the one Jamie's taken on to look after the baby, wants you to go up to the farm as soon as possible.'

Doctor Haney was unruffled though his weather-beaten face revealed his feelings of pity. 'Won't do much good,' he said, 'the poor woman is past helping, the sooner she's taken the better.' He moved to the sideboard and poured himself a brandy. Whisky would have been better, or so the old wives would have it; whisky it seemed set the blood flowing while brandy made the blood sluggish and slow. Still a brandy might help him face his trip to the farm-house.

It wasn't poor Katherine he was worried about, it was that husband of hers. Jamie would take it badly, he was a devoted husband and father if ever Haney saw one. Why did bad things always happen to those who didn't deserve it? But then wasn't he past asking that sort of question? If there was a God up there, he didn't ever listen to Dr Terence Haney.

'Hadn't you better get up to the farm then?' his wife asked, a trifle impatiently, Haney thought, something in the young girl's demeanour must have impressed her greatly.

Haney sighed. 'Aye, I'll get up there, no good putting it off I don't suppose.'

He picked up his hat and bag from the hallway and sighed; a doctor was a man not a miracle worker, there was only so much that could be done for a woman suffering an incurable sickness. Perhaps he would do just as well to go back to the old-time remedies used by his grandfather.

Haney smiled grimly to himself; imagine picking some agrimony, distilling the leaves or roots or some such thing and administering it to his patients. Yet were the methods he now had in his possession any more effective? Not, he feared, in this case.

He was just about to climb aboard the trap when he saw the figure of the young girl from the farm running towards him. Haney spent a moment watching the slim figure, admiring the honey-coloured hair and the soft lift of young breasts against linen and the occasional glimpse of a slim ankle beneath white petticoats. He sighed for days gone by and took up the reins of the horse knowing he had a duty to do.

Fon was so relieved to see the doctor, she came to a sudden, breathless stop. 'It's Katherine!' she said, 'Jamie sent me to fetch you, will you come?'

The doctor gestured for her to climb up beside him, moving his bag a little way to accommodate her. Fon took a shuddering breath.

'It may be too late,' she said softly, 'Katherine is very bad.'

She saw Dr Haney nod almost imperceptibly as he shook the reins and clicked his tongue at the animal, causing the horse to jolt forward.

The roadway back up the hill was winding and slow and Fon forced her shaking hands together knowing there was nothing to do but accept the way things were. She could change nothing, not even the doctor could alter the course of events, not now. It was too late, Fon thought, her mind on the green bottle, far too late.

The doctor was a silent man, moody, some said, but Fon had witnessed Dr Haney being kindness itself to Katherine and she had a great deal of respect for him.

At last, he drew the horse to a stop outside the whitewashed farmhouse and climbed down on to the pathway, holding up his hand to Fon.

She jumped down easily and followed the doctor into the dimness of the house.

She heard the sound of wailing and knew with a leap

of her heart that it was a man's voice crying out in anguish. She felt the doctor falter for a moment and then move forward again and close behind him, she entered the bedroom where Katherine lay.

Jamie was clinging to the now sleeping baby, staring down at the figure in the bed. Katherine's eyes were closed, her lids pale blue, almost transparent, but a slight breath ruffled the collar of her cotton nightgown. Katherine was still alive.

Dr Haney laid a hand on Jamie's shoulder, letting it rest there for a moment. Then, he went through the motions of examining Katherine, listening to her faint breathing and touching her emaciated wrist with robust brown fingers that had become as delicate as feathers.

He stepped back and shook his head and Fon saw him glance at the green bottle before picking it up and putting it away in his case. The responsibility now was not all hers, she thought with a tremendous feeling of release.

Katherine's eyes flickered open and for a moment they were clear and lucid. They moved from one to the other, lingering on Fon.

'Remember your promise,' she said. She smiled radiantly at the man she loved and then softly and quietly, Katherine died.

For a long moment there was silence in the room, no-one moved, as if to move would be some sort of sacrilege. It was Dr Haney who broke the spell and covered Katherine's face with the sheet.

'God rest your soul,' he said and turned away quickly. 'Your wife, Jamie,' he said, 'was the bravest woman I know.'

He walked to the door. 'You'll have arrangements to make,' he said, 'make them at once, Jamie, that's my advice.' He left then and Jamie stood as though in a daze.

Fon took Patrick away from him and settled him into

his cot. She brushed the sweat-dampened curls away from his forehead and reluctantly returned to where Jamie was standing like a lost soul in the kitchen.

'She's gone,' he said gesturing in bewilderment, 'Katherine's gone and I don't know what I'm going to do without her.'

Fon stood there uncertainly for a moment and then, feeling as though unseen hands were guiding her, she moved towards him.

'Come on,' she said gently, 'I'm here, I'll look after you.'

He came to her like a child, a big, awkward child and, as Fon folded him in her arms, she knew without a shadow of a doubt that she had found her destiny.

CHAPTER TWENTY-SIX

Eline sat looking through the window of the cottage and wondered at her temerity in leaving Will's shop once and for all.

If she had needed convincing, it was finding Gwyneth and William one morning pouring over the order books together that did it. Their heads were bent close together, shoulders touching and a wave of sick jealousy had washed through her so that for a moment she couldn't breathe. Then common sense reasserted itself, Will was a free agent, she had made it quite clear there could never be anything between them.

Eline knew in that instant, she must leave the shop and allow Will to get on with his life, the best he may. Eline was Joe's wife and always would be until death did them part, so why should she feel she was cutting part of her life adrift?

'You can't mean it,' he said softly when she told him of her decision. It was more difficult to hold firm to her resolve than she had anticipated. 'You need to work and Eline, I need to have you near me, you must realize that.'

Eline shook her head. 'No, what I do realize is that there's no future for us, we always knew it really, didn't we?'

'But how will you manage?' Will asked anxiously. 'I mean how will you live?'

'I'm getting work from Mrs Grenfell and Mrs Miller now,' Eline said firmly. 'I *have* to make my own way in the world, you must see that?' She played her trump card. 'You wouldn't stand in my way, would you, Will?'

She saw the hurt in his face and longed to put her

hands on his cheeks and kiss his dear mouth. She took a deep breath forcing herself to wait for his answer.

'No,' he said at last, 'I wouldn't stand in your way, Eline. I'll make up your wages as soon as possible and see that someone brings them along to you. I take it you want to leave immediately.'

'That would be best.' She forced herself to speak calmly as though every nerve within her wasn't screaming out for him to take her into his arms and hold her close.

Eline found herself out in the grey of the November day, her coat clutched around her against the cold wind coming in from the sea. There was an iciness within her that had nothing to do with the weather. She had seen the look of victory on Gwyneth Parks's face and knew instinctively that the girl would lose no time in making up to Will for Eline's absence.

Joe was sitting up in his chair when Eline reached home and Nina Parks was in the kitchen singing happily to herself. All at once, Eline knew she could not work from home, she was out of place now in the little cottage, and in any case she couldn't put up with Nina Parks's triumphant smile at having cut the ground from under Eline's feet. Eline squared her shoulders knowing she would have to make other arrangements.

'Hallo, not working today?' Nina looked up from the oven, her face flushed with the heat, her hair curling prettily around her forehead and her words were like an accusation.

'I have patterns to take to Mrs Grenfell,' Eline felt bound to explain. 'I just called back for them.

'Want a cup of tea?' Nina asked grudgingly and it was as if Eline was the guest and she the mistress of the house.

'Not just at the moment.' Eline bent to kiss Joe's cheek. 'You're looking better today, love, there's a bit of colour in your cheeks,' she said encouragingly.

285

'Aye, been sitting outside in the fresh sea air,' Joe said, 'watching the boats go out.' There was a world of sadness in his voice and Eline felt guilty that she was so removed from her husband's pain.

'Is there anything you want?' she asked and Joe looked up at her with far-seeing eyes. He shook his head.

'No thanks, *cariad*, I'm being well looked after, couldn't ask for better than I'm getting.'

Was there a reproach in his words? Eline wondered, but Joe suddenly reached out his hand to her. 'And you are earning us a living, what more could I ask?'

Eline picked up her patterns and looked around her, the house gleamed with cleanliness, the smell of cooking permeated the air and her own presence seemed entirely unnecessary. Eline returned to the street and, without a backward glance, walked briskly towards the train terminus. If there was bitterness in Joe's voice, she mused, she couldn't blame him, his life was full of frustrations. And yet so was hers. She had to think for them both, work to make enough money to keep them sheltered and clothed. It was a job she would not shirk but she could not help being saddened and angry that her efforts were taken for granted.

Eline had tried to persuade Joe to sell the *Emmeline*, tried to make him see that the boat would take a great deal of maintenance being so old. 'In any case,' she had said, 'when you are better you will be in a position to buy another boat, what with the insurance on the *Oyster Sunrise* and all.'

To Joe, selling the *Emmeline* was like selling his past as well as his future and stubbornly, he refused to hear of it.

As Eline waited for the train, she made up her mind that with some of the wages she had saved, she would rent herself an office. It would need to be something modest at first but soon, as her work improved, her orders would increase and she would gradually build herself a good viable business.

Emily Miller, through Hari Grenfell, had offered Eline the job of changing the windows of the emporium every few weeks – that would bring in a steady, if small, income for a start. If only, Eline thought, she could find an office in Swansea, she would be at hand to do window dressing whenever it was required.

When she had somewhere private to work, she could set up an easel, work out her designs. She could even work in coloured leathers, she realized with a flash of excitement.

There was the latest design she had worked on with Hari Grenfell, the ladies' remedial boot, perhaps a different coloured cuff could be added to make the boots match any outfit.

Hari had promised that Eline would share in the profits so at least she was off to a bit of a start. A feeling of hope filled Eline, she might never have happiness in her private life but, by heavens, she would be a successful business woman if effort was anything to go by.

Hari Grenfell was patently pleased to see Eline. She was seated in the large office of her boot and shoe store and there was an open letter on the desk before her.

'Just the person I wanted to talk to.' Hari smiled warmly. 'Sit down, Eline, I've some good news for you.'

Eline clasped her hands in her lap and sat on the very edge of the plushly upholstered chair. The carpet beneath her feet felt soft and deep and Eline marvelled that a woman from the slum areas of Swansea could have achieved such wonders in a comparatively short time. For Hari Grenfell was still a young woman, elegant, well-dressed and poised, but still young. One day, Eline thought, she might find herself in the same circumstances as Hari.

Then Eline thought of Will Davies who might be falling in love with Gwyneth Parks and she knew that whatever success she might have, she would not find the personal happiness that Hari had achieved.

'The Ladies' Cuffed Boot has found favour with some of the big shoe companies,' Hari said holding up the letter. 'At least two of them wish to buy the pattern.'

Eline was bewildered. 'But surely there are not that many ladies who need adapted footwear, are there?' she asked and Hari's smile widened.

'Indeed not,' she agreed, 'but the shoe is so beautiful, such a new fashion idea, that it seems to have taken the fancy of some of the most influential boot and shoe-makers in the country. You are going to become a household name, Eline, are you happy?'

Eline bit her lip against the rush of tears that threatened to engulf her, she didn't want Hari Grenfell to think she was a silly, sentimental girl, did she? But Hari seemed to understand.

'I know you have more than your share of problems lately, Eline,' Hari said, 'but this' – she waved the letter – 'secures your future.' She leaned back in her chair. 'It won't make you rich overnight, but it's a very good start, a very good start indeed, better than any I had.'

Eline looked at her doubtfully. 'But you are so successful,' she looked around her, 'you have everything you could possibly want.'

Hari shrugged. 'I couldn't have done it without the help of some very good friends and that's what I hope I can be to you, Eline, a good friend. You are a very talented person, you deserve to succeed and I'm sure you will if you put all you have into it.'

'I'll do that all right,' Eline said ruefully, 'I need to earn a living for Joe and me.'

Hari sighed. 'Just as I needed to earn a living for my baby and myself. It's for the sake of others we push, so it seems, not for ourselves.'

Eline was aware of Hari looking at her steadily. 'What are your plans?' Hari asked and it was as though she was waiting for some sign tht Eline was serious about her career.

'I've decided to find myself an office,' she said, 'I realized this morning that I can't work at home not with Joe there and Nina pottering round.' She glanced up at Hari. 'Nina takes care of Joe,' she explained wondering how much gossip Hari might have heard. But Hari was nothing if not discreet.

'I'd say that was the wisest move you could make,' she said, 'it looks professional and it gives you the peace of mind you need to make your designs. I'll keep my ears and eyes open in case anything suitable comes up.'

'What about working in coloured leather?' Eline asked, changing the subject; she didn't want Hari to think she was asking for any favours. 'Is that a realistic prospect?'

Hari leaned forward eagerly. 'Have you anything specific in mind?'

'I thought we might have a removable cuff for the boot,' Eline replied, 'with different coloured leather to match various outfits.'

'Excellent,' Hari said, 'we could definitely have several options of colour with pigskin.' Her eyes were alight with enthusiasm. 'I know I'm going to enjoy working with you, Eline,' Hari added warmly.

When Eline left the emporium, she made her way along the business section of the town looking for offices that were for rent. She wanted something with plenty of light, south facing if possible, but nothing that would eat into all her savings too drastically. She sighed with a mixture of apprehension and excitement, her life was going to need some sorting out, but at least she had made a start at it, and, according to Hari Grenfell, a very good start indeed.

Sarah smiled and nodded, leaning coquettishly towards Geoffrey Frogmore. He really was a boring young man but so rich! She saw Emily glance at her in disapproval – Emily thought she should be mourning over the death of Tom Parks. Sarah was sorry about him, of course, but there was nothing she could do to bring him back, was there? Ignoring her step-mother's frown, Sarah continued to smile at Geoffrey as though she was besotted by him.

Mind, she had to give all credit to Emily, she had certainly set out to impress the Frogmores. The table was groaning with fine china and gleaming silver and the cook had really excelled herself with the mutton cut fine and wrapped around minced meat beaten together with mint jelly.

'Is your father really going to buy us the manor house?' Sarah asked quietly, widening her eyes in a pretence of awe. 'Can he really afford such a place, after all, you both live very modestly at Mrs Marsh's boarding house.'

'That's one of the things I love about you,' Geoffrey said, 'you are so innocent. At least I know you are not marrying me for my money because you didn't know I had any.'

'That's true, darling,' Sarah said, quickly kissing the corner of his mouth and thinking at the same time what a trusting fool he was. She had taken great pains to find out all about Geoffrey Frogmore, helped by her father's, or rather Emily's, connections.

Geoffrey Frogmore was a rich man in his own right, his mother had been connected to minor aristocracy, foreigners it was true, but as the only male heir it was rumoured that Geoffrey had inherited a small fortune.

His father, too, was in the possession of a considerable amount of money and property and had decided to come to live at the seaside in the small Welsh village because of Jack's failing health.

The rooms at the house of motherly Mrs Marsh were simply a stop gap, a convenient place to rest and to assess the lie of the land. After all it might have been that the Frogmores wouldn't have been happy in the area.

Geoffrey, of course, had been delighted with Oyster-mouth, he loved the seaside village, loved the gently sloping cliffs that rose above the ocean and now he loved Sarah Miller, daughter of a prosperous father and step-daughter of the well-bred Emily Miller *née* Grenfell.

Sarah was well aware that Geoffrey's father had pointed out her family were 'in trade', but Geoffrey had replied with the opinion that these days such things didn't really matter. In any case, it seemed that his father had grown heartily tired of waiting for his son to prove his manhood and was only too willing to accept any young girl of excellent means as his daughter-in-law.

Well, Sarah thought to herself, she was not as rich as she had led Geoffrey to believe, but that didn't matter one jot. She tossed her head; one day, she would be rich, because the only other person who could inherit Emily's fortune was Pammy, Sarah's natural child.

Not that she'd ever admit as much to Geoffrey, he thought Sarah a sweet innocent virgin. She smiled to herself; he was probably so inexperienced in the ways of women that it wouldn't be too difficult to make him go on believing the story.

Emily was gesturing for Sarah to rise and leave the gentlemen to their port and cigars, a stupid idea, Sarah thought, she would have none of it when she was running her own home.

'Sarah, are you sure that this is what you want?' Emily asked tucking a stray curl into place. 'Geoffrey seems very nice, but isn't he a little dull?'

'But so rich,' Sarah said drily, 'and I'm fed up with being broke, waiting for you to hand out your little bit of charity. In any case,' she settled into the rich tapestry-covered chair, 'you should be glad I'm going to be married, at least you know you'll be safe with Pammy.'

Emily didn't respond, she simply rang the bell and

asked the deferential maid who entered the room to bring her some tea.

'I expect I'll give Geoffrey a son and heir in my own good time,' Sarah continued, 'keep him and the old man happy, then I can have anything I want.'

'Just be careful,' Emily said, 'there's something about Geoffrey that I can't quite fathom, I don't know what it is.'

'I'll fathom him, all right,' Sarah said smiling. 'Keep a man happy between the sheets and that's all that's required.'

'If you really believe that then I'm sorry for you,' Emily spoke quite sharply, 'it means you haven't had any decent men in your life.'

Sarah felt a flash of annoyance, Emily spoke as though she was much older and wiser than Sarah, but really there wasn't a big age difference between them.

'I have enjoyed my life,' Sarah said, 'well, parts of it anyway, but now I'm taking your advice and settling down to a good marriage. That *is* what you advised me to do, wasn't it?'

'I suppose so,' Emily said and then lapsed into silence until the menfolk entered the room. Sarah couldn't understand Emily, she came alive when John Miller was around and yet to Sarah, John was an old man, but she supposed she could only see him as her father not as a handsome, attractive man.

Geoffrey came to her and took her hands in his. 'I want to set the date of our wedding,' he said happily. 'Will you do me the honour of becoming my wife as soon as possible.'

'Of course I will, my darling,' Sarah said smiling around her. 'I'm greatly honoured by your proposal and I want nothing more than to make you happy.' She seemed to have made the correct response because Geoffrey produced a box from his pocket with the air of a magician producing a white rabbit from a hat.

But when Sarah opened the velvet box, her amusement vanished for nestling in the plush interior was a ring with the most gorgeous square-cut emerald surrounded by twelve perfect diamonds.

'Geoffrey, how wonderful,' she breathed. He looked down at her with pride.

'It was my mother's,' he said softly and, taking the ring from the case, slipped it on to her finger where it sparkled and gleamed, the dark green of the emerald fired by the surrounding diamonds. Sarah allowed herself a smile, she was going to enjoy being Mrs Geoffrey Frogmore very much.

CHAPTER TWENTY-SEVEN

Fon couldn't believe how lonely the farm was without Katherine. She devoted her time to looking after Patrick who was growing bigger and stronger by the day and Fon felt a certain satisfaction in knowing that Katherine would have been happy at the way her son continued to thrive.

Jamie was another matter; he was unable to eat or sleep and was distraught almost to the point of giving up everything he had worked for at Honey's Farm. Fon, coming upon him one night with his head sunken on his chest, the books unopened before him on the table, suddenly remembered the letter Katherine had given her before she died.

Rubbing at his haunted eyes with shaking fingers, Jamie looked up at her.

'I can't do nothing right, Fon, not without my Katherine, I can't.'

Fon moved quietly towards him and held up the letter. It trembled between her fingers and Fon's mouth was suddenly dry with apprehension. What would Katherine have written? How would it change her life? For change her life it would, Fon felt certain of that.

'Take it,' she urged, 'Katherine said we were to read it when . . . when she was gone. Open it, Jamie, please, for I can't.'

He tore it open eagerly, like a man dying of thirst in the desert, anxious for anything at all that was part of his wife. He read in silence and then looking up at Fon as though he had never seen her before, he handed her the letter.

My dearest Jamie and my dear Fon, I know you must grieve when I'm gone from you at last but I don't want you to be unhappy for too long, remember, I will be at peace. What I want is for you, Jamie, my beloved, to marry Fon. This is the plan I formed from the beginning. This is why I was so fussy about the girl I chose to come and help on the farm and this is why I encouraged you both to be together so much.

I know this will be a shock to you both, but you must realize, Fon, that as a single girl you can not stay indefinitely at the farm with Jamie, it would not be seemly. And Jamie, to be practical, you can not manage alone.

My darling baby loves you, Fon, you have become his mother and this, too, was part of my plan. I cannot write any more, but my last words to you are that you must look after each other and you'll see that love will come in time.

God bless you both,

Katherine.

Fon found that she was crying, tears ran unchecked down her cheeks and into her mouth. She sank down at the table and put her head into her hands and the sobs shook her so that she was crying out loud.

After a moment, Jamie took her in his arms, he held her tenderly. They clung together for a long time bound by their grief. There was no passion in Jamie's touch and Fon was glad because passion would have frightened her.

'We both loved her so much,' he said at last, 'that we can't think straight, not yet at least but perhaps, in time.' He moved a damp curl away from Fon's cheek and released her.

Carefully, he folded her letter and placed it in the satin-lined box where he kept his private papers.

'I'll make us a cup of tea,' he said softly and though

his voice was hoarse, there was an edge of something in it that Fon recognized in herself, it was a feeling of hope that the future, after all, was not going to be entirely bleak.

Eline was seated at the desk in her brand-new office at the back of Salubrious Passage which was a narrow alleyway between two buildings with an arched gas-light over the front.

The building was not quite what she had in mind but she had learned that premises were not easily come by. It was only because of an introduction to the landlord by Hari Grenfell that Eline was given the opportunity to rent the place at all and at least there was a big window shedding in some much-needed light.

She had placed her drawing board under the window and had a new sign painted on a board outside which stated: ELINE HARRIES BOOT AND SHOE ARTIST.

She smiled to herself. The only order she'd had was one for a painting of a fine old house on the slopes of Kilvey Hill. It was apparent to her at once that the word ARTIST was being taken literally.

Still, she had accepted the commission given to her by a gentleman called Mr Frogmore who, it seemed, had bought Kilver House for his son who was about to get married. He had not told her a great deal about himself but it was clear that he was a gentleman of means by his dress and his manner and the courteous way he had given her the address of Kilver House and told her to bill him for all travelling expenses as well as for the painting itself.

As for designs for leatherwear, Eline had been given nothing to do whatsoever except for the work Emily Miller and Hari Grenfell put her way. Eline had decided, however, that along with the cuffed boot she would design matching kid gloves, a plan of which Emily heartedly approved.

She sighed; she missed seeing Will so badly that it was like a pain within her, a pain, she assured herself, that would fade in time. She had once caught sight of him through the window of his shop but, although she thought that their eyes had met, he had turned away without any sign of recognition.

She rose from her desk. It was a fine day, an unusual day when the early December sun was shining with cool clarity, bathing the roof of the building opposite in a mellow glow. Outside in Salubrious Passage, a group of ladies walked by, not noticing Eline's office at all. She felt disappointed. She certainly wouldn't make any sort of living for herself this way.

She packed up her coloured chalks and decided to take a walk up to Kilver House, the exercise would do her good and anything was better than sitting twiddling her thumbs.

Outside, it was colder than she had realized and she pulled a woollen scarf around her neck, glad of its warmth. But after walking briskly for half an hour, she loosened the scarf and breathed deeply, glad of the coolness on her hot cheeks.

Kilver House was much further than she had anticipated and when her legs began to ache, she told herself sternly that she was getting soft.

The gently sloping hill of Kilvey was almost barren with stunted unhealthy grass growing in patches like a man going bald. Here and there a camomile flowered but the flowers were bleached white by the fumes from the copper works spread out below her on the banks of the River Tawe.

Kilver House, when at last it came into view, was settled against the fold of the hill. It was a large house with many windows and built of mellow stone that appeared sun-bathed although it stood in the shade of the hillside.

Eline moved up to peer through the windows. The

297

house seemed unoccupied, no flames glowed in the marbled, ornate fireplace and there was no sign of movement. Still that would make no different to Eline, she was to draw the outside.

She chose a hillock on which she could sit comfortably with her pad on her knee and began to work swiftly with her crayons. The house had good, well-balanced lines and yet the crenellated effect of the end walls gave it the appearance of a small castle.

Eline soon forgot the cold air upon which her breath hung in tiny puffs and although the fingers holding the crayons were blue, she was engrossed in her work, so much so that she didn't notice a carriage draw up at the end of the driveway and a group of figures alight.

She looked up startled when a hand touched her shoulder, only to see old Mr Frogmore smiling down at her in approval.

'Dedicated to your work, I see, Mrs Harries.' He smiled warmly and peered over her shoulder. 'Excellent, you have caught the spirit of Kilver House and of the hillside behind it very well indeed. I congratulate you.'

'Let me see.' The young, feminine voice was familiar, But the light was in Eline's eyes as the woman bent forward. 'Very good, I like it.'

Eline rose to her feet, not enjoying having her half-finished work poured over by curious eyes. Then she recognized Sarah Miller, she was clinging to the arm of a young man, looking like the cat that had stolen the cream.

'This is my son, Geoffrey Frogmore,' old Mr Frogmore said politely, 'and his wife-to-be, Sarah Miller.'

Eline mumbled something polite but non-committal and Sarah smiled at her in an infuriatingly patronizing manner.

'Oh, I recognize you, of course, you used to work the oyster beds, didn't you?' Her remark was apparently innocent but it put Eline at a disadvantage inferring that

298

she had come up from humble origins and had set herself up as an artist.

'My husband was the master of two oyster skiffs, yes,' Eline said, 'but unfortunately Joe was hurt in an accident at sea and now I do my best to make an honest living.'

'Laudable indeed,' old Mr Frogmore said heartily, 'and a very talented artist you are. If I can recommend you to any of my aquaintances then I will, my dear.'

Far from harming her image, Eline thought in satisfaction, Sarah's spitefulness had enhanced it, at least in Mr Frogmore's eyes.

'Come along,' Sarah said, gazing up at Geoffrey Frogmore, 'let's step inside and see our beautiful home at close quarters, shall we?'

Mr Frogmore smiled at Eline. 'Please accompany us, my dear and then perhaps I might offer you a ride back into Oystermouth.'

Eline packed up her crayons, she was too cold to work any longer and, in any case, the temptation of not having to walk all the way home was too much to resist. It was even worth enduring Sarah Miller's smug satisfaction at her rise into wealthy society so long as she could sink back into the warmth and comfort of the gracious carriage that waited at the end of the drive.

Following the little trio, Eline smiled to herself. Sarah's efforts to embarrass her had come to nought, but Sarah, it seemed, was about to make up for it by rubbing in the fruits of her good fortune.

As Christmas drew nearer, Fon, though settling into the routine of the farm without Katherine, began to feel despair at Jamie's continued gloom. Katherine's letter, initially, had seemed to make him content, if not happy, but lately, he had become quiet and morose again.

Fon made paper chains to amuse Patrick and hung them around the walls. She decorated the mirrors with holly, the polished leaves and bright berries making a colourful splash against the drabness of the walls that badly needed repainting.

She knitted Jamie a thick wool scarf and wrapped it in bright paper and spent hours in the kitchen baking pies and boiling puddings so that the house was redolent with the smell of fruit. But still Jamie moved about the place as though he himself had died and become a ghost.

The day before Christmas Eve, Fon made the journey home to Oystermouth to see her mother. She had accumulated a clutch of small presents, embroidered handkerchiefs for Sal and Gwyneth and some stockings she'd bought for Mam while she'd still been receiving wages. Since Katherine's death, Fon hadn't the heart to remind Jamie she'd not been paid.

The little house was empty; the fire was laid, the floors swept but there was no sign anywhere of the Christmas festivities.

Fon searched for some newspaper and cut it up into strips pasting the edges together with flour and water. Outside was a hedge of holly from which she cut some sprigs and hung them over the dour old pictures in her mother's kitchen.

She waited about an hour and then made her way reluctantly to Joe's house further along the village street. Fon heartily disapproved of Joe Harries, he had treated her mother shabbily enough in all conscience, but now that he was confined to his bed it wasn't Christian to bear a grudge.

A greatly different picture to that in Mam's own kitchen met Fon's eyes as she stood in the doorway of Joe Harries's house. Cheerful flames roared up the chimney, flickering through the black-leaded bars of the fireplace and crackling with the scent of apple boughs.

The succulent smell of roasting meat and the sound of it spitting in the dish made her realize how hungry she was. A huge plum pudding stood on the table, still steaming from the pot, and Joe and Mam were seated side by side drinking a glass of port.

'Fon!' Nina rose to her feet and held out her arms and Fon went to her, hugging her warmly. 'Have you come to spend Christmas with me?'

Fon shook her head and saw something like relief in her mother's face. 'I can't, there's the baby, Jamie couldn't manage Patrick on his own. In any case, it's his first Christmas without Katherine, I think I should be there.'

Joe, Fon noticed, was sitting in a chair with wheels fixed to it and after a moment, he nodded to her and wheeled himself out of the room. He was obviously as uncomfortable with her as she was with him, Fon decided.

'Is it wise being up there all alone with a man?' Nina asked softly. Fon knew that she meant well and yet anger flared through her.

'I don't think you're one to worry about gossip, are you, Mam?' she said briskly. She saw Nina's colour rise.

'Look, Fon, I'm an old married woman, you are different, you have your life before you, you must keep your reputation or you'll never get yourself a husband.'

'I'm going to marry Jamie,' Fon said flatly. 'We've both agreed and it's what Katherine wished on her death-bed.'

Nina looked discomfited. 'But, love it's what *you* want that counts,' she said biting her lip, 'you mustn't sacrifice yourself to this man however loyal you feel to his wife's wishes.'

'It's all right, Mam,' Fon said, 'I love Jamie, I want to marry him.'

'I see,' Nina spoke slowly and it was clear she didn't see at all. Fon realized that Mam couldn't understand that this was her destiny, Fon, Jamie and Patrick were meant to be together for always.

Nina sighed. 'I suppose I should talk to you about –

301

well – about life. Love between a man and a woman isn't always the romance it seems, there's the marriage bed to think about.'

Fon shook her head. 'Don't, Mam, there's no need, I've seen enough to know what life is about, I am living on a farm, mind.' She didn't add that, in any case, Mam and Joe had made a good job of teaching her all about babies and such.

'I know, but you got to have patience with a man, they sometimes act a bit rough-like in bed, but they don't mean it and when you get used to it, it's, well, it's *nice*.'

Fon could not envisage Jamie ever being rough, he was far too kind and considerate for that. But she kept her own counsel, she knew that her mother meant well, was trying to warn her so that she wouldn't be hurt.

'I'll be all right, Mam.' She handed over the presents. 'I won't see our Sal I don't suppose so perhaps you'll give her this, but I'll call in on Gwyneth on the way back, she'll be at the shop, I expect.

'Aye, she will that,' Nina said, 'folks will be rushing to spend their money for Christmas I don't doubt.' She handed Sal's present back to Fon. 'Take it with you, I saw Sal and she's going to come up to Honey's Farm tomorrow. Give her the gift yourself.'

Fon concealed her surprise; Sal had become almost a stranger to her, she had kept out of the way of all the gossip and scandal and had lived her own life in her comfortable position in one of the big houses and was safely walking out with a nice, respectable man.

'Have a good Christmas then, Mam,' Fon said. 'God bless, see you soon.'

It was cold out in the street after the warmth of the kitchen and Fon drew her coat round her, pushing her hands into the sleeves to keep them warm. She looked at the pewter sea, full of the promise of snow and shivered, wishing she was back at the farmhouse. It was, she realized, her home now, it was where she belonged.

302

Fon didn't know what to make of Sal's proposed visit; still they were sisters, Fon would make Sal welcome at the farm, of course, and yet did she really want anyone interrupting the life she was building with Jamie?

The windows of William Davies's Boot and Shoe Store were ablaze with lights, sprigs of holly framed the stands that held the merchandise and from somewhere in a back street a barrel organ was playing a festive tune. Fon stood silent for a moment, staring within at the flurry of women in crinolines, toffs who had come to buy last-minute gifts for their family and friends.

She hesitated and then she saw Gwyneth, her face all aglow as she looked up at Will Davies. He was handing a customer a parcel and then he smiled down at Gwyneth as though together they had achieved something wonderful. Gwyneth, Fon saw at once, was deeply in love with William Davies and no good could come of it.

She moved tentatively into the store and managed to catch her sister's eye. Quickly, she pressed the small gift into Gwyneth's hand and kissed her cheek.

'God bless and keep you over the festive season,' she said in a hushed tone. Gwyneth hugged her impulsively and disappeared for a moment behind one of the counters. Fon stared around her, embarrassed to be standing among the rich ladies of Swansea who, it appeared, were clearing the shelves of all the goods in sight.

'This is your present.' Gwyneth pressed a box into Fon's hands. 'It's all right, we're having a sale and they didn't cost me a fortune so you needn't worry.' She laughed happily. 'But you mustn't open the packet until Christmas morning, mind.'

Gwyneth's attention was demanded by a customer and, with a quick kiss on Fon's cheek, she was whisked away to sell yet another pair of shoes.

In the street once more, Fon clutched the box close and hurried towards the terminus of the Mumbles train.

It was getting colder, the night was drawing in and she would be glad to be back at the farmhouse. She looked across at the sea, dark now except for a path of yellow splashed intermittently from the lighthouse. How Fon longed to be home and, in that moment, she knew she could never leave the farm, whatever happened.

Christmas morning passed with scarcely a ripple in the routine of life on Honey's Farm. Fon was disappointed with Jamie's reaction to the festive season and although he obediently prayed with her, he refused to attend church or to celebrate in any way.

In was after a fine cooked dinner that Sal arrived and with her she had a handsome young man whose arms were full of gifts.

'Fon, my lovely, you're so thin and *pale*.' Sal clasped her close. 'Why aren't you having some port or a little sherry, something to at least prove that you realize it's Christmas?'

Fon glanced uneasily at Jamie who was rising to his feet, a dour look on his face.

'This is Sal, my sister,' she said, 'and her young man has come to visit with her. Look, Jamie, Sal's brought us all presents. Isn't that kind of her?'

Jamie thrust his hands into his pockets without speaking and Fon glanced apologetically at her sister.

'Jamie's recently lost his wife,' she explained and Sal instantly drew herself up to her full height. Sal was a big girl, raw-boned like Nina, but twice the size.

'I know that,' Sal said, 'and I'm sorry, but I'm sorrier still to see him making a misery of my little sister.'

Jamie looked at her sharply. 'Yes, you, I'm talking about, you,' she said hands on hips. 'Are you going through life for ever with your chin on your boots, then? Are Fon and that lovely little baby of yours going to live with misery for the rest of their lives? If so I'm taking our Fon out of here right now.'

304

'Sal,' Fon said softly, 'please Sal, Jamie is grieving for his wife, he can't help it if . . .'

'Oh, but he can help it,' Sal said firmly. 'Let him show some backbone, is it? Other men lose their wives but they don't wallow in misery. Feeling sorry for yourself is a sin and worse, it's morbid.' She glared at Jamie.

'Is this what your wife would wish for you then? Did she want you to mourn her for ever more?'

'No,' Jamie said fiercely, 'she wanted me to marry Fon. She wanted me,' he gestured to Fon and the baby, 'us, to be happy.'

'Then for pity's sake make a go of it before you lose everything,' Sal said. 'Now, let's open this bottle I've brought, let's have a bit of cheerfulness in here, is it?'

When Sal had gone, Fon felt as though a breath of fresh air had blown through the farmhouse.

She sank into a chair bewildered by the look of dawning awareness on Jamie's face. After a moment, he reached over and took her hand.

'Your sister is right, you know,' he said softly, 'this isn't what Kath would have wished for me and you. Let's try and be happy, Fon.' His fingers curled and gripped hers and Fon felt happiness flare through her.

Gratitude for Sal's interference warmed her and as Fon's eyes met Jamie's she knew that however small it was, this was a beginning, a real beginning for both of them.

CHAPTER TWENTY-EIGHT

Eline was tired, she had worked hard on the picture of Kilver House and at last, she had finished it. After numerous sketches in crayon, Eline had painted the picture in subdued colours and the paint was drying nicely on the canvas.

She was quite pleased with her efforts, she had caught the mellow glow of the building and had even hinted at the frost in the grass edging the gravel pathways around the old house. She sighed and closed her eyes, it was time she went home.

Home, the small house in Oystermouth Village was in reality no longer *her* home. It belonged to Nina and Joe and Nina's ebullient family. They all inhabited the place as though Eline was a mere lodger. And so she was, if she was truthful.

Eline drew on her coat and wound a scarf around her neck to keep out the winter chill. Christmas Day had been a prime example of the way she had become an outsider in her own home, she thought moodily; she had taken a back seat while Nina and her daughters had entertained Joe with songs, monologues and silly, foolish, happy jokes. If anything was guaranteed to make her feel like an intruder, it was the way Joe's eyes rested in gratitude on Nina Parks.

The train was cold as it travelled back following the shore towards Oystermouth. All along the roadway were lights, strung out like a necklace on the curve of the bay. Behind closed curtains, people were together, families, close and loving, and Eline felt so alone, so empty as she huddled in her seat.

She alighted at Oystermouth at last with a handful of other passengers who quickly dispersed leaving her by herself in the silent street. Eline walked slowly past Will's shop and stared longingly into the dark, glassy-eyed windows as though seeking comfort from the place where Will spent much of his time. He wasn't there, of course, he was out celebrating, probably with his rich friends from Swansea. It was only she, Eline Harries, who was alone and friendless.

'For heaven's sake!' she heard her own voice say. 'Stop being so self-pitying.' Suddenly the door to Will's shop sprung open and Will himself stood there, as surprised as she was at their unexpected meeting.

'Eline!' He spoke her name softly and she looked up at him, her heart racing. As his tall figure emerged from the darkened shop, she saw Will's eyes were alight with happiness. 'Eline, I was just locking up the back door of the shop when I caught sight of you. I *had* to speak to you.' He moved a step closer. 'It's been so long,' he said. 'How are you, Eline?' She couldn't see his eyes now as Will stood in the shadows and Eline wanted to move towards him into his arms.

'I am very well,' she replied politely. 'I hope you had a good festive season?' The words sounded stilted and foolish, the small talk of strangers.

'Yes, thank you. You, too?' he said and then he swore softly. 'All this is so banal, so useless, when all I really want to do is take you in my arms.'

Eline's heart lifted, but did he mean it? Last time she'd seen him he was close in conversation with Gwyneth Parks.

'Are you managing all right, with work, I mean?' Will asked breaking the uneasy silence that had fallen between them.

'Very well,' Eline said quickly, almost defensively, 'I've just completed a commission to do a picture of Kilver House for a Mr Frogmore.'

307

'Oh, yes, Mr Frogmore.' There was something odd about Will's tone.

'You don't like him?' Eline asked wondering if Will's dislike was engendered by jealousy. He had been in love with Sarah Miller once himself and now she was marrying young Geoffrey Frogmore.

'I don't like what he's doing to the neighbourhood,' Will said, 'if what the rumours say are true. Eline, we can't stand here talking trivialities in the cold, come with me to my rooms, let me give you a hot drink.'

'Don't be silly,' Eline said bluntly, 'we'd have the gossips waggling their tongues determined to be first with the news that Mrs Harries was alone with a young gentleman in his quarters. Don't you ever learn Will?'

'Damn the gossips!' Will said taking her arm, 'Eline . . .'

'No, Will!' she held up her hand, 'nothing's changed. We both know there can be nothing between us. I'm sorry.' She hurried away and for a moment she wondered if he would come after her. If he did, she felt she would melt into his arms, she was so lonely, so very lonely.

Would it be wrong, she wondered, to steal just a little bit of happiness for herself, to spend just a little time talking to William? But he did not come and taking a deep breath, Eline almost ran the rest of the way along the road and breathless, let herself into the house, feeling the warmth wrapping itself around her.

She stood in the kitchen which was usually the hub of all activity and listened to the sounds of laughter coming from the parlour. Eline slumped against the door feeling even more acutely that she was a stranger in her own home.

After a moment, she took off her coat and hung it over the old rocking-chair and, forcing a bright expression on her face, made her way into the parlour.

The scene that greeted her was one of a happy united

family. Nina sat opposite Joe's chair and grouped around him were Nina's two daughters.

Sal was a big girl with a friendly smile but Gwyneth as usual was immediately hostile, her smile fading as she looked at Eline.

'Eline!' Joe said, and there was a look of pleasure on his face, 'I've got a surprise for you, just watch this.'

Placing his hands on the arms of his chair, Joe struggled to rise, the veins stood out on the backs of his hands and his muscles bulged. Eline would have moved forward but a look from Nina stopped her.

Joe was breathing heavily, his face was red and the pulse throbbed in his throat. He struggled for several minutes but, at last, he was upright. His entire body trembled but there was such a look of delight in his eyes at his achievement Eline was moved to tears.

'Joe!' she said. 'How wonderful!' She watched anxiously as he slumped back into his chair and wiped the beads of sweat from his brow.

'Give it a few more weeks and I'll be walking again,' Joe said breathlessly, 'and it's all thanks to Nina.'

Eline felt a pang of pain, Nina was the hated mistress, but to Joe, Nina had been a strength and a support when he most needed help. It seemed that now Eline must be grateful to her for Nina had given Joe a new lease of life. Eline forced a smile and yet her heart was heavy; was she doomed to spend her life as someone for ever on the outside looking in?

Throughout January ice and snow held the sea at Oystermouth in its cruel hold and prevented the skiffs from going out. The village settled in and the fires in the small cottages sent smoke issuing from the chimneys.

Eline had returned from the office to her home to a barrage of gossip concerning Mr Frogmore; it seemed he was buying up as much property in Swansea as he could. It was rumoured that he had even approached the landowners of Oystermouth with a view to making a whole new string of properties along the sea front.

'Damn cheek!' Nina was rubbing her hands against her apron and Carys Morgan was sitting with her baby in the old rocking-chair, her face flushed with the heat of the fire. There was no sign of Joe and when Eline could get a word in, she asked where he was.

'Oh, he's with Sam, I wrapped him up well, mind.' Nina smiled reassuringly. 'Sam insisted on wheeling him down to the public for a drink of ale before supper and good riddance to them, too!' Nina paused. 'Sick of us going on about this Mr Frogmore, the men are, says it's all a storm in a teacup. There'll be a storm all right if we have dancing places and such disturbing the quiet of the village.'

'Is that what Mr Frogmore wants then?' Eline asked doubtfully; he hadn't seemed that sort of man to her at all. She made up her mind to ask him about his plans when she delivered the painting to his rooms in Mrs Marsh's boarding house. He would be quite within his rights to tell her to mind her own business, but Eline had the feeling that Mr Frogmore liked her and what's more valued her opinion. In any case, a man who had bought a lovely old building like Kilver House couldn't possibly be the sort to destroy the peace of a small village like Oystermouth.

'Joe's coming on well with his walking,' Carys said, her plump, good-natured face creased into dimples as she smiled. 'Sam won't have to take Joe in his chair for much longer, kills Joe, being pushed in that chair does. Nina's done a fine job.'

'Yes, she has,' Eline said feeling once more as though she was being edged out of Joe's life even in the eyes of dear, kind Carys Morgan. But then Eline was an oddity, a woman who worked for a living and more a woman who left her man in the hands of his mistress. It was no wonder she was the recipient of strange looks

310

whenever she walked down the street, Eline thought ruefully.

And yet she knew she was doing the right thing. Nina was good for Joe, she was the only woman who would have put up with his moods for Nina loved Joe, loved him more than Eline would or could ever love him. What a mess life was.

Carys rose to her feet. 'I'd better be getting back, the men will be home for supper any time now and my Sam will be starving as he always is after a pint or two of ale.'

As if to confirm what she had said, the door was pushed suddenly open and Joe was wheeled into the kitchen. His face was red from the roughness of the wind and yet there was a euphoric smile on his face, put there no doubt by the amount of ale he'd drunk.

'Here's the hero home safe and sound,' Sam said heartily, swaying a little, unaware of the cold air blasting in through the open door.

'Thanks, Sam, you're a good man.' It was Nina who spoke, who naturally assumed the air of a woman welcoming home her man and his friends. 'Have a bite of rabbit stew with us, it's hot on the hob and plenty of it.'

Sam shook his head reluctantly. 'Got to get my head down, weather is going to be better tomorrow according to Skipper George and I might get a bit of dredging in if I'm lucky.'

He punched Joe lightly on the shoulder. 'See you, old fellow, we'll get out to the public again if we can throw off these dragons that we call our womenfolk.'

It was quiet in the kitchen once Carys and Sam had left. Joe had declined supper and wanted only to go to bed. Eline watched quietly as Nina wheeled Joe through to the parlour where his bed was and she stood helplessly by as she heard Nina undressing Joe, washing him down, talking to him in soft encouraging tones. Only when Nina had Joe settled would she walk the short distance back to her own cottage.

311

Eline sighed; she was useless, she might as well move out, live near the office in Swansea, leave Joe entirely to Nina. It would be the best thing all round.

She hardly slept that night and by morning she had made up her mind to ask Mrs Miller if she might have a room in the emporium as before. She would not expect the elegant suite she'd once been given, any room would do, however small, for, Eline decided, she was out of place in her own home and perhaps she always would be.

Nina was not sorry to see Eline leave Oystermouth and indeed, she hoped it was for good. Naturally the girl would come and visit Joe from time to time, she was duty bound to do so if only to bring money for Joe's support, but Nina felt a sense of triumph. To all intents and purposes Joe was hers again now.

'I can't understand it.' Joe was seated near the table, picking at his breakfast of bacon and eggs and crispy brown fried bread. 'What a way for a wife to treat her husband – deserted me, she has, left me alone to fend for myself. What if I didn't have you, I ask you, what would I do then?'

Joe like all men was too wrapped up in himself to realize that if it wasn't for Nina, wild horses wouldn't have dragged Eline away from him.

'Well, don't you fret, I'm going to move in with you for good, we'll live together like we used to and damn what people think. In any case,' she smiled, 'folks round here seem to be accepting me now, they can see I'm taking good care of you, Joe.'

'Aye, well, I've done with Eline, she can go and live her own life and good luck to her, but she needn't think she's getting anything from me.'

'What do you mean, Joe?' Nina asked bluntly. 'You haven't got any money, have you?'

'No, but I got this house, haven't I? Worth a bit of

money it is, mind, and Eline will see none of it when I go.'

'But . . .' Nina stopped herself from blurting out that Eline had been keeping him since his injury, working to support him. It was none of her business to defend Eline to Joe, after all.

'But nothing,' Joe smiled. 'You have stuck by me more than I have ever done by you, Nina love. You gave me a son, God rest his soul, and that's more then Eline ever gave me.' He sighed and held Nina close as she rested her cheek against his head.

'Eline was my dream, my picture of a perfect woman, but she *was* just a dream. You, Nina, you are the reality and you shall have your reward, don't you worry.'

'Don't!' Nina said in genuine fear. 'Don't talk like that, Joe, do you think I want your house then? I want *you* Joe, you are my life, don't you know that yet?'

'I do.' He pulled her down on to his knee, wincing a little at the pain in his back. 'That's why I want you to know where the deeds are kept.'

'No, don't talk like that, Joe.' Nina kissed his mouth to stop the flow of words but he held her away from him determinedly.

'I hope to go on for years yet and to be able to walk again, but just in case it don't work out that way I want you to go to the tin trunk upstairs. There you'll find a copy of the letter I've lodged with Mr Kenyon, the solicitor.' He smiled, 'In it, I've said the house is to be yours.'

Nina could see that Joe was becoming quite agitated and she rested her hand on his shoulder, trying to calm him. 'All right, Joe, but hush now is it?' she begged. 'I don't want to hear such talk, it frightens me.'

'Still,' Joe caught her arms, 'I want you to promise that you'll go and get it if anything happens to me sudden, like.'

'But what about Eline?' Nina said suppressing the

glow of pride that Joe wanted *her* to have everything and not his wife.

'Eline will have what's left of my boats,' he said, 'and in any case, she has her career to think of, she's made that quite clear.' There was a tinge of bitterness in his tone and Nina bit her lip.

'That isn't very fair, Joe.' She found herself springing to Eline's defence; in spite of everything she had come to respect the girl if not to like her.

'Why isn't it fair?' Joe demanded. 'Did she consult me about going to work? Oh no, madam went her own headstrong way. Well, she'll survive, she's self-centred enough not to go without.'

He raised her hand to his lips and kissed it lightly on the palm, a gesture that moved Nina unbearably.

'In any case, old girl, she's younger and stronger than us, she can marry again and very probably will.' He smiled up at Nina. 'I can't see you wanting to get hitched again, can you?'

'No,' Nina conceded. 'Without you Joe, I'd be lost.'

'Right then, that's settled, let's not hear any more about it, right?'

Nina gave in. 'You are the boss, whatever you say goes. Now I'd better get on and do something round here or we'll end up living in a pigsty.'

And yet within Nina there was an uneasiness, a faint worrying sense of doom. It wasn't like Joe to talk about death. She sighed, with Joe, it was a case of living one day at a time and that's all she could do except what she had always done, loved him with all her being.

Mr Frogmore smiled warmly when he took the painting from Eline's hands and set it on the broad mantelshelf in his rooms in Mrs Marsh's boarding house.

'That is extremely lovely, my dear, it does complete justice to the old house. Let me pay you at once, I'm getting old and inclined to forgetfulness.'

Eline doubted that; Mr Frogmore was a fiery old man with glinting eyes that took in everything.

'I have a few friends who would love you to paint for them,' he said. 'Would you be prepared to travel, my dear Mrs Harries?'

Eline felt a dart of excitement. 'If it was necessary,' she said. 'Although I would prefer to remain within the boundaries of Swansea as much as possible, I would certainly be willing to travel to other parts of the country.'

'Excellent, well done.' Frogmore handed her an envelope and Eline was surprised at the generosity of his payment. She glanced up at him quickly. 'But ten guineas is far too much!' she protested at once and he looked amused.

'Nonsense my dear, are you aware of what London artists are charging these days? No, you take my advice and charge double that amount in future.'

Eline took a deep breath, she'd never believed such money could be earned from the hobby she enjoyed so much.

'Now, I will let my friends know about you, my dear, and if your paintings are as pleasing to them as they are to me, you will be well away.' He looked at his pocket watch and Eline felt it was time to take her leave.

'One thing,' at the door she turned, 'there is some disquiet in the village, people are talking about the property you are buying, they fear you will open up dance halls and such.'

To Eline's surprise, Mr Frogmore laughed out loud. 'Nothing could be further from the truth,' he said, 'I belong to the Society of Friends, a Quaker as it is commonly called and I'm looking for suitable premises for a meeting house, that's all.'

'I see,' Eline felt foolish, 'well, forgive me for asking, but may I tell the villagers this? It would set their minds at rest.'

Mr Frogmore waved his hands. 'If you must, my dear, it will soon be common knowledge anyway.'

When she stood outside on the landing, Eline wondered whether to call to see Joe as she was here in Oystermouth, yet she was longing to return to her rooms in Mrs Miller's emporium and hug the knowledge that she could consider her future as a painter.

'Eline.' The sound of her name, softly spoken, made her jump. She glanced round, her heart beating swiftly, knowing at once that Will was standing behind her in the gloom of the landing.

'Eline, what a surprise to see you here.' He accompanied her as she walked down the stairs. 'I hear you've left your husband and are living in Swansea.'

'You hear correctly,' Eline said, afraid to look up at him in case she softened and allowed him to embrace her. 'And I'm here on business, as it happens.' Her tone was a rebuff and Will, taking it as such, moved away from her without another word.

As Eline hurried out into the street, she was unable to see clearly because of the tears that suddenly rose up to choke her. Will would doubtless wash his hands of her – even he could only take so much of her rudeness. And yet the knowledge that she had hurt him left an aching void within her that nothing would ever fill.

CHAPTER TWENTY-NINE

Sarah was very happy with her lot, she had Geoffrey just where she wanted him and what's more, she believed that marriage to such an eligible man who, along with his father, was so patently wealthy would give her entry to the best homes in Swansea.

Most of the gentry knew that Sarah's father had been a cobbler but they knew also that John Miller was now a highly successful business man. The spiteful few would say it was a case of like father like daughter and that advantageous marriages were the key to a better life, but Sarah felt she could ignore any unkind gossip especially now that she was wearing Geoffrey's emerald ring on her fingers.

They were to be married with an unexpected degree of modesty in the meeting house of the Society of Friends, an austere establishment which eventually would give place to the new meeting house Mr Frogmore senior was planning to inaugurate.

Sarah had displeased Geoffrey by demanding petulantly to be married in St Mary's or at least in St Paul's, both of which were elegant buildings and well thought of in the town. It was only when she saw a glint of anger in Geoffrey's normally kindly eyes did she sense the danger signals.

'Of course, Geoffrey, I want to please you in all things,' she said hastily. 'We will naturally be married wherever you decide.'

Geoffrey had smiled at her warmly then and kissed her hand. As he bent forward, Sarah could not help noticing the balding patch at the top of his head. She suppressed a desire to giggle; she had upset her future husband once, she'd better not do it again.

Sarah was married on a cold day in February. Frost rimed the cobbles and she felt the horses slip on the icy surface with a sense of apprehension. For the first time she wondered if she was doing the right thing, then she glanced down at the ring gleaming on her finger and knew that with Geoffrey, she would be set up for life. She could do just as she liked when they were man and wife; she was sure he didn't have the nerve or character to deny her anything.

Emily was smiling warmly, no doubt glad to have a troublesome step-daughter out of harm's way. For a moment, Sarah's expression softened as her eyes rested on her father. John Miller looked so prosperous, so elegant and distinguished that no one would have believed he had begun life as a humble apprentice in the cobbling trade.

The service was as spartan as the meeting room and an icy blast came in through the open doorway. Sarah was glad that she had worn a frock in white velvet, trimmed with white fur and covered with a small white fur jacket. She looked both bridal and smart and yet she did not feel the bite of the keen edge of the freezing weather too harshly.

As the man standing before her intoned passages from the Bible, Sarah looked down at her white kid boots with the fashionable cuff sweeping almost to the ground and smiled to herself, the boots were all the rage in Swansea now. Some said they were designed by Emmeline Harries, but Sarah believed the idea had come from the pen of Hari Grenfell. That little Harries oddity didn't have the brains or the means to have made something so beautiful.

She was aware that Geoffrey was taking her hand and slipping a wedding band into place. Her finger looked strangely bare without the glorious emerald ring that now rested in a velvet box within the folds of the white fur reticule hanging from Sarah's arm. But soon all that would change, she would be virtually ablaze with gem-stones, Sarah promised herself.

She needed some reward, she mused, for marrying a dry old stick like Geoffrey Frogmore, but she smiled up at him concealing her feelings as adroitly as she'd ever done.

Geoffrey lead her out of the church into the cold spring air. She looked around her at the guests, they were pitifully few, just her father with Emily at his side and one or two of their friends. And, of course, old Mr Frogmore who at least was smiling with genuine warmth and with him Geoffrey's friend, Chas, a thin-faced man who had stood at Geoffrey's side during the ceremony looking more as though he was at a funeral rather than at a wedding.

Emily moved forward to congratulate Sarah and if there was a reserve in her tone it made Sarah amused more than angry. She no longer needed Emily's largesse, she had her own husband now and would never want for anything again.

She was being swept into a carriage then taken home to Kilver House up on the hill. The refurbishment was not entirely finished but the main rooms, including the master bedroom, were ready for occupation.

Sarah suppressed a grimace, tonight she would have to begin sharing a bed with her sallow-faced husband – such a prospect was not pleasing. But then, one man was very like another, she comforted herself, so long as they got what they wanted in the bedroom, they were quite easy to handle.

It was fortunate, she mused, that Geoffrey had not heard any of the old scandal about her but then she had been away from Swansea for some time and perhaps the gossips had grown tired of what was, after all, yesterday's news.

A simple meal was set out in the dining room that faced the sea and Sarah sat with Geoffrey listening while her father welcomed him to the family and hoped the couple would be blessed with children. She bet he did, he and Emily would have Pammy for keeps. Well, they were welcome.

Mr Frogmore spoke some pious claptrap about the union being blessed in heaven and Sarah was impatient; all she wanted was to begin her life as lady of the manor.

Geoffrey was staring at her, a strange look in his eye, and she smiled up at him in what she thought was a modest, wifely manner. She rested her hand on his arm, admiring the way the diamonds in her ring sparkled and shimmered as she moved her fingers.

'I wish we could be alone,' she said softly and he nodded curtly as though she had said something quite mundane. Did he have any feelings at all? Sarah wondered, a trifle anxiously. Had she made a dreadful mistake?

The meal dragged on interminably with discreet servants bringing in course after course; the old man had put on a good show where the feeding of the guests was concerned, Sarah conceded. But then, at last, to her relief, the guests began to leave.

Emily and John were the last to go and for a moment, John hugged Sarah.

'Be happy, love,' he whispered in her ear, 'and remember to obey your husband in all things, that way you can't go wrong.'

Sarah watched from the window as her father waved from the coach until it was out of sight. She turned to see Geoffrey standing in the half-darkness watching her.

'You gave me a start,' she said quickly, 'lurking there like that. What are you thinking of, Geoffrey?'

'My father is going back to the lodging house now,' Geoffrey said. 'Chas is going with him but only for a few days, thereafter he will make his home here with us.'

'Really? Is that a good idea, do you think?' Sarah asked piqued that she had not been consulted. Geoffrey didn't reply but walked to the front door talking in a low voice to his father, his arm casually draped around the shoulder of his friend. Chas was glowering, as though reluctant to leave, and Geoffrey squeezed his shoulder encouragingly.

Sarah closed her lips in a firm line; Geoffrey would have to be taught a lesson, he couldn't just decide that his friend was to live with them. Sarah was no silly girl to be treated in such a way, she intended to be mistress of her own home.

Still, she mused, let Geoffrey have the benefit of her love first, let him see how Sarah could thrill him with her caresses, then she would have him where she wanted him. Wasn't it the same with all men?

When they were alone, Geoffrey seemed all solicitude, he brought her a gleaming glass of port and urged her to drink it. 'It will help to take away the tensions of the day,' he said quietly. He refilled her glass as soon as it was empty and then when she would have sipped it coaxed her into drinking it down.

Sarah was amused; if Geoffrey thought he would make her drunk with a few glasses of port then he had another think coming. Sarah had indulged with the best of them and drunk many a man under the table. But, of course, that was something Geoffrey would never know.

He took her arm. 'It's time to retire, my dear,' he said and, with a pang of something akin to pity, she realized he was nervous. He took her arm to lead her to the curving staircase and Sarah wondered if she should feign a timidness she didn't feel, but Geoffrey had pushed open the door to the master bedroom and stood aside for her to enter. After a moment, he began almost reluctantly, it seemed, to undress.

'Why not go into the dressing room, dear?' Sarah said feeling slightly uneasy. Geoffrey didn't reply but carefully took off his spectacles and folded them neatly away in their case.

'It's all right, Sarah,' he said, 'I know what you are, a woman of experience and what's more, a woman with good connections. That's why I married you.'

Sarah felt her mouth drop open. 'What do you mean?' she asked in a small voice. 'Why do you say I'm experienced and why should you need *me* when you have so much money of your own?'

Geoffrey shook his head. 'My dear,' he said gently, 'my father has all the money, I shan't get a penny of it until I produce a son.'

'But you led me to believe . . .' Sarah's voice drifted away under Geoffrey's ironic smile.

'And *you* led me to believe that you were an untouched virgin,' he said calmly. 'You were silly to think that men in public bars would refrain from gossiping about you. It was a juicy bit of scandal after all, Sarah Miller handing over her bastard child to be reared by her step-mother. The late Tom Parks was your last little peccadillo, I believe?'

'If you knew all that, then why did you marry me?' Sarah said hotly, her cheeks flushed, her heart beating uncomfortably fast. 'Why not find some prim little maiden to get you a son?'

'I wanted an experienced woman,' Geoffrey said without rancour, 'a whore in the bedroom and a lady in the drawing room. In any case my father was getting tired of waiting for me to find the right partner.'

Geoffrey sighed heavily. 'Poor innocent father had no notion of who *was* the right partner for me.' He smiled wryly.

'Listen to me, Sarah, I am not as other men, I can't love you as a woman because that is not my inclination. But with your help, I *can* father a child, do you understand?'

'No!' Sarah said, suddenly afraid. 'I won't listen to

you!' She had heard of such men, of course; working in public bars the talk was lewd and coarse and left nothing to the imagination.

'Oh yes, you will.' Geoffrey's voice was full of entreaty. 'You will try to understand me and my dear friend, Chas. If you want to live the good life you will find you'll do a great deal you don't want to do – like being faithful to our marriage vows.

'Look, my dear,' he continued, 'if you co-operate with me, we shall conceive a child quite quickly, then when we have a son, I will leave you alone. You shall have everything money can buy, my father will see to that, he will be so grateful to you.'

Sarah sighed in resignation; what Geoffrey said made sense, they were married now. What was the point in causing a scandal by walking out on him on their wedding night and becoming the laughing stock of Swansea?

Quickly, she took off her clothes and, as she removed the last garment, she was aware of her naked vulnerability as she had never been before.

She slid beneath the sheets and began to shiver, not from the cold linen but from the look in Geoffrey's eyes.

'You will thank me, one day, Sarah, I promise you, for you will be made into an honest wife instead of remaining a whore all your life.'

He lay beside her like a tentative boy and Sarah realized it was up to her to make the first move, for Geoffrey could not. She turned to him and, with her eyes closed, put her arms around him.

Later, when it was all over, she turned her back on her husband knowing that he had cheated her and, for that, she would never forgive him.

He gently lifted her face to his, his hand steady now on her chin. 'I'm sorry, Sarah, I really am sorry, but I promise you this, I'll be a good husband and a good father to our children and I'll always be kind to you.'

Sarah turned away from him and closed her eyes. How could he know that her hot blood cried out for satisfaction and she could never be happy in such a travesty of a marriage? Never.

Eline was thrilled to see how popular her new boots had become. The cuffed boot became *the* fashion for the winter months and teamed up with the matching kid gloves, the design soon began to spread in popularity to other towns across the country.

Hari congratulated her warmly as they sat in before the fire in the suite of rooms above Emily's emporium.

'You seem to have your life mapped out for you,' Hari said softly. 'I'm so pleased for you, Eline, you deserve everything you can get, such talent as yours is rare.'

'I'm so grateful,' Eline said softly, 'if it wasn't for you and for Mrs Miller I don't know where I'd be, still living in the cottage in Oystermouth, the third part in the triangle that my life with Joe and Nina had become.'

'It takes a great deal of courage to break away from convention,' Hari said, 'I know from first-hand experience.'

'What do you know from first-hand experience?' Emily poked her head around the door. 'I hope you don't mind, Eline, I wanted a word and the door was open.'

'Please come in,' Eline said quickly, 'it is *your* house, after all.'

'But these are your rooms for as long as you want them,' Emily said. 'It suits me to have an expert window dresser living on the premises.'

She held out a note to Eline. 'A messenger came from old Mr Frogmore. It seems he's living up at the lodge of Kilver House now he's given up the rooms with Mrs Marsh.'

Eline opened the letter and looked up smiling. 'A friend of old Mr Frogmore wants me to paint a portrait for her,' she said doubtfully. 'I can draw and paint houses and landscapes all right but I don't know about people.' She glanced down at the note again. 'She's offering me an awful lot of money, I feel I'd be taking it under false pretences.'

'Nonsense!' Emily replied quickly. 'You must accept travelling expenses as well as a fee for the actual portrait. Where does this friend live?'

'In Bristol.' Eline read the address. 'I suppose that's not too far away.'

'Nearer than Street in Somerset,' Emily affirmed. 'It's just across the channel, perhaps you could get a steam packet over, in that way you'd cut down on the travelling time.'

Hari leaned forward and put a hand over Eline's. 'In any case you must give it a go,' she urged. 'You must use your talent in any way you can.'

'I suppose so.' Eline sounded nervous and Hari leaned back in her chair. 'I tell you what, you could practise by doing a portrait of my son. I can't promise he'll sit still for long, but David is a good child and if his nose is in a book, he forgets all about time.'

Eline smiled, wondering why it was that in this house with these people who were comparative strangers, she felt more at home than she'd ever done since she left Honey's Farm to marry Joe.

Later, when she was alone, Eline took out her sketch-pad and began to draw her reflection in the dimness of the lamplit dressing-table mirror. After a while, she stopped, her eyes aching, and she frowned as she looked down and saw such sadness in her own image. She quickly put down the paper and pencil.

Much as she was fulfilled with her work, Eline knew that without William it was all emptiness. She would give up everything – even her promising future – if only she was free to marry the man she loved.

CHAPTER THIRTY

Eline arrived in Bristol on a fine crisp day when the
winter snows of February were thawing into the kinder
days of blustery March. Daffodils waved splendid golden
trumpets at the skies and stood firm against the winds
that threatened to uproot their bulbs.

Eline took a cab through the windswept streets to the
outskirts of the town. Mrs Charlotte Brentford lived in
a beautiful house which stood on a softly folding hillside.
Against the backdrop of the grassy slopes, the old
building rose magnificent, more a mansion than a house.

Avon Manor was grander even than Summer Lodge.
It equalled the fine Vivian mansion that stood in the
parklands that rolled down towards the sea in Swansea.

Eline wondered what her reception would be as the
cab jerked to a halt outside the arched doorway. She was
so used to being alone and independent that it hadn't
occurred to her to bring a companion. In any case, who
would she bring? She bit her lip, she supposed she could
have begged one of Emily Miller's maids to accompany
her, perhaps it would have appeared more seemly. But
it was too late now, the cab door was opened and she
was helped to alight by a footman in scarlet-and-blue
livery.

She was welcomed in a whirl of activity. Eline was
aware of a large hallway lit by many lamps and of rich
drapes and heavy doors, then she was relieved of her
luggage and swept into an enormous drawing room. In
one corner there was a splendid spinet and beside it a
harp.

Charlotte Brentford introduced herself; she was a

beautiful widowed lady who had three unmarried daughters, all of them wishing to have their portraits painted. Mrs Brentford's voice was soft and beneath the cultured tones was the charming rhythm of the west country.

'Let Mrs Harries catch her breath, girls.' Mrs Brentford admonished her daughters good-naturedly. 'You will all have your turn to say exactly how you would like Mrs Harries to present you.'

'The girls want miniature portraits,' Mrs Brentford explained, 'they are to be sent to cousins abroad.'

'Cousins and prospective husbands,' one of the girls said excitedly.

Looking at the girls objectively, Eline guessed they were about her own age, given a year or two either way. And yet she felt so much older than any of them.

'You are all so lovely I'm sure you'll have no trouble finding husbands,' she said softly.

'Now girls,' Mrs Brentford held up her hand, 'allow Mrs Harries to sit down and have some refreshment, she has come a long way to see you, let her at least have some space to gather herself together!' She gestured for Eline to be seated and then arranged her multitude of skirts elegantly around her on the plush love seat.

Looking around her, Eline felt a sense of excitement; this was going to be a very happy assignment.

Over the next few days, Eline found it quite an experience to be a guest in the Brentford household. She was treated with every courtesy; her bedroom was luxurious and had the added advantage of a dressing room attached. Along the corridor was a bathroom with a huge, highly decorated bath and every morning, a maid brought hot water to Eline's room.

The fire in the grate was constantly alight though how the servants managed to get any sleep, Eline could not help but wonder.

After a few days, she had the Brentford daughters sorted out in her mind and had begun work on the portrait of Maria, the eldest girl, who had an abundance of rich, brown hair that fell upon creamy shoulders. Maria was a dark-eyed beauty and an incurable chatterbox.

Eline was tempted to tell her that unless she kept her mouth closed for more than a few seconds at a time, it would be difficult to capture the fullness of her lips and the wide generosity of her smile.

The girl had an excellent sense of fun; the work took shape much more quickly and with much more success than Eline had anticipated. She did numerous sketches searching for the best angle at which to catch Maria's impish sense of humour.

It was at night, lying in the luxury of the huge bedroom with the lamp turned down low and the glow from the fire sending a rosy light flickering across the ceiling, only then, when she was alone, did Eline think of home.

She sighed as she wondered how Joe was faring with his attempts to walk again. She feared for him in his single-minded determination to be as other men. Joe had lost much of his strength; his will might be strong, but was his constitution ready for the strains he was imposing upon himself?

Inevitably, Eline thought of William, she longed for him in a way that she knew was wrong. She wanted his arms around her and his lips upon hers and sometimes she turned her face into the pillow and wept with the futility of it all.

It took Eline almost a month to complete the portraits and when they were finished, she could not help but be pleased with them. The faces of the three Brentford girls were captured for all time in paint, and they had richness and colour and depth.

'The portraits are exquisite!' Mrs Brentford said happily. 'You have caught the spirit of youthfulness in my girls, you are *so* talented, Mrs Harries, I congratulate you.'

Maria gazed at her image, her eyes wide. 'Do I really look as lovely as that?' she asked wistfully, 'or is it your artistry that brings out the best in people?'

Eline laughed. 'I paint only what I see, Maria, and if it's compliments on your looks you want, I suggest you wait until your cousins and prospective husbands hand them out to you.'

At last, her work was finished and it was a sad moment for Eline as she prepared to leave Avon Manor. She had been happy in the weeks she had spent in Bristol, except for some lonely moments in the still of the night.

'Come again any time you wish,' Mrs Brentford said, taking her hands, 'and be sure, you'll have many more commissions when my friends see what you have done for my daughters.'

As the coach drew away from the lovely old building, Eline glanced back and saw the glowing walls and strong, stone turrets of Avon Manor. She felt that she was leaving an oasis of peace where for a time she had done nothing but be herself. And in the comfort and peace of Avon Manor she had had time to think. But now she must go home, she must see her husband, take up her old responsibilities and make sure that Joe had money enough for his needs.

Eline sank back in the cold leather seat suddenly; it was as though the weight of the world was pressing in upon her.

'Joe, I told you you were doing too much!' Nina shook her fist at the man in the bed and the gesture was only half-playful. 'I wish you wouldn't drive yourself so hard. You see what's happened now, you've had a set back and you *must* rest.'

'I'm all right, girl,' Joe said edgily, 'I'm not an old man yet, I can still flex the muscles when I need to.'

'Aye, but you must take things more slowly.' Nina emphasized the point by banging her hand on the bedside table. 'You have been hurt, your body is weak and needs building up again, you shouldn't try to rush things.'

Joe sighed. 'I'm sick of sitting here like a lost cause, I can't live like it, Nina, if I can't walk again then I might as well be dead.'

'Don't talk like that!' Nina said angrily. 'How do you think that makes me feel?' She put her hands on her hips. 'I *care* about you, Joe Harries, not that you deserve it, mind, a selfish pig you are sometimes.'

'Well,' Joe said moodily, 'you must be the only one in the world who does care about me.' He pushed back his greying hair. 'Where's that wife of mine these days, I ask you? She hasn't come near here in weeks.'

'She's away in Bristol, you know that well enough, Joe. Working that girl is, to support herself and you which is not easy, mind.'

'Why should I care and why should I feel guilty?' Joe asked sourly. 'When did Eline ever consider my feelings? She wanted to work, didn't she?'

Nina moved to the door. 'I give up on you, sorry for yourself now, is it? Well, don't moan to me, I got no patience with self-pity.'

Joe gave a roar. 'I'll show you that I'm not feeling sorry for myself, I'll damn well walk if it kills me.'

He pushed aside the blankets and with an effort that made the veins stand out in his neck, slowly swung his legs over the side of the bed.

'Joe, you stop that!' Nina said urgently. 'The doctor told you to rest, now stay put until you are feeling better.'

Joe made no reply but sighed heavily as his feet touched the floor. He paused for a moment and then pressing his hands against the bed, forced himself upwards.

'Please, Joe,' Nina sounded desperate, 'get back into bed, please.'

Joe's muscles were straining, his arms once so strong

were trembling with the effort to push himself upright. He grunted and his breathing was heavy, his colour high, his eyes glittering as though with tears.

Nina, watching him, felt fear drag at her, Joe was in no fit state for such an effort. Hadn't the doctor told him that his heart was strained and needed a complete rest?

Joe's colour receded and his skin took on a sheen of sweat that emphasized his sudden paleness, but he was on his feet, standing unaided.

'I feel bad, Nina,' he said suddenly and his voice was little more than a groan. He slumped back then, sitting awkwardly on the bed and his eyes seemed strange as if Joe was no longer inhabiting his body.

Slowly, so slowly that he scarcely seemed to move, he toppled over backwards, arms outstretched at his sides.

'Joe?' Fearfully, Nina made her way towards him, her breath ragged with horror as she stood beside him for a long moment, looking down at him, and she knew, with a strange sense of unreality, that the man she had loved for so long, her darling Joe was dead.

'Joe, my lovely, don't leave me.' Her voice was a whisper. She sank down on the bed beside him and put her arms around him, holding his beloved head against her breast. 'Joe, oh Joe, why did you do it? You know I can't live without you.'

She rocked him to and fro as though he was a baby, his head heavy against her, his thick grey hair springing back from his forehead. She smoothed his hair; it was alive and strong giving her the fleeting impression that Joe was as alive and vibrant as ever.

Nina closed her eyes, her fingers twined in Joe's hair and prayed that the nightmare would end, that she would wake and everything would be all right.

It was there that Eline found her some hours later and in one horrified glance, Eline saw that her husband was dead. She had returned from Bristol to find everything

331

had changed in her absence, nothing would ever be the same again.

'Come away, Nina,' she said softly, prising the older woman's hand away from Joe's hair, 'there's nothing you can do for Joe now.'

Eline went into the street and, tapping the window of the next house, called for Carys Morgan to come and to bring help. Soon the tiny cottage was filled with people.

Voices surrounded Eline, voices asking questions, making suggestions. The doctor came and went and then Eline and Nina were ushered into the kitchen while old Mrs Mortimer saw to the laying out.

Nina's eyes were glazed, she sat as though in a trance and didn't take the cup of tea that Eline tried to hand her.

'Someone fetch Gwyneth,' Eline said softly. 'Nina is going to need one of her own.'

Sam Morgan touched Eline's arm. 'Sit down, *merchi*, you look worn out, no good you getting sick, is it?'

Eline suddenly felt very tired. She sank into a chair and put her head into her hands unaware that Gwyneth had entered the kitchen until she spoke.

'Look at *her*!' The voice was scornful. 'It's always the same, whenever something's wrong *she's* here pretending to be the grieving wife when we all knew that she didn't give a fig for Joe Harries.

'Who looked after him? I ask you that. Who cared for Joe and waited on him hand, foot and finger? My mam, that's who.'

Gwyneth looked down at Eline and her face was red with fury. 'And now, I suppose, you'll tell my mam to get out of *your* house, her usefulness is ended now. Is that why you sent for me?'

Eline shook her head, unable to speak a word in her own defence. She had not been there when Joe died, she never was there when she was needed.

'Now don't be hasty.' It was Sam Morgan who spoke. 'Grief does a lot of funny things and there's nothing to be gained by trying to place blame. Joe is dead, nothing can change that and bitterness now will only add to the pain.'

Eline rose stiffly to her feet. 'I'll go,' she said softly, 'Gwyneth is right, it's Nina who was the true wife to Joe, her place is here in his home.'

'Stop it, all of you!' Nina was on her feet, her eyes glinting with tears. 'Stop talking about my Joe, going over his name will do nothing to bring him back. Get out of here, all of you, just leave me alone with him.' She dissolved into tears. 'Just leave me alone with him,' she repeated brokenly.

Out in the street, Eline felt conscious of the eyes of the villagers upon her as she made her way along the street in the direction of the train terminus. She saw women turn their backs as she passed or go inside and close their doors. Tears caught her throat, Eline knew she had never been truly accepted in Oystermouth Village, but never had she felt such an outsider as she did now.

She stood for what seemed a long time waiting to hear the clipclop of the horse's hoofs heralding the approach of the Mumbles train and at last, sighing, she set off to walk the five miles into Swansea.

Eline felt disorientated, she had always known, even in the most difficult moments of her marriage that Joe was there, comfortingly strong in the background of her life. And now he was gone.

Eline swallowed hard, she could not bear to think about Joe dying and she not there to be with him at the last. It was Nina who was at his side, she who had held him in her arms and her grief at losing him had been plain for all to see. Eline, on the other hand, had appeared composed, almost unfeeling; could she honestly blame the villagers for treating her as an outcast?

333

She was just reaching the outskirts of Swansea when a coach stopped beside her and she looked up to see William climbing down and coming briskly towards her.

'Eline!' he called, pausing as he drew close to her. 'I've just heard about Joe, I'm so sorry.'

Eline stood silently, looking down at her feet, unable even now to believe that Joe was dead.

Suddenly she was crying, great gulping sobs that shook her small frame, she was wracked with guilt; here she was newly widowed and longing to be in another man's arms.

'Leave me alone!' She was aware that her voice was rising hysterically. 'I never want to see you again, do you understand that?'

'Eline, what are you talking about?' Will was bewildered by her rebuff, reaching out his hand as if to touch her.

'I was such a bad wife,' she said harshly, rubbing her eyes with her fingers. 'I should have been with him and instead I was thinking only of myself.' She hit out at Will as he lifted his arm to comfort her.

'Can't you see, I can never be with you now, there would always be the ghost of my husband between us. It's my fault he died, my fault! No wonder the villagers despise me.'

'No,' Will said, 'of course they don't despise you, you worked to support your husband. How could anyone blame you for that?'

'Go away, don't keep on about it.' Eline cried in anguish. 'Just leave me alone, can't you? I don't want you around me, don't you understand? I'll never forgive myself for leaving Joe when he most needed me.'

'He preferred Nina to be with him, face facts,' Will said and it was clear he was growing angry. 'They were comfortable together, he was in love with her in a way he had never been with you.'

'How do you know that?' Eline said furiously. 'How could anyone know how Joe felt, least of all you?'

'You were his obsession,' Will insisted, 'his dream. Joe wanted you on a pedestal, not tending to a sick man's needs, you didn't fit into that picture at all.'

'What makes you think you understood my husband?' Eline felt as though her head was about to explode. 'You only wanted to take his wife away from him, didn't you?'

Will looked stricken and Eline felt the need to lash out at him, to hurt him as she was hurting.

'How do you know that your actions didn't contribute to his death?'

Once the words were spoken, Eline was appalled at what she had said, but it was too late, far too late to take the hurtful words back.

Will stared at her for a long moment and then turning on his heel, strode away, his back straight, his shoulders set, revealing the depths of his anger.

Eline moved in a daze and found herself on the beach, staring out to sea. She could not think straight and for the moment she was content to let her mind drift away from stark reality to some dream world where it was always summer and where she did not have to face the heavy burden of guilt that would always be with her. Only one thing was clear, she and Will were finished, it was all over between them before it had really ever begun.

CHAPTER THIRTY-ONE

Fon and Jamie were just finishing the books for the week and Jamie sank back in his chair and sighed, rubbing his hand through his hair.

'There we can go to bed now, Katherine?' he said and then colour suffused his cheeks. 'I called you Katherine, how could I, Fon?'

Then, slowly Jamie began to smile, a rueful, diffident smile. 'How she would laugh if she could hear me, dim wit that I am.' He leaned forward and took Fon's hand, kissing the palm gently.

'I don't know what I would have done without you in these past months,' he continued, 'what a wise woman my wife was to plan our futures for us the way she did, she was right, wasn't she Fon?'

Fon felt a little frightened; this was the first time Jamie had looked at her, really looked at her as a woman and it was unnerving.

'We'll see, Jamie,' she said softly, 'just give it time, be patient.'

He stroked her hair gently. 'I know you are an innocent, sweet girl,' he murmured, 'isn't that why Katherine was so fond of you, so sure you were the right one?'

'I can't ever take her place, Jamie,' Fon said earnestly, 'and I wouldn't want to, but in time perhaps everything will sort itself out.'

Fon resisted the urge to throw herself into Jamie's arms; she knew in her heart that she loved him as she would love no other man, her place was at Honey's Farm by his side, it was pre-ordained, she was sure of it. She sighed heavily then.

'You know I have to go down to Oystermouth for a few days, don't you, Jamie?'

He nodded. 'Aye, with your mam still grieving over Joe Harries and him dead these past months I suppose you have no choice. Got to take your turn in keeping her company.'

Fon shook back her hair. 'Our Sal has been marvellous, mind, full of common sense that girl and then Gwyneth does more than her share; living with Mam like she does, she carries all the responsibilities.'

'Still, your mam is well set up. I'll give the man that much credit, he paid his dues to the one who cared for him while he was sick.'

'I know,' Fon said, 'I think everyone was surprised when Joe's letter was read by a proper solicitor naming Mam as the one who inherited his house. Mam must feel very strange owning her own home and her living in a rented cottage all her life.'

Fon took a deep breath. 'Fair play to Eline, mind, she didn't make any fuss about it, said Joe's word was law and that Mam deserved to be rewarded for all she'd done. It's a wonder she's not bitter about it all, her going out to work to support him and that.'

'Well, love, those problems you must leave to other folk to sort out, all you have to do is visit your mother, show her that you care. If you like, you can bring her up here for a few days – perhaps a change of air will do her good.'

'We'll see,' Fon smiled, 'I don't think she'll leave Oystermouth, but thank you for the offer, it's so kind of you to think of it.'

'This is your home, Fon,' Jamie said firmly, 'if you want to invite your mam, then you have every right.' He sighed. 'I know I miss *my* mam and dad, I wish they were still alive.' He looked up at Fon. 'I've only you and Patrick to care for now.'

She looked at him, her face soft with love and wished

that he would say the words that would make her heart fly up with the birds. Until he actually spoke out she wouldn't know if he loved her or was simply taking the easiest way out of his loneliness.

'I'll run you down to Oystermouth tomorrow,' he broke the silence, 'don't stay away too long, will you, Fon? I don't know what I'll do without you.'

When she was in bed, Fon stared into the darkness, wondering what it would be like to lie in Jamie's arms, to be his wife with all that implied. She was nervous, she had never gone out with followers, not like Sal and Gwyneth who had taken to courting as naturally as ducks swim on ponds.

Fon sighed and turned over on to her side, her face buried in the pillow wondering what it felt like to be loved by a man. Would she let Jamie down? After all, he had been married to Katherine for some time, he was an experienced man.

Fon felt her colour rise even though she was alone in the darkness. She pushed away the uncomfortable thoughts of failing to please Jamie and forced her eyes shut. And yet sleep wouldn't come, she was worried and afraid, but perhaps it would help if she talked matters over with Mam tomorrow.

And yet, in her heart, Fon knew that when the time came to speak of such things, her tongue would cleave to the roof of her mouth with nerves and she would be unable to utter a word.

At last she slept and in her dreams she was in church with Jamie at her side and a Bible clutched in her hand. The vicar was offering a blessing on the union between Fon Parks and Jamie and everything was bathed in the light of romance and dreams, and there was no reality to spoil the moment.

Eline knew she must make up her mind what to do about Joe's boat and that meant a trip into Oystermouth. She

338

had not set foot in the place since Joe had died, partly because she knew she wouldn't be welcome and partly because she was riddled with guilt that she had not been with Joe at the end.

But, she had to be practical, she knew that the boat would deteriorate if she didn't decide what to do with it and, after all, the *Emmeline* had been Joe's pride and joy. Hopefully, she could sell the boat, get it off her hands and then perhaps she could begin to come to terms with her guilt.

On top of the train, looking out over the sea, Eline clasped her hands together and tried to suppress the nervousness that seemed to grip her. She feared the hostility of the villagers but, perhaps even more, she feared coming face to face with Will Davies. Her heart thudded at the thought of the row they'd had and she immediately felt ashamed; she shouldn't have hurt him, but it had been imperative that he realized it was all over between them.

And yet how she wanted him! She rubbed at her face self-consciously and stared more intently at the ebbing waves without really seeing them.

When Eline alighted from the train, she walked briskly along the road towards the small cottage where she had gone on her wedding day. The door was open, the house deserted and, after a moment's hesitation, Eline went inside.

There was no sign of Nina, but Eline knew she must talk to her, ask her advice about the boat. In a way, it would hurt to dispose of it, it was all Eline had left of her life with Joe. And yet what would she do with an oyster skiff? She could scarcely take it out to sea herself.

She sat in the small kitchen and stared down at the slate floor that she had scrubbed to within an inch of its life and wondered what had happened to all those weeks and months of her life when she had been married to Joe. Was it all wasted now?

She forced herself to think of other things, her grief and guilt were almost intolerable, but returning to the village brought all her memories flooding back, the early days with Joe when she had looked up to him, grateful for his protection.

The money for the boat, she told herself briskly, she would plough back into the business. Not that it needed it, between the design work and the portraits she was called on increasingly to paint, she scarcely had time to do any window dressing.

She would never be rich and famous, not like Hari Grenfell but what did it matter? What did anything matter any more?

'Pull yourself together!' she said aloud, forcing herself to think about her business. She had wondered for some time which way she should go, aware that she must begin to construct her life into more ordered lines. She needed to specialize in only one field to make any real impact. But what should she devote herself to – design, window dressing or portraits? She just wasn't clear about it at all, her thoughts were so chaotic these days.

'*Bore da*, Eline, what a surprise to see you. How are you this morning?' Carys was standing in the doorway, she was smiling in her usual good-natured way and yet she looked a little peaky. Startled from her thoughts, Eline looked up quickly.

'Carys, I was waiting for Nina but perhaps I'd better come back another day.'

'Come into my house and wait,' Carys said, 'the baby is sleeping so we'll have some peace, at least for a little while.'

Gratefully, Eline followed Carys into the warm homeliness of the next-door kitchen. The fire burned up cheerfully and the wooden table was spread with a bright, checked cloth upon which stood a bowl of flowers.

'Sit you down, Eline, you look pale and tired, not still beating yourself with the stick of guilt, are you?'

Eline wondered at Carys's perception, homely she might be, but Carys was kindness itself. 'How can I help it? I left my husband and went off selfishly to follow my own plans. What sort of wife is that?'

'Now come on,' Carys made the tea deftly and quickly, swirling the hot water around the brown china pot before carefully adding the tea leaves, 'if my Sam had taken up with Nina Parks I might have walked out too, but,' she smiled, 'I don't think I'd have had the guts.'

'I can't pretend I was being unselfish or self-sacrificing,' Eline said, 'I *was* thinking of myself, I was glad to get away from Oystermouth and I can't forget I wasn't here to look after Joe when he died.'

'And could you have prevented what happened if you *were* here?' Carys reasoned. 'Of course not, no one could. Get on with your life, Eline, forget the past, it's the only way.'

'I know you're right,' Eline said softly. 'What have I really to keep me tied to Oystermouth except a few friends like you and Sam?'

There's Will Davies. For a moment, Eline wondered if she'd spoken then aloud but Carys was handing her a cup without changing the expression on her kindly face.

'Drink up, love, give yourself a breathing space, think things over and then make up your mind what to do when you're sure what you want.'

'Will I ever be sure of what I want?' Eline said. 'I seem to be at sixes and sevens with myself, I can't seem to think clearly any more.'

'It's not really surprising,' Carys said, easing herself stiffly into the rocking-chair, 'you have suffered a lot of worries lately, as I said, you *must* give yourself time to get over the shock of poor Joe's death, then you will be able to think straight, you'll see.'

341

Eline leaned forward, suddenly concerned; Carys was definitely not herself, there were lines of worry around her eyes and mouth.

'Here's me going on about my troubles,' Eline said, 'what's wrong with you?' Aware that her words might sound abrupt Eline qualified her question. 'I mean is anything troubling you? You look, I don't know, anxious I suppose is the word.'

'It's the oysters, the supply is drying up,' Carys seemed happy to talk, 'everyone is feeling the pinch, some of the village folks are so bad off they're not even eating the oysters themselves but keeping the catch to sell.'

Eline was shocked, she had been so wrapped up in herself that she hadn't noticed what was going on in the village.

'The authorities may even stop the men fishing in the Swansea Bay if the situation gets any worse,' Carys sighed. 'I don't know what things are coming to.'

'But you and Sam are all right, aren't you?' Eline asked anxiously and Carys smiled ruefully.

'Aye, all right for now but the beds have been over dredged, the oysters haven't been allowed to breed properly.' Her voice grew unusually angry.

'It's not the regular fishermen like Sam who've been working the beds out of season but the casuals that come from other parts.'

Eline felt quiet, unable to find the words to comfort Carys for she knew that without oysters, the village would probably die. People would move to the town and Oystermouth would be nothing but a ghost town.

'Poor Mrs Marsh is selling up her boarding house,' Carys continued talking, as if glad to get her worries out into the open. 'Not many guests staying there any longer, the regulars have either died off or set up in their own homes and with no one new coming to the village, there's nothing to keep her going here any longer in that big old house.'

'What about Will Davies?' Eline asked with a sudden feeling of panic. 'Where is he staying?'

Carys shrugged. 'I don't know, he might still be at the boarding house, at least until it is sold.' Her shoulders slumped. 'If the fishing dries up completely, what will happen to us all?'

Eline bit her lip, her sense of panic abating. Will had not left the district but, perhaps, on reflection, it would be better for everyone if he had.

'Don't worry, Carys,' Eline leaned forward, 'there's bound to be a better harvest next year, particularly if Swansea Bay is closed. I know it will be tough now but give the oysters a chance to breed and matters are bound to improve.'

'No,' Carys shook her head, 'the oysters take years to mature, nothing will happen by next year, lovie.'

Eline realized how very little she knew about the business of oyster breeding and fishing and her cheeks flamed.

'I'm sorry, Carys, it was stupid of me to comment on something I know nothing about.'

'You were only trying to cheer me up,' Carys said. She straightened her shoulders. 'And quite right too, I'm being stupid, not you.' She smiled. 'I can always go and work in the quarry, I'm not helpless.' She poured some more tea.

'Anyway, Nina Parks got no money worries from what I hear, she has no rent to pay a demanding landlord.'

Eline took the fresh tea and sipped it before answering. 'Joe felt that Nina was entitled to have the house and I don't blame him.'

'Very generous of you,' Carys said drily, 'many a woman would have fought such a thing tooth and nail, you were his legal wife, mind.'

'I know,' Eline said, 'but I wanted to abide by Joe's wishes. He did leave me the boat after all.'

'And a fat lot of good that's going to do you now,'

Carys dismissed. 'Who wants an oyster skiff when there's no oysters?'

Eline put down her cup and rose to her feet, shaking out the creases in her skirt. 'If I can help in any way, Carys, just let me know, all right?' Eline made up her mind to bring a basket of fruit and vegetables with her next time she called. It would be difficult to get Carys to accept what she'd look on as charity, but if Eline concocted some story about having too much food herself perhaps Carys would relent and take the gift.

Eline stood for a moment outside the small cottage she had shared with Joe and looked around her wistfully, she had been so happy to come here as a bride, so proud of the ring on her finger and her status as a married woman. And yet she had failed Joe miserably; could she ever forgive herself for that?

Eline began to walk back along the roadway in the direction of the train terminus. She looked around her seeing everything with fresh eyes after her talk with Carys and for the first time Eline realized that real poverty was beginning to stalk the small village. Oystermouth was on the verge of disaster.

CHAPTER THIRTY-TWO

Eline held the letter in her hand and re-read it for the second time. She still could not believe the good news it contained.

A carriage drew to a halt outside Eline's office and glancing up, she saw Hari Grenfell alight, her skirt held high to reveal the now fashionable cuff boot in softest kid, dyed brown to match Mrs Grenfell's outfit.

Eagerly, Eline opened the door and smiled. 'Come in, but excuse the mess.' She gestured at the littered desk. 'It's not always this bad, but I've had a few ideas lately and I seem to have used up an awful lot of paper working them out.

'That's all right, it reminds me of my workroom at home. I can't stay long, I've just come to tell you how well your design is going, it's been taken up by a French house now and your future as a designer is secured abroad as well as at home.' She smiled. 'I'm so proud to have had a hand in all this, really I am.'

'Please sit down.' Eline moved some papers from a chair and realized that she still had the letter clutched in her hand.

'Perhaps you can advise me,' Eline said quickly, 'I'm in a bit of a muddle, I don't know what to think.'

'What is it,' Hari asked, 'anything wrong?'

Eline shook her head, 'Quite the opposite.' She seated herself behind the desk and looked down at the letter. 'I did some portraits a while ago for a lady in Bristol, a Mrs Charlotte Brentford.'

She glanced at Hari. 'I wasn't sure I could do it but the portrait I painted of Maria, their eldest daughter,

345

was sent to her prospective husband and he liked the portrait so much that he came down from London immediately to meet Maria. Well, it seems they fell in love right away and they are to be married.'

'Congratulations,' Hari said, 'I see your talents are endless. I think it's wonderful, but why does all this put you in a muddle?'

'Well,' Eline rushed on, 'this man, Lord Greyfield, is a patron of the arts and it seems he would like to set me up in a gallery in Swansea so that I can do my paintings and sell them both here and in London. He would handle that end for me.'

'And take a commission I expect,' Hari said gently. 'Still this is a wonderful opportunity, if you want to take it. The question is, do you?'

Eline sighed. 'I don't know if I'll ever be good enough to sell work in London, but I've always loved painting pictures. I remember doing sketches when I was a child living on the farm.' She looked up suddenly in surprise and smiled. 'Yes, I think it *is* what I want to do.'

Hari looked disappointed. 'Well, the arts world's gain will be a loss to the shoemaking industry, but if it is really what you want then you must go all out to make it a success. Perhaps you would still help me in an advisory capacity from time to time, keep the designing as a second string to your bow. It's always useful to have more than one outlet.

'In time you may well have enough capital to develop both talents, run a thriving studio and when times are quiet, as they are at the moment, use your talents in the shoe trade. Footwear is always needed.'

'You talk a lot of sense,' Eline said softly, 'but you have such a fine talent yourself that I'm sure you don't need me.'

Hari smiled. 'It's kind of you to say so, Eline, but one day I'm going to be the one who is honoured to be mentioned in the same breath as you.'

346

She rose to her feet. 'I must get back home, I promised Craig I wouldn't be out long but remember, Eline, all my good wishes go with you.'

She paused. 'You can look on your work with designing and window dressing as a good grounding in the years to come, I feel sure of that. Take care, Eline, and if there is anything I can do to help you, don't hesitate to come to see me.'

When Eline was alone, she read the letter again and she was filled with a sudden surge of energy; she must look for suitable premises, that was the first thing she must do.

She looked out of the window at the wall of the building opposite and wondered where the best site would be for her gallery. She would need somewhere where there was plenty of space and light, room to work and room to exhibit, somewhere the rich of Swansea could come and gaze in comfort.

Mrs Marsh's boarding house! The thought sprang into her mind like a breath of scented breeze and she smiled. She thought of the large attic that looked out over the sea, facing south, and of the high-ceilinged elegant rooms – she knew she had found just the place.

She chewed the end of her pencil, her mind racing. She would need staff, some one to clean the rooms, some one who would be unobtrusive and reliable. Carys Morgan, of course! And Sam, her husband, perhaps he would be able and willing to frame the paintings when they were dry. It would provide practical help for the couple until the oyster industry picked up again. Perhaps in time, Eline would be able to afford to increase her staff and where better to provide work than the village which was beginning to feel the pinch of poverty? Perhaps in time the villagers would even forget their hostility towards her – it was a happy thought.

It was only a few days later that Eline was seated in the front parlour of the boarding house trying to convince Mrs Marsh that to sell her home would be the best thing for her to do in the circumstances.

'But where would I live if I sell the boarding house?' Mrs Marsh asked helplessly. 'I don't want to leave the village and I owe such a lot to the bank I won't be able to afford much.' It seemed as though the decline in the oyster industry had already caused more misery than Eline had imagined.

'What about the cottage Nina Parks used to rent?' Eline suggested. 'I believe it's still empty. You would still be living in the village and your expenses would be so much less.'

'But then there's Mr Davies, I can't throw him out into the street, can I? He's been with me a long time now, a fine young man he is, too.' It was Mrs Marsh's last protest and Eline recognized that with a small dart of satisfaction.

'I will talk to Mr Davies and I won't just turn him out into the street, you can be sure of that,' she said, her heart beating uncomfortably fast.

'Right then, that settles it.' Mrs Marsh leaned back in her chair, the lines of worry easing out of her forehead. 'Mrs Harries, you have my word on it that the boarding house is yours.'

As Eline walked out into the street, she felt a strange mixture of feelings; she was on her way, she had taken the first steps towards owning her gallery and yet now there was the problem of facing Will. She stood in the street and looked up at the tall, elegant building set on three floors. There would be ample room for a discreet gallery on the ground and first floors and the top floor could be her living space.

The attic with its excellent light and the view of the beach would be her work room where she would paint her pictures. A cold hand touched her; she supposed the commissions would come in, but what if they didn't?

And what would she say to William? He could hardly

348

stay in the boarding house, he would certainly object to sharing his living accommodation with the public and in any case they both couldn't live in the same building.

Perhaps the obstacles were too formidable. Was she reaching for the unobtainable, carried away by foolish dreams that had no foundation in reality?

Tea rooms – her mind leapt forward again, revelling in the project, unable to let it go. The kitchen and scullery at the back of the house could easily be turned into a tea room especially if she extended them into the small back garden. You see? she told herself, it will work, it has to work.

It was more difficult than Eline had anticipated to sell the boat and it was only with the help of Mr Frogmore that at last the *Emmeline* was bought by a sailor from Bristol. Eline recognized that it was the end of an era, her life as the wife of an oyster fisherman was over and a new phase was beginning.

After that, the purchase of the boarding house moved ahead so swiftly that Eline scarcely had time to think. She sometimes felt a dart of panic that she was chancing too much, far too soon. She had taken on a lot of debt in order to buy the house, but she felt with the commissions that were in the pipeline and the money from the sale of the cuff boot, she could easily meet her commitments.

She was sitting in her office, working on the design for a cuff bag to go with the boots and gloves, thinking how wise Hari had been to urge her to keep up her design work, when the door opened and a tall figure stood blocking out the light.

'Good morning,' Eline said formally, trying to see through the gloom.

The man came forward and with a small shock, Eline recognized William. Instinctively she rose to her feet, disturbed at the anger in his face.

'I kept away from you, fool that I was, I believed you needed time to mourn.' Will's voice was bitter. 'Instead, you were busy planning your future, buying the boarding house from Mrs Marsh without even bothering to talk to me. But then why should you worry if you were putting me out on to the street? Clearly you've never given a damn about me.' His tone was heavy with sarcasm.

'I'm sorry,' Eline said, her mouth dry. 'I meant to talk to you about it.'

'How very kind of you! Did you think the blow of losing my home would be any the less if you broke the news to me?' He spoke abruptly. 'It seems to me you have always been intent on doing just what *you* wanted to do.'

'That's not true!' Eline protested, her thoughts racing. 'I just didn't think you . . .'

'No, you didn't think at all,' he said. 'Well, you needn't worry about me, I shall move out as soon as I can, I won't inconvenience you or stand in the way of any of your precious plans.'

'Get out!' Eline said harshly but he had already turned away and was striding through the door, his shoulders taut with anger.

Eline collapsed into her seat, her designs forgotten as she put her head in her hands. It seemed she was doomed to disappoint everyone for whom she cared. She suddenly felt tears well up in her throat, she was struggling to succeed and what for? Was the price of success a lifetime of loneliness?

Emily sat opposite her step-daughter and stared at Sarah with cautious eyes. 'What is it you want?' she asked guardedly.

'I can't stand this awful marriage,' Sarah said truculently. 'Geoffrey is an unfeeling monster, I can't live with him, he cares more about that man Chas than he does

350

about my welfare.' Her face was downcast, a tear trembled on her lashes, she looked like a small child about to have a tantrum.

Emily sighed. Sarah as always was inclined to exaggerate everything, she revelled in airing what she saw as her problems.

'Is your husband violent?' Emily asked as gently as she could. Sarah shook her head.

'No, but he's not interested in me, he's more interested in his precious friend!'

How absurdly jealous and petty, Emily thought, but she contained her impatience. 'I'm sure he's just like most men, dear,' she said, 'men can be thoughtless at times and Geoffrey has been used to a bachelor life, adjustments have to be made on both sides. Have you spoken to him, asked him what *he* wants?'

'*He* only wants a son,' Sarah said, her lip thrust out mutinously. Emily leaned back in her chair. 'Is that so unreasonable?' she asked. 'After all most men would like a son.'

Her words were touched with a ruefulness that was lost on Sarah, John would love nothing more than to have a son, but Emily simply could not give him one. Instead, she and John loved Pammy to distraction and sometimes Emily could almost believe Pammy was her own child and not Sarah's illegitimate daughter.

Emily was always uneasy when Sarah was in her house, she felt threatened by her as if at any moment, Sarah might change her mind and snatch the little girl away from Emily. That was one overriding reason for trying to keep Sarah's marriage intact.

'Look what Geoffrey has given you,' she said persuasively, 'that wonderful Kilver House, a fine carriage, everything your heart could desire.'

'Everything but a healthy vigorous man in my bed!' Sarah burst out.

Emily concealed her disgust. Didn't Sarah ever think

351

about anything but her own gratification? 'It will come, give Geoffrey time,' she urged. 'These things can't be rushed. He has,' she paused, 'he *has* come to your bed, hasn't he?'

'Yes,' Sarah pouted, 'and I hate it whenever he touches me.'

'As I said,' Emily repeated, 'these things take time, be patient, Sarah.'

Sarah rose from her chair in a swift angry movement. 'You don't understand,' she said, her words clipped and furious.

Emily was about to reply when Sarah swayed towards her, her face suddenly white.

'What is it?' Emily took her arm and led her to a seat. 'You look so pale, Sarah, are you falling sick with something? Sit still, I'll have the doctor fetched at once.'

The doctor arrived within the hour and was closeted with Sarah for less than five minutes. Anxiously, Emily looked up at him and he smiled as he put on his hat.

'She'll live,' he said bluntly. 'Don't look so worried, Mrs Miller, go in and see her.

Sarah had regained her colour and indeed, she looked quite radiant.

'You all right, Sarah?' Emily asked anxiously and Sarah's eyes were suddenly triumphant.

'I'm going to have a child,' she said. 'Send someone for Geoffrey to bring me home.'

'You are going home to him?' Emily asked bewildered at the turn-round in Sarah's attitude.

'Of course I am,' Sarah said, smiling for the first time since she'd entered the house. 'This changes everything, Geoffrey will be in my power now. Once I give him a son I will be able to twist him round my little finger.' She sighed contentedly. 'I know how much a son means to him, and to his father; I shall have them both in the palm of my hand.'

Emily rose and pulled the silken-tasselled cord to

summon the maid. 'Where is Geoffrey now? Where shall I send a message for him?' she asked.

Sarah looked at her. 'He'll be at his club, no doubt, along with his *dear* friend. Tell him he must come at once.'

'Are you sure?' Emily sounded surprised. Sarah nodded emphatically. 'Of course I'm sure, this changes everything.'

Emily's thoughts were racing as she gave the maid her instructions. 'Send Coland to the gentleman's club in Wind Street,' she said, 'tell the footman that Mr Geoffrey Frogmore should come at his earliest convenience to fetch Mrs Frogmore and hurry!'

Emily sighed as the maid left the room; if only Sarah would remain content now that she was having Geoffrey's child. Hopefully it would be a son then all would be well and Pammy would be safe once more.

When Sarah was alone with her husband in the plush drawing room of Kilver House, she seated herself in the large armchair and looked up at him triumphantly.

'Well, Geoffrey, are you pleased with me?' she asked smugly. He allowed himself a smile.

'It remains to be seen if you have got me an heir,' he said slowly. 'I hope so for both our sakes.'

Sarah felt her spirits fall sharply; this was not going to be as easy as she'd thought.

'I'd like you to remove your, your friend from our house,' she said almost pleadingly and saw her husband frown with annoyance. 'I don't think it would be right for our son to grow up in a house that was divided, so to speak,' she added lamely.

Geoffrey nodded slowly. 'You may be right, Sarah, perhaps it would not be wise to influence unduly a young boy in any way.' He squared his shoulders. 'But as I said, it's early days yet, we shall have to see how you do as a mother, won't we?'

He smiled. 'At least tonight, when my father comes to dinner I shall have good news for him.'

'Oh, yes,' Sarah's voice had an edge to it, 'your father will be pleased all right and rather relieved, I should imagine, to know that you are going to have a child. He must have doubted that the day would ever come.'

'Don't be clever,' Geoffrey said evenly. 'It does you no good to scoff at things you do not understand.'

'But you will give him up, your friend,' Sarah refused to acknowledge the man by name, 'once the child is born, I mean.'

'Give Chas up, no,' Geoffrey said flatly. 'Removing him from our house, that I shall consider, certainly.'

Sarah rose from her chair. 'I shall take a rest before dinner,' she said quietly, knowing that she had won all the concessions she could for the time being.

She remained in her room, hearing masculine voices from downstairs, and knew that Geoffrey was talking to that awful man, no doubt telling him the news about the child. Well, perhaps now life wouldn't be so bad, Geoffrey would visit the man somewhere other than under her roof and at least he would no longer come to *her* bed. It was a wonder, she thought angrily, that she had conceived a child at all under the circumstances.

She dressed carefully for dinner, knowing that old Mr Frogmore would be generous in his gratitude to her for providing an heir. She rested her hands on her stomach. 'Please,' she whispered, 'let it be a son.'

CHAPTER THIRTY-THREE

Emily felt free at last. She hugged the little girl she'd come to think of as her own and stared down at her lovingly. 'My darling Pammy, I pray your mother will never want to take you away, not now she is with child again.'

Emily felt better now that the midwife had seen Sarah and confirmed her pregnancy; sometimes the greatly experienced nurses knew more than the doctors about such matters. Sarah was never going to be happy with her lot but at least she had found what she seemed to want, a good marriage to a rich man. Perhaps love would come but somehow, Emily doubted it.

Emily heard the doorbell ring followed by the sound of voices in the hallway and, with a sinking heart, she recognized the high, almost petulant, pitch of Sarah's voice.

Emily left Pammy to the ministrations of her nanny and hurried down the stairs, her heart beating uncomfortably fast. What could Sarah possibly want with her this time?

'Sarah,' she said as warmly as she could, 'how are you feeling? Come into the drawing room and sit down, we must have some refreshments.'

'I don't want anything at all, no cordial or tea, it all makes me feel as sick as a dog,' she said pettishly, almost throwing her coat at the waiting maid.

She swept through to the drawing room and dropped into a seat. Her waistline was already thickening and her breasts were straining against the confines of her silk bodice.

'You look very well,' Emily said encouragingly and took a seat on the opposite side of the fireplace, bracing herself to face yet a new demand. It was dreadful of her to think it but Emily knew from experience that the only time she saw Sarah was when she wanted something.

'I'm fed up with being in the house alone,' Sarah started, 'Geoffrey is always at his club or out with his friend somewhere or another, he doesn't consider me at all.'

Emily smiled soothingly. 'Sometimes husbands can be like that,' she replied, trying to remain cheerful although her spirits were sinking even lower for any minute now Sarah would come to the real reason for her visit. She did, quite abruptly.

'You must make the girl your responsibility, legally,' she said firmly folding her hands over her stomach. 'Geoffrey insists on it.' She frowned. 'His exact words were "I'm not going to be responsible for the upkeep of another man's by-blow".'

Emily felt elation sweep through her though she knew better than to reveal her real feelings; it didn't do to let Sarah realize how keen she was to make Pammy her own. Sarah didn't want her child at any price but she could be contrary if she had a mind.

'Go on,' Emily said as calmly as she could but excitement was rising within her. She had never expected such a gift to fall into her lap. Within a matter of weeks perhaps, Pammy could be hers by law and then Sarah could never take her away.

'I shall have to talk to John, of course, but I don't see any problem in making our guardianship of Pammy legal.'

Sarah stared at her, seeing right through her. 'It's what you always wanted, isn't it?'

'It is,' Emily conceded inclining her head, 'and I'm very pleased that you want it too.'

Sarah shrugged. 'I've never been close to the child.'

She patted her stomach. 'I shan't be close to this one either, I don't really want children, but at least Geoffrey can afford the best sort of help for me. With luck I won't have anything to do with it once it's born.'

She sank back in her chair, the main purpose of her visit over. 'Perhaps I will try some hot black coffee, no sugar, mind.'

Emily rose at once and pulled the silken cord, then she turned to Sarah.

'I suppose you want all this taken care of right away?' she said cautiously.

Sarah nodded emphatically. 'Aye, the sooner the better, Geoffrey is afraid that another man's child might somehow benefit from his money, that's how mean-spirited he is.'

Emily could well understand how he felt, but she kept her own counsel. 'I shall send someone to the solicitors with a message this afternoon,' she said with a calmness she was far from feeling. 'We'll set the wheels in motion right away.'

Even as she sat drinking coffee with Sarah, Emily forced herself to contain her excitement; she still couldn't believe the stroke of good fortune that had come her way. Sarah was willing, no, anxious to be rid of her daughter for ever.

It would have been sad except that Pammy had known no other mother than Emily and now she never would. And John had been a better father than any man could be – after all, the little girl was his own flesh and blood, his grandchild.

Sarah seemed to cheer up when she'd drunk her coffee. 'Look,' she held back her hair and Emily saw that on Sarah's small ears were gorgeous matching emerald and diamond clips.

'A gift from my father-in-law,' she said smugly. 'And better than that, once the boy is born, Mr Frogmore intends to settle some money and lands on him to be

357

held in trust by me.' She smiled thinly. 'Geoffrey isn't too happy with that, but there's nothing he can do about it, his father is adamant.'

'So you are content then?' Emily asked delicately. 'In your marriage, I mean.'

'Aye, as content as I can be,' Sarah said flatly. 'Geoffrey isn't a knight in shining armour, but then what man is?'

And Sarah had experienced enough of men to know, Emily thought ruefully.

Later, when Sarah had gone, Emily sat down at her desk and drafted a letter to her solicitor; the sooner Pammy was legally hers, the better.

The boarding house took very little converting; once the furniture was removed, fresh paint applied to the walls and new carpet laid on the floors, the place appeared entirely different.

Eline hung a few of her paintings on the wall, the ones she had worked on when she lived at Honey's Farm, and stood back to admire the effect.

Standing there, in the slant of light from the large front window, doubt seized her; would anyone really wish to buy her paintings? But then she wouldn't only sell her own work, she would have some canvases by famous artists, most of them depicting some aspect of the beautiful Welsh coastline.

Eline had already been offered some paintings on marine subjects, gorgeous works with richly painted stormy seas and ships which dipped and rose in the waters around Mumbles Head. But in spite of everything she was not happy.

There was a sudden knocking on the half-opened door and moving into the hallway, she saw a tall figure outlined against the sunlight. Her heart started to beat swiftly and her throat was dry even as she forced herself to speak evenly.

'You'd better come in, don't stand there in the doorway where everyone can see you.' She led the way through to the front room and stood in the window looking across at the sea.

'I've come to collect my things.' He spoke abruptly as though she was a stranger and she looked down at her feet.

'Then please collect them and get out of my house as soon as you possibly can, I don't want you anywhere near me.' She was hurt and anger iced her words.

'Your manner is as charming as ever.' As her chin lifted abruptly at the insult, Will stood looking down at her, his eyes unreadable. 'I see you've wasted no time in converting the place, most considerate of you, just as well I didn't wish to stay under the same roof as you, isn't it?'

'I'm very sorry,' Eline said, her voice heated. 'I should have arranged my future so that I didn't disrupt your life, is that it?'

'I would have liked a fair chance to make other arrangements, I would have liked to talk to you about all this,' he gestured around him, 'I would have been reasonable, you must realize that, I certainly wouldn't have stood in your way, ever.' He sighed heavily. 'I resented your assumption that I would be willing to fit in with whatever plans you decided upon.'

Eline felt her anger drain away as she sensed the hurt behind his words. 'We don't have to quarrel, William,' she said softly, 'I'm going to need friends more than ever now.'

He moved to the staircase. 'Then perhaps you should learn to give them a little consideration.' He spoke slowly, seeming to relent a little.

'Carys, Mrs Morgan, she's not well,' he said quietly, 'in fact, she is so thin that you wouldn't recognize her. Things are bad all round in the village, very bad, people are losing their livelihood, the oysters are scarcer than gold now. But then, I suppose you are too busy with your own ambitions to notice such things.'

He placed one foot on the bottom stair; he was so tall, so handsome, so very dear, that Eline almost moved to put her arms around him. She wanted to tell him he was right, she should be noticing what was happening around her. Then he spoke again.

'I shan't be any bother, I'll get my belongings and then you'll have another room free so that you can advance your career without hindrance.' The sarcasm in his tone made Eline go cold. She lifted her chin, too proud to show him that she was near to tears.

'That suits me,' she said stiffly. Eline heard Will moving about upstairs and fought the instinct to run after him. He had made it quite plain that he had no time for her; she'd asked for his friendship and he had turned on her, as though blaming her for the state of the village. She swallowed hard, trying to force back the tears.

'Let yourself out,' she called up the stairs. 'I have an important client to see.' She walked from the house and down towards the beach, forcing back the tears. For a long time, she sat on the sands staring at the boats out in the bay without really seeing them. Was her career going to be enough for her for it seemed that's all she would have?

She would make it enough, she told herself sternly, she didn't need anyone, she would do it all alone. And yet her brave words rang hollow even to herself.

Loneliness rose like a spectre before her as she realized she had no one in the world who really cared about her. But self-pity would get her nowhere. She rose to her feet and dusting the fine sand from her skirts, Eline turned back to the road and squaring her shoulders returned to the boarding house.

There was no sign of Will or of his possessions, he was gone from her life for good. Sitting on the bed, because she had no other furniture as yet, Eline stared down at the bare wooden floorboards and suddenly the future reared up before her full of doubts and uncertainties, and slowly, she gave way to the hot, insistent tears.

It took Eline almost a month to get the gallery functioning and by then she had a steady stream of callers from Swansea and the surrounding areas. Sometimes a dealer from London would come down and Eline found that she was beginning to make the business work.

'Eline.' With a mop and bucket in her hand, Carys was standing in the back kitchen, the floor glistening beneath her feet. 'Can I talk to you?'

Eline smiled at her, happy in the knowledge that she was doing something practical for Carys by giving her a job in the gallery. 'I'll pop the kettle on and we'll have a nice cup of tea, you deserve a break.'

Carys had been working for Eline for about two weeks. She had jumped at the idea when Eline had suggested it to her and Eline had made sure that the work wasn't too gruelling for Carys, as Will had said, had become thin and wan, her once plump cheeks hollow and pale.

Carys had been glad of work, glad of some money in her pocket but now, she came to Eline, a rueful look on her face.

'I got to give up my job here,' Carys said awkwardly. 'Sam thinks he can get work in the quarry, taking on some more men they are now, see, and there'll be nobody to mind the baby.' She avoided Eline's eyes, her thin face flushed with embarrassment.

'Come on,' Eline said quietly, 'what's the real reason, Carys? There is no work in the quarry, I know that. I won't be angry or offended, but I'd rather you tell me the truth.'

'Well, the baby's right bad, see, grizzling all the time he is and Sam can't manage him.' Carys looked up and faced Eline. 'And Sam, he don't like me working here, see, people are talking.'

'What do you mean, talking?' Eline said, her mouth dry.

'Against you, they are,' Carys said, slowly. 'You know you've never really fitted in here, lovie.'

'I know that but what makes them all so angry now?' Eline asked in bewilderment. 'What am I doing wrong?'

'You are getting rich,' Carys said simply, 'between your fame with the shoes and then you are bringing strangers, posh strangers into the village.' Carys looked down at her roughened hands.

'Ashamed we are of our poverty and us not wanting the whole world to see it. You forget, Eline, we are proud of our heritage, proud of the oyster fishing.' She took a ragged breath. 'The strangers know nothing, they are blaming us for the lack of oysters in the beds, saying it's our greed that's destroyed the oysters. "Over fishing," they call it.' She sighed heavily. 'The oysters are the only way we know how to earn our keep and we have to eat, don't we?'

'But, Carys, you need this job,' Eline protested, 'you need the money to buy food for you and your child, it's foolishness to give it up because of a bit of gossip.'

Carys nodded. 'I know but I got to listen to Sam, see. In any case, I'm getting black looks from my neighbours, they are not earning any money and they think I'm a traitor by working for you.' She gave a wry smile.

'That Nina Parks is loudest of all, you can just imagine it, can't you? Never liked you, not been the dearest of friends, like, have you?' Carys moved to the door.

'Still, she's as hungry as the next one, I suppose. She's got her cottage that Joe left her but nothing else. No work on the beds, nothing but what her daughters can spare her, by the look of it.'

'I suppose Gwyneth Parks has enough to say, too?' Eline asked and Carys smiled her old cheerful smile.

'Oh aye, mouthy is Gwyneth just like her mam. She's busy telling folks how you threw that nice Mr Davies out of his lodgings without so much as a day's notice and him the darling of the village for letting people have boots on tick.'

Eline felt herself grow cold. 'That isn't true,' she said and Carys nodded.

'I know but Mr Davies is staying, along with old Mrs Marsh whose boarding house you took, in the house Nina used to rent and Gwyneth has moved in with her mam. Gives people food for thought, that sort of thing, mind.'

Carys touched Eline's arm. 'I'm sorry, mind, not to be working for you any longer and grateful, too, for what you tried to do for me but I can't stay.'

'Wait, just a minute,' Eline said and from a drawer brought Carys some money. 'Take it,' she said, 'it's not much but you are entitled to your wages and it will help tide you over for a few days, anyway.'

Carys turned away quickly to hide the glint of tears in her eyes. 'You always was kind, Eline, and for what it's worth, I think the villagers are wrong to treat you like an outcast.'

She hurried away, her thin shoulders hunched. Eline went inside and closed the door, leaning against it, her thoughts racing.

So Will was living in Nina's old home, was he and Gwyneth moving out to accommodate him? That suggested that they were very close, very close indeed. The thought pained Eline although she knew it was foolish of her; if she and Will had ever shared anything, any tender feelings of love, it was now over.

She moved slowly through the rooms of the gallery; later, the customers would come in greater numbers, mostly from Swansea and the surrounding areas, to look and sometimes to buy and they would not notice the poverty that was slowly gripping Oystermouth.

She sat on one of the elegant chairs with which she'd furnished the main gallery and suddenly, all her achievements seemed to mock her, her life was full of ambition and although she'd felt satisfaction at her success, now she knew that without someone to love, her life was nothing but a barren waste.

Fon was busy in the kitchen, her hair dishevelled, her apron rumpled as she took the meat pie out of the hot oven. The table was laid for the evening meal, the red and white checked cloth, crisp and clean, hung in neat folds, the floor gleamed with washing and the old furniture shone with polishing.

Sighing with relief, Fan took the potatoes from the fire and set them on the black leaded hob. Everything was ready for Jamie's return.

She took off her apron and crept up stairs to check on Patrick; she'd given him his supper some time ago and had washed him and put him down for the night.

She stood, her face softening as she looked down at him curled up in his bed, his hair plastered to his forehead, his lashes fanning out on his plump cheeks. She resisted the urge to kiss him, he was so dear to her, so very dear. She held her hands together in an attitude of prayer. 'Thank you, God, and thank you, Katherine, for giving me all this,' she whispered.

She heard the sound of the pump in the yard gushing water and with a lifting of her heart, she knew that Jamie was home from the fields. She pressed her fingers to her lips and blew the sleeping child a kiss and then retraced her steps to the kitchen.

She was putting out the pie when Jamie came in, his dark hair curling on his forehead; he looked just like his son, Fon thought tenderly. Beads of water bejewelled Jamie's hair and his face was ruddy, having rubbed it with a towel. There was a scent of soap about him mingled with the sweet smell of grass and Fon loved him so much that she ached.

He looked at her and she became aware of her tangled hair and her flushed cheeks. 'I must look terrible,' she said self-consciously.

Suddenly, he looked at her as if he'd never seen her before. 'No,' he said thickly, 'you look beautiful.'

Rich colour suffused her skin from her throat to the roots of her hair. Fon stood awkwardly, not knowing what to say as Jamie came slowly towards her.

He took her nervous fingers in his strong hands and rubbed the back of her wrist with his thumb. 'Fon,' he spoke haltingly, 'it's taken me a long time to say this but I mean it from the bottom of my heart.' He drew her closer so that he was holding her now in the circle of his arms.

'Fon, I love you.' The words were simple but they were the finest words she had ever heard.

Fon rested her head against his broad chest, her eyes closed in delight. 'And I love you, Jamie,' she said, 'I think I've always loved you.'

She felt his big hand smooth her hair and as she tipped her face up for his kiss, she knew that she had found happiness, at last.

CHAPTER THIRTY-FOUR

Sarah sat up in bed with a gasp, the contractions had started, she was sure of it. She clutched the silken spread close to her swollen body and looked wildly around her.

'Geoffrey!' She called his name sharply and, after a moment, he appeared in her doorway, tying the cord of his dressing gown firmly around him. 'Geoffrey, my pains have started, the baby's coming early.'

He moved at once, calling for a servant to fetch the doctor; he was efficient, she would give him that. Sarah eased herself back against the pillows, she mustn't panic, she must take deep breaths, keep calm, she would do her child no good by getting hysterical.

She mentally counted the months, her baby would be a month premature. She put her fingers to her mouth in fear, all the old midwives said that it was worse to have an eight-month rather than a seven-month baby.

One of the maids entered the room with a hot drink balancing precariously on a tray. It was obvious that she had dressed hastily, her cap was at an untidy angle on her head and her apron was bunched to one side. But Sarah, who normally would have upbraided the girl for her sloppy appearance, looked at her gratefully.

'Thank you, Cassie,' she said, taking the cup with trembling fingers, 'how did you manage to make me a drink so quickly?'

'I hadn't gorn to bed very long and the fire was still alight, madam,' the girl answered shyly, unused to displays of gratitude from her mistress. 'I managed to catch it and make it burn up again.'

'Perhaps you can see to my fire?' Sarah asked humbly. 'I feel a bit cold and shivery.'

Cassie bobbed and obediently moved over to the small grate, placing coals with care on the dying embers. Sarah watched her, she had done the same sort of task herself as a young girl, both in the homes of the rich where she'd worked and earlier in her father's house.

But now, both her father and she herself were better placed; John, the respected husband of Emily, who was once a Grenfell and she, Sarah, the wife of Geoffrey Frogmore. How things changed, she thought ironically.

And yet, was she any happier? she asked herself with rare introspection. What did she have? A husband who preferred his friend and a life of loneliness ahead of her.

The pain came again, tightening her body into a spasm, twisting her face as she attempted to suppress the moans that were forcing themselves between her lips.

The timid Cassie was at her side at once, her small face anxious. 'You'll be all right now, madam,' she said in an attempt to be reassuring, 'the master has sent for the doctor.'

Where was Geoffrey? Sarah looked towards the door, feeling that for all that their relationship could not be, his duty, as the father, was to be at her side.

As if answering an unspoken call, Geoffrey came into the room, neatly dressed now, with his hair combed. Looking at him objectively, Sarah saw that he could be quite good looking, especially without his spectacles. She held out her hand to him.

'Be with me, Geoffrey, please?' she said quietly. He took her hand reluctantly and she drew him towards her. 'I need you at my side right now, you *are* my husband after all.'

Geoffrey, as always alive to possible gossip, glanced at the maid. 'Of course I'll stay with you, dear,' he said, 'so long as I'm not in the way.'

The pains became stronger and Sarah clung to

Geoffrey's hand, wishing quite suddenly that theirs was a real marriage built on love. Perhaps, she thought, when all this was over, they could try to make a go of it.

The doctor came at last and with him the midwife, her stiffly starched apron crackling as she walked. It was she who took charge while the doctor stood and talked to Geoffrey.

'Out!' the midwife ordered and Geoffrey went gladly, along with Cassie who threw Sarah a sympathetic glance before closing the door behind her.

The midwife examined Sarah swiftly and efficiently and nodded her head in satisfaction.

'The husband can come back in and hear what I have to say,' she told the doctor autocratically.

'The baby is coming a few weeks early,' the midwife said briskly, 'but there is no reason why it should not be a perfectly healthy child.' She looked sternly at Sarah. 'But you will need to take great care of him, feed him with your own milk, none of this wetnurse nonsense, mind.'

Sarah couldn't speak, another pain was racking her, tearing at her, breaking her bones apart. She held out her hand and Geoffrey took it firmly. Beads of perspiration dampened her hair so that curls clung around her face. She laboured to bring her child into the world, feeling as though she would die in the attempt. The pain seemed to go on and on until Sarah felt she could no longer bear it.

'Good girl,' the midwife urged, 'the head is nearly here, I can see it, a big, strong head. It will be a fine child, you'll see.'

'Come on, Sarah,' Geoffrey's face was animated, alight with excitement, 'you can do it, bear down now as the midwife tells you.'

There was one last wrenching surge and then a feeling of utter peace. Sarah lay for a moment, breathing in the luxury of not being in pain and then, the silence was broken by a sharp cry that seemed to tear at her breasts which yearned to suckle her young.

'There!' The midwife sounded triumphant, as if she had borne the child herself. 'You have a fine son.'

She put the child into Sarah's arms and as she looked down at the crumpled, indignant face, Sarah felt a rush of pure happiness and love that brought tears to her eyes. She had never felt like this before, certainly not when she'd given birth to her first child.

'You have done well,' Geoffrey said softly, 'you are a good, brave woman, Sarah.'

'Right,' the midwife intervened, 'enough fussing now, your child is safe and well and your wife needs attention. Go on out and tell everyone that you have fathered a fine boy, that I find is all husbands are good for at a time like this.'

Geoffrey smiled. 'I'll let my father know, he'll be so proud to have an heir.'

Sarah felt the weak tears come to her eyes, it seemed that her husband's approbation was more important to her than she would ever have guessed.

Emily looked down at the papers in her hand, a smile of joy on her lips.

'You look like the cat that got the cream,' John said softly and Emily held out her hand to him.

'She's ours, Pammy is really and truly our daughter, John, now no one can take her away from us.'

John took her hand in his. 'I know, love, and I can't help feeling a bit sorry for our Sarah. What sort of mother gives up her first born in such a way?'

'You are a dear, sentimental man,' Emily said indulgently. 'Look, love, Sarah was too young when she had Pammy, she wasn't ready for the responsibility of bringing up a child properly. Sarah was not able to forge a bond with her baby then, but this time it will be different, she will love her new son to distraction, you'll see.'

John's face brightened. 'Aye, she seems proud of him, all right and he's a fine boy, healthy and with such lungs on him, he'll be a tenor in the choir, if I'm any judge.'

Emily felt a stirring of pain within her, she was very conscious that she could never give John the son he so obviously wanted. She rose and looked at herself in the elegant mirror that hung over the fireplace; she was a young woman, in the prime of her childbearing years, it wasn't fair that by some freak of nature she could not have a child of her own.

For a moment, her joy at having adopted Pammy was swamped by feelings of frustration, then she pushed the dark thoughts away.

John, as always, sensed her mood. He rose and took her in his arms, cradling her close to him. 'You are all I ever wanted, Emily,' he said softly. 'You know that.'

She touched his cheek lightly and a great sense of happiness filled her. 'I do know, my love.' She put her arms around his neck and clung to him telling herself that she should count her blessings, she was the luckiest woman in the world.

Sarah held her son close, coaxing him to suckle at her breast. His small, rosebud mouth sought and found and he clamped on to her with such determination that Sarah laughed out loud in joy.

'Look at him, Geoffrey,' she exclaimed, 'he will grow up a fine child, he knows where to find his nourishment, all right.'

Geoffrey was fascinated by the boy, he stared down at his son in wonder and Sarah exulted at the feeling of power that Geoffrey's softened attitude gave her.

'Geoffrey,' she said softly, tentatively, 'come here.' She held out her hand and Geoffrey drew nearer the bed touching her fingers lightly with his own.

'Will we have more children, Geoffrey?' she asked him quietly.

'Perhaps,' he said reaching out a finger to touch his son's petal-soft cheek.

'Geoffrey,' Sarah looked at him pleadingly, 'couldn't we try to make a good marriage together? Our son deserves parents who will be close and care for him.'

Geoffrey looked at her with a strange expression in his eyes. 'Sarah, I must confess that I have a new respect for you after witnessing your bravery during childbirth. I want us to have a successful marriage as much as you do.' He paused and rubbed his forehead. 'I must be honest with you, however, I can never love you as a man should love a woman, I do not have that power within me. You must accept that I am different from other men, I have other needs, it is something I can't help and in any case wouldn't change.'

He smiled without any of his usual sarcasm. 'I will be good to you, Sarah, as a friend is good. I will provide for you and our son and I would fight to the death for both of you if you were in danger.' He shrugged. 'That is all I can promise you.'

Sarah felt tears sting her eyes. 'Very well, Geoffrey,' she said with new determination, 'I will try to be a good wife and I *will* be a good mother, that *I* will promise you.' If there was regret in her voice, Geoffrey chose to ignore it.

There was a knock on the bedroom door and Sarah covered her breasts quickly.

'It is my father,' Geoffrey said, a pleased smile on his face, 'the old boy can't keep away from his grandson.'

Old Mr Frogmore seemed rejuvenated, his face lit up as he saw the picture of an apparently happy family scene, his son sitting at the bedside of his wife and child, his hand holding that of his wife, his other hand on his child's cheek.

'You don't know how happy you have made me, both of you.' His glance encompassed Geoffrey and Sarah then came to rest on the sleeping face of the baby.

'May I hold him?' he asked and Sarah smiled, gently handing over her son.

'Be careful with him, he has just been feeding, don't shake him about too much.'

Old Mr Frogmore's eyes misted with tears as the baby waved indignant fists at him, eyes screwed up as though trying to see into the distance.

'He's so handsome,' Mr Frogmore said raggedly, his voice trembling, 'so very handsome.'

He handed the baby back to Sarah and made a visible effort to control his emotions. 'What are you going to call him?'

'We thought, Jack Winford after you, father,' Geoffrey answered quickly and Sarah, catching his warning glance, remained silent. On reflection, she rather liked the names, just as she liked old Mr Frogmore. 'Winford is a fine, strong name,' she said softly. 'I'd be honoured to call my son after you.' She hesitated a moment. 'Father,' she added almost shyly.

Mr Frogmore seemed to swell with pride. 'I will keep my promise and sign over to you some money and lands at once, Sarah. Some securities I will put in trust for my grandson so that his future is assured.'

He dipped his hand into his pocket and brought out a long velvet box. 'In the mean time, this little bauble is for you, my dear.'

Sarah's gaze softened, her father-in-law was so kind to her. She prized open the box and saw glittering within its plush interior a necklace of emeralds and diamonds which matched both her earrings and the ring Geoffrey had given her.

'I wish I could say they were family heirlooms, my dear,' Mr Frogmore said, 'but I must admit I came by them in London a few years ago.' He smiled drily. 'I do believe they once belonged to your step-mother, Mrs Emily Miller. As they say, it's an ill wind that blows no good.'

Sarah felt momentarily sorry for Emily, to have lost such priceless gems must have hurt unbearably. But then Emily had made a great fortune, she could afford to buy all the gems she wanted now, so why feel sorry for her?

'They are beautiful and I will treasure them,' she said and lay back against the pillows suddenly tired.

'I will leave you to rest, now.' Mr Frogmore was nothing if not perceptive. 'Conserve your energy, my dear, you must look after yourself so that you regain your strength quickly.'

He left the room and Geoffrey smiled at her in approval before following his father from the room.

Sarah looked down at the sparkling emeralds and diamonds and then at the face of her sleeping son and for the first time in her life, she knew that possessions were worthless baubles, that the real riches of life came only with love.

CHAPTER THIRTY-FIVE

'Well, I say we ought to run her and her gallery out of the neighbourhood.' Nina Parks's strident voice echoed among the people gathered in the church hall. 'That Eline Harries has brought nothing but ill luck to this village from the moment she came here.'

'How is getting rid of the gallery going to fill the bellies of our children?' It was Carys Morgan who broke the uneasy silence. She looked down at the child in her arms, her expression anxious.

'My little one is wasting away under my very eyes,' she said brokenly, 'and my Sam drinking what little money we have. He is hoping the drink will take away the pain and shame.'

'What has Eline Harries ever done for us?' Nina demanded, hands on hips. 'What has she brought to this village? She's an outsider and she's bringing in other outsiders to look down their noses on us.'

Nina paused, her anger gathering momentum. 'What do the outsiders care that we starve while they buy pictures costing enough money to keep us in food for a year? Why should we put up with it? Answer me that.'

'Eline gave *me* a job,' Carys said, 'and I was daft enough to listen to your grumbles and pack it in. Why didn't I stick to my guns? I don't know. After all, I was bringing good money into the house.'

'Aye and your man would have been more ashamed than ever, then, wouldn't he?' Nina Parks said bitterly. 'His wife kotowing to the likes of *her,* it's not right.'

'Well, you've got *her* cottage, haven't you? Didn't turn that down, mind,' Carys said with some of her old spirit.

'*That* was given to me by Joe,' Nina retorted sharply, '*I* was really wife to him, especially at the end, *she* did nothing but run away from the thought of hard work and the suffering of her man.'

Carys rose abruptly from the hard, upright wooden chair upon which she had been sitting.

'Well, if you call this a meeting then I'm a Dutchman,' she said. 'I thought we were going to talk about ways around our problems, instead all we've done is throw mud at Eline Harries. Drinking sour wine I call that, pure jealousy because she's making a success of things.'

Carys made her way slowly to the door and once outside stood looking along the street as though wondering what to do. The child in her arms cried fretfully and Carys put her cheek against the little boy's head, it was burning as though with a fever.

She turned and hurried towards home; the sooner she got the baby into the house, the better, she should never have brought him out in such bitter weather and him with a bad cough on his chest.

The fire was burning low in the grate when Carys entered her house and she quickly pushed another log into place. Thank God that at least the wood from the trees was free not like coal which the merchants thought was gold-dust these days, the price they were charging.

Carys put the child into bed and set to work rubbing his small chest with goosegrease. A bit of warm flannel wrapped around her son's small body seemed to ease the rattling cough and soon the child fell into a gentle sleep.

Carys boiled the kettle and made herself some hot cordial of dandelion leaves, sipping it gratefully. She would have loved a cup of tea but there was not even a dusting of leaves in the once full tin.

Carys felt herself sway, she was so weak, it was days since she'd had anything to eat, her last meal was nothing but a crust of stale bread.

375

Sam had been given the only bit of cawl in the house for his dinner but now the pantry was empty and not even Carys's ingenuity could produce a meal from nothing.

She must have dozed a little in her chair for she sat up startled to hear the rattle of the door latch. Sam came into the kitchen and Carys noticed the deep lines of worry around his eyes.

Reluctant to add to his misery, she held her tongue about the baby and instead, handed him a drink of cordial.

'What to eat, girl?' he asked, his voice low, his shoulders, once so proudly held, slumped as he leaned over the scrubbed table.

'I was just going up the road for something,' she improvised quickly. She took her shawl from the back door and rested her hand for a moment on Sam's bent head. 'I won't be long, love.'

In the chill of the street, she hurried towards the gallery, her mind suddenly made up. She would ask Eline most humbly for her job back.

The gallery door stood open, the front window, enlarged now, was filled with painting. Ships rode out storms on green and grey seas and sails billowed as though they were real not simply paint on canvas.

From inside, Carys heard the sound of voices, cultured and low and she hesitated in the doorway, embarrassed at intruding. Hunger growled in her belly impelling Carys to go inside. From the back of the house came the succulent smell of food and Carys leaned against the wall, suddenly overcome with faintness.

'Carys, what is it?' She heard the voice as though from a distance and then she was being led to a chair in the hot, steamy kitchen behind the tea rooms and there on the large hob bubbled a cauldron of soup.

'I was just going to have something to eat,' Eline said matter of factly, 'I hope you'll share some with me,

Carys, because Penny here thinks she's working for a family of ten!'

The girl at the stove turned around, her face beaming. 'Mind,' she said, 'Mrs Harries lets me take the leftovers home with me, tells me to make too much, she does.'

Suddenly, without any warning, Carys found herself on the verge of tears knowing that there was no job – Eline had found someone else to clean for her and who could blame her?

'Good God, Eline, there's enough soup there to feed half the village,' Carys said, gulping at the lump in her throat, 'they'd give their eye teeth for the chance of such a feast.' She couldn't now tell Eline why she had come.

Eline sighed. 'Are things really that bad?' she said ladling out a bowlful of the steaming soup and putting it on the table before Carys.

'They couldn't be worse, that's for sure.' Carys took up her spoon and looked longingly at the plate of thick crusty bread.

Eline seated opposite her, pushed the bread across the table before picking up her own spoon and beginning to eat.

Carys felt she had never tasted anything so wonderful in all her life. The bread melted in her mouth and the hot soup seemed to hit her stomach with a feeling of warmth.

Eline watched her; Carys knew she was staring even though Eline kept looking discreetly away and not catching her eye.

'You've given me an idea,' Eline said at last, 'what if I have some soup taken to the church hall? The villagers can come there to eat whenever they want.'

She rose to her feet, obviously impatient to put her plans into action. 'I'll get on to everyone who I think has influence and we can all help to pay for the food.'

'Oh, Eline,' Carys said, 'it would save our lives if you did that.'

Carys finished her soup and rested for a moment against the back of her chair, feeling a renewed sense of energy sweep through her. 'I must get back,' she said, 'Sam is starving and the baby isn't well but thank you for the soup, it was lovely.' She hesitated, not wanting to ask for charity but Eline read her mind.

'Look, I'll put out a few jugs full of soup and we'll take it down the road to your place, it won't take a minute. We can spare it, there's plenty here.'

Within minutes, Carys found herself out in the roadway with Eline at her side. She felt elated, her belly was full and now Sam would eat too.

'Why did you come to see me, Carys?' Eline asked softly and Carys looked at her doubtfully before answering.

'Oh, I was just passing, like, and I felt a bit bad so I came inside, I hope you don't mind.'

'You came for your job back, didn't you?' Eline didn't wait for a reply. 'And thank goodness you did. I'm going to need another pair of hands, believe me, I'm so busy I don't know if I'm coming or going.'

'What would I be doing?' Carys asked gripping the jug close to her, imagining how Sam would relish the thick vegetable and meat soup.

'Well, I'd like you to serve the teas to the visitors,' Eline said quickly. 'Penny is good at cooking but not so good with people, she gets very nervous when there are ladies in fine dresses around. Would you like the job?'

Carys smiled widely. 'When shall I start?' she said cheerfully.

Sam was upstairs when Carys led the way into the kitchen. Carys put down the soup feeling a sudden sense of forboding.

'The baby,' she said, her breathing suddenly restricted, fear running through her like wine. She hurried up the stairs unaware that Eline was behind her and burst into the bedroom to see Sam bending over the bed.

'Thank God you've come,' Sam said and he was white to his lips. 'The baby . . .'

Carys pushed him aside and leaned over her son listening for the breathing that had become faint and ragged.

'Go for the doctor, Sam,' Eline was saying, softly. 'Tell him Mrs Harries wants him to come at once.'

Carys, looking at the pallid face of her child, knew that it was too late for doctors, weeks of near starvation had taken their toll and her baby was too weak to fight the racking cough any more.

As though in a daze, Carys was aware that the doctor had come and was ministering to her child but she sat motionless in the chair, staring at anything but the face of the baby.

'His chest is very badly congested,' the doctor said and Carys, looking up at him, saw him shake his head.

She rose and went to the bed and picked up her son feeling the small head fall heavily against her breast. He was so beautiful, so perfect, and Carys had waited so long for him, it wasn't fair that he should be taken away from her.

The baby sighed softly, just once and became heavier in Carys's arms. 'He's gone,' Carys said tonelessly, 'my baby's gone from me,' she looked up at Sam, 'and it's all because of stupid pride.' The bitterness in her voice hung heavily in the silent room.

Carys spoke again, her voice low. 'If I hadn't given in to the feeling in the village against Eline Harries, I'd have been earning money working in the gallery and this would never have happened.'

Her voice rose. 'We'd have had food in plenty and my baby would be alive. I'll never forgive myself for this, Sam, never.'

She felt Sam trying to take the baby from her arms but Carys held her child firmly. 'No, leave me alone with my son,' she said, 'just leave me.'

The room was empty then and that's how it should be, Carys knew that, no one could share in this moment of desolation, she had to endure the pain alone.

She bent her head over the child and kissed the still-warm skin and her eyes burned with hot tears that she would not, could not, shed.

It took Eline only a day to organize the distribution of the soup in the church hall. She had won the support of many of the councillors and prominent citizens of the area and now, as she stood before the haphazard assortment of tables, with the cauldrons of soup waiting, she clasped her hands together, praying the people would come.

The vicar and his helpers from the village church stood anxiously waiting to serve the food and Eline stared around her in desperation. Why was the hall still empty?

She went to the door and looked outside, the street was deserted, the doors closed and with a sense of despair, she knew that the people were too proud or too hostile to take the food she was offering.

She returned inside. 'It's no good,' she said, 'I don't think anyone is going to come.'

'Well, more fool them.' Penny was at her side, her young head lifted in indignation. 'It's good food I've cooked and plenty of it and if I've wasted my time I'll never forgive the lot of 'em here in this village. We wouldn't behave like that in Swansea, mind.'

'But the villagers are strong and independent,' Eline said defensively, 'they have never had to ask for anything before and it's not easy for them to swallow their pride.'

'Well,' Penny said, 'I'd listen to my empty belly before my pride any day.'

The door swung open and a stooped figure, swathed in black, stood there for a moment before walking determinedly into the hall. Eline looked up, her heart thumping with hope, someone at least had come to accept her food.

'Good God,' Penny said, 'it's Mrs Carys Morgan, the poor soul that's just lost her baby, there's brave, isn't she?'

Carys came up the table and picked up a bowl, her face was white and her eyes, though red-rimmed, were clear.

'I'll have some of that soup, Penny,' she said, her voice hoarse, 'it seems Eline Harries is the only one in the village with some sense in her head and me, I've no pride left, see.' She turned to the vicar. 'I've found that pride is an empty thing.'

She took the bowl and moved to the door and stood outside in full view of the villagers who now were looking from behind closed curtains watching as Carys unashamedly ate the soup.

The vicar took up a bowl and stood with Carys in the roadway and after a few moments, Penny hurried forward to stand on tiptoe and peer over their shoulders. She came back to Eline and she was smiling.

'They're coming out of their houses,' she said as though it was something of a personal triumph. 'The villagers are following Mrs Morgan's lead, they're coming to eat our soup.'

It was Sam Morgan who came through the door first, his hand resting for a moment on his wife's thin shoulder. There was pride in his eyes and the glint of tears on his weather-beaten cheeks.

Behind him came a straggle of villagers, hesitating uncertainly in the doorway. Sam led the way, looking grey and sick, but he held out his bowl towards Eline with a steady hand.

'You are a good woman,' he said, loudly, 'and I for one am grateful to you.' He touched his cap and moved away and stood beside his wife. They exchanged a loving look but neither of them could speak, words were unnecessary.

Eline took a deep breath as she saw Gwyneth Parks stand sheepishly in the doorway for a moment and then, drawn by hunger, move to the end of the queue.

Skipper George, his eyes warm with admiration, spoke out clearly as he accepted his food.

'Eline Harries deserves our respect as well as our gratitude,' he said loudly, 'none of us has been very neighbourly to her and yet she has turned out to be more of a good Samaritan and more generous than any of us have ever been.'

Eline found herself choked with emotion at his words, and her eyes blurred with tears. But soon, she was too busy filling bowls and jugs with hot soup to think of anything else. The ladle hung heavily in her hand, her arm ached with lifting but she kept dipping into the cauldron and filling vessels until her back hurt.

'So, it's you giving out charity, is it?' the voice of Nina Parks was unmistakable and, as though by a command, the chattering of voices and the clinking of spoons against china fell silent. All eyes were turned on the two women who seemed to stand isolated in a gap in the crowd.

'Well, we have never been friends and never will be,' Nina continued, 'but I'll say this by here in front of everyone, you are all right, Eline Harries, you are one of us.'

She held out a bowl and Eline filled it to the brim, swallowing hard, and, as she held out a plate of bread, Nina took a hunk of the crusty loaf, inclining her head in thanks. And then she was walking away, her piece said.

The chattering voices rose to a crescendo, folk were smiling again. Villagers crowded around Eline congratulating her, thanking her and, with red cheeks, Eline protested that it wasn't she but the rest of the townfolk of Swansea who had worked the miracle.

Eline leaned against the table, her shoulders weary, her arms aching but she was happier than she'd been for a long time. She felt a hand warm on her shoulder and turned to see Will standing beside her. A shock ran through her as she looked into his eyes and saw love reflected there.

'I've been so pig-headed, so damn intolerant.' He spoke quietly. 'I love you, Eline, and I know you love me.'

Eline swallowed her tears, searching vainly for the right words to say to this man who meant more than anything in the world to her.

Will spoke again, this time more loudly. 'I'm proud of you, Eline,' he said, his clear voice carrying across the crowded hall. 'You are a fine, generous woman and I want you to be my wife.'

'William,' her voice broke as she stood quite still, the tears now unchecked, running into her mouth.

'Come here.' He held out his arms and after a moment, Eline went into them. She closed her eyes, breathing in the scent of him, listened to the sound of Will's heart beating so close that it might have been within her own breast.

It was time now for new beginnings. Joe would have wanted things this way, Eline knew that as clearly as if he'd spoken to her.

'Go on, marry the man, you are meant for each other!' Nina Parks called across the hall. And it was Nina who began the clapping that warmed Eline's heart with happiness.

Someone cheered and as the sound of hands and voices rose and filled the church hall, rising high into the rafters, Eline clung to William, her mouth turned up to his.

'Of course I'll marry you,' she whispered, 'I love you more than life itself.' And as their lips met, Eline knew that with William, she had found her destiny, she had come home.

THE END